Also available from

*The Masters at Arms*

GALLANT MATCH
GUARDED HEART
ROGUE'S SALUTE
DAWN ENCOUNTER
CHALLENGE TO HONOR

*Louisiana Gentlemen*

WADE
CLAY
ROAN
LUKE
KANE

GARDEN OF SCANDAL

*Watch for Jennifer's brand-new trilogy set in the sexy and scandalous court of Henry VII*

BY HIS MAJESTY'S GRACE

*Coming in 2011*

*Available in paperback from MIRA Books*

# JENNIFER BLAKE

## TRIUMPH IN ARMS

MIRA®

ISBN-13: 978-0-7783-2748-6

TRIUMPH IN ARMS

www.MIRABooks.com

**Printed in U.S.A.**

For my readers around the world who appreciate the romantic gesture, the passion and promise of love unrequited, the mystery of human relationships, and the olden days when such things mattered.

# Prologue

*New Orleans, Louisiana*
*April 1847*

Christien Lenoir waited with his thumbs in his waist-coat pockets and his back propped against a Doric column of the Théâtre d'Orléans's arcaded entrance. Tension sang along his nerve endings. The lady should appear at any moment. A single glimpse was all he required; it would decide whether he proceeded or called a halt.

Around him the crème de la crème of the Vieux Carré streamed from the theater, pouring out into the damp night. Family groups, courting couples trailed by their duennas, widows and gentlemen on the town, they moved in a murmur of animated conversation and hummed snatches of the music just heard in *L'elisir d'amore*. The flickering gaslights mounted above the arched theater entrance cast a yellow-orange glow over the opera crowd, glinting on jewels, shimmering on silks, satins and velvets, turning white linen a sickly hue. In the street beyond the wide banquette, it reflected with a glasslike sheen from the wet carriages as swearing drivers jockeyed for position, preparing to take up their owners. Rain had passed over during the performance, leaving puddles between the paving stones that rose in glittering wavelets as horses' hooves and carriage wheels splashed through them.

Abruptly, Christien straightened. There she was, Madame Reine Marie Cassard Pingre, just emerging into the lamplight's glow. Her young daughter walked beside her. They came closer, passing where Christien stood, so near he could hear the silken whisper of the lady's petticoats, catch a delicate wafting of roses and lavender. Face set, looking neither left nor right, she seemed intent on reaching the near corner where the rue d'Orleans crossed rue Royale.

She was beautiful, he saw, as all things unattainable are beautiful. Following her with narrowed eyes, Christien felt a prickling at the back of his neck not unlike the warning when he faced an adversary of unknown skill, uncalculated power.

The mother and child he watched were strikingly similar. Bright hair, light brown touched with gold, curled in fine tendrils around their faces. Though the lady's tresses crowned the top of her head in an intricate arrangement nestled with pink camellias, the child's drifted around her in the night wind in fine intimation of how her mother's might appear if released from its pins. Wide-spaced eyes, delicately molded noses and determined chins marked them both. Their slender forms, encased in the lavender-gray silk of demi-mourning, were made to appear fashionably fragile and elegant by some modiste's clever fingers. The affection between them was plain to see as the lady glanced down at the child, no more than four or five years old, whose small, glove-encased hand rested in hers.

Christien's every sense took on a razor-sharp edge. The streetlamps seemed brighter, the night air fresher, the murmur of the crowd around him like a roar. His heartbeat increased in tempo while a piercing ache of need spread from its heated center.

It stunned him, that sudden hunger of the heart. As a *maître d'armes,* one of the infamous fencing masters of New Orleans, his days were devoted to masculine pursuits. Little time was left for feminine company and none at all for respectable females. He had schooled himself to do without such tender influences, seldom allowed them to cross his mind, never permitted them to hold his thoughts or his desires hostage. He was immune, or so he'd felt, to the *coup de foudre,* that thunderclap of infatuation that made fools of other men.

He had not taken an attraction to his quarry into account. Nor had he considered how long he had been alone. It could be a dangerous oversight.

Mere lust was not the difficulty, though he could not take his eyes from the lady, felt suddenly parched for the taste of her, the feel of her skin against his. Rather, it was a near-desperate urge to stand beside mother and daughter, to walk homeward with them, protect them and, yes, claim them as his own and be claimed by them.

Christien swallowed on the tightness that invaded

his throat. He understood to a nicety who the mother and daughter were, knew their status in the *haut ton* of French Creole society. That he was unacceptable in the close circle of their acquaintance was a given. Yet the exclusion struck him now as such things had not in some time, making him feel the less for it.

Madame Pingre had been widowed two seasons ago, so was just beginning to leave off her mourning. The whispers concerning the death of her husband fretted the edges of Christien's mind, rumors of bloody and convenient murder. Seeing her so close, he felt a flicker of disquiet. She was the kind of woman a man might kill to possess, yet he required her to be innocent; it was the only way the business at hand could succeed. If she was not as expected, he might live to regret his involvement.

The pair lived in one of the town houses on rue Royale, a pied-à-terre kept for the *saison des visites,* the annual escape from country life into the city for the social season now winding down with the advance of spring. Not for them the interminable wait to have a carriage brought around, peering down the street for its arrival among the others that clattered up the mud-streaked thoroughfare. They would simply walk home along the wet banquette.

The lady was certainly headed in that direction. The slight smile that curved her lips had a strained edge to it, Christien thought, and her attention was centered on the child with little left over for those around her. She moved in an aura of isolation and seemed to prefer it that way.

A male escort should have been with them. No doubt the lady's father, Monsieur Cassard, was around somewhere but delayed as he spoke to acquaintances. Madame Pingre and her daughter were left unprotected for the moment. Christien's frown deepened as he saw it.

Just ahead of her, a dowager in moss-green cut-velvet and cascades of pearls turned and called a greeting. Reine Pingre flushed a little, but paused in her escape. Her expression was polite as she exchanged compliments and listened to a spate of complaint that seemed directed toward the acting ability of the tenor they had just heard. The child, young Marguerite Pingre, stood swinging her mother's hand as she gazed around her in bored impatience.

She glanced Christien's way, her attention snared perhaps by his intent appraisal. She blinked, then returned it in solemn interest. Christien smiled and inclined his head, a consciously gallant gesture.

Young Marguerite's mouth turned down. She spun around, putting her back to him. Clutching her mother's fingers with both hands, she put her forehead against the bunched wrist of her opera-length kid glove. For long seconds, she hid her face there. Then she risked another quick glance over her shoulder.

It seemed a great victory, one more flattering than any coquette's show of interest. Christien felt his mouth curve again in wry appreciation.

The youngster's gaze slid away somewhere past his right shoulder. Abruptly, she stiffened. Her face drained of color. With a small cry, she jerked free of her mother's hold. In a flutter of skirts above small, white satin shoes, she darted from the banquette into the street.

Just down the way, a cabriolet pulled by matched grays rounded the street corner on two wheels. It straightened, racing toward the theater. The child jerked her head toward the sound. She halted on tiptoe, a small, pale statue in the center of the muddy street.

Madame Pingre swung, searching for her daughter with a startled gaze. Her eyes widened as she caught sight of her in the path of the jangling carriage. Snatching at her skirts, she sprang from the banquette.

Christien was already moving, shoving his way through the stunned onlookers. With a single glance for the wild-eyed carriage horses and the cursing driver sawing on their reins, he launched himself after the lady. Reaching with long arms hardened by unrelenting practice with foil and rapier, he caught her around the waist just as she jerked up her daughter. He flung himself toward the far edge, clutching the pair in an iron hold as he plunged, turning in midair.

The street came up to meet him, slamming into his back in a welter of slime and dirty water. Breath left him in a hard grunt, and the night sky above him spun for an instant. Lying with mother and child locked to his chest and his pulse thudding in his ears, he felt the carriage wheels grind past so close they brushed his hair, and the vibration shuddered through every fiber of his body.

The clatter of hooves died away as the carriage came to a standstill down the street. Somewhere a young boy whistled in shrill admiration. People were babbling, shouting, applauding. A stray dog barked its excitement. Men ran to halt other wheeled traffic, gathered close with urgent queries to know if the three of them were injured, were alive.

Christien had only a distant awareness of the commotion. His arms were full, as was his heart, which shuddered against his ribs. A deliciously rounded, most definitely adult female form was pressed against him from chest to ankles on his right side, a warm armful of soft curves under a welter of silk topped by a mass of shining curls that tickled the underside of his chin. On his left, a smaller shape trembled against him, pressing a small, tear-wet face into his neck.

"Papa," the child whispered, her lips moving against his skin with the delicate brush of butterfly wings. "Oh, Papa."

# 1

"Somebody coming, *madame*, stranger coming down the road!"

Reine Marie Cassard Pingre put down her pen as the warning was called out from downstairs. She closed the ledger in which she was copying figures from the bills of lading for goods that had been delivered at the plantation steamboat landing that morning. Rising to her feet, she grimaced at the ink staining her fingers. She should hurry and wash her hands before descending to greet the visitor.

But really, what was the point? The gentleman was doubtless only a crony of her father's. He would join him where he rested on the lower gallery, which was comfortably shaded by massive live oaks at this hour. With glasses of Madeira in hand, the two of them would discuss the price of cotton and the latest political scandals. She would be free to return to her desk work once the obligatory compliments were out of the way.

Stretching a little, she moved to her sitting room's French doors, which stood open to the morning air. Sunlight lay in a broad swath over the canvas that carpeted the gallery floor, reflecting from its white surface with blinding brilliance. Reine shaded her eyes with one hand as she gazed out at the front drive that curved its way down to the river road.

A horseman cantered toward the house, kicking up puffs of dust that formed a small comet tail behind him. Tall and broad of shoulder, he sat his saddle with the ease of one born to it. A wide-brimmed planter's hat of summer straw shaded his face, while the folds of a long gray dust coat protected his clothing. He was too far away for his features to be visible, yet something about him seemed familiar.

Reine felt a small frisson run down her spine. She was not a fanciful female by any means, yet it seemed the sun dimmed as if a cloud passed over it. The heat of the day waned, leaving her chilled and unaccountably disturbed.

A goose walking on her grave, she told herself with an abrupt shake of her head. That was all. Turning with decision, she crossed to the hallway and made her way down the stairs.

Alonzo, the white-haired butler who had been a fixture at River's Edge since before she was born, awaited her at their foot. She asked him to see that refreshments were provided on the lower gallery. As he moved away to do her bidding, she drew a deep breath and walked out the open front door, pausing on the steps of the white-columned portico.

The visitor had just reached the gate that closed off the pathway through the front garden. He was definitely not a friend of her father's, Reine saw; the muscular grace with which he swung from the saddle was that of a man in his prime, one no stranger to physical exertion. He did not lack for assurance, for he tossed his reins to the stable boy who came running and pushed open the gate in the picket fence as if returning home instead of paying a social call. The way he gazed around him, taking in the grass-covered rise of the Mississippi River levee, the front garden behind its fencing, the big white house and waving fields of young cane behind it, was keenly appraising. No master on watch for signs of negligence could have been more thorough.

Alonzo, his assignment completed, stepped through the front door and came to a halt behind Reine. She was heartily glad of his silent support. The arrival of Chalmette, her brother's big, rawboned bloodhound that emerged from his cool wallow under the hydrangea shrubs, also improved her feelings. She did not reprove the dog as he raised his ruff with a low growl and planted himself in front of her.

"Good day, *monsieur*," she greeted the visitor in polite tones. "May we be of service?"

He turned toward her, reaching at the same time to remove his hat. Lowering it to rest against the swinging fullness of his long dust coat, he stood square-shouldered and grim of face before her.

"You!"

Shock wrenched that single word from her. The

tone of her voice disturbed the hound, for he growled again in deep-throated warning. She put a quieting hand on his head.

"As you say, Madame Pingre," the visitor answered with a brief tip of his head. "Christien Lenoir, at your service."

Dark hair with the black satin gleam of a swamp panther's pelt, deep-set dark eyes, strong features that carried a copper-bronze tint: this was the man who lived nightly in Reine's dreams, yes, and her nightmares. It was he who had saved her and Marguerite from being mangled by carriage wheels or worse on that terrible night four months ago. For an instant, she was back in his arms again, lying against his hard length, caught to him in a hold so secure it seemed nothing could harm her, not then, not ever.

The urge to sink into that infinite protection had been so seductive she was forced to steel herself against it. Anger at her weakness and the impossibility of ever having someone to share her blighted existence washed over her in that instant. Though it pained her to remember it now, she had screamed at this man like a harridan as she scrambled up and dragged her daughter away from him.

The heat of a flush rose to her hairline. It was all she could do to sustain his piercing gaze. What mischance had brought him to River's edge she could not imagine, but the sooner he was on his way, the better. "I ask again if I may direct you, *monsieur.*"

"I've come on a matter of business with your father. That is, if he is at home."

"What could you possibly have to discuss with him?" The question was less than gracious, though the best Reine could manage at the moment.

"You doubt my invitation to call?"

A dangerous undertone shaded Christien Lenoir's voice, she thought. It was a reminder of a similar dark peril seen in his eyes as they had faced each other in a muddy street. Fear had meshed with the anger inside her as she recognized it, but beneath both had been a strange exhilaration. They had been muddy, disheveled, bruised and shaken, but for a brief instant there flashed between them an awareness so searing she had felt branded by it. They had stood staring at each other, a heartbeat away from quarreling, until Marguerite began to cry.

Just thinking of it now made Reine feel as if her blood had turned hot and scouring in her veins, mounting to her brain. It was difficult to recall what he had just asked.

"I…I must confess to being surprised," she said finally. "My father is expecting you, then?"

"He should be," he said in cryptic reply.

She hesitated, then stepped back, gesturing toward the side gallery. "That way, if you please. Alonzo will take your hat and dust coat, then show you to him."

"You're very kind, *madame*."

His voice was dry, the look in his eyes ironic as he came up the steps toward her. He seemed a veritable paladin, impossibly tall and wide of shoulder and with his coat flowing around his heels like a cloak. If the presence of the bloodhound troubled him, he gave no sign but only held out a hand for him to sniff. Chalmette availed himself of that privilege, gave a wag of his tail, then trailed away in the direction of the hydrangea again.

Reine gave the dog a jaundiced look. As she glanced back at the visitor, she caught a glimpse of amusement in his eyes, as if he understood her annoyance at Chalmette's defection. She only inclined her head in leave-taking before turning away to reenter the house.

It was possible he paused to watch her departure. She could not be sure for she did not look back.

The visitor's arrival was such a distraction that it was difficult to return to her paperwork. When she had placed half a dozen sums in the wrong column, entered one set twice and added a column three times with as many different answers, she flung down her pen and left the writing table once more.

A small mirror hung in a gilded frame above the console table between the French doors. She stepped to it, frowning at her reflection. Her hair, never particularly neat, had sprung into a mass of wild wisps around her face in the souplike summer air. Her face was flushed in a less-than-attractive fashion, and, yes, that was a smudge of India ink on her chin.

With an exclamation of annoyance, she slipped her handkerchief from the embroidered, drawstring pocket that dangled at her waist along with her keys. She moistened it with her tongue and scrubbed hard at the stain. Not that she cared what she looked like, of course. She had never been more than passably attractive, but she preferred at least to be clean.

What business could Monsieur Lenoir possibly have at River's Edge? She could not think her father required instruction in the use of fencing foil or sword; he had been proficient once, though that was years ago. He owned no property on the Passage de la Bourse that might be rented out as a sword master's atelier as far as she was aware. He was of too mild of a temper to contemplate engaging a *maître d'armes* to rid himself of an enemy. That was, of course, if Monsieur Lenoir could be brought to hire out his sword for such a purpose; only the least respectable of the fencing masters were so lost to honor as to stoop to such arrangements.

The only other thing she could imagine was a debt of honor. Her father was a fine man but had one vice, an addiction to games of chance. It had been years since he allowed it to overcome his better judgment, though Reine's mother sometimes spoke of the days before their marriage when he had won and lost several fortunes. Regardless, he came up short of funds now and again after a particularly long night of play. Yes, and there had been that evening not so long ago when he had come home only as the roosters crowed.

Dismay seeped over Reine as she became certain she had hit upon the reason for the sword master's visit. Her father owed a gambling debt.

Cash to pay it off was in short supply; she knew that well enough, having spent the morning toting up the accounts. Not that such a state of affairs was unusual; most planters lived on their expectation of future profit. Harvest time usually saw their hopes rewarded, but not always. A single crop destroyed by drought, insects, disease or storms, and ruin could overtake them. That was unless friends or a benevolent banker came to their rescue.

Her father had been fortunate in his friends and business acquaintances thus far. A convivial man, he was generous to a fault when in funds, always cheerful in company and as affable when losing as when winning at the card table. He made few enemies, which he often proclaimed to be the secret of a good life.

Reality and her dear papa were not on close terms, however; he made a habit of ignoring unpleasant facts for as long as possible. More than that, he did not believe in burdening females with financial worries. This in spite of it being Reine who kept track of plantation profits and expenditures. Though her affection was deep and abiding, her knowledge of his faults gave her a bad feeling about this unusual visit.

The need to know precisely how matters stood between her father and Monsieur Lenoir became more acute with every passing moment. It was a relief when Alonzo appeared to tell her that she was required on the gallery.

The visitor and her father rose at her approach, then sank back into their seats as she took a wicker chair and folded her hands in her lap. Her father made a hearty show of recalling the identity of their guest to her memory and expressing yet again his gratitude for his good services in preventing injury to Reine and Marguerite outside the theater. With that out of the way, he fell uncharacteristically silent, glancing from her to his visitor with a worried frown between faded blue eyes. He shifted his gaze out over the gallery railing to the moving patches of sunlight under the oaks. He looked at the caller again, cleared his throat and pursed his lips.

Her father was growing older, Reine noticed with a small clutch at her heart. Liver spots marked the backs of his hands, his features were grooved with lines and his dark hair streaked with silver. A bon vivant as a young man, he had married rather late in life so had been almost forty when she was born. Events these past few years had taken their toll, stealing the spring from his step and the sprightliness and laughter from his smile. For much of that she was to blame, as she knew far too well.

"Yes, Papa?" she asked after a moment. "You have something you wish to tell me?"

"Indeed. There is a matter… That is, I must relate… Oh, it's a damnable thing, and I'm more sorry than I can say. It concerns you more than any other, and it seemed best that I let you know first so you can… Ah, *chère!*"

Reine's apprehension, already strong, turned to alarm. She sat forward. "What is it? Has something happened? Tell me at once!"

Her father opened his mouth and closed it again with a shake of his head. Reine, feeling the gaze of the sword master upon her face, swung toward him in hope of clarification.

Thankfully, he did not disappoint her.

"What your father is trying to tell you, Madame Pingre," he said, his voice as steady as his black gaze, "is that he has lost title to this property. The house, its furnishings, workers and acreage has passed from him over the gaming table. His loss is my gain. I am the new owner of River's Edge."

The words he spoke were clear enough, but her mind refused to accept their meaning. This was worse, so much worse, than she had feared. "What? What did you say?"

"It's true," her father said in mournful concurrence as she turned back to him. "Everything is gone. The town house in the Vieux Carré, as well."

"I am sorry," Lenoir said.

Reine closed her eyes, unable to bear what was surely the spurious regret in his voice or the implacability in his features. "Gaming," she said, the damning word no more than a whisper in her own ears.

"Euchre." Her father's voice regained strength now that the news was out. "My luck was abominable. Truly, I never saw it so bad. I was sure it would turn as the night went on, but alas, it never happened." He gave a fatalistic shrug.

"How could you?" she demanded in shaken tones as her lashes swept up again. "Had you no concern for me or for Marguerite? As for *Maman,* I cannot imagine how you are to tell her."

Uneasiness passed over her father's face. "Things are not so bad as they appear."

"How could they be worse? We will have to leave here, and where are we to go? We may be able to put up for a few days in a hotel, but if you have lost so much—" Reine stopped, closing her lips in a tight line to prevent herself from saying more. It went against the grain to expose the full extent of the disaster to their guest. *On lave son linge sale en famille,* the old wives said, wash your linen within the family circle only.

Her father rubbed the back of his neck, a harassed look tightening his features. "Nothing so drastic should be required. Monsieur Lenoir and I have come to an agreement that seems workable."

"For more time to arrange your affairs, you mean? I'm sure that's very accommodating of him, but hardly improves matters." She sent the sword master a fulminating glance. The more she considered it, the more unlikely it seemed that her father had wagered everything, particularly in a game with this man. It was too coincidental, unless, of course, they had fallen into play because of the incident outside the Théâtre d'Orléans.

"The matter is delicate, *chère,* but should prove satisfactory if it works out as planned." Her father rose to his feet so quickly that his knees popped. "I should go to your mother before she decides to come down to greet our visitor. Monsieur Lenoir will be better able to put the situation to you in a way that…that must meet with favor. I'll leave him to state his case as he put it to me."

Reine's heart beat high in her throat as she watched her father depart in such haste that the tail of his frock coat flapped around him. When his footsteps had faded away inside the house, she turned to the man in the chair next to hers.

Christien Lenoir leaned forward slightly with his elbows on the wicker arms. A rueful smile curved his mouth as he met her gaze, though it did little to change the expression in his eyes. That remained watchful, as assessing as if she were his opponent on a dueling field.

"Well, *monsieur?*"

"This may be awkward, is almost certain to be in all truth. I trust you won't hold that against me."

"I can hardly promise since I have no idea what you mean." She was distracted by the feel of her heart thumping against the wall of her chest, also by the odd magnetism of the man that made it almost impossible to look away from him.

"No, I suppose not. The thing is, my proposal seemed perfectly rational and straightforward when it first came to mind. Discussing it with your father was a matter of business. Now it appears more problematical."

"That will not, I feel sure, prevent you from making it."

"By no means. After seeing you again, I'm more inclined than ever."

She searched his features one by one. His eyes, black as a moonless night, were shuttered by a thick fringe of lashes, holding all feeling in abeyance. The sun's glow, which slanted across the strong planes of his face and glinted in the shining blackness of his hair, provided no illumination for his thoughts or intentions. His nose, between thick, expressive brows, might have been large in a less masculine face; its bladelike jut had the look of an eagle's beak and the same commanding arrogance. The tilt of his chin was determined, almost threatening.

Christien Lenoir was not handsome in the pale and refined fashion of the moment, yet he had a dark attraction made up of harsh planes and strong bone structure like a son of Lucifer himself. His masculine presence, the sense of steel-hard resolve under a thin layer of civilized intentions, seemed to overshadow the morning. Nothing she saw gave her reason to hope that he would relent to the point of erasing her father's gambling debt.

Lowering her gaze, she allowed it to rest for an instant on the cuff of his shirtsleeve, which rested on the chair arm closest to her. The linen was paper-thin and frayed at the edges. His cravat, she saw, had the reddish tint of age under its black dye. The knees of his woolen pantaloons were worn more than was acceptable, and his boots could use new heels. It was quite probable he had just as much need of River's Edge as they did, was just as determined to hold on to it. What, then, could he want of her?

An odd thought shifted through her mind, one that sent heat rushing along her veins. He had mentioned a proposal. What if he meant that quite literally?

No, it could not be.

Unclenching her teeth, she said, "I can't begin to guess what you have in mind, unless you mean to suggest that my father lease River's Edge from you."

"That would not suit me at all."

"I feared not, for you would have no need to involve me in such a plan. Do you mean to set up as a planter so require his expertise? Well, and perhaps my aid in arranging your household?"

"Something along that line."

"You can't expect Papa to become your overseer," she said in dismissal. "Not because he would wish to be disobliging, you understand, but because he has not the skill. He is, always has been, a gentleman."

"So forbidden to earn his keep like a common laborer. I am aware of the distinction."

She ignored the rough note in his voice as she went on. "Still less would my mother ever consent to move into the overseer's cottage. It just isn't…isn't suitable."

"Madame Cassard would rather become the pensioner of some relative than give up the benefit of a household with an abundance of servants to do her bidding. Perfectly understandable. But in that case, she and your father, also your young daughter, may as well become my pensioners."

Reine clasped her hands in her lap, clenching them as irritation surged through her. "They aren't…that is, we aren't dependent on your charity."

"Aren't you?"

The question was accompanied by another disturbing flash of sympathy, an infinitesimal softening of his eyes that revealed hints of gold in their darkest depths. She rejected it with only the slightest hesitation. "By no means."

"I'll agree the matter is different with you, given

that you have something to offer in return. You would, of course, become the mistress of River's Edge."

She stared at him a long instant. "Mistress," she said in tight incomprehension.

"Rather than your mother, who currently holds that position, I mean to say. The responsibility would naturally fall to you as my wife."

She held his black gaze, uncertain the words he had spoken in such soft precision could have the meaning she thought. At the same time, a peculiar flowering sensation moved over her, tightening her nipples, settling hot and heavy in her lower body. It made her feel a little dizzy, so she reached to grasp her chair arm with tight fingers.

"Your wife," she said faintly.

"It's the obvious solution, you must agree. As your husband, I would take possession here without ousting your family. Very little need change except that we will be joined by a legal tie."

*Take possession.* What a very suggestive phrase, one that curled her toes inside her slippers.

Reine had been married. The last thing she needed was anyone to take possession of her ever again. Her vision blurred at the edges, and she gave her head a quick shake to clear it. "Impossible."

"Unlikely, perhaps," the swordsman returned with no relenting in his expression, "but not at all impossible."

"You don't understand. I have no desire whatever to marry again."

"You would see your parents and your daughter put out of their home instead?"

"No, but I don't…really can't…"

"You are revolted at the idea of being wed to a man who has made his living as a sword master."

"It isn't that." She meant it, for her ideas concerning social stigma had changed since the death of her husband. Becoming a pariah could do that to someone.

Still, it seemed strange that she should receive a proposal from such a man. Theodore had always had a particular fear of sword masters. They had formed a special Brotherhood made up of a select few who went about exacting vengeance for the wrongs done to those weaker than themselves, especially to women and children without male protection. And they were not, so he said, too particular about their methods, showed little regard for the status and dignity of their victims.

"I revolt you personally," Christien Lenoir went on.

She gave him a scathing look that encompassed the symmetry of his face, his powerful shoulders and long, hard-muscled legs outlined so faithfully by thin wool. "Don't be absurd. My preferences don't come into this."

"I don't revolt you, then. We make progress."

His light tone was like a match to tinder. She lifted her chin while fiery temper rose above the turmoil inside her. "If you must know, I am said to have had my first husband killed. That is, of course, if I didn't bludgeon him to death with my own hands. You would be sharing your bed with an accused murderess."

She had said the wrong thing; she knew it instantly. It was because Theodore had been killed while he slept, but this swordsman wasn't to know that. With suffocating chagrin, she waited for his reply.

He didn't keep her waiting.

"But I should be harder to kill, so am willing to accept the risk," he said, a wickedly amused smile curving his mouth, lighting the darkness of his eyes with a startling glow like aged cognac. "In fact, I can think of nothing more certain to please me than to have you share my bed."

# 2

"You don't believe me."

Christien could not deny the charge. It seemed ridiculous on the face of it, that the lady before him could have the fortitude to strike a death blow. What interested him about her claim, beyond the hot flush on her cheekbones for her inadvertent placement of him in her bed, was that she thought it might deter him from marrying her. Well, and the fact that she would go to such lengths to put him off the idea.

"Let us say it seems doubtful," he allowed. "Unless your husband was a much smaller man?"

"Not smaller than I am, but certainly not so large as you."

He could almost feel her gaze travel across his shoulders and along the length of his outstretched leg as she spoke. The tingling sensation left in its wake was difficult to ignore.

"But all men must sleep sometime," she went on. "He was attacked in our bedchamber, you understand."

"So you dispatched him while he snored beside you. Then what? Lay back down and waited until someone came to find him?"

"Certainly not. I didn't—"

She stopped, drew a breath that swelled the gentle curves of her breasts against her bodice in a manner far too enticing for his comfort. High color stained her cheekbones again, and her eyes were the dark gray-blue of a storm sky, revealing her annoyance. Christien didn't mind. It was better than the stricken pallor that had been in her face a moment ago. To continue the effect seemed a worthy cause.

"There," he said with the greatest affability, "I knew you could not be so callous, just as you won't reject my suit out of hand."

"Is that what you are presenting, your suit? I thought it an ultimatum."

He shook his head. "I am offering you my hand and everything I possess. You have only to be reasonable enough to accept them."

"Everything you possess," she repeated in bitter condemnation.

He watched the compression of the lovely lines of her mouth with tight interest and a drawing sensation in his lower abdomen. "Your father's losses are a debt of honor, Madame Pingre, and as such must be paid. No one forced him to wager so deep or remain at the table so long."

"You only took advantage of it."

"That I did," he agreed with instant candor. "Someone was going to have his holdings at the end of the evening. I decided it might as well be me."

She met his gaze for a long moment, her own fathomless as she studied him. He wondered if she heard the stark truth in his voice, could recognize somehow that taking a hand in the game with Cassard had been more than mere happenstance. It was he who looked away first, allowing his gaze to drift again to her lips, so lush and inviting in their graceful curves and smooth surfaces that he had to steel himself against the impulse to reach out, pull her close and take them.

She drew a swift breath, looked away in her turn, shifted to put a little more distance between them. "If you had any consideration at all, you would allow Papa to give you his note of hand for the value of his losses. To dispossess him at his age, much less my mother who is…is not well, is heartless beyond belief."

"But I'm not dispossessing either of them. I'm trying to see to it they need never leave their home here. All you have to do is—"

"Is offer myself up as a sacrifice for their security," she interrupted.

"It seems reasonable enough, given the alternative."

"It isn't reasonable at all! I'd thought to be a widow for the rest of my days."

He frowned, aware of a hollow sensation opening in the center of his chest. "You buried your heart in your beloved's grave."

"Please," she said with a weary gesture.

"Nothing so melodramatic? Nor are you so spineless, I'll warrant."

"I should hope not."

"Being married was a disappointment?"

"No, not at all."

He heard the insistent denial but judged it false. And he wanted her as his wife, wanted to erase all her past knowledge of a husband with a fierceness so sudden it was like a sword thrust to the vitals. "No," he echoed on a hard-drawn breath. "I'm at a loss, then, to see why you are so opposed to what is, after all, a perfectly acceptable arrangement."

"To a man I don't know and with whom I have nothing in common? Yes, and for reasons that give no consideration to compatibility of mind or circumstances, much less affection. Our ideas of what is acceptable differ greatly, *monsieur.*"

"You prefer a love match."

"I hope I have more common sense. Yet a man of my own kind would be preferable."

"So you want to enjoy the pleasures of the social round for a season or two before you choose him, now that your mourning is at an end. Or do you have someone in mind already?"

"Certainly not!" The blue of her eyes carried more heat than the summer sky. "I was speaking in the abstract. I did say I have no interest in another husband."

"But I am at liberty to doubt it. You are far too attractive a woman to wear the willow."

She shook her head in rejection of both compliment and conclusion. "The way my first marriage ended is not likely to make me welcome another offer."

He noted that she made no mention of going back into society. The reason for that was clear enough; few invitations would be extended to a woman suspected of murder. Avoiding that subject seemed best for the moment. "It's my heritage that offends," he went on in dogged persistence.

"Not precisely, though I fail to see why you expect me to be comfortable with a man from a background so unlike my own."

"I have spent several years making a place for myself in the Vieux Carré, Madame Pingre, and have succeeded well enough to draw many gentlemen of good family to my salon," he answered while something cold and hard settled inside him. "Though possibly that's the crux of the matter, after all, the detail that I labor for my living. Yes, and in such an *outré* profession."

"It isn't in your favor." The look in her eyes dared him to make something of it. "What kind of life might I have tied to a husband who believes every quarrel can be settled at sword point? It would be worse than…"

"Worse than your first, perhaps? I do see the objection. About my birth I can do nothing. I am of the ancient native people, the Natchez. Yet French Creole ladies have married and civilized those of other nations before." He gave her a tight smile in recognition that such civilization might be required. "As for my profession, I will pledge to put down my sword on our wedding day and never again raise it against any man."

A startled look rose in her eyes as she stared at him. "You would do that?"

"If you require it." There were few things he would not undertake to gain her agreement.

"And suppose I required…"

"What?" He had to ask the question as she trailed to a halt, though he suspected the answer.

"To…to occupy our marriage bed alone."

The image of her lying in that bed in lawn and lace, with her hair spread in a curling mass around her, shimmering in the lamplight in all its wild glory, rose in his mind's eye. She might start out alone, but it would not be for long if he had any say in the matter. Breathing deep to control the surge of his body in reaction to such thoughts, he said, "So you would condemn us both to celibacy and childlessness?"

"I have a child, my daughter, Marguerite." Her gaze was directed somewhere past his shoulder.

"And I will be proud to be a father to her if it pleases you and she will permit it, but hope to have other children."

She looked down at her hands. "I see."

"It's not an unreasonable expectation," he said quietly.

"It would not be if the situation were normal."

"The situation is ours to command. It can become normal if we will it so."

She looked up, her gaze wary yet shaded with the barest hint of humor. "You have an answer for everything."

"It's a failing of mine," he said in solemn agreement, "and not the only one."

"There are more?"

That small show of interest seemed promising, if not particularly flattering. "I am an early riser and like to ride before breakfast. Idleness is difficult for me. I must always be doing something, so will expect to be involved in the day-to-day operation of the plantation. I enjoy working with my hands and hope you won't be embarrassed if I am seen at it. Though I have no objection to attending a social event now and then, my preference is for quiet evenings at home. I am, in spite of what you may suppose from my occupation, a rather dull man."

"You will forgive me if I find that unlikely?"

"You are free to think whatever you please," he said in dry concession. "Oh, and I should add that I have certain obligations to friends in and around New Orleans so must spend an occasional evening away from you."

"I shall try to bear up under your absence."

He thought his heart failed to beat for a second. "Does that mean you agree?"

"No, no, not in such haste," she answered as confusion amounting to near panic flashed across her face. "I merely— It was only a comment. No, I must have time to think, to discuss the matter with my parents. Something so important, so...so permanent as this, can hardly be decided in a half hour."

"You're wrong. It can be decided in a moment." He knew that much with absolute certainty. It was the reason he was here, the reason he owned River's Edge.

"By some, perhaps, but not by me." She looked down, watching her fingers as she smoothed over the worn wicker that wrapped the arm of her chair. Abruptly she clenched her hand into a fist. "Why?" she demanded. "Why are you doing this?"

"Rather than simply turning you all out into the road? Consider it a whim."

"I don't think you are a man who has whims," she countered, searching his face, "much less one who acts on them. Is it that you require a wife to maintain your home? Perhaps you feel I owe you for your quick action outside the theater so will agree to anything."

"I have no expectation of your gratitude and no use for it."

"Yet you must have a reason."

Oh, he did that, but it was not one he cared to explain. Such knowledge could become a weapon in the wrong hands. He answered with a question of his own. "You don't feel the chance to improve my position is enough?"

"In society, I suppose."

"No marriage vow is likely to make me acceptable among the *haut ton*. The only position of interest to me is as owner of River's Edge. To be a landowner and beholden to none is enough." His lack of status was an essential truth he'd accepted long ago. To speak of it caused no particular distress.

"And this outcast state is one you expect me to suffer as your wife."

"I had thought," he said with quiet reason, "that you were already beyond the pale due to the odd nature of your husband's death. We seemed to be a pair of outcasts, you and I."

Her eyes darkened and she pressed her lips together in a thin line. Somewhere a squirrel chattered, a crow called and a woman with a rich and mellow voice sang a mournful ballad. The warm summer breeze sighed through the trees, then died away again.

"You are quite right," she said abruptly, looking away from him. "Nevertheless, I need time to consider. If you will return tomorrow…"

"I have your father's invitation to remain as a guest at River's Edge until matters have been arranged, one way or another."

She swung back to study his face. "Is that by chance a threat?"

"A statement of fact, rather." Christien allowed a shading of irony to darken his tone. "Though reluctant to wound your sensibilities, I must point out once more that you could all be considered as my guests."

"So we could." She came swiftly to her feet, so he was forced to do the same. "I will give you an answer at the earliest possible instant."

"I would be grateful for it," he said, and had never been more sincere in his life.

If she heard, there was no sign. Turning in a whirl of skirts so wide and fast they polished the dust from his boot tops, she walked from the gallery. He watched her go, noting the straight set of her shoulders, militant tilt of her head and ladylike glide that could not quite conceal the faint, seductive sway of her hips. He felt as strung out as if he had been in a fight to the death. His neck was stiff, and he was uncomfortably aware of another, even more rigid portion of his anatomy.

Whether he had won or lost was impossible to say; he would have to wait on the lady's pleasure for that answer. In the meantime, he was established at the plantation. He was a part of the family, at least temporarily. He was under the same roof as Madame Pingre and her daughter, could breathe the same air, eat at the same table, sleep only a few doors away.

He should have been satisfied, and was in one sense. He also felt like the worst kind of interloper. And why not, when that was exactly the part he played?

# 3

In due time, Monsieur Cassard returned to collect Christien from the gallery, suggesting a stroll to survey the property. It was an unexpected concession to his role as new owner and Christien was duly grateful. He had a thousand questions, but it seemed crass to plunge into them at once. Instead, he made a comment about local politics, which segued into a discussion of the war in Mexico.

"I'm surprised a young man like you isn't with the army," Cassard said as he strolled with the full skirt of his frock coat pushed behind him and his hands clasped under it. "I would be if I were younger."

"It's not my quarrel," Christien answered.

"Such an adventure doesn't come around in every generation."

"True enough." He had considered signing on with the Louisiana Legion that was now fighting below the border. He'd been to the big rallies at Hewlett's Exchange, where many of his friends and fellow *maîtres d'armes* had signed on for the fight, had listened to the speeches and felt his heart pound to the beat of the drums. It seemed a noble thing, to join the struggle of the young United States against old ideas, old forces. To build a country that stretched from sea to sea was a seductive dream. Regardless, he had other plans. Yes, and dreams of his own.

"You think old Scott is the man to finish the job down there?" Cassard asked, referring to General Winfield Scott, commander of the army's eastern division in Mexico.

"He's a seasoned soldier, so he should know what he's about," Christien answered briefly. "He had little enough trouble at Buena Vista."

"Oh, he's ruthless enough, heaven knows. Appalling, the way he took Veracruz. Six thousand shells lobbed into the city, so they say, and such a death toll that the town fathers surrendered so people might save their dead from the vultures. I don't care for this making war on women and children. Truly, it sickens the soul."

It did indeed, Christien thought. To picture a lovely body like that of Reine Cassard torn by exploding shells was more than he could stomach. Her skin was so soft, her curves so sweetly fashioned for a man's hand, and her mouth...

Recovering his wits with an effort, he picked up the thread of the conversation. "President Polk must have known how it would be. Scott, you may recall, commanded the cavalry troop that carried out the forced march of the Southeast Indian tribes to the Indian Territory a decade ago. The deaths of a few hundred more women, children and old people mean nothing to him."

What Christien did not say was that the prospect of fighting under the general was a major reason he was not with the army. Scott's name was spoken with a curse by those of his lineage.

"No doubt you've made a pretty penny out of all the recruits marching off to face Mexican steel."

Christien tamped down a spurt of anger at the suggestion that he was benefiting from the conflict. To take offense would not help his cause. "Business has been good on the Passage these past few years, agreed. But I like to think I may have saved a life or two by teaching men to defend themselves against an enemy with a sword as part of his kit."

Cassard pursed his lips. "Regardless, Scott may find Mexico City a more difficult proposition."

"Santa Ana's forces will defend it with their last breath, and who can blame them?" Christien said in agreement.

"They say he cannot hold out for long."

"They say a lot of things."

"Indeed," the older man with a snort. "Now that express riders bring dispatches from the border ports several times a week, every man who spends a picayune for a news sheet thinks himself a military strategist. To hear them, you would swear they had personally ordered the army of the west to New Mexico and California, the center to the northern territories of Mexico, and the eastern division to Veracruz for the drive on Mexico City. As for the navy blockade—"

"They curse it for depriving them of goods from that part of the world," Christien supplied with a wry smile. "Most seem to be predicting the fall of Mexico City before the summer is done, or hoping for it."

"Pray God they are right," Cassard said. "I grow weary of the whole business."

It seemed a good time to change the subject. Accordingly, Christien inquired about the state of the plantation's ditches, the repairs to the river levee that were required of landowners, the numbers and health of the mule herd, the repair of the sugar mill set some distance away from the main house and the rate of use of the plantation nursery, infirmary and chapel. While deep in discussion of these and other matters, he and his host visited the stable, barns and various other out-buildings. The last of these, the chapel, was a small wooden building with attached steeple whose bell not only called the hands for services, but also rang them in from the fields and warned of fire, flood and other calamities.

Christien was glad enough to inspect it. It was here, in this simple, whitewashed structure with its plain altar and one window of stained glass, that he and Reine would be married. That was, of course, if she agreed.

Leaving the chapel, they walked slowly down the track that fronted the row of neat, whitewashed cabins that housed the slaves on River's Edge. An enormously tall, broad-shouldered hand, so dark his skin had a purple cast to it, was wielding a hoe along a row of vegetables outside the end cabin. Cassard paused to introduce the man as Samson, second in command under the overseer and the driver responsible for seeing work was carried out in the fields. Knowing the prosperity of the place rested as much on this man's shoulders as any other, Christien took a moment to talk to him, sizing him up. He liked what he saw, and said so as he and Cassard walked on again.

"He's a good man, is Samson. He takes pride in his position."

"He was working a garden patch. You allow one for every cabin?" Christien looked up ahead, noting the patches of beans, squash and okra that flanked the structures, many of them brightened with morning glories and yellow daisies.

Monsieur Cassard gave a considered nod. "And a pig or two, as well. It adds to their larder and keeps them healthier and more content, or so my father always claimed. I'm happy to follow his lead, even if…"

"Yes?"

"Well. My…that is, our overseer, feels the practice uses effort that could be put to better use. He may attempt to persuade you to his view. I hope you will leave things as they are."

"I see no reason to change," Christien said readily enough.

"You relieve my mind. I lean toward the French manner of plantation management, not unnaturally, which allows for elasticity in the use of time. The overseer is *Américain* so less tolerant, as was his father, who held the position before him. The attitude was gained from my father-in-law, I regret to say, as he once owned the property. River's Edge was a wedding gift, part of my wife's dowry."

"A handsome one."

"It was," Cassard agreed. "Not that he missed it. He had two or three other places along the river in his possession, was forever buying and selling."

"An enterprising gentleman."

"To a fault, yes. Everything must be made to pay. Maximum effort must always be expended, and he saw that it was so, being a strict taskmaster who preferred to control all in his purview, from the least of his children to the oldest of his slaves. Bonhomie was not his style, you comprehend, nor social grace. He never quite adapted to French Creole ways, though he came from Virginia decades ago, just after Louisiana was turned over to *les Américains*."

The comments seemed noticeably grim, given Cassard's easygoing temperament. Christien wondered what lay behind it. Inquiring too deeply didn't seem politic at this juncture.

The heritage of the plantation's original owner no doubt accounted for the design of River's Edge, he thought, glancing back at the white bulk of the house rising through the trees. It was Georgian in style, with rooms that opened on either side of a long hallway on the lower floor, as he'd noticed earlier, and likely the same upstairs. The basic plan had been altered to suit the climate, however, with French doors rather than windows to admit every chance current of air and wide galleries, or verandas, to protect the walls from semitropical downpours. That the galleries functioned in the French mode, as convenient outside hallways for moving from room to room, was incidental.

"I was not aware your wife was American," Christien went on after a moment.

Maurice Cassard's smile was tender. "My Nora has spoken French in our family circle for such a long time she's almost forgotten it was not her first language."

"Your daughter must be modeled upon her."

"What makes you say that?" Cassard gave him a keen look.

"She seems a forthright lady, if I may say so, with little use for coquettish airs."

"Quite right, though it's her grandmother, my wife's mother, you must look to for that pattern card. That lady was Irish and formidable in her strength of character. My Nora, I fear, is made of more fragile clay."

Christien gave him a quick look, but Reine's father was staring out over the cane fields ahead of them with such an unhappy expression on his face it was plain the description gave him no pleasure. "Was? The grandmother is deceased?" he inquired.

"She died in childbirth, a change-of-life baby that perished with her."

Condolences were necessary, though Christien allowed only the smallest of pauses before he went on. "And Madame Pingre's grandfather, this *Américain?* He lives nearby?"

"At one time he did, only a few miles down the river road. He, too, is gone."

"A pity," Christien replied with perfunctory courtesy.

"These things happen," Cassard said with a shrug.

"You may wonder that my wife and I are so dependent on your good will, given her father's extensive holdings. She came of a large family, you understand, with ten brothers and sisters who lived to adulthood. By the time everything was portioned out among them, there was scarce enough in any one allotment to matter."

Christien suspected a certain amount of Madame Cassard's portion had vanished over the gaming tables. That was none of his business, though he also thought the fact that Cassard had done nothing to earn the honey fall made wagering it on the turn of a card easier. The same applied to River's Edge, of course. Not that he faulted Reine's father for the way he lived. For one thing, idleness and reckless plunging at cards was the way of the aristocratic French Creoles, and Cassard would be condemned for acting otherwise. Then, he himself was hardly in a position to feel superior given the way he had gained the place.

"You will forgive me for bringing up another death," Christien said as they strolled on a few more steps, "but I have a certain curiosity over the passing of your daughter's late husband. He was killed, I believe."

"So it's supposed. I prefer to think it a tragic accident."

"Your daughter is credited with aiding his passing."

Cassard made a sound of disgust. "Nonsense, utter nonsense."

"Why should anyone think otherwise?"

Reine's father shot him a quick glance from under lowered brows. "You know what people are, always looking for scandal in anything the least unusual."

"True, though I gather the affair was something of a three-day wonder." Persistence, Christien had noted, sometimes had its rewards.

"Oh, it was a damnable business. Theodore—her husband, that is, Theodore Pingre—simply disappeared from the house one night. All that was left to indicate what happened to him was a welter of blood and gore on his bed linens and a poker stuck with bits of flesh and hair on the carpet beside it. Nothing was heard from him for several days. A body was pulled from the river then, and identified only by the alliance ring on his finger. Turtles and catfish had got at him, you understand."

Christien was unmoved by the image. He'd seen his share of bodies that floated up from the river's bottom, the occurrence being all too common along the New Orleans waterfront. Bloated, waterlogged, the victims were often so changed it was difficult for their own mothers to identify them. "When you speak of the house, I take you to mean from their home?"

"No, no, they were here at River's Edge."

"Indeed." He allowed idle curiosity to layer his tone.

Cassard frowned a little but answered readily enough. "Young Marguerite was ill with a stomach complaint. Her life was feared for as these sicknesses take so many little ones. Reine and Theodore were living at Bonne Espèrance, her husband's family place that borders with River's Edge. It was the usual ménage, including Monsieur and Madame Pingre, a widowed sister of *madame,* a bedridden uncle and his daughters who looked after him. All that was lacking were brothers and sisters to Theodore, this because he was the only child to live to maturity. No great tragedy, that, as Madame Pingre is a woman who should, perhaps, never have been a mother. Monsieur Pingre, before he died, lavished a fortune on the boy to make up for it."

Christien nodded his understanding as Cassard paused. The last circumstance might provide some explanation for how Pingre had become a man who cared nothing for the young females he despoiled. "Madame Pingre, his mother, is still in residence there?"

"By no means. She embarked for Paris not long after her son died. The house has been closed up these two years and more."

"I don't suppose she has any idea of selling?" It seemed possible one of his friends from the Passage de la Bourse might have an interest. It was always a good thing to choose one's neighbors.

"If so, I've heard nothing of it," Cassard said.

He would keep it in mind, nevertheless, Christien thought. At least Cassard had the same opinion of the lady that he had acquired. "I didn't mean to interrupt your story," Christien said with a slight bow of apology. "You were saying?"

"Where was I? Oh, yes, Theodore. He was never one to abide illness, so took himself off to town. His uncle, already ill with a wasting sickness, came down with Marguerite's childish complaint and was carried off by it in a matter of hours. Reine, being apologetic over the death and feeling the funereal atmosphere was unlikely to aid her little one's recovery, bundled her up and brought her here where she might have the aid and support of her family."

"Your son-in-law returned and came to River's Edge to be with them, I suppose."

"It would appear so."

Christien lifted a brow. "Meaning?"

"No one saw him arrive on that night, just as no one saw him leave. Or be taken away, as the case may be."

"How did he get into the house? Was the butler not on duty?"

"Alonzo had been sent to bed after more than twenty-four hours on his feet, carrying trays up and down, also endless cans of hot water. The doors were not locked as Reine and the baby's old nursemaid, Demeter, were still going in and out to the kitchen. Everything was at sixes and sevens, you perceive, as we feared for Marguerite's life."

Christien gave a nod as he pictured it. To close off access to the outdoor kitchen would not have been practical. "No one saw or heard anything unusual?" he asked after a moment.

Cassard shook his white head. "The sheriff came and put the same question to the house servants and everyone else on the place. Yes, and with the same lack of results. Monsieur…"

Christien lifted a brow as he waited for his host to arrange his thoughts. When he failed to continue, he said, "You meant to say?"

"I hesitate to speak for reasons that may be obvious,

yet honor compels that I be frank with you. The circumstances here are more difficult than you imagine. Because of it, I shall not hold you to your offer of marriage. That's if you think to withdraw it."

"No." It was the last thing Christien intended.

"You are not put off by the notoriety surrounding Pingre's death?"

"It was a trying time, I'm sure, but I can't imagine your daughter was at fault. My concern is only for how she came to be implicated in such a bloody affair." As he was not inclined to pursue his release from his proposal, he went on with hardly a pause. "What do you believe happened?"

His future father-in-law looked at him for a second while relief eased the lines of strain in his face. Glancing away again, he said, "I cannot answer that, I'm sorry to say. I was not at home that evening."

"You were in town?"

"Gaming, you mean?" Cassard grimaced. "I can hardly fault you for wondering, but no. The upset with Marguerite had brought on one of my wife's nervous spells. She had but a single dose left of the laudanum she takes at bedtime. I drove to town late that evening and slept at the town house overnight so as to purchase a new supply the instant the apothecary opened next morning. By the time I returned with it, the sad business was done."

It made sense, Christien saw. If Cassard had been on the premises, the murderer would surely have thought twice about entering the house. "Exactly how long ago did all this take place?"

"Over two years now, as Marguerite was five her

last birthday. She saw it, you know, or we must suppose so as she was in the same room. You might think she would recall nothing, being so young. Nevertheless, she has horrific dreams, sees monsters everywhere since that night. Why, she even claimed she saw one the night you saved her outside the theater. I'd thought her release from mourning black might improve matters, but…" He trailed off with a shake of his head.

*Papa. Oh, Papa.*

The child's soft cry echoed in Christien's memory, the undercurrent of his every thought concerning that night outside the opera house. He'd thought he might have reminded Marguerite of her father, but it seemed unlikely given what he'd just heard. What did it really mean?

"Marguerite and her father," he said with a frown, "they were close?"

Cassard gave Christien a quick glance from under lowered brows. "Theodore was not what one might call a doting parent. He was far more occupied with his friends and their round of cockfights and barrel houses."

"Wild, in a word."

"Immature, I would say instead," he answered with a sigh of weary tolerance. "It's a failing of men who marry young, before they have time to become jaded with town pursuits or to settle into the role of husband and father. They improve with age."

"Hard on their wives."

"Who are equally young and inexperienced, yes, though usually have their families to support them."

"It was an arranged marriage, I suppose?"

"It seemed a good match," Cassard said in immediate defense. "Theodore was his parents' only heir, as I told you before. He and Reine played together from the time they left their cradles, were of the same age and didn't dislike each other. His family had been friends and neighbors for many years. Worse alliances have prospered."

Indeed they had, Christien thought, and this one must have been compatible enough given that it had produced Marguerite. Before he could express that unpalatable thought, however, he caught the thud of quick footsteps. He turned to see the object of his thoughts racing toward them down the lane they had been following.

Marguerite Pingre wore a ruffled pinafore over full skirts and pantaloons and narrow boots of white kid on her small feet. The pink ribbon that held her bright, flying hair away from her face was tied in a bow on top of her head. It threatened to come loose from its moorings with every pounding step. Gamboling around her was the big red bloodhound that had greeted Christien on his arrival. With his tongue lolling out and his eyes bright with joy, he had no aspect of fearsome watchdog whatever.

"Help, *Grand-père*, help me!" the child called. "I've run away from Babette to see the gentleman with the sword she and Cook talk about. I run fast, fast so she can't catch me. She says I'm naughty and the *loup-garou* will get me."

Monsieur Cassard bent and closed his arms around the child as she threw herself against his legs. Lifting her, he gave her a firm buss on one flushed cheek, smiling into her piquant little face. "What would any old werewolf want with the likes of you, *hein?* Such a small kitten as you are would hardly be a mouthful for him. Now say hello to Monsieur Lenoir, *ma chère,* for he is our visitor and we must make him welcome."

The child lifted clear blue eyes fringed with fine, dark lashes to him. They widened and she gave a quick gulp. She made no other sound, but held so still she might have been a small wax effigy.

"Have you nothing to say, Marguerite? It's impolite to ignore a guest."

"It's the man," she whispered, her face serious as she leaned to confide this news into her grandfather's ear.

"*C'est vrai?* But which man, *ma petite?*"

"The man who knocked me down in the street. Yes, and *Maman,* too, so the horses wouldn't hurt us. Is he the man with the sword? Will he kill the *loup-garou?*"

Cassard shot Christien an amused glance. "You must ask him, yes?"

The hope in the child's deep blue eyes as she turned them on him was too much for Christien to resist. "But certainly I will slay the beast for you," he said, making her his best bow. "Only show him to me, and he won't live a minute."

Her expression was uncertain, and still she didn't smile. "Truly?"

"I swear it on my honor." It seemed a safe enough vow considering werewolves existed only in childish nightmares. The best thing to be done to rid young

Marguerite of these fantasies, and perhaps her nightmares as well, would be to see to it her nursemaid ceased using the threat of monsters to frighten her into obedience. That was, of course, if he was allowed a stepfather's right of interference, or any right at all where she and her mother were concerned.

"I like you," the child said with abrupt decision.

"You are very kind, *mademoiselle*," he answered, his voice as grave as hers had been, "just as a lady should be."

"*Maman* isn't always, or *Grand-mère*."

"Marguerite!" Monsieur Cassard exclaimed in protest.

"I'm sure they have their reasons." To prevent irony from surfacing in his voice took more effort than Christien expected.

"I am a trial, and so is *Grand-père*. Will you be a trial?"

"My angel, please."

Christien shook his head, both for the child and to allow Cassard to know there was no need for his concern. "I shall endeavor not to be one."

"*Maman* will like you, then."

"We must hope that's the case." Seldom had he meant anything more.

They returned to the house, the child walking between Christien and her grandfather and the big hound trailing protectively at their heels. She was not a chattering sort, he discovered as they moved slowly toward the graceful white structure seen through the screen of oak branches. She was thinner than he remembered, as well, and seemed to have a pinched look to her small features that he did not recall. Her thoughts did not make her happy, apparently, for she frowned as she walked.

Yet now and then she looked up at him with an expression in her small face that bordered on wonder. The expectation in it flicked Christien's heart on the raw, troubling him more than he cared to admit.

Guilt was never a comfortable companion.

# 4

Dinner, served at the usual hour of three in the afternoon, was a sumptuous meal in several courses, beginning with creamed soup and continuing with two fish dishes, two of poultry, three baked or smoked meats, a medley of vegetable selections, syllabub in dainty cups and a final tray of cheese and nuts.

A great, shield-shaped *chasse-mouche* of mahogany, pulled by a velvet rope in the hand of a small, yawning kitchen boy, swung back and forth over the polished board to discourage the circling flies and also to cool the diners. Regardless, beads of sweat ran down the water glasses filled with cool spring water and oozed in golden beads of oil from the cheese. Perspiration also shone on the faces of the servants, who moved quietly around the table, removing plates, offering dishes and replenishing water and wine-glasses.

Christien was impressed. His own meals were Spartan indeed in comparison, and that was on the rare occasion when he dined in his rooms instead of a restaurant. Familial boards were not a large part of his life in spite of invitations from friends and former sword masters Gavin Blackford and Nicholas Pasquale, Caid O'Neill and the Conde de Lérida, and also the Kentuckian Kerr Wallace when he and his Sonia were in town for the winter. Christen was reasonably certain any leftover food would be enjoyed in the kitchen by the more privileged house servants, yet the array was a telling indication of the bounty produced at River's Edge.

They were six at the table. Monsieur Cassard had tried to relinquish the head of the board to him, but Christien had refused in favor of a place at the right hand of his hostess. Across from him was Reine, with Marguerite seated on a cushion beside her mother. By default, the remaining place was taken by Reine's brother, Paul Cassard.

The younger Monsieur Cassard was no longer a boy, but perhaps a year or two away from his majority. With a thatch of brown hair and hazel-green eyes, he seemed more suited to the outdoors than to the salon; certainly his frock coat and pantaloons were those of an unpretentious countryman rather than a town dandy. He had, so it appeared from a brief exchange with his father, been responsible for the fish that was a part of the meal, only returning from a foray upon the river in his skiff in time for his catch to be cooked.

He had witnessed the boy's return, Christien realized, though he'd not known who he was at the time. Glancing out his bedchamber window while washing for the meal, he had seen him trotting toward the house. In his hand had been a willow branch stripped of its bark and left with a thumblike projection of side limb to hold the fine catch of bass and bream that wriggled upon it. Loose-limbed, sunburned, with hair a rough tangle and his clothes stained with river water, he'd seemed carefree and cheerful.

The boy was less so now. No doubt he'd been informed of the situation at hand. He could not be pleased to learn the house and land he might have been expected to inherit were lost to him. It was regrettable, but a problem that could be dealt with later.

"Your accommodations are quite comfortable, Monsieur Lenoir?"

The query came from the frail lady seated at the foot of the table. Madame Cassard appeared older than she should as the mother of a young son and a daughter barely in her twenties. Her hands shook as she manipulated her spoon and fork, her skin had a grayish cast and her thinning tresses were augmented by rolls of false hair tucked into the massed curls on top of her head. Her pale blue eyes seemed uncomfortably searching in their appraisal as they rested upon him. Though her husband had said she was not to be told of present events, Christien wondered if she had not gleaned the knowledge by some other means.

"They could not be more so." It was not mere politeness. He'd been pleasantly surprised by the size of the bedchamber and connecting dressing room allotted him.

"If there is anything you require, you have only to ask for it. But permit me to say that you seem familiar, *monsieur.* Who was your father, if you please?"

"It's unlikely you ever met him, Madame Cassard," he said, keeping his voice rigorously even. "He was Jules Lenoir, a defrocked priest and former missionary to the tribes along the Mississippi. That was until he made his home to the north, in the swamplands of central Louisiana."

The lady lifted her brows, her features set as she digested that piece of news. After a moment, she went on. "And your mother?"

"Her name would mean even less, I fear." It was, Christien reminded himself, the kind of catechism that might be expected by any visitor, but particularly one who came as a suitor for her daughter's hand. Widowed or not, she must be protected from those who were unworthy. He would certainly be counted among that number under normal circumstances.

"She or your father must have been of Spanish blood, yes? You are, if you'll forgive me for saying so, as dark as a Moor."

"*Maman,* you must not say such things," Reine said, reaching to put her hand on her mother's arm. The glance she sent across the table to Christien carried only the slightest trace of apology.

"But how else am I to learn anything? I can hardly ask others about him in the usual way, now, can I?"

"Answer that if you can," Paul Cassard told his sister without looking up from his plate. "Does King know he's here?"

"I think not. At least, not as yet," Reine answered in clipped tones.

"Bet he won't be happy."

"King?" Christien inquired, his tone mild in deliberate contrast to his heightened interest.

"Merely Owen Kingsley, the overseer," Reine answered. "As for my mother's questions, you are not obliged to answer if they offend you."

"I have no particular objection." Christien committed the overseer's name to memory before turning back to Madame Cassard. "You asked about my coloring, *madame.* My mother was not Spanish but rather descended from the last Great Sun of the Natchez."

The gaze of his hostess turned bewildered. "I beg your pardon?"

"Truly?" Paul demanded, his eyes wide as he looked up at last. Cassard paused with his spoon halfway to his mouth, his expression arrested. Only Reine continued to eat, having heard something of it before.

The copper tint of his skin, a different hue from the olive cast of those claiming Spanish ancestry, had been a sore point since his arrival in New Orleans. He'd endured less polite inquiries about it than that of his hostess. Too many were obsessed with skin color in their fear of whispers concerning a touch of the tar brush. To be descended from one of the older native tribes of the area was no great step upward in their estimation.

"The Natchez tribe is no more," he went on evenly. "You may recall that they were scattered more than a hundred years ago, after they rose against the French at Fort Rosalie. Some were sold into slavery in the

Caribbean, while others fled to tribes in Louisiana and Mississippi, where they remained until more recent years. My father lived among them, and my mother was a member of his flock. She was baptized with a Christian name a short time before they were wed."

"Quite a romance." Paul's voice held barely repressed doubt. "No wonder he was defrocked."

"As you say." Christien gave him a level look before he continued. "The last remnants of the Natchez were rounded up almost ten years ago, along with the Tunica and a half dozen other tribes along the Mississippi and Arkansas rivers, then sent with the Cherokee on the long march to the Indian Territory some call the Trail of Tears. As a woman married to a white man, my mother might have been spared, but her family would certainly have been taken. They all fled into the swamps."

"They escaped the march, then?"

That question came from Reine. Christien was glad of the excuse to turn to her. "For what good it did them. They made a home in the back reaches of the swamp that lies along the river named for the Duc du Maine, but it eventually defeated them."

"You were with them?"

A fugitive sympathy seemed to lay pooled in her eyes, but it might have been an illusion caused by the moving shadow of the *chasse-mouche* swinging above them. He inclined his head. "I was there, being only a year or so older than your brother when we went into the swamps."

"But you didn't remain."

"I could not. All but a handful were gone after a few years, dead of fevers, snakebite, blood poisoning and a half-dozen other things it would be impolite to speak of at the dinner table." Nor did he care to speak of them. The images of death and dying were burned into his soul. The only escape was in banishing them from memory.

"How came you to avoid these perils?"

It sounded rather like an accusation, though that might have been in his ears only. "I was sent away so the last of the Great Sun's bloodline would not die out in Louisiana. My mother, sister to the last man officially selected in secret to wear the mantle of the Great Sun and the only female of her family left alive, chose me to carry on the tradition. It was her right in accordance with Natchez tradition. Though the Great Sun is male, the title descends through the female line."

He had been sent into the world alone, banished from his remaining family and heritage. He'd not heard from them again except to be told they were gone. He thought some few others of his mother's people had arrived in the Indian Territory, but had no idea if they still lived. For all he knew, he might indeed be the last of his kind, the last of the Great Sun's line.

"Extraordinary," Monsieur Cassard said.

Paul Cassard nodded in agreement as he watched Christien with an unwavering gaze. "I'll say. You have a Natchez name?"

He inclined his head. "You would translate is as *faucon nuit.*"

"Nighthawk. How picturesque. Did you choose it yourself?"

"By no means." He looked from one to the other, his features rigorously composed. "You don't believe me."

Paul Cassard's eyes narrowed in concentration. "You know, it almost seems to me I've heard that name...."

Monsieur Cassard stepped in before his son could complete the thought. "Don't take us up so quickly, *mon cher.* It's only that we had not thought to meet one such as yourself."

The French Creole gentleman had never expected to have someone like him as a guest under his roof or be forced to accept him as a possible son-in-law, Christien thought. It would be interesting to know if Cassard would have agreed so readily to his unusual proposal had he known his background. It seemed doubtful.

"I'm sure I've seen you somewhere," Madame Cassard insisted, her voice fretful. If she had heard or understood a single word of what had been said in the few moments just past, it was impossible to tell it from her expression.

Reine's gaze was just as shuttered, though for other reasons altogether, he was sure. She was deliberately concealing her thoughts concerning the prospect of a Natchez for a husband, also her belief concerning his hereditary position as ruler of a tribe that no longer existed. He would have given much to know her impressions, though they mattered little in the long run. He meant to have her, whatever she might think of him.

The meal came to an end and Christien retreated

to his bedchamber. Someone, Alonzo perhaps, had brought up his valise from where it had been tied behind his saddle and placed the contents in the armoire that anchored one wall. His sword case, an item never far from his side, rested on the table beside the bed. Inside was a pair of matched rapiers that he had bought from his friend Gavin Blackford, or rather Gavin's wife, since they had belonged originally to the lady. Of French manufacture, with blades of finest steel ornately chased along half their length, they had hilts of wrought silver enameled in black, and leather-wrapped handles. They were as beautiful as they were deadly.

The room was spacious but dim as the tall French doors that opened out onto the front gallery were closed against the late afternoon heat. Its walls were wainscoted, with cypress planking below a chair rail and plaster above that was painted with a series of murals after Watteau. A convenient commode table with pitcher and bowl, an armchair, a rosewood armoire and matching half-tester bed completed the furnishings. Comfort underfoot was provided by an Axminster carpet in shades of cream and green. Connecting to the bedchamber was a small dressing room with a chest of drawers, bootjack, coffin-shaped zinc tub for bathing and hinged screen to prevent chilling drafts.

It was not the master bedchamber. Christien had not expected it would be. Still, he could not help wondering if that more commodious room would be turned over to him in due time. Nor could he prevent himself from speculating on whether the master's lady would sleep there with him, or if she would have her own bedchamber accessed through an interior door.

The confrontation with Reine rose up in his mind. It had gone as well as could be expected, he thought. She had been cool to his proposal, which was hardly surprising, but had not screamed, cried or begged to be spared, had given him no outright refusal.

Thank God the task of putting the proposition before her and her father was over. He'd been steeling himself to it for a week or more, dreading how it might be received. Now he had only to possess his soul in patience until he had an answer.

Christien had not slept well the night before. The great half-tester bed beckoned with its pristine white counterpane and gently moving mosquito *baire*. He slipped from his frock coat, removed his cravat and the studs from his shirt, levered off his boots. Mounting the bed steps in one bound, he stretched out on the mattress with his fingers laced behind his head.

He was still covered in perspiration. Levering up to one elbow, he stripped off his shirt, scrubbed his chest and arms with it and flung it toward the nearby chair. He lay back again, wiping his face with his hands.

The half-tester overhead had a lining of pleated yellow muslin and side curtains of gold damask over a mosquito *baire* of pale yellow netting, all of which were drawn back at the midpoint. The mattress beneath him seemed stuffed with high-grade cotton for sublime softness. A faint breeze sifted through the louvers at the shuttered windows, stirring the under curtains at the windows so they wafted in lazy waves.

It was so pleasant that he closed his eyes for a few minutes. The others in the household were doing the same after the heavy meal, he was sure. A late-afternoon rest was a must in the blood-simmering heat, as well as a pleasant custom left over from old Spanish days.

He came awake with a scream ringing in his ears. Heaving himself off the bed, he hit the floor with the thud of his stocking feet, then hovered there, startled by the strange bedchamber and the darkness that filled it. He was stiff and headachy, a sign of how long and hard he'd slept. It must be near midnight, at least.

The wail came again, thin, high-pitched, ringing down the hallway outside his bedchamber. Snatching open his sword case on the bedside table, he hefted one of the matched blades. He strode to the door, pulled it wide and moved into the long, dark corridor.

Something small and white wavered in the dimness. Abruptly, it sprang toward him.

It was Marguerite, flinging herself against him, clinging to his legs with desperate strength. She shook with sobs between the keening cries, almost too high for human ears, which whistled in her throat.

Down the hall, a door flung open. Light streamed out, a long beam that came closer. Christien turned toward it with his sword in his fist and his free hand holding the child against his side.

Reine stood in the doorway with the lamp held high. Its light spilled over her, catching with blue and orange fire in the shimmering tresses that tumbled around her shoulders, casting mysterious shadows down the white batiste fullness of her nightgown. She stood as still as a statue for an instant, her wide gaze brushing over his bare shoulders, his set features, the sword he held in readiness.

Directly across from where he stood, another door swung open. A moan came from the dark interior of the room. "Angel of Death! I knew it, I knew it! He's come, come at last. Angel of Death, come for me. I said it, I knew him. I told you, didn't I? I knew it, I *knew...*"

The anguished and near incoherent muttering grew louder as Madame Cassard staggered into the hall. Her eyes were wide and she clutched a rosary of ivory beads in her hand. She stared at Christien in the dim glow from her daughter's lamp, her features slack and eyes wide as her voice dropped to a whisper.

Just down the hall, Monsieur Cassard hovered in the door of his own room, his face a mask of concern. At the edge of his vision, Christien was also aware of a dark shadow that materialized into the butler, Alonzo, coming down the narrow set of stairs from what must be the house servant's rooms in the attic.

The trembling in the child grew more violent. Her keening rose once more to a scream stifled only as she buried her face against Christien's thigh. She clutched him with the strength of desperation in her small hands.

Ignoring the others, he sank to his heels beside her. He drew her to him, folding her to his chest with his sword still in his hand. "I've got you," he said into her hair as he rocked her. "You're safe now. Hush, *ma petite,* don't cry. The *loup-garou* will never get you, I won't let it. It's gone and I have you now."

Marguerite hiccuped and circled his neck tightly with a small arm, huddling close. She rested her head on his shoulder, heaved a sigh and was silent.

Reine Pingre moved then, coming toward them in a spreading circle of lamplight that cast her moving shadow over the walls, appearing half avenging goddess, half Madonna. Tears filled her eyes and her features were blank with the force of her relief. Kneeling beside the two of them in a billow of fine white fabric, she placed the lamp on the floor, then touched her daughter's fair hair, smoothing it gently.

"She will be all right, I think," Christien said in a low tone.

"I believe so." Reine lifted her lashes, meeting Christien's gaze while stark gratitude shone in the pure blue of her eyes. "And because of it, you have won River's Edge in truth, Christien Lenoir. If you can keep her safe, keep us all safe, then I will marry you."

# 5

What had possessed her?

Reine could not quite explain it even to herself as she lay staring at the dark ceiling of her bedchamber with her sleeping daughter huddled against her. Circumstances compelled her to accept Lenoir's offer, of course, but it also seemed imperative that the half-naked swordsman should not leave River's Edge.

A large part of it was that he had stopped Marguerite's hysteria with a few soft words, something she could not do. No, nor anyone else in the house. It had been the way her daughter clung to him as to a savior, as well. It had also been her mother's rambling denunciation, the darkness pressing around them and the terror for Marguerite that had surged along her veins. The memory of his deep voice naming them both as outcasts played into it, as well, as did the feeling that nothing would ever be the same if she failed to give her promise.

It was a desperate gamble. Perhaps she was more her father's daughter than she knew.

Her decision had not been affected at all by the

sight of a broad chest and muscled arms, a hard hand holding a sword or a handsome face set in such steadfast resolve that it seemed nothing could daunt him, nothing defeat him. She had seen a man undressed to the waist before. She was no virgin miss to swoon at her first sight of an abdomen like corrugated iron or a man's bare feet. She had shared a bedchamber with her husband where they dressed and undressed, bathed, occupied the same bed and all the rest of it.

Seeing Theodore half-dressed had been nothing like the glimpse she had of Christien Lenoir. No, nothing at all.

She pushed the thought from her with determination. They were both men, no more and no less. How different could they be?

Well, yes, Christien's body was honed by practice on the fencing strip. It had also been sculpted with muscle turned steel-hard with fortitude and protective instinct. He was taller, wider and stronger by many degrees than the man she had married, a stripling who had never lifted a finger except to turn a card or take a drink. It was possible he was different in other ways, as well.

She would not dwell on that. She was also different from the green girl who had accepted the husband chosen for her because it had been expected from childhood, because she had been told her parents knew best. She was a grown woman with a daughter. She had spent two years helping manage River's Edge, making decisions, ordering supplies, distributing food, care and comfort to all who depended upon her. She had survived the death of her husband, Marguerite's nightmares, her father's lax attitudes and her mother's increasing frailty. She would never again bow to a husband's will, no matter how he sneered, shouted or rode off to other women.

The wedding would cause a sensation. Little else would be talked of in the neighborhood for weeks, even months. That the woman whose husband had died so mysteriously should take a fencing master of Natchez blood as his replacement, one to whom her father had lost everything in a card game, would be delicious beyond words. How they would whisper and smirk, vowing she deserved no better.

Why, why had she agreed?

It was the hard purpose allied to fierce tenderness in Christien's eyes as he held Marguerite, so very like the expression on his face that night outside the theater, that had moved her. Yes, that was it. Could he ever wear that look for the sake of a woman grown?

Not for her, of course. She had no expectation of anything other than tolerance. Well, and the sort of coupling in the dark that had produced her daughter— dutiful, uncomfortable and maddeningly short-lived.

She flung a hand across her eyes as she thought of the physical side of her marriage. To be used with scarce a caress or kiss, merely the clumsy lift of her nightgown and fast, hard mounting, had too often left her feeling bruised and bereft. Some deep instinct told her it should be different, a sybaritic feast of passion taken in slow, bone-deep gratification. Theodore had batted aside her small efforts in that direction, grunting as he took what he wanted in such furious effort it seemed he feared to fail before he achieved it. And perhaps he had cause, for he sometimes lost his seed upon the sheets before he could fumble his way into her.

Even with such disappointment, Reine had caught, now and again, the intimation of something just out of her reach. It seemed it might be touched if only she could turn to the arms of another man immediately after Theodore rolled away from her.

Wicked, wicked to think such a thing! She must be utterly lost to grace that she had yearned for more than a single man seemed able to provide. What husband could respect, much less care for, a wife with such wanton imagination, such fervid excess of desire?

She must keep the weakness to herself now as she had before. That should not be difficult. In her brief experience, men neither noticed nor cared what occupied the minds of the women around them, had no interest in their secret longings. If such inclinations should happen to be brought to their attention, they were put down to female irrationality, so of no concern. There was safety in such an attitude, though it was annoying in the extreme.

What on earth was she to say to her future husband when she met him at breakfast? Deciding when, where and how they would marry might occupy them for a short while, but what then?

She had no idea. He was a stranger, after all.

She had agreed to marry a stranger with copper skin and dark, dark eyes. Yes, and splendid shoulders. And a hard fist when he held a sword in his hand. Nighthawk, how barbaric it sounded. And yet there was something in his eyes, some shadow of sadness when he spoke of his vanished people, some isolation of the soul that touched an answering chord inside her.

Sleep would not come. She turned and sighed and adjusted her pillow a dozen times while the minutes ticked away, marked by a small clock on the fireplace mantel. She flung her arms up on the pillow beside her head.

Her alliance ring made a clicking noise as it hit the headboard. She reached with her right hand to finger the familiar shape in the dark, its gold scrollwork and curved shape designed to be paired with Theodore's matching band. Slowly, she inched it off.

She was to marry Christien Lenoir. She need no longer wear the ring that marked her as Theodore's wife.

Sitting up with care to avoid disturbing Marguerite, she pushed aside the mosquito netting and eased from the bed. She moved, sure-footed in the dark, to her dressing table and felt for her pin dish, dropping the ring into it. She would lock it away properly in the morning as a remembrance for her daughter.

She was turning back to the bed when she heard the big bloodhound, Chalmette, bark with the sound of warning. Glancing at the bed to be sure the noise had not disturbed Marguerite, she eased from the bedchamber into the connecting sitting room. At its

French doors, she drew back the heavy curtains, opened a shutter and peered out.

A horseman rode at a quiet walk from the direction of the stable. Rounding the house, he turned down the drive toward the river road. As he reached the wider roadway, he picked up his pace to a canter.

The man was only a dark, upright shape in the saddle under the dim light of a sickle moon, but that was enough for Reine to identify him. It was her newly betrothed bridegroom, riding out on some business almost certain to be clandestine. Why else would he sneak from his bedchamber in the early morning hours, making every effort not to disturb the house?

What was he about? A woman more vivacious and accommodating than she had been, perhaps? Cards, drinking, laughing and talking with his swordsmen friends?

Desolation seeped through Reine's veins. She closed her eyes and rested her head against the curtain folds that were pulled tight in her hand. So it began again, the lies, the desertions, the betrayals. The aching loneliness. She had expected better of Christien Lenoir, though why she could not have said. Perhaps she had only hoped.

Could she bear it all again? Could she accept glib explanations instead of the truth? Could she smile and pretend everything was as it should be? Could she stand being made to feel again that she was lacking because her husband preferred more amusing company?

It was the fate of women, or so she had been told. Men were men, *n'est-ce pas?* They must have outlets for their terrible male energy. Whatever excitement they might find elsewhere, they must always return to their wives, yes? It was a woman's duty to wait on that moment. A wise one took pleasure and comfort in her children and learned to enjoy her occasional freedom from the demands of the bedchamber.

The answer to that, Reine had always thought, was almost childishly simple. If marriage was supposed to be passed in such solitary waiting, then why take a husband at all? And in fact, life had been much more peaceful with Theodore gone. No demands that she come to bed at once, no disparaging remarks about her failure to follow the current modes, no teasing and tickling Marguerite until she was in tears, no wrestling with Paul until he was red-faced with anger over unkind jeers from a man ten years his senior and half again his size.

No sneering at her *Américain* mother, and no curses if she dared question where Theodore had been, suggested he limit the glasses of cognac he drank after dinner or asked that he refrain from leading her father into the most infamous of the Vieux Carré's gambling dens.

Much more peaceful, yes.

Now it would begin again.

Releasing the curtain she held, she smoothed the brocade folds with trembling fingers and turned to make her way back to her bed. She didn't sleep, however. The first breezes of dawn, drifting into the room, stirred the ghostlike folds of her mosquito *baire*, seeped inside its white tent to cool the tears on her face.

# 6

Pale lamplight shone from the balcony doors, which stood open to the hot night air. Vinot was still up, Christien thought, or more likely had never gone to bed. He bracketed his lips with his hands and whistled in a soft signal. The old fencing master's shadow shifted, a gray ghost of movement against the salon's high ceiling as he picked up the lamp and left the room. A few minutes later, the street door swung open on oiled hinges.

"You're back, my son," Lucien Vinot said, his voice as gentle as his eyes were sharp. "I had not expected you so soon."

Christien stepped inside, took the door and closed it behind him.

"The first part is accomplished. More than that, I've been given a bedchamber at River's Edge."

"So you are established there. Excellent." The *maître* turned and shuffled back down the long hallway that led under the upper floor of the house, ending at a set of stairs that curved their way upward. Over his shoulder, he said, "You had no difficulty with Cassard?"

"None at all. He was expecting me, of course."

"And his daughter, she was agreeable?"

Christien followed after his onetime mentor, reaching around to take the lamp as the older man grasped the banister to pull himself up the stairs. "I wouldn't put it quite that way, but she allowed herself to be persuaded."

"I'll warrant she did. You have a convincing way about you."

"She was more taken by the fact that her daughter likes me. It's a damnable business. I could almost wish it undone."

The *maître* stopped at the head of the stairs to look back down at him, his gray hair loose, long and free of pomade, making a silver nimbus around his head and shoulders. "But not enough to undo everything?"

Christien thought of Reine standing like a goddess with the folds of her near-transparent nightgown swirling around her feet and a lamp like a beacon in her hand. He recalled the womanly fragrance of her, and the sheen of her hair as it was burnished by lamplight. He felt again the touch of her hand that seemed a permanent brand on his skin. "No," he said shortly.

Vinot gave a pleased nod as he stalked into the room that served him as both salon and bedchamber. Gesturing toward the table in the center as a place for Christien to deposit the lamp, he poured two glasses of sherry from the decanter next to it and handed one to him. "Did you have time to look around?"

Christien inclined his head. "For what good it did me. Everything seemed just as it should."

"Nothing unusual in their manner? No sign of disturbance?"

"Naturally, they were disturbed. I've taken everything they own and foisted myself on them as a houseguest and future bridegroom. It would be incredible if they accepted it without kicking up some kind of dust."

The *maître* frowned as he dropped into a chair at the table. "You sound as if they have your sympathy. I would remind you that Cassard made our plans possible with his weakness for cards. Moreover, these are the people who helped hide the man who killed my daughter."

"You don't know that. Certainly, I saw no sign of it."

"I know that arrogant, cowardly young scoundrel. He refused to meet me, refused to give me satisfaction after taking my Sophie's innocence and deserting her in her time of need. He cared not a whit that she died and his bastard with her. She wasn't good enough."

"*Maître…*" Christien began.

"Nor was I his equal, if you please," the old man went on, unheeding. "He was not required to accept my challenge under the code duello. No, certainly not." A sardonic laugh shook him. "The truth is, he was so terrified he couldn't get away from me fast enough. He was petrified I would find a way to force a meeting, positive I would kill him. And so I would, so I would. But now he's healed and bored with hiding, so has begun to appear here and there in town at night. He thinks I have forgotten him, more fool he."

"He has been making mischief elsewhere, as well,"

Christien said with a scowl. "He prowls around River's Edge at night, frightening young Marguerite, I think. What can he mean by it?"

"Nothing good, I'll wager."

"He must have little ready cash, else fear of your reprisal would have sent him on the run as soon as he was able. The income he once had from Bonne Espèrance is gone as his mother closed the house, shut down crop production and sold off the hands before she left for Paris. If she is sending anything for his support, no whisper of it has been heard."

"She may also believe him to be dead," Vinot pointed out.

"Or she may have washed her hands of him. Cassard indicated that she was not a doting mother. Suppose…"

"What?" his old mentor asked, his gaze keen.

"Suppose Theodore thinks to terrorize Marguerite then, when his daughter and his wife are suitably distraught, rise from the dead and demand money for staying away? Well, or for leaving the area, never to trouble them again?"

"It sounds possible if you assume the wife knows nothing. Taking advantage of the fair sex was ever his specialty."

"It sounds damnable," Christien said in fierce condemnation, "the act of a madman."

"Which he may be, if he was struck about the head as it seems from what Cassard told you. Why the blows could not have killed him in truth…" Vinot trailed off with a shake of his gray head. "But no matter. The monster's luck will not last. I shall see to it."

Christien tucked the idea of Theodore's madness into a corner of his mind while he listened to the old sword master's obsessed ramblings. Vinot was so intent on revenge that he couldn't sleep, ate little, went nowhere and thought of nothing, spoke of nothing else. He was fading away, losing strength, skill and purpose for living. It seemed something must be done to assuage his grief and settle his mind before he dwindled into insanity himself or even death.

Christien owed the old sword master that reprieve. Vinot had found him shivering on the street when he first arrived in New Orleans, had taken him in, fed him, taught him everything he knew. His daughter, Sophie, bright, vivacious Sophie, had been like a younger sister to him. She had made a game of teaching him how to bow, how to take a lady's hand, to talk lightly of nothing. His own father had taught him his letters and the rudiments of reading, but there had been few books in the swamp for practicing the skill. Sophie had shared hers, had nagged him into attempting harder words and passages, had made him perfect his hand with a pen and insisted he become proficient in ciphering. In return, he had taught her the march of the seasons, ways of animals, how to tie knots, to swim, catch fish and protect herself in a fight.

He had taught her to trust young men and assume they would always control their passions. He had made her unafraid, even daring. He had been the architect of her downfall if not the instrument of it.

Christien wondered now if he hadn't been a little mad himself when he had agreed to this scheme of retribution that he and the *maître* had set in place. Or perhaps he only wished he had that excuse.

"What if you are wrong?" he asked now, his gaze on the red-brown sherry in his glass. "What if Theodore Pingre is dead as they've said all along?"

"Then you will be the owner of a fine plantation and have a nice young wife with a new-made family. What could be better than that?"

"And if you're right, then the lady will be a bigamist and I will be no husband at all. You'll forgive me if I see that as less than satisfactory."

"She appeals to you?" his mentor asked, his gaze keen.

Christien gave him a satirical look but made no answer. Let the old man make of that what he would. Some things were private.

"It's to be hoped the final sacrifice, that of actually marrying the Pingre woman, will not be necessary. Have I expressed my gratitude to you for carrying the matter to this point?"

"There is no need."

"But there is. My indebtedness is so great I can hardly express it. This whole affair—" Vinot paused for a brief, encompassing gesture "—none of it would be possible without you."

"Please. I have my reasons."

"The Brotherhood and its tenets against such conduct as Pingre's, yes, of course. Nighthawk on the wing without the cover of darkness."

Christien shrugged away the name that was connected to both his childhood and exploits for the

Brotherhood. It had its uses, but he had ceased to feel any attachment to it long ago. "For Sophie, as well," he said. "She was dear to me and did not deserve her fate. But I do wonder about Reine Pingre."

"If the woman and her family are hiding Theodore Pingre, then she deserves to lose what good name remains to her, just as my Sophie lost hers. If not, then you may make it up to her in any way you please. Or not at all, it's up to you. Either way, you'll still have River's Edge."

Vinot made it sound so simple. Christien had known it would not be from the moment he set eyes on Reine outside Davis's theater. Since then, he had spoken to her, smiled at her across a table and heard her promise to be his wife. He had caught a glimpse of the place, and the family, he might have had if things had been different.

It could well turn out impossible to do either of the things his old mentor suggested, he thought, impossible to hold Reine Cassard Pingre, impossible to let her go.

# 7

Christien had not returned by the time Reine descended to breakfast. Everyone else seemed to be sleeping late after the night's excitement. She had her morning repast of warm rolls and café au lait on the lower gallery with only Chalmette at her feet for company. She ate slowly, sipping from her cup, watching over the rim as squirrels chased one another up and down the live oaks, breaking off a crust now and then for the hound, who caught them in the air with a snap of large white teeth. Birds sang in the trees, insects hummed and voices called from somewhere behind the main house.

After a time, she realized she was waiting, that she was unconsciously listening for something more, possibly the sound of hoofbeats from the river road. She was listening for Christien's return.

Chalmette growled in warning an instant before a footstep scraped on the pathway that led from the rear of the house. The tread was familiar enough. She turned to face the man who appeared around the corner, coming to a halt, hat in hand, at the edge of the gallery's brick floor. "Monsieur Kingsley, good day."

"Might be for some," Kingsley, sometimes known as King, answered in harsh tones. "Don't much look that way to me."

He was a burly figure with thick shoulders and neck, a belly that hung over the top of his trousers, sandy hair plastered to his head above a broad, bland face and pale eyes somewhere between gray and green. Their expression just now was less than pleasant.

"You refer, I suppose, to the arrival of Monsieur Lenoir." Another time, she might have called for an extra cup and invited him to be seated to share the last of the brew in its silver pot. His pugnacious manner affected her with such annoyed unease that she withheld the gesture.

"I hear you're to marry him."

"How did you…?"

She stopped as she recalled the shadowy form of Alonzo on the dark attic stairs the night before. He had told the cook, no doubt, as she was his sister, and Cook had related it to the kitchen maid. The maid had found the knowledge too deliciously important to keep. While drawing water at the well or some other errand, she had passed on the story to others. And why should they not be interested, after all? Anything that happened in the big house affected them, as well.

"Never mind that," Kingsley said with a scowl. "What I'd like is the straight of it. Is it so?"

"You forget yourself, *monsieur*," she said, her voice even. She reached at the same time to put a staying hand on Chalmette's big head as he rose with a low rumble in his throat to stand at her knee. The dog had never cared for the overseer, or for Theodore, either, for that matter.

"Do I, now? I think it's you that's forgettin', Madame Pingre."

"Would that I could."

He watched her a long moment, then looked away with a wag of his head. "We can't, neither one of us. What's done is done. Thing is, you taking a husband makes it harder. That's unless you told him about that night."

"No."

"Thought as much. So what are you up to?"

"The alliance was arranged by my father," she said, her lips as stiff as her tone. "I have no power to refuse it."

"You tried, did you?"

She declined to answer such an insolent query, could hardly believe it had been put to her. The overseer had always been respectful and eager to please. That had not changed even after Theodore disappeared. Since leaving off her black, however, she had begun to notice a certain familiarity in his manner and a disturbing, almost possessive look in his eyes.

Kingsley had been at River's Edge as long as she could remember, had been born there, she thought, the son of the *Américain* who had held the position before him, a man come from Virginia with her grandfather. Others whispered a different tale of his birth, one concerning his mother and old Monsieur Pingre, Theodore's grandfather. If true, that would make Kingsley the uncle of Reine's dead husband.

Her own father had always put the greatest faith in the overseer's knowledge of growing methods, management and his loyalty. So had she, particularly the latter. It was possible their trust had been misplaced.

"It came from a gambling debt of my father's, if you must know," she told him. "Either I marry Monsieur Lenoir or we will all have to leave River's Edge. Which would you have me do, if you please? Particularly as there's no guarantee you would be kept on as overseer once my family and I departed."

Kingsley narrowed his eyes, lifting a hand to rub his knuckles over the bristles of his unshaven chin. "I see the problem."

"I thought you might."

"So what are you going to do about it?"

She gave him a swift look. "What *can* I do?"

"Well, you can't go through with it."

"I have no choice. It's out of my hands. Can you not understand?"

He frowned at the wall above her head. The rasping noise of his hard knuckles across his chin tore at her nerves until she thought she must order him to stop. Then he lowered his hand, spreading his fingers wide.

"Somebody needs to make this joker see he's not welcome in these parts."

"I don't recommend the attempt. He's a master swordsman, you know."

"Wouldn't have to be a sword anywhere in it."

"In what? What are you thinking?"

"Never you mind, Madame Pingre. I'll take care of it."

"You can't just…just attack him. Besides, I don't believe he's a man who can be frightened off with crude force. He will retaliate, you may be sure of it."

"He can try."

"Monsieur Kingsley…"

"King. Whatever happened to you calling me King?"

She had never done such a thing, and well he knew it. The *petit nom* had begun with Paul as a sly jest, then her father had taken it up as a habit. "Monsieur Kingsley, I must ask you to have nothing more than the most necessary contact with my…my fiancé. He will eventually be made privy to everything that happened here, but in the meantime…"

"Oh, he will, will he?"

"Naturally. A wife should not have secrets from her husband."

"What if he gets on his high horse, maybe takes off when he hears?"

It seemed a distinct possibility, given the pride she had seen in every line of Christien Lenoir's body. Reine swallowed hard, unaccountably disturbed by the thought. "That will be his choice."

"The way I see it, then, the sooner you tell him, the better."

"Even if his next move is to send the sheriff to evict us?"

"It won't come to that. I'll see to it." The overseer didn't wait for a reply. Ducking his head in a crude bow, he slapped on his hat and strode away back down the path that led eventually to the plantation outbuildings.

Reine watched him go with a frown between her brows. What had he meant, he'd see to the matter? She didn't like the sound of it, no, not at all.

Still, he was correct in saying she should explain what had taken place at River's Edge on the night Theodore died. It would be best done before the wedding so as to have a clean start between the bridegroom and herself.

She couldn't risk it, she realized as she turned her gaze to Chalmette, who had flopped back down beside her, reaching down to smooth a hand over his big head. Others were involved, and there was no way to say what having the details of the incident made public would do to them. She must wait until she knew her betrothed better, until she could trust he would not expose everything, wreaking the kind of havoc she had sacrificed so much to avoid.

She wondered when that would be, if ever.

"That man, he be trouble."

The comment came from a shadow that hovered just inside the French door beyond Reine's table, a dark figure in a white apron over a dress of solid black. Reine lifted her head with a jerk that said as much about the state of her nerves as it did her surprise. An instant later, she relaxed again.

"*Alors,* you'll give me a heart attack one day," she said. You never knew where old Demeter would turn up, for she had a habit of slipping in and out of the house unnoticed. Chalmette paid her no attention beyond giving a single thump of his tail.

"Not so. You are strong and I am old. My heart will stop its beating before yours."

"Don't say such things."

"Why not, when it's so?"

Reine didn't like hearing it, had no wish to face the possibility of another death. Nonetheless, it was true that Demeter was withering away like a leaf of tobacco, becoming ever more brown, wrinkled and bent in body with each passing year. Her hair was white in sharp contrast to the dusky color of her skin, and the opaque look of cataracts dulled her eyes. Her full apron, once kept stiffly starched and sun-bleached, was wrinkled from long wear and dusted with the snuff she used.

Demeter had tried to continue as nursemaid to Marguerite after Theodore's death, but it had been too much for her. Grief had taken its toll, for she had loved him as if he were her own; she had lain down on her bed and refused to get up for weeks after he disappeared. She had never lived at River's Edge, but had taken possession years ago of the small cabin on the Pingre property built as a playhouse for Theodore's sisters, who had died as children. There she took in stray cats and grew herbs and vegetables, especially the greens she claimed she must have at every meal. Some few went to her for potions of one kind or another, but she was so very witchlike in her tiny gray house, like something from a dreary fairy tale, that she was left alone in the main.

"'Tis true, so why not?" she said now with a shrug. "Though I worry."

"About what?"

"Never you mind. I come to tell you that you do wrong. You must not marry wi' this man."

"I thought you spoke just now of Monsieur Kingsley, saying he was troublesome."

"So I did, me, and so he be. He strut like a rooster, that one. But now I speak of the other, this big and so handsome man with his sword and his promises."

It was ever so with older slaves, Reine knew; they had lived so close within the family circle for so long, were so intimately acquainted with all its details, that they felt privileged to speak their minds. "How can you say we should not wed? You've not met him."

"Don' matter. You must not marry."

"I've been a widow more than the two years required, Demeter. Isn't it enough? Would you have me mourn forever?"

"Sometimes it must be. I mourn still."

"But as you pointed out, you're not young." It was an unkind thing to say, perhaps, but so was Demeter's attitude unkind, unaccountably so. "Besides, you don't know everything. I must marry Monsieur Lenoir."

Demeter listened to the tale of the gambling debt with her head cocked to one side and her rheumy, half-blind eyes on the flashing movement where a pair of wrens swooped and dived at a blue jay to drive it away from their nest. When Reine was done, she shook her head. "This be bad."

"I'll admit I was taken aback at first. Still, Marguerite likes the man. Can you believe she went to him last night when she had her nightmare, instead of to me?"

"Little ones be wise in these t'ings sometimes. But she saw the *loup-garou* again, yes?"

Reine gave an unhappy nod. "She was terrified until

she ran to Monsieur Lenoir and he put his arms around her. She quieted at once, and you know it's always taken hours to calm her."

"You t'ink he take away her fear."

"I saw him do it. He was there when she needed him. I suppose…I suppose a man with a sword in hand must seem a better match against demons than a mere mother. Perhaps a father is what she needs."

If the old nursemaid heard the catch in Reine's voice or noticed her distress at the thought of being supplanted, she chose to ignore it. "She have one."

"But he's gone. She doesn't remember Theodore at all."

"Don' be saying that!"

"She was barely three when he died. Children that age have little recall, and then there was that terrible night. It's best that she doesn't remember." Reine preferred to think so, anyway.

"He gave her life, did M'sieur Theodore," Demeter insisted with a quaver in her voice.

Reine's smile was a little crooked. "I rather thought I did that."

"She be the only one of his line, his only child and he an only child, too. Better that she'd been a boy."

Theodore had also made clear his disappointment that Marguerite was not a son. Being reminded added a cool edge to Reine's voice as she replied. "You will not say that in her hearing, if you please. As she is my daughter, she can be of my line."

"For shame, that you would take that from M'sieur Theodore."

"I take nothing from him that he didn't give up of his own accord. He wanted nothing to do with Marguerite. I recall that, even if you don't." Demeter had always been on Theodore's side in any dispute. Nor could she ever be brought to see any wrong in him.

"He was young, hadn't settled himself."

"So was I young, but had to be settled enough for both of us."

Demeter turned her clouded gaze in Reine's direction, a cunning look on her features. "You did fine. I always be sayin' that, I do. You don't need a husband."

"Nor do I want one, but I'm telling you I must marry and that's an end to it."

The finality in her voice seemed to have the desired effect, for Demeter said no more. With a thrust-out lower lip and wagging head, she wandered off in the direction of the kitchen.

Reine watch her go with a sigh. The old nursemaid would sit for a while with the cook, she knew, graciously accepting sugar cookies or a slice of pie as her due and downing them with a glass of buttermilk fresh from the churn. The two of them, old friends for years, would discuss what was happening with the people of the big house. After a while, Demeter, having a formidable sweet tooth, would gather up whatever extra cookies and cake she could beg and take herself back to her little house, her greens and her cats.

Reine wished she could leave her own doubts and fears behind as easily.

# 8

The only member of the family at hand to greet Christien on his return to the plantation was Paul Cassard. A brooding look lay in the boy's hazel eyes as he came down the steps toward him. Before he spoke, he waited until Christien's black stallion had been taken away and Alonzo had carried the box and carpetbag he had brought back with him into the house.

"I hear you and Reine are getting married."

"She has done me the honor of agreeing to my proposal, yes," Christien answered in wary precision. The boy must be a heavy sleeper that he had missed the excitement of the night before. Thinking back, he realized he had not appeared in the hallway while it took place.

"Some proposal, marry you or get out."

"I hope it was not put so crudely."

"Did you have to make Reine marry you?"

That was a good question, though the answer was not one Christien cared to share with his future brother-in-law. "It was the best way to allow her and everyone else to remain here, maybe the only way."

"You might have courted her."

"And you think it would have served?" Christien asked with a dry note in his voice.

"Maybe not, but she deserved more than she got. She deserved the right to decide, and maybe to refuse."

"Oh, agreed." What Madame Pingre deserved was a different matter from what he could have allowed.

Paul stared at him in keen assessment of a kind that could easily have come from a gentleman much his senior. "You'll be good to her?"

"I give you my word."

"She's had enough of bad husbands."

A frown drew Christien's brows together as he considered the reason her brother might have for making such a statement. He didn't much care for where it led him. "I shall strive not to be one."

"Do that, and it may be all right," Paul said with a slow nod. "Best you not rush her into anything."

"Meaning?"

"She'll do what's expected, but she won't be pushed into being a wife to you. Try it and you'll be the loser."

He was talking, Christien thought, about what would take place in the marriage bed. He could hardly blame the boy for being concerned, though he resented the implication that he might be capable of forcing himself on a woman. "The fencing strip teaches patience," he said with deliberation, "also the trick of reading a partner's emotions and intentions. And the *maîtres d'armes* who live longest make a habit of learning from other men's mistakes."

Paul pursed his lips, then gave a slow nod. "That's

all right, then, I guess. But you hurt Reine, and you'll answer to me."

He stuck out his chin, as if he expected Christien to make light of the threat. It was a gesture he must have made before, for an inch-long scar could be clearly seen on its close-shaven underside.

"She is fortunate in her brother," Christien said as he put out his hand in friendship, "though I hope she won't require you as her champion in the future. That should be my role."

"She may need one more than you think. More than she thinks, too."

"I will be there," he answered, even as he absorbed the warning.

"Could be you will, at that," the boy said, his gaze narrowing as he slowly reached to accept Christien's hand, clasping hard. "Could be it's a good thing you've skill with a sword. Nighthawk."

Christien did not respond to the name. Nor did he make the mistake of trying to overpower his future brother-in-law in the handshake. There was more than one point being made here, he thought, as well as a bargain being sealed. He hesitated a moment before he said, "If there is something you would like to tell me, I'm willing to listen."

"Never mind that. Just you take care of Reine."

His nod of agreement was instant, since he had intended no less. Holding Paul Cassard's gaze, he allowed the boy to decide when the pledge was done and so end it. He did that an instant later, stepping back at the same time. He began to turn away.

"Do you fence?" Christien asked abruptly.

The boy turned back, his features stiff with reluctant interest overlaid by pride. "Not yet. *Maman* felt I was too young for the salons this past season, though Papa promised I could attend next winter."

"I could show you the rudiments. I closed my salon this morning but need to keep in practice. A sparring partner would not come amiss."

Color flooded Paul's face so the freckles stood out across the bridge of his nose like bits of brown wrapping paper. For an instant, it appeared he would agree. Then his face changed. "I think not," he said, looking down at the toes of his boots.

"Now, why? I am an interloper, true, but will soon be family."

"It's not that."

"You think I'm so cow-handed I'll ruin your style before you can develop it?"

The boy had the grace to smile at the suggestion. "I've seen you in New Orleans and know your reputation."

"Something more serious, then. You feel I've taken what should be your inheritance."

A moody shrug was the only answer.

"There's not much I can do about that except to apologize. I am sorry, you know."

"But not enough to give it up."

It was such a mutter that Christien had to strain his ears to catch it. "No," he said simply. "I have as much need of it as you, perhaps more."

"What I thought."

"Can you say you would not feel the same in my shoes?"

Paul Cassard gave him a brief stare from under his brows before shaking his head. "That still doesn't make it right."

It was too true for denial. "I will admit that much, though it changes nothing. In the meantime, are you sure I can't entice you into a few minutes of practice with a foil? You could slash away at me all you like. Who knows, you might even get in a few touches by way of retaliation."

"Not likely, as I've never held a foil in my life. That's if I wanted to try."

The words had a sullen sound, as though the boy feared Christien might think less of him for the admission. Or that he felt less of himself for it. "We are none of us born knowing the correct moves," Christien said at once. "You will catch on quickly, I'm sure. And I'll try not to inflict too much damage before you gain prowess."

"I'm not afraid," he replied, flaring up with a scowl.

It was the response Christen wanted and expected. "Good. Shall we meet under the oaks at the side of the house in half an hour? I must see to my belongings, but will be ready by then."

Young Cassard's nod of agreement was so stiff that Christien had to control a smile. If only his sister was so easy to read, and to lead.

A short hour later, the two of them were hard at it. Shuffling back and forth over the grass, they beat the tips of their blades together in the most elemental of fencing moves. Sweat poured down their faces, wet the hair at the back of their necks and made the sword grips slippery in their hands. The smell of crushed grass rose around them, mingling with the scent of sautéed onions from the outdoor kitchen no great distance away.

Paul must have frequented the salons as an onlooker, Christien thought, even if his father had forbidden lessons. Or perhaps he'd seen a clandestine duel or two during his winter sojourns in New Orleans. It would not be unusual, since word always got out when notable swordsmen were to meet. At least young Cassard had some acquaintance with the form and etiquette necessary on the fencing strip, also with the more basic positions.

Christien had brought foils from town, the equipment to keep them in good shape and a single suit of padding. The last he'd given to Paul to wear. It was unlikely the young man would be able to touch him with his blade, and though the last thing he intended was to harm Reine's brother in any way, accidents could happen. Explaining why he'd drawn Paul's blood was not the way he preferred to start his marriage.

He was just demonstrating a parry in seconde when he caught a flurry of movement from the corner of his eye. It was Reine, moving swiftly from sunlight into the deeper shadows of the oaks with her skirts swirling around her feet. She came to an abrupt halt no more than an arm's length from where their improvised piste, or fencing strip, was marked off in the grass with lines of powdered lime.

"What in the name of heaven are you doing?"

Paul answered her, his voice breathless with strain and excitement. "What does it look like? A duel, perhaps?"

"Don't be ridiculous. I can see it isn't." Her eyes flashed with bright blue annoyance, and the lush curves of her lips were tight at the corners.

"Monsieur Lenoir offered me a lesson."

"And you agreed! Are you quite mad? Stop! Stop this instant!"

Though she spoke to her brother, her gaze flashed over Christien. He could swear he felt its sting everywhere it touched, on his hot, perspiring face, his shoulders and chest, and lower, where his exertions had caused his pantaloons to cling to his leg muscles. With an abrupt gesture, he gave the signal to disengage. He stepped back in form with his sword tip trailing on the ground.

"It was only for exercise," Paul protested, wiping his face with his shirtsleeve as he also relaxed his guard position. The exhilaration of the match was strong in his veins, however, for he continued in breathless enthusiasm. "No one could be hurt. Monsieur Lenoir knows to the inch where he's striking. He beat out forty other masters to take first prize in the tournament of fencing masters this spring, you know. That makes him the best swordsman in New Orleans."

"It isn't your skin I'm worried about."

Christien gave her a swift look, his heart leaping in his chest. She didn't mean that the way it sounded, or did she? Reine avoided his gaze, her attention on her brother. Her features were dewy with heat and temper, her hair gilded by the dappling of sun through the tree limbs overhead. She breathed in a quick cadence that lifted the gentle curves of her breasts in an intriguing rhythm, but that was as apt to be from hurry as from concern of his hide.

"What, then?" Paul asked, scowling. Then his face changed. "Oh. *Maman*."

"Yes, *Maman*. You know how she is. What if she looked out and saw you?"

Paul flushed, glancing from his sister's stern gaze to Christien as he spoke in explanation. "Our mother is alarmed by violence in any form, and undone by the sight of blood. I should have thought."

"This was mere exercise." Christien kept his voice mild with an effort, the better to hide his disappointment.

"But she is unlikely to understand that," Reine said at once. Turning back to Paul, she went on in brisk tones, "You are sweating like a pig and have the odor of one. You should go and bathe. Or have you forgotten that you have a lesson of a different sort with Father Damien?"

"Latin and sums when I could be fencing? No, really. Could a message not be sent to—"

"We have done enough for one day." Christien cut across the boy's protest as he moved to lay down his foil and pick up his frock coat. He put it on not only because it was impolite to appear in shirtsleeves before a lady, but because Paul wasn't the only sweaty male under the oaks who might smell like livestock. "I didn't realize you had other obligations," he continued as he slid his left arm into the sleeve and adjusted the fit on his shoulders. "You should have told me."

"I am tutored three days a week by the parish priest," Paul said without enthusiasm.

"If he completes his studies before his eighteenth birthday, the good father will escort him on his grand tour," Reine added, then paused, her features stiffening. "At least, that was the plan before you...before River's Edge changed ownership."

"I see no reason why it should change," Christien replied in even tones.

"Father Damien will be pleased."

The comment was austere. Her brother more than made up for it, however.

"You mean it?" he cried in strangled relief while rich color surged into his face. "I'd thought...that is, I was sure the trip would be off. I have to tell Father Damien. Yes, and Gaston and Ambrose, since they go with us." He started off, then turned back to execute a jerky bow. "*Merci*, Monsieur Lenoir, thank you for everything."

A grand tour. It seemed the disappointment of missing it had been behind Paul's resentment as much as for the loss of his future inheritance. Who would have guessed?

"I must apologize for the upset," Christien said to Reine when her brother had vanished into the house. "It wasn't my intention to create more problems for you."

"I'm sure it wasn't. You could not know how these things upset *Maman*."

"She isn't well, I believe."

"She seldom leaves the house, has never been strong. Her childhood was not a happy one, she has always feared…everything, and her nerves were quite shattered by Theodore's death. She was first on the scene where he…he died, saw Marguerite asleep next to a pool of blood, you understand. For an instant she thought her injured, even dead. Then she screamed and Marguerite woke."

"I quite see," he said, trying to ignore the creeping sensation that moved over his scalp at the images she invoked. He paused for an instant before he went on. "So you don't object to the fencing lesson, then, only to its location."

Her features remained stiff. "I can't say that. My brother needs no encouragement to think himself a swordsman, courting challenges among his friends for the excitement and chance to prove his courage."

"He seems too sensible for such foolishness. More than that, the code I practice, the one I teach, warns against it. Fencing is a valuable tool for turning boys into men, teaching them responsibility, self-discipline, manners, endurance and a dozen other things."

"And you think my brother has need of these."

What Christien thought, gauging the concern in her eyes, before resting his gaze on the fine skin of her face and silken length of her lashes, was that Paul was lucky to have such a sister to worry over him. "Most do," he answered, "and he seems at loose ends."

"He frets about things over which he has no control."

"It's a failing of young men, to care beyond what

might be expected, to take responsibility for things they can't change. Learning skill with a blade will give him direction. I should also point out that it may save his life if he crosses the path of a man who has not been taught to curb his conceit or his temper."

"Pray God he never does," she said with a small shake of her head. "Still, I refuse to allow that you, who met my brother only yesterday, know more of what he requires than I."

"But you will concede that we are both male, so must have similar impulses."

An intriguing shade of wild rose appeared on her cheekbones before she spoke. "I can hardly argue with that."

"We will move farther from the house for his lessons, if that will serve."

"You may do as you like. I'm sure you will, regardless." Her voice carried a distinct edge, and she looked away as she replied, as if she could not bear the sight of him.

Christien watched her a long moment, noting the tightness at the corners of her mouth and firm clasp of her hands in front of her. His gaze wandered to the luscious, peachlike curve of her cheek, the tender, blue-veined valley between her breasts that was exposed by the rounded neckline of her gown. He swallowed, clearing his throat and collecting his thoughts before he could frame the question in his mind.

"Is something wrong?" he asked after a second. "Or, perhaps I should say, something more?"

"Of course not."

"I'm not sure I believe that. If you've changed your mind…"

"It isn't that."

"But there is something. Come, out with it. I can't fight what I can't see."

The look she gave him was scathing. "Nor can you help being male or going about your so very male business at all hours."

"Ah," he said, studying the accusation in the blue depths of her eyes. "You know I left the house last night."

"I saw you go."

"And you think the worst."

"It's usually correct, in my experience."

"But you have no experience with me. If I tell you I couldn't sleep after my long evening nap and the excitement that interrupted it, that I went into town to pack the remainder of my things and arrange my affairs in order to be more settled here, would you believe me?"

She stared at him with doubt in her eyes, and who could blame her? His explanation might be true in part, but left out much. That it couldn't be helped did not make it easier to stand behind the lie of omission.

"You're quite right," she said abruptly, "I don't know you at all." Turning from him, she leaned her back against the trunk of the great oak that spread its protective umbrella overhead. "It's wrong to judge you based on other men. I've been meaning to tell you…to say that I regret screaming at you like a fishwife on the night we met. You had done nothing to deserve it, and everything to earn my eternal gratitude. It's just that I was so…so shaken and terrified for Marguerite that I hardly knew what I was saying."

"You were also embarrassed to be the focus of so much attention. You've had, I think, more of such public notice than is comfortable." His attempt to pass it off was sincere enough; her gratitude was not what he wanted. Even as he spoke, moving after her to lean a shoulder against the tree trunk next to her, he was aware she had not said she believed his story of where he had been.

"You can have no idea," she said with a sigh.

"Now it will begin again with our wedding."

"Yes."

"People will look elsewhere for entertainment once the novelty of it palls. Speaking of the wedding…"

"Yes, I suppose we must speak of it."

Her reluctance was hardly flattering, but he had little right to complain. "Have you a date in mind?"

"I expect it had better be soon," she said, the unhappiness in her face deepening. She sent him a look that barely met his eyes before flitting away again. "Because of the gossip, I mean to say. There will be all manner of speculation and counting on fingers if you remain in the house too long before the wedding."

"A serious consideration," he said, his voice at its most grave.

"Indeed." She sent him a brief glance. "You are laughing about it."

She was quick, his future wife, and more sensitive

to his moods than expected. "No, no, only thinking that a small gaffe such as our living under the same roof pales before the rest."

"So it does." She lifted a hand to rub between her eyes with her fingertips, as if a headache had begun to throb there.

"I would do nothing to cause further embarrassment for you," he said softly as he reached to take her hand, holding it between his, "but only what may make this easier."

"Short of going away and never coming back, I suppose."

His smile took on an ironic curve. "Yes, short of that. I am grateful, you know, for your agreement to my odd proposal." He lifted her hand to his mouth, brushing his lips across the backs of her fingers. Smooth and silken, they carried the scent of roses. And they trembled a little in his before she tugged them free. "Don't," she said, her voice carrying a husky note. "There's no need to play the gallant."

"What if I'm not playing?" He hardly knew what he was saying, only that he must spout something to keep her with him.

"Flirtation is also not a requirement. The arrangement between us is financial in nature, nothing more. Pretending otherwise will not help."

"As you wish, though your brother feels you deserve to be courted."

"Paul is still young enough to be a romantic."

"You, on the other hand, at the great age of—what, two- or three-and-twenty?—are not. It seems a shame."

"I should think you would prefer it under the circumstances." Her voice, though sharp, held the barest hint of a question.

"A politely distant marriage will not suit me. I thought I made that clear." His parents had enjoyed a rapport that spread love and laughter to every corner of their lives. The memories of it had kept him warm at night in the years when he'd first left the swamp. He'd always assumed his would be the same. By keeping that image before him, he could at least sound like a prospective groom.

"As to that, we must wait and see." A flush stained her skin and she swallowed as she looked away, a movement perfectly clear in the elegant line of her throat. She went on at once. "We will be married in the chapel here at River's Edge, if you have no objection. The wedding should be small, with only close family and friends present. Father Damien will of course preside."

"Perfection."

"You have someone who will stand with you?"

"I will arrange it."

Her nod of acceptance was brief. "I see no need for a *corbeille de noce,* as that implies a normal betrothal and is an unnecessary expense besides. As for—"

"My prerogative, I believe." His voice had a distinct edge. She apparently thought he lacked romantic spirit, as well, or else was without funds to supply the usual basket of gifts for the bride from her groom. It irritated him either way, putting him on his mettle.

She gave him a quick glance. "As you please. I was only trying to make this as simple as possible."

"It's simple enough as it stands. Don't stint on anything that will make it better for you and your family, not on my account."

"No, no, I won't," she said, her gaze meditative.

He met her eyes for an instant, seeing his dark shape reflected there like an image caught in a pool of rain-water, blurred and insubstantial. It did nothing to help his feelings. "There is the matter of the wedding journey afterward," he said finally.

"Unnecessary. I have no particular relatives I care to visit."

"But you made the usual jaunt up and down the river with Pingre, I suppose, presenting him to your distant family members, being presented to his?" His voice was calm, a matter for self-congratulation.

"Of course. It was expected."

"Regardless, you have none that you would wish to become better acquainted with me."

A startled expression appeared on her face. "It isn't that, truly. I just…" She stopped, drew a breath that lifted her breasts against the fine lawn of her day gown. "What I mean to say is, not one of them offered their support when Theodore died and the whispers of murder began. I see no reason to pay them any particular honor now."

If it was a falsehood, it was a good one. The tightness in Christien's chest eased a fraction. "We could stay a few days in town."

"Fever has been reported in New Orleans. I could not expose Marguerite to it, even if we wanted to risk it. And if you are going to say that she could remain here, I prefer not to leave her. Nor would I want to take the chance of our bringing disease with us on our return."

"No honeymoon sojourn, then," he said, inclining his head in token of his agreement. "But what of the wedding supper and customary three days of seclusion following it?"

Color rose in her face and her lashes came down to conceal her expression. "A great inconvenience, I know, but people will expect no less. To ignore them might cause as much talk as the wedding."

"I didn't intend to ignore them," he said, his voice deep and a shade gruff.

"No? It drives most men quite mad, being unable to leave the bedchamber, having nothing to do except—"

"I'm sure we can find something to fill the time."

"Except sleep, I meant to say...."

"Sleeping," he said, the words like raw silk tearing, "was not in my mind."

# 9

Reine was seated on the upper gallery with a pile of linen in her lap and needle and thread in her hand when her father walked out onto the canvas flooring. He glanced in her direction, but did not speak until she had threaded her needle and begun to set stitches along a ripped seam.

"What's that you're mending?"

"A shirt," she said shortly, her gaze on what she was doing.

"I don't recall an accident of that nature," he said with a lifted brow.

"It isn't yours."

He rocked on his heels with his thumbs hooked in his waistcoat pockets, straining it across the rounded shape of his belly. "Feeling testy this morning, are you? It's this marriage, I suppose."

She looked up with an ironic lift of one brow. He had the grace to flush and look away.

"Yes, well. I'm truly sorry, *chère*. I didn't think, didn't quite realize how it would turn out, or I'd never have agreed to it."

"It really was Monsieur Lenoir who suggested it?" She did not look up from the flash of her needle in and out of the fabric. The backs of her fingers seemed to bear the imprint of his mouth still. His lips had been so firm and smooth, so very warm. She could not prevent herself from imagining how they would feel on her mouth. She pricked herself a little as she pulled her needle through the linen, but it was not enough to draw blood.

"Didn't I tell you so?" her father replied.

"Yes, but it would make more sense the other way around. You're quite sure you didn't put the idea into his head?"

"Now, why would I do that?"

"Why would you not?" she asked with a severe look in his direction. "Such a union relieves you of your debt, makes it unnecessary for you to move *Maman* to another household and disposes of a daughter whom you feel should have another husband instead of pining for the one who died. You come out of it very well as far as I can see." What she did not say, but thought privately, was that if it had come about in that manner, then Christien was as caught in this coil as she was.

"That wasn't the way of it," her father said with a slow movement of his grizzled head. "Lenoir seemed set on having you, said everything possible to gain my permission to address you. It was clear he'd had a great deal of time to marshal his arguments."

"Why do you say that?" She formed a series of stitches with extra attention, trying to appear only vaguely interested.

"He came right to the point for one thing, not that it signifies in the least," her father answered with a dismissive wave of one hand. "The thing is, I didn't realize you would be so against it. If you really can't stomach the arrangement, we will call it off."

"Call it off?" She dropped her hands into her lap, her fingers clenching her needle. "Is that possible?"

"Nothing easier. I'll just inform Lenoir it's not in the cards. He's a sensible man. I'm sure he'll bow out with no great to-do. Though, I must say he seemed reluctant when I offered to let him off the hook two days ago."

"You did that."

His gaze upon her was chiding. "I am not an ogre, *chère.*"

"No," she said with a misty smile, "you are the best of fathers. But what about River's Edge?"

"I never liked the place above half, to tell the truth, only accepted it because your mother was attached to it. It might be as well if you leave here, anyway, leave all the bad memories behind, start over somewhere else."

"Where people don't know us, you mean." There was a certain seduction in the idea, she had to admit.

"Natchez, maybe. I hear it's booming, and I've friends there. Or Havana, a tropical port. Bound to be opportunities there. Paris, even. What would you say to Paris?"

Reine smiled a little at the enthusiasm in his voice. Her father had always been one for big plans. Still, she shook her head as she took up her sewing again, allowing her fingers to go about the task with little direction from her conscious thoughts. "*Maman* wouldn't like it, you know she wouldn't."

"No, I suppose not." Her father sighed, settling back onto his heels.

"She would hate leaving everything behind, would likely make herself frantic over the strangeness of a new place. And it isn't as if I have any real objection to Christien—Monsieur Lenoir. He's been a complete gentleman in this business."

"He rates high in Paul's book."

"Anyone with a swordsman's skill would," she pointed out in a dry tone. "Still, Christien put himself to the trouble of earning his good will. Not many men would have." Unspoken between them was the knowledge that Theodore had not bothered. A brother-in-law had been a nuisance to him. He'd behaved as if the two of them were in competition, and was jealous of any affection she displayed toward Paul. They had descended to fisticuffs more than once.

"Then you are resigned."

"That's as good a way as any of putting it, I suppose."

"I must admit to relief," her father said, rubbing a finger alongside his nose with a rueful air. "Lenoir is pleasant enough, but he can poker up in a frightful way. I'd not relish taking something from him that he really wanted."

"But if it's all a question of indebtedness…"

"Doesn't mean the marriage doesn't suit him," her father said with a judicious air. "Matter of fact, I think he may have taken a fancy to you, *chère.*"

"You're wrong, surely."

"You don't think it possible?"

"I'm no great beauty, and have done nothing to attract him." She hesitated, then went on. "He rode into town late last night."

Her father sent her a quick glance, then looked away again. "It doesn't mean he's dissatisfied, only that he requires other…pleasures."

He meant the kind of pleasure not to be found at River's Edge until after the wedding. Reine pressed her lips tightly together for an instant before she spoke. "I would like to think such outings will come to an end. Afterward, I mean."

"I'm sure Lenoir will be an ideal husband once the knot is tied. And it's a wife's part to see that he's content at home."

Her gaze narrowed a fraction. "Are you saying it was my fault Theodore preferred the beds of other women?"

"Never, only that he was young and had never known the bridle. He'd have surely settled down in time."

"Possibly," she said, though she was far from convinced. Her father did not know all the hurtful things Theodore had said, especially before flinging himself off to town on that last evening at Bonne Espèrance. Even during the three days when a bride and groom were traditionally shut up together, when they were supposed to be learning to be comfortable with each other, to grow used to the intimacies of marriage and overcome the embarrassment of them, he had slipped out, leaving her alone. She had cried into her pillow, too ashamed to allow anyone to hear. Things had never been the same between them.

"Besides, Lenoir is not your usual idle gentleman," her father went on. "He may have other obligations about which we know nothing. Why, he may be instructing a client who prefers private lessons after salon hours."

"I suppose." After an instant, she added, "Do you know anything of his finances? I mean, he doesn't seem to be especially well off."

Her father walked to lean on the post next to her chair. "Why would you say that?"

"Only look at his linen." She held up the shirt she was mending. The light behind it showed fabric that was nearly transparent. "Quite threadbare, you see, and the sleeve almost torn from the armhole. Do you think he would mind a new shirt as a wedding gift?" She was doing her best to come to grips with the idea that Christien might be as dependent on the blessings of River's Edge as the rest of them.

"I think anything you did for him would meet with favor, yet I am all amazement. One could be forgiven for thinking you've added your newly betrothed bridegroom to the list of those you look after."

"I wouldn't want him to be embarrassed in front of our wedding guests. Besides, it's only a shirt."

"And a pair of knitted stockings to wear with his boots will be next, I suppose. Oh, yes, and possibly a cravat. What after that, unmentionables?"

"Papa!"

"Forgive me, I couldn't resist when you are being so domestic. Still, I'm puzzled over how you intend to judge the size of this shirt you will make."

"I shall use this one as a pattern, of course."

Her father's gaze took on a humorous slant. "And I was making a private bet over who would win out should you decide to take the gentleman's measure."

"It might be better to have it," she said, ignoring his double entendre as she frowned at the shirt she held. "Only think of the waste of time and linen if this shirt has shrunk in the wash or the sleeve gave way because he is larger in size than when it was made?"

"He could be wider in shoulder, perhaps," her father said, "but nowhere else. The man hasn't a superfluous inch." He sighed, patting his small paunch. "But if you are to do the job, you'd better hurry. I saw Alonzo in the kitchen heating shaving water just now. Another quarter hour and your groom will be riding over the plantation. I never saw such a man for getting out into the morning dew." He twinkled at her as he pushed from the post where he rested. "You've had your breakfast, I suppose. I'll leave you to go in search of mine."

She gave a distracted answer as he strolled into the house. Her papa was indulging his droll humor in advising her to seek Christien out for measuring. He had no thought at all that she would actually do it. She wasn't sure she dared, yet the idea of working from an accurate pattern grew in her mind with all the hardihood of an oak seedling. If the replacement shirt did not fit Christien, there would be no time to alter it.

It wasn't as if she had never undertaken such a task before. She measured Paul and her father for nightshirts on occasion, though their other linen was made in town. Accurate guides for cutting the fabric made all the difference in the world.

She did want her future husband to be well turned out for the wedding. If the guests assumed she had accepted his proposal because of his fine, crisp linen as well as his wickedly handsome face and strong physique, she wouldn't mind. It would be better than pity for being forced to exchange the duties of a wife for the well-being of her family. When viewed that way, it seemed the garment she would make should fit with absolute perfection.

She was not one to allow second thoughts to sap her resolve. Ten minutes after her father left her, she finished mending the shirt, picked up her sewing basket with its cotton tape for measuring and went in search of Christien.

At the door of his chamber, she paused with her sewing basket in the crook of her arm and lifted her hand to knock. What if he was still abed? What if he were unclothed? What if he refused to be measured? Her father was right. Her groom was formidable when displeased, with a black scowl and a will of iron.

She wasn't afraid of him, was she? To stand quaking at the mere thought of his frown was no way to begin a marriage. She rapped on the door.

A deep voice called for her to enter. She did not hesitate, but turned the knob and swept into the room.

Christien stood with a razor in his hand, stooping

a little due to his great height as he peered into the oval shaving mirror that sat atop the bureau. Shirtless and barefoot, he was covered only by fawn pantaloons from which dangled the looped braces that normally held them up. Alerted by her light footfalls, or perhaps by her abrupt stillness, he swung toward the door.

"Good day to you, *monsieur,*" Reine said as she jerked into forward motion. She kept her voice even in spite of the wave of heat that mounted to her forehead. How ridiculous to be affected by the sight of a pair of wide shoulders ridged with muscle and the sculpted column of his back as it swept down to his waist. She had seen unclothed men before, from her late husband to slaves injured in the field and brought to the infirmary.

"*Madame,*" he said with a lifted brow. "I thought… that is, I expected Alonzo with more hot water."

"He will be along shortly. Meanwhile, I have a small task to perform."

He eyed the sewing basket under her arm. "I don't believe I'm in need of stitching."

"I should hope not. But pray go on with your task. I will wait." She moved to the half-tester bed and placed her basket on the high mattress. The sheets were rumpled and the pillow still held the indentation of his head, but she refused to picture him in the bed. No, she would not.

He watched her for an instant before reaching for a towel, wiping it over the scattered trails of lather still on his face. "If you will allow me to dress, I'll come to you wherever you choose."

With great resolution, she turned to face him. "I would rather you didn't."

*"Madame?"*

"Didn't dress," she amplified, resting her gaze for an unguarded instant upon his wide chest, its flat planes gilded with morning light through the windows, glinting with water droplets. No furring of hair concealed its impressive musculature, a phenomenon she had noted before in the drawings of woodland natives. Her fingers tingled with the need to trail them over that smooth, hard surface, and she wondered in a paralyzing flash of desire just what it would be like to lick away the water with her tongue or to press her bare breasts against it.

"I am at your service, of course," he with a smile lighting his eyes, "but it might be useful to know what brought on this sudden…desire."

Confusion clouded her mind. She directed her gaze past his shoulder while heat simmered inside her. "A shirt. I only wish to measure you for a shirt. Nothing more."

"A shirt." His voice turned wry.

She wondered briefly if he was disappointed that she required nothing else of him. The idea that he willingly would have answered her desire was seductive beyond reason. She swallowed before forcing a reply from her throat. "It's the custom for the bride to make a gift for the groom. A shirt seems appropriate."

"Does it now?" His features were unreadable as he studied her. "Why would that be?"

"You need one. Why else?"

"I need many things."

"This happens to be something I can supply."

He lifted a brow while irony rose to gleam in his eyes. "First you want me undressed, and now you are offering personal services. You really should think before you make such comments, *madame*."

She felt as if her face could be used to melt candle wax. "You know I never meant— I fear I've had little occasion to watch my tongue before now."

"It will be my pleasure to teach you greater care."

She didn't trust the rich anticipation in his voice or the way his gaze lingered on her mouth. No, nor her own curiosity about exactly how he might carry out his threat. "I am forewarned. Now, if you will allow me?"

"There is really no need to go to such trouble."

"My choice, I believe, as with you and the *corbeille de noce*."

He seemed to have no answer for that, for which she was grateful. Or she was until he tossed the towel aside, then came toward her with arms outstretched. His expression was all acquiescence but devilment was in his black eyes. Her heart beat high in her throat as she wondered when he would stop, if he would stop, of if he meant to take her into his arms.

He halted a mere pace away.

She drew a ragged breath while reprieve and disappointment warred inside her. Really, the sooner she was done and out of this bedchamber, the better it would be.

Abruptly, his face changed and he took a pace back, lowering his arms. "Forgive me. I should not tease, but you blush so easily that it's irresistible." He glanced around as if in search of something. "I should slip on my shirt, at least."

"It will be better without, though I have it here." She gestured toward her basket. "Alonzo brought it to me earlier that I might sew up a ripped seam."

"I thought he meant to do that himself," he said with a frown.

"He lacks the skill."

Christien's lips firmed and a hint of dark color crept under the copper-bronze of his skin. "There's no call for you to see to my linen."

"It will soon be my duty. What difference can a few days make?" She had not thought he could be embarrassed. It was a revelation.

"Duty," he repeated.

"Should I have said my pleasure? But I'm not that fond of sewing."

"Still, you will stitch all the seams it takes to make a new shirt for me."

"That's different. It seems the tear I repaired may be from a less-than-ideal fit across the shoulders, which is why a more accurate measurement is required." She lifted her chin, her gaze steady as she waited for him to make something of her explanation.

"You are very practical."

"So I am," she replied with finality before turning to take the tape of cotton twill from her basket and facing him again. "As I said, the replacement shirt will be a gift. Now, if you'll lift your arms, please?"

He stared down at her, his black gaze moving over

her face. She was flushed again, she knew; she could feel the heat as she stood waiting. She refused to acknowledge it, however, just as she refused to back down.

After a moment, he inclined his head. Raising his arms, he spread them wide in a gesture of ironic surrender.

It felt like a victory. Reine drew a silent breath, then stepped close. She leaned to pass the tape around him. Adjusting it under his arms, she brought the ends to the front, carefully making one of them meet a hash mark. She reached behind her for the lead pencil from her basket that she would use to note the measurement.

He bent his head, his gaze on her left hand that held the tape. Abruptly, he reached to catch her wrist. "Your wedding ring," he said, his voice low, almost rough, "you took it off."

"It seemed appropriate given the circumstances." She held perfectly still in his grasp, her gaze on the satisfaction that suddenly flared in his eyes. It was, perhaps, a natural male reaction; men did not care to see the mark of another man on a woman they proposed to claim. It was disturbing all the same.

"Yes, of course." He allowed his eyelids to fall, shielding his expression as he shifted his grasp, skimming his thumb back and forth over the bare spot on her finger. Then he loosened his hold, released her.

It was a moment before she could recall what she should be doing. Taking a quick breath, she jotted down the measurement. She lowered the tape to his waistline next.

As she bent her head to see the mark, the shorter hair at her forehead brushed his chest. His male nipples tightened into brown buds centered in the flat coins of their areolae. She blinked at the phenomenon; she had not realized men's bodies reacted in the same way as women's. An instant of quiet fell in which she noticed he was barely breathing. She flung a quick glance upward to discover the cause.

He released a short, winded-sounding laugh while amusement danced in the black centers of his eyes. He said nothing, however, only held his place like some ancient statue of a half-naked Olympian.

He really was magnificent, his arms wrapped with corded muscle upon which stood the tracery of veins, his hair that lay against his skull in blue-black waves, the molding of his nose and the chiseled contours of his mouth. She could see the place where his heart throbbed under his breastbone, a firm and steady beat. If she placed her hand in the center of his chest, she would be able to feel it. If she leaned forward a fraction, she could touch her tongue to one tight nipple, tasting it, tasting him.

An odd dizziness assailed her. As she inhaled sharply in the effort to banish it, she absorbed his scent. It seemed compounded of bay leaves and island spices from his shaving soap, the herbal smell of the vetiver used to keep insects out of the armoire where his pantaloons must have reposed overnight, clean male skin and a hint of the fresh outdoors. She stepped back to the high bed, steadying her calves against its lower edge.

"What is it?" he asked, putting out a hand in support, his fingers closing on her elbow.

"Nothing." She removed her arm from his grasp.

"You aren't used to this. Maybe you should sit down."

"I've seen a man's chest before," she said with a snap in her voice. It wasn't just his bare skin that bothered her. It was the concern in his eyes, the warmth of his body that wafted around her, his masculine presence that seemed to take up all the space in the room, and all the air.

"Your husband's, I would imagine. It would have been a different matter."

That much was certainly true. Compared to Christien Lenoir, Theodore had been a mere stripling and almost flabby in his lack of muscular development. But she wouldn't think of that, not now. At least she would recall no more than was necessary to calculate the extra yardage required to make this damnable shirt.

"Theodore was younger," she said, infusing briskness into her tone, "not that it signifies. Turn, please, so I may complete my task."

He hesitated, his dark gaze searching hers. Finally, he pivoted on one foot, squared his shoulders and waited.

What shoulders they were, almost as wide as the French door beyond him. Smooth, shaded copper-gold, they gave mute testimony to endless hours of labor, though whether at sword play or something more manual was impossible to say. Her hands shook a little as she lifted her tape and spread it from the edge of one firm, muscle-clad expanse to the other.

The contrast between her own pale flesh tones and

the rich color of his skin fascinated her. He was like a figure in bronze. Did that hue extend under the waist of his pantaloons? How would he appear if unclothed in the manner of the classical male nudes displayed as objets d'art in French Quarter salons?

Depraved, she must be depraved to consider such a thing. It would not do. Her mind should be strictly on her task. She would keep it there if it required every ounce of discipline she possessed. She would indeed.

With the shoulder measurement recorded, she brushed aside the black-satin hair that grew low on his neck, too aware of its weight and warmth as she took his measure from the nape down to his waistline. By all rights, she ought to smooth the tape down over his backside to the point where the tail of his shirt would be hemmed. That was hardly likely to aid her resolve. More than that, she was not so brave. She would just allow her gaze to linger on the taut curves under the drape of his pantaloon to gauge the extra length required. That would have to do as an estimate.

"Now the arm length," she said with an unaccountably husky note in her voice.

Obligingly, he lifted an arm and bent it at the elbow according to her guidance. She reached high with her tape, held one end on the top of his shoulder while she trailed the rest around the turn and then to the wrist.

It was impossible not to compare her height to his as she held the length of twill in place long enough to mark it. The top of her head would graze the bottom of his chin if she stood close against him. His arm would no doubt lie perfectly across her shoulders should he lower it. Reaching around her would be nothing at all for him. His hands would span her waist, she was almost sure of it.

How very warm the morning had grown already. The shutters should really be closed to preserve what was left of the night coolness. She must see to it, just as soon as she was done. All that was left was the wristbands. Well, and the neck.

"If you will turn and bend your head," she began when that last measurement was reached.

"I doubt it will suffice," he said, his voice grave as he faced her. With the pantherlike grace that was peculiarly his own, he went to one knee before her. "Better?"

It was stunning, to suddenly be looking down at him instead of upward. He was closer, too, with his bent knee intruding into the fullness of her skirts. His eyes seemed larger and more liquid from this angle, their velvety black-brown irises shimmering with hints of gold, faceted about the pupils with topaz. His lashes were a forest of black that tangled at the corners where they came together, and his brows gave such dark definition to the facial bones they covered that he seemed like some ancient warrior prince, ageless and invincible. And yet he knelt before her as if in homage.

He took her breath. She could not move, couldn't remember what it was she should be doing. Slow heat mounted to her forehead as she fought the urge to take his hands and raise him up. He should not be on his knees, not to her, not ever.

Somewhere on the lower floor an outside door

opened. The draft it caused stirred the curtains at the bedchamber's open French doors, swept through the room to slam shut the door into the hallway. She jerked as if she had been shot.

"Madame Pingre? Reine?"

A shudder moved over her from head to heels. She subdued it with ruthless determination. Clearing her throat, she ran her tongue over lips suddenly gone dry. "Yes," she said, a ragged sound as she looked away from the minute narrowing of his eyes on her mouth. "Your neck, I must know how tight to make the collar band."

"By all means." He waited with an expectant air.

When had control of this situation shifted to the swordsman? Reine could not recall, but it seemed imperative that she take it back. She leaned with decision to circle the strong column of his neck, looping the tape loosely before drawing it snug.

"Wait," he said as she reached for her pencil. "I could use a bit more breathing room." He tucked two fingers behind the tape, easing it away from his skin a fraction of an inch.

The tape had not been that tight, but he did seem to be having difficulty with his breathing. For an instant, she wondered if she had the same effect on him that he was having on her.

The idea sent a small rush of pleasure over her before she quelled it. He must be used to far more exciting women.

Reine loosed her hold on the cotton strip and inserted her own fingers behind it to assess the fit.

Against their backs, she could feel the steady pulse that beat in his neck. Clearing her throat again, she asked, "Better?"

A smile tilted his mouth, apparently for her repeat of his question moments ago. It had been inadvertent, she thought, or perhaps not. She hardly knew what she was saying.

"Much better," he replied. "Reine?"

"Yes?" With the tape marked, she put aside her pencil and removed the length of cotton in a slow slide. She had nothing else to measure, no excuse to linger. It seemed a shame.

"I believe a small acknowledgement of our engagement is in order. With your permission?"

"What? Oh…" Comprehension came as he rose to his full height, took her hand and placed it on his shoulder, then encircled her waist with a strong arm. He cupped her face, his eyes darkly serious as he met her startled gaze. He looked at her mouth and the gold in his eyes took on a molten gleam. Then he lowered his head and matched his lips to hers.

Warm, he was so incredibly warm, and sweet as heated honey. The surfaces of her mouth tingled and her bones dissolved so she swayed against him. His chest was a solid wall of warmth, as gratifying as she had imagined in its hardness. His arms were so firm in their support that she felt enclosed in safety.

She should protest, should step away. Instead, she spread her palms over his shoulders, absorbing the sensation of velvet over steel. In a short time he would have a husband's right to more than this, much more.

At the thought, a surge of such wild longing rose inside her that she felt it press against the back of her throat. Tears caught her unprepared, and with them came a low moan that she could not hold inside.

He drew back, tipped his head in an attempt to see her face. "I'm sorry. My best intentions seem to be unreliable around you."

*"No, no, Reine, no!"*

That moan, so like an echo of the one in Reine's head, came from the doorway. She sprang away from Christien, whirling toward the sound.

*"Maman,* I didn't see you!"

"Alonzo said you were alone with this barbarian. I could not believe... But so it is, and he half-naked. Yes, and with the door closed, too! Have you no shame? You are not yet wed, are barely betrothed. What will the servants think, or the neighbors? What will everyone think!"

# 10

Her mother was wringing her hands and shaking her head while tears poured down her cheeks, dripped from her chin. She would work herself up to a bout of hysteria ending in a migraine; Reine knew the signs too well.

With a fleeting glance of apology for Christien, she moved to her side, taking her arm and turning her back toward the hall. "Don't upset yourself, *chère Maman.* No one will think anything. There's no reason they need ever hear. It's not as you believe, not at all. I was but measuring Christien for a shirt."

"Christien?"

"Monsieur Lenoir, my betrothed. You remember...."

"Yes, yes, of course I remember. I'm not an idiot."

"Alonzo must surely have told you what I was about. As for the door, it was the wind that blew it shut, that's all."

"But I saw you. I did see you..."

"Yes, of course. I...I stumbled, so clumsy of me." She flung a look of harried appeal at Christien. At the same time, she hoped her mother would not notice the swollen fullness of her lips.

"We will be wed soon in any case, Madame Cassard," he said, stepping forward. "Then it won't matter if we are shut up together."

"Not here," she said with a fretful shake of her head. "The master bedchamber, the best in the house, Maurice said. It should be yours."

"I thank you for the thought, but would not put you to the trouble of moving." He inclined his head so a bright sheen slid over the black waves of his hair. "I'm perfectly fine here."

"I believe the room I use as my bedchamber has a better aspect," Reine said prosaically. "It faces east so will not be so hot at night." She gave him a quick glance, afraid she had given away the fact that she had considered more than the mere comfort of her room.

"It will be as you prefer in all things," he said. Though the phrase was delivered with all the politesse expected of a bridegroom, the look in his eyes was not at all polite. Reine felt a small shiver run down her spine in spite of the growing warmth of the day. She skimmed her tongue over her lower lip and tasted his sweetness there, could almost feel the pressure of his mouth again, the seductive, mind-numbing flick of his tongue.

Her mother wagged her head from side to side. "Oh, but Reine, my Reine. It isn't right, this talk of rooms and weddings. You mustn't…it can't be right. Why does it have to be this way?"

"Papa told you, I know he did. Don't upset yourself. All will be well."

Her mother groaned again, putting a hand to her head. "I need my tisane. My head feels as if it will burst. Come away, Reine, come with me now. I have to lie down, and you must make my tisane."

It was the only thing to be done when her mother was taken in this way. Reine, murmuring her agreement and a great many other words of comfort, turned her back down the hall toward her own room.

As they moved off, she looked back over her shoulder. Christien stood where they had left him, with the morning light gilding his bare shoulders and a thoughtful look shading the black-coffee-and-aged-brandy darkness of his eyes.

Her chest tightened around her heart. He was so large and outrageously masculine, with latent power in every sinew as he held the center of the bedchamber with his bare toes sunk among the fat cabbage roses of the carpet. She felt a distinct heated sensation in her lower body merely from looking at him. Yet he was not all brawn by any means. He missed little, this master at arms, she thought. He would require answers later concerning her mother's distress.

The trouble was that she could not be sure how she would answer him.

In the master bedchamber, Reine rang the bell and ordered a kettle put on to boil while she undressed her mother and helped her into bed. That done, she went down to the outdoor kitchen and returned with the herbal tea, or tisane, her mother preferred, along with a selection of small cakes as additional distraction. She had hoped her mother might have fallen into a doze in her absence so her sewing box and measurements could be retrieved from Christien's room and she might, perhaps, have a few words with him. Instead, her mother sat propped against her pillows, her eyes closed as she clutched her head and rocked slowly from side to side.

"Here you are," Reine said, placing the small tray she carried on the table beside the bed and lifting the cup from it. "Drink it quickly. It's hot, but not scalding."

Her mother reached blindly for the drink, a concoction of Demeter's made from willow bark shavings, mint leaves, lemon balm and a few other things the old nursemaid refused to name. She sipped from it and sank back on the pillows as if the mere taste was enough to bring relief.

"Thank you, *chère*," she said after a moment. "You are a good daughter. Yes, perhaps too good."

"If you speak of this marriage…"

"Your papa should not have asked it of you."

"He didn't. That was Monsieur Lenoir's solution to our predicament."

"But you agreed. Why did you agree? Why could you not have refused and kept on refusing until—"

"Until what? Until we were riding down the drive while perched on top of our belongings? No, no, this will be better."

"I fear— Oh, *chère*. You can't know…" She trailed off, sighed and began again. "Your papa and I have been happy. I wanted you to be happy in your next husband. But not now, not like this, no, no. It's too soon. I can't think—"

Happy? What did that mean? Could happiness be in a kiss that tasted of shaving soap and honey-sweet man, of mind-drugging ardor and potential surrender? Was it in physical completion? If so, Reine thought she might have some small chance of it. She still felt drugged by Christien's kiss, bemused by the certainty that she had never had another like it, not in all the time of her courtship and marriage to Theodore.

"Don't think, then. Let it go, *Maman.*"

"I must, someone must. Oh, *chère,* what if he comes back?"

Her mother's question wrenched Reine's thoughts away from the man she had just left. Goose bumps ran across her shoulders and down her arms. "Who? You can't mean Theodore. He's dead, *Maman.* You remember. He's been dead these two years."

"He wasn't there. The bed, all that blood. But he wasn't there."

This was an aspect her mother returned to again and again. Reine could hardly blame her; it was the point that had never been adequately explained. If she had been there, in the bedchamber she and Theodore had sometimes shared at River's Edge, all might have been made plain, might have been different. But she had not.

For an instant she was back in that terrible time. Marguerite had been so ill, with high fever, vomiting and flux. Her crying could be heard all over the house at Bonne Espèrance. Everyone had been kept awake by it: Theodore's mother, the elderly uncle dying in an upper bedchamber of the French Creole–style house, the pair of cousins who looked after the old man. The noise and upset in the household had so exasperated Theodore that he finally rode into town and remained there for several days. Or perhaps he had only wanted to avoid contamination as he could never bear being ill.

Reine, doubtful about the remedies pressed upon her by old Demeter and reluctant to burden a household already dealing with one invalid, had longed to be at River's Edge. When the old uncle died in the midst of the turmoil, she picked up Marguerite and went home. Not that it had done much good; the sickness had simply run its course. Reine had not slept for days and nights together, had spent every moment rocking Marguerite, bathing her in cool water, spooning minute sips of sweetened lemon water into her mouth, trying to find something she could keep in her stomach. All track of time was lost in the endless round of days and nights.

When the fever finally broke and Marguerite slept, Reine eased away from where she had been holding her, lying in the great tester in her bedchamber. She'd realized then that she had eaten nothing all that day. After a small meal in the outdoor kitchen at the end of the walk, she put her head down on the table for just a moment, savoring the relief that the crisis was past. In a moment, she would return to the house, she thought, would climb the stairs back to her bed.

She woke at dawn to a keening scream. Jumping up, she ran back inside with her heart in her throat. She had found her mother holding Marguerite while blood smeared them both. She shuddered even now to think of it.

It was some time before a coherent story could be made of what had happened. Theodore had returned from New Orleans, stopping at Bonne Espèrance, where he learned Reine and Marguerite had left. He arrived at River's Edge, they knew, because a sleepy stable boy had taken his horse. He entered the house and made his way to the bedchamber Reine had occupied without doubt, for his discarded clothing lay on the floor where he'd dropped it. The mattress was imprinted with the shape of his narrow form, an indication that he had lain there. Theodore was never seen again, however. At least he was never seen alive.

"You know he's dead, *Maman.* He was found in the river, remember?" Reine spoke over her shoulder as she moved to close the shutters over the windows, shutting out the light as well as the steadily increasing heat. Pausing an instant before latching them, she gazed though the crack at the silver flood of the Mississippi, a bright swath in the morning light, just visible over the levee from this second-floor window. The dock for River's Edge was directly opposite the house, and Theodore had been found no great distance below it. Reine closed her eyes tightly, then opened them again before she went on. "Paul saw him when they pulled him out."

"Yes, yes, my poor Paul. It troubles him still, I know it does."

Reine could only agree. It troubled all of them in one way or another.

"Theodore may not have been the best of husbands, not patient and kind like Maurice. But he was not…not a terrible one, was he?"

"What do you mean, terrible?"

"He never struck you?"

Reine shook her head. Theodore had been thoughtless, high tempered and quick to find fault. He had been so catered to all his life that he expected all things to revolve around his wishes, and was outraged when it was otherwise. That didn't make him a bad husband.

And yet her mother's comment made it sound as if she knew Reine's marriage had been lacking. She wasn't sure how, for it was nothing they ever talked about. Such things were too upsetting for her mother. More than that, they were no one's business but her own.

It was good to think that her parents' marriage was more blessed, that her mother had been happy, or as happy as someone of her unstable temperament could be. It had always been a gentle union due to her mother's fragile condition, but her father obviously adored her, would do anything to keep her calm and content. If passion was not a large part of their union, it was their affair. At least a mild version must have enlivened it when they were younger, Reine felt, or she and Paul would not have made their appearance in the world.

It wasn't what she wanted for herself, a selfless and tepid union, she realized as she moved back toward the bed. No, not at all, in spite of what she might have thought a day or two ago.

She was not fragile or overly genteel, didn't shrink from emotions that were wild and hot and free. Perhaps it was her French blood from her father's side of the family, but she felt such things were regulated by nature. She should be more ladylike about them, perhaps, should keep them inside where they would not embarrass her or her future husband. Still, that didn't mean she shouldn't feel them.

Did it?

She wondered how Christien viewed the matter.

"People say the most revolting things," her mother went on, turning her head back and forth against the tall headboard. "They should not talk about what happened here, about you. I can't bear it."

"I suppose it's natural to speculate when something so odd takes place. I'm sure they mean nothing by it." Reine seated herself on the edge of the bed, lifting the cup to encourage her mother to drink more of the cooling tisane.

"Are you? I am not. They should understand you could have nothing to do with it, that you aren't capable of…of what they whisper behind their hands. Poor Theodore must have been injured by a prowler. The blood on his pillow—he must have been beaten about the head and face. He wandered out to seek aid, or perhaps he didn't know what he was doing, where he was going, and so fell into the river."

It was what they had all said in one form or another since that night. Repeating it seemed to give her mother a measure of peace, as well. Nothing else made sense.

Because she had found Marguerite lying in Theodore's blood, it had naturally preyed on her mind. The peace when it finally faded away, seldom to be mentioned, had been tremendous. Now the impending marriage, and perhaps the sight of Reine with another man in the room where Theodore had been fatally injured, had brought it all back again.

The wedding would be a reminder for everyone—friends, neighbors, acquaintances, even perfect strangers. They would begin the round of questions again. How had Theodore been killed without waking the child in the bed beside him? Had he actually left the house under his own power? If not, who had removed the body? How was it that no one in the house had seen or heard anything? How could his own wife have slept while he was being murdered in their bed?

It was that last question that haunted Reine. She hadn't known how to answer then, couldn't tell anyone now. She could say she had been so very tired, had been away from the main house in the outdoor kitchen, that she never dreamed anything so dreadful might take place. She could maintain that she had not known Theodore would return or come on to River's Edge after learning she had taken the baby there.

It made no difference. No one seemed to understand. She could hardly blame them, for she had never quite understood it herself.

Reine sat holding her mother's hand, making soothing noises while trying to say nothing that would incite fearful remembrances. After a time, the tisane did its work. When she was certain her mother slept, Reine took the cup from her lax fingers and went quietly from the room.

"Is she all right?"

She inhaled sharply, almost dropping the small tisane tray she carried before she recognized the deep voice. It was Christien, leaning with his back against the wall a few feet down the hall from her mother's door. He had finished his shave, reclaimed his shirt and donned frock coat and boots, but she could not quite banish the image in her mind of his half-naked splendor. The concern indicated by his waiting in the hall for news surprised her, but was also oddly gratifying. It was a second before she could find words to answer him.

"She is perfectly well, thank you."

"No demand to have me horsewhipped or thrown out on my ear?"

"She could hardly do that even if she wanted." Reine gave him a sardonic smile as she moved away from the door to prevent their voices from disturbing her mother. "It's your house, after all."

He ignored that as he caught up with her in a single smooth stride, keeping pace as she continued down the hall. "No message sending for the priest, either?"

"For a hasty wedding, you mean? No."

"Too bad."

She stopped, turned to face him as he halted in his turn. "You wouldn't mind?"

"I would prefer it," he answered, his gaze steady. "What of you?"

What did she really want? On one hand, she felt as if she was being hauled to the altar with her feet dragging. On the other, the whole affair seemed to be moving at a snail's pace. The sword master might be fearless on the dueling field, but could easily change his mind and put them off the property once the gossip mill began to grind out all the old rumors and accusations. Delay could lead to calamity.

She moistened her lips, which had suddenly gone dry, speaking with her gaze on his cravat. "No. It would suit me, as well. Shall we say in a week's time?"

"The only thing better would be if it took place tomorrow."

He was an impatient bridegroom. She should be flattered, and would be if not certain he wanted primarily to have the matter settled. As with most men of decision, once resolved on a course of action, his instinct would be to move forward with all speed.

Oh, she did not doubt he wanted her; she was not so foolish as to think that he would have offered marriage otherwise. It was only that she was fairly sure he wanted River's Edge more. And why would he not? It was a valuable property, and he apparently had nothing except his reputation as one of the deadliest swordsmen in New Orleans.

She knew all that, so it was ridiculous to be so affected by his declaration. Yet she could not deny the intoxicating anticipation that ran in her veins at the thought of their wedding night. If a dread of what he might think of her afterward blended with it, that was her secret.

Drawing a deep, sustaining breath, she tipped her head in agreement. "Excellent. In the chapel here, then, as we said before. You will naturally invite whomever you please."

"I have a few friends who might like to witness the deed."

"If you will draw up a list, I'll see they receive notice."

"I'll take care of it. Unless you prefer to be more formal?"

"Not at all. It won't be a particularly formal affair. To wear an elaborate gown and enter into the usual celebrations would be inappropriate under the circumstances, as I'm sure you must realize."

He reached to put a knuckle under her chin, tilting it up so she was forced to meet his rich brown-black gaze. "Whatever you wear, you will be beautiful," he said. "And I will try not to humiliate you with my attire."

"I don't… I'm not… If you mean the shirt—" she began as fiery color surged to her hairline. She wished rather frantically that she had never called attention to the state of his linen, no matter how pure her motives.

"Never mind. I will wear with pride whatever you make for me. As for the rest, you'll have to trust me."

"Yes," she whispered, lost in the darkness of his eyes.

He smiled and brushed her lips with his in a kiss with the sweet, tingling taste of promise. Inclining his head, he let her go.

Reine's throat felt tight and her chest leaden as she continued toward the stairs and the outside kitchen. It was a lie she had spoken and she knew it well. Trusting him was the last thing she could do.

# 11

The muffled squeal, followed by a despairing protest, came from the stable. Christien drew up so abruptly that his big black danced a few steps along the fenced wagon path before coming to a halt. Though wary of another hysterical scene similar to the one after Madame Cassard's discovery of Reine in his bed-chamber yesterday morning, he could hardly pass by without investigation. He was by no means sure it was the older lady he'd heard, anyway. It might have been Reine or even Marguerite. In fact, it was more likely to be one or the other, since Madame Cassard rarely, if ever, left the house.

The murmur of voices, one female, the other over-riding and gruffly male, came from the stable's great open center, which was wide enough to drive a wagon through. The breathless fear in the lighter one decided Christien. With a silent command, he set the black in motion again, ducking a little as he rode into the twilight dimness of the outbuilding's interior.

It was a second before his eyes could adjust from the dazzling summer morning outside. He could barely make out the dark shape of a carriage, a line of stalls, the shapes of harness and riding tack on hooks, the cavernous rise of a loft or mound of hay in one corner. A cat sat cleaning its paw in a patch of sunshine while a chicken stalked around it with a wary air. The air was thick with the smells of hay, leather, old manure and dust.

A flurry of movement at the edge of the haystack caught his attention. It became two struggling figures, a white man in the rough garb of a laborer who straddled a young black kitchen maid with her skirts up to her waist and her apron twisted around as she pushed and shoved at him.

"You there!" Christien rapped out in hard command. "Let the girl go. Come out where I can see you."

The man cursed and rolled off the woman before climbing to his feet. The girl scrambled away, dragging her skirts down, sobbing under her breath. Grabbing up an overturned basket, she hurriedly picked up the clutch of eggs that had spilled from it, leaving the broken ones lying in their cracked shells. With a single wide-eyed glance at Christien, she fled through the rear opening of the stable and disappeared from sight.

"What the hell do you want?"

The question was surly and held an *Américain* twang. The man who asked it was thick and squat, with a shock of sandy gray hair and pale eyes. His manner showed a marked lack of respect, almost as if he felt he was the aggrieved party. Christien looked him up and down and was unimpressed by what he saw.

"You'll be the overseer," he said in grim recognition. "Kingsley, I believe it was." He swung down from his horse and tethered the black to a support post with a quick twist of the reins.

"What's it to you?"

"Bend your mind to it. I'm sure it will come to you."

The man laughed, a jarring sound without humor. "Oh, yeah, the gent that won the place off old man Cassard. The one who'll be marryin' Madame Pingre. I guess you think you're sittin' purty."

Christien's voice, never loud, grew softer still. His friends could have told the overseer it was not a good sign.

"We will leave Madame Pingre out of this. All you need understand is that I am the owner of River's Edge. Whatever may have been tolerated in the past in the way of conduct toward females on this property no longer applies. You will leave them strictly alone. Is that understood?"

"Aw, don't pay no mind to that gal. She wanted it, no matter how much she squalled about it."

"It appeared otherwise." Christien, noting details about a possible opponent without conscious thought, let his gaze linger a moment on the odd pattern of calluses on the man's hands. They had the look of hard labor with a hoe or, just possibly, strenuous practice with a sword. Both seemed equally unlikely.

"I tell you—"

"Don't," Christien recommended. "Listen well, because this is the last time I will say it. Leave the women alone."

"Or what? What you goin' to do, huh? Fire me? You

better be talkin' to that bride of yours, let her tell you how things stand around here."

Christien moved with deceptive lack of speed, yet one moment the overseer was rocking on his heels, sneering, and the next he was stretched out on the ground. Kingsley stared up at him with shock and rage in his eyes. Pushing to one elbow, he swiped at his nose and came away with blood on his fingers.

"That," Christien said gently, "is how things stand."

Behind him, there came a choked sound that might have been an objection, but could also have been a laugh. He spared a brief glance toward the stable doorway. Paul Cassard stood poised there as if he didn't know whether to run or dance a jig.

Kingsley gave them both a sour look but settled his most malevolent stare on Christien. "You'll live to regret this," he said, his voice thick.

"Will I? Collect what you're owed and get off the place. You have until dark to be gone."

"*Monsieur,*" Paul said, coming a step closer, "Christien?"

"The boy knows. He'll tell you."

"Nothing he can say will make a difference. You aren't welcome at River's Edge." One of the eggs from the kitchen maid's basket had been spoiled. Its smell permeated the air, overriding the normal odors. It was not, Christien thought, the only thing rotten in the stable.

"You don't know what you doin'," the overseer insisted.

"Your mistake. I know full well." A man who felt

he had the right to behave as he pleased with any female could not be allowed to remain in the vicinity of Reine and Marguerite. It could not be allowed, no matter the consequences.

"You better be checkin' with Madame Pingre. I know a thing or two about that lady and her doings that she'd not like anybody to—"

He got no further. Christien reached to close hard fingers on the man's shirtfront. Hauling him to his feet, he slammed him against the wall behind him. He shoved his face close to that of the overseer. "Do not speak of the woman who is to be my wife. Don't breathe her name. Don't utter a word of anything that may concern her. If I hear that you have spread any tale of her whatever, I will personally find you and slice the hide from your miserable body in strips so small they can be used for fish bait. Do I make myself clear?"

The man's face was reddish purple, the veins swollen in his neck and forehead from the twisted tightness of his shirt collar. He tried to speak, but only made a choking sound.

"Do you understand?" Christien repeated.

Kingsley gave a bobbing nod, though his eyes shone with murderous, fear-tinged fury. He grasped Christien's wrist, trying to break his hold.

*"Monsieur,"* Paul said in worried tones. Moving forward, he touched Christien's shoulder.

Christien shuddered. With an abrupt gesture, he shoved the overseer from him in revulsion.

Kingsley stumbled back, caught his balance. With

a last look of narrow-eyed hatred, he backed toward the stable's rear door. Staggering as he turned, he shambled off and was lost to view.

*"Sacré,"* Paul Cassard said in a wondering tone. "You fired him."

"I trust your father won't be too displeased. Or Reine."

"They may worry about what he'll tell around the countryside."

"I did my best to discourage that, though I don't know what he can say that hasn't been whispered up and down the river already."

"No." The boy gave him a wary glance. "Not that I think there's anything to be told. *Mais,* you put King on the ground. I never thought to see it."

"He was taken by surprise." Paul meant to deflect his interest in gossip. Christien would allow it, for now.

The boy nodded. "He didn't expect you to face him down."

"Maybe it was time someone did," Christien said, his thoughts still on other things.

"Guess he figured you might run him through with a sword next time you saw him. Makes me wonder, too. Would you?"

"Possibly."

"Figured it." The boy gave a wise nod. "Lucky for us it was you who won at cards the other night. At least, I think so."

Christien turned his head to give Paul his full attention. "Do you indeed? I'm honored. Now, if only your sister felt the same."

"Could be she will." Paul ducked his head. "I mean, she's bound to come around sooner or later."

"Your confidence is overwhelming." Christien could not prevent the dry note that echoed in his voice.

"Yeah. Don't suppose you feel like sparring this morning?"

"You are offering to be my partner?" It was a victory of sorts, and Christien was grateful for it.

Paul gave a short nod. "I saw where you'd been to town, brought back more padding, masks and what not. That should please Reine." He paused to give him a sly upward look. "Seeing as that means something to you."

"Scamp," Christien said without heat. "Come along, then, and we'll see if we can make a swordsman of you."

A shy smile came and went across the boy's face as he turned in the direction of the house. Christien followed, lingering only long enough to hand his mount off to a stable boy who appeared as if from hiding. He frowned as he walked, however. And as he could not tell which direction the overseer had taken as he left the stable, he did not let down his guard.

# 12

Reine waited, stitching furiously on the shirt for her husband-to-be, until she heard her father leave the smoking room and mount the stairs to bed. Setting her sewing aside, she rose and left the salon.

The door to the male domain stood open. A small, square room at the back corner of the house beyond the dining room, it held a gaming table covered with green baize and set with sturdy chairs, a chest on which stood a tray holding liquor decanters beside a teakwood tobacco humidor and a pair of wing chairs tufted in maroon velvet that were drawn up near a fireplace. A black marble mantel surmounted the empty firebox with a small portrait of Theodore staring down from above it. Christien stood at the card table, where he gathered the cards he and her father had used, fitting them back into their velvet-lined case.

Without bothering to knock, she walked into the room. "You take too much upon yourself, *monsieur*," she began without preamble.

He looked up, his features still and closed in, as if she was the last person he wished to see. "How so?"

"I am told you have let the overseer go."

"The man was abusing one of the female slaves. I didn't care to have him around." He reached for the ivory chips scattered over the tabletop, stacking them into their slots with strong brown fingers that showed the pale scars of innumerable sword cuts. She stared at them an instant, aware of a drawing sensation deep inside her until she forced it from her.

She had suspected Kingsley of taking female slaves into his bed, a habit all too common among overseers. Certainly the presence of light-skinned babies in the slave nursery was damning evidence. Such arrangements were usually of mutual benefit, mutual consent, however, as the favor of the overseer usually meant freedom from field labor for the woman. That Kingsley might have been using force sickened her. She was fiercely glad that Christien had put a stop to it. Still, there were other considerations.

"What will we do for someone to see to it the cane is harvested and made into sugar, the corn brought in, mules and oxen looked after?" she asked. "Then there is the wood to be cut and hauled for the winter for the house and cabins, and a thousand other tasks. You might at least have found a replacement before dismissing him."

Christien looked up. "You want him brought back?"

"I didn't say that." Something in the dark pools of his eyes sent a trickle of alarm along her nerves.

"Good. I can see to the things you mentioned. But is that your real concern, or are you afraid he may talk out of turn?"

She drew a sharp breath. Her heart threatened to choke her with its suffocating beat, so it was a moment before she could find her voice. "What do you mean?"

"He threatened it."

"Did he?"

"I believe I convinced him it would not be wise."

Her relief was staggering. She moved to one of the wing chairs, sinking down into it. It crossed her mind to ask how Kingsley's silence had been assured. Given Christien's deadly reputation with a sword, however, she was not certain she wanted to hear.

From the corner of her eye, she was aware of Theodore's portrait. It had been painted at the time of their wedding, and given to her by her mother-in-law later while she packed for Paris. The likeness showed him standing with one hand resting on a Roman plinth, a Byronic figure with long brown waves hanging around his face, dark eyes set rather close together, an undershot jaw and full red lips. He wore evening clothes of somewhat florid style that had been cut with triangular lapels to make his shoulders appear wider. His expression was brooding and a little petulant, as if he was bored with sitting for the portrait yet arrogantly certain his form was worth recording for posterity.

The likeness was excellent. It had been sent, so his mother said, as a reminder to Marguerite of the man who had been her father. Reine had relegated it to this room because it seemed to increase the nightmares that plagued her daughter.

Setting the last of the chips into the box, Christien

closed the lid. "It might have gone better if I'd had some idea of what the man intended to say."

"He didn't tell you."

"He seemed to think you should do that. At least, that was my impression." Turning, he leaned his hips against the table and crossed his arms over his chest.

He was obviously waiting to be informed. She had no wish to go into the matter, could not bear to at this moment. "It's nothing, really."

"It's nothing, but has kept your father from letting the man go, in spite of his behavior."

"He has been here all his life, knows exactly what should be done. My father has a fine grasp of the principles of farming but is hardly the man to force others to labor in the sun." She shook her head. "You must realize that, surely, by now. You have been at the card table with him for much of the past three days."

"That troubles you?"

"I had thought losing everything to you might make him cautious at the gaming table. That can hardly happen if you encourage him." She made the point with emphasis, glad to think that she had distracted him from his earlier question.

"Gaming is a fever for some," Christien answered, "the eternal turn of the cards being the appeal rather than winning. It seemed best to indulge him here at River's Edge where it can do no harm since we play for penny stakes. You will note that he hasn't gone into town since I arrived."

What she noted was the thought the sword master had given the problem and the way he had acted upon it, without fanfare but with every consideration for her father's welfare. A peculiar sensation moved over her, one compounded of reluctant gratitude and something more she could not name. "You think it may last?"

"That remains to be seen. He seems satisfied for the moment."

It was also true that her father enjoyed Christien's company. Perhaps he had need of masculine companionship. Paul was always available, of course, but her brother was still rather young and had no taste for card games. The saints be praised.

"What I had hoped to discover," Christien said, leaving his stern pose to move toward her, "is that you were feeling neglected as I've spent so much time with your father."

"Don't be absurd." She distrusted the curl of his smile, the dark look in his eyes. Why did he have to be so attractive in this mood? It was most unfair when she wanted to be annoyed with him. "You also spend time with Paul and Marguerite, and I have not complained there."

"But you are keeping an accounting." His face bemused, he reached with his long, hard fingers to pluck a stray sewing thread from the fullness of her skirt, rolling it between them before dropping it to the Brussels carpet.

"No such thing," she said in exasperation, brushing where he touched in case there were more threads. "I was merely observing—"

"Now I am under observation."

He was, though not in the way he meant. She seemed unable to sleep until she knew he was in the house at night. Twice in these past few days he had left at midnight and not returned until the early morning.

Face flaming, she said, "What you do and with whom is none of my concern."

"Oh, but it is." He took her hand in a warm grasp. "I give you leave to concern yourself with every minute of my days, especially those spent alone like this."

His days, but not his nights. In her recognition of that point, it was an instant before she realized he was drawing her toward the gaming table. He released her as they reached its edge, placed his hands at her waist and lifted her with effortless strength so she was seated upon it.

"What are you doing?" She meant it to be a demand, but it came out as a choked exclamation.

"Making certain you can't suddenly remember a duty elsewhere in the middle of our conversation," he answered, wading into her skirts until he stood between her knees.

"Let me down at once. What if someone should come in?" With his arms still around her, there seemed nothing to do with her hands except to place them on his upper arms. Her breasts grazed his coat front so her nipples tightened into small, tingling buds at the friction. An aching vulnerability invaded the space between her spread thighs. With it came an urgent need for heat and pressure there, just there at their apex where he was not quite touching her.

"They have been allowing us time to become

acquainted. Haven't you noticed? Having been strictly forbidden to be gallant, I believe it's time I took base advantage of it."

A protest hovered on her lips, but died away unspoken as he bent his head, hesitated, then set his mouth to hers. Her gasp of mingled shock and pleasure gave him deeper access and he accepted it without pause. The taste of him melted on her tongue, sweet and rich, flavored with sunshine, earthiness and rampant desire. He eased nearer, deepening the joining, investigating the tender surfaces of her mouth, the glasslike edges of her teeth, abrading her tongue with sinuous invitation to return the favor. She took it in a perilous, half-reluctant foray, then ventured more boldly as pleasure bloomed inside her.

His arms became a haven once more as on that first night, one so perfect it sent her to the edge of delirium in the space of heartbeat. Tears rose in her eyes for the rightness of it, the exquisite flavor and the promise. She could not move, could not breathe or reason. Her fingers closed upon the worsted of his coat sleeve, holding him, slowly drawing him closer against her.

He smoothed one hand from the indentation of her waist up the rigid slope of her back, spreading his fingers to press her closer still. With the other, he skimmed her rib cage, slid higher, brushed the outer curve of her breast. His thumb circled her nipple, its callused edge scraping the pale gray-green India muslin of her dinner gown.

Hot need rushed through her with such force that she stiffened, stunned by its effect. Languor spread through her, dissolving her bones, sapping her will.

She should call a halt, push away, she knew, but the resolution for it seemed beyond her reach.

She could feel the percussive thunder of his heart, sense the fervid heat of him and the firmness at the juncture of his thighs even through her skirts. Under her clenched fingers, the muscles of his arms were like tempered steel, forged harder than iron with his exacting control.

Such containment was not what she required. She throbbed with need so long suppressed that her blood boiled in her veins. She longed to be touched, yearned mindlessly for that most intimate *touché* from this *maître*, the gesture of victory where the ultimate impalement was prohibited. One touch, only one.

It came, the pressure of a hard palm at the center of her being, a slow and deliberate clasping through layers of silk and linen. She cried out, a sound muffled by his mouth, while bright, shuddering pleasure poured through her in endless waves.

He released her lips, but remained bent over her with one strong hand pressing her forehead against his chest as it rose and fell with the attempt he made to control his ragged breathing. After a moment, she stirred, pushed at him as she attempted to break away.

"Don't," he said in low command. "Not yet."

"Please. I must… You don't understand." She was almost incoherent with humiliation, wanting nothing more than to vanish from his sight, hiding away until she could regain her dignity and self-respect.

He took a single step back. "The fault here is mine. I never intended to go so far."

"Whatever fault there may be, I share it. Try, please, to put it from your mind."

"As if I could," he said on a rough sound that was half laugh, half groan.

"I'm aware it may be difficult, but you need not fear a repeat of these few moments."

"Fear it? By all the saints, I would fight the archangel himself for the chance of living them over again."

She stared at him, afraid to let herself believe what he implied. "You weren't…aren't put off? Theodore said… That is, he assured me my responses were too…too eager, that I was held in such thrall by my own deep responses that I—I unmanned him."

"No," Christien said, the word a growl deep in his throat. "You don't put me off in any fashion."

She slid from the card table, carefully avoiding his eyes as she shook out her skirts. "It's kind of you to say so."

"I am not being kind."

"Diplomatic, then." She had to get away before the hard knot in her chest dissolved into tears she could not control. Blindly, she turned toward the door.

"Nor that, either. I speak the bare truth for once in this miserable business. You were lovely, even unforgettable, in your ladylike desire."

"Gallant, after all." She attempted a smile, though it was directed at the carpet. Moving with more speed than grace, she set a path for the door. Her hand was on the handle, had almost opened it, when he called after her.

"Reine!"

She turned back, but he was no more than a blur in the center of the room. "Monsieur Lenoir?"

He gave the ghost of a laugh. "You might call me Christien, considering what just passed between us. On this subject, I must tell you that all men are not alike. Some give rein to their passion with no thought of control, others exercise control without passion. Some fortunate few combine them. For any man, a woman's fervent response is, or should be, his goal and most cherished reward. You may have cared for your Theodore, were doubtless innocent enough when wed to believe whatever he told you. It's even possible he believed it himself from sheer ignorance. Yet I will undertake to show you soon that your late husband was an arrogant fool."

# 13

*Your late husband was an arrogant fool....*

What had Christien meant? Reine, safe behind the closed door of her sitting room, pondered the possibilities. No exact idea presented itself, but just remembering the deep timbre of his voice and the pledge that lay in the inky darkness of his eyes were enough to keep her wide-awake.

She sat with her slippers kicked off, her feet on the settee and a palmetto fan in one hand, waving it before her face against the still, sullen heat of the evening. Beyond her room, she could hear the noises of the house as everyone settled down for the night. Marguerite had been sent to bed in the nursery some time ago, and now her nursemaid, done with her chores of straightening the nursery and putting out her charge's clothing for the next day, climbed with slow steps to her attic room. The murmuring voices of her parents died away, became gentle, near-matching snores. Christien's even footsteps passed down the central hallway to his bedchamber. Alonzo could be heard closing the shutters and locking the French doors. In

due time, he climbed the stairs and his treads continued on up to the attic.

The night quiet was broken only by the whir of
insects and vibrato cries of frogs hoping for rain. After
a time, a dog howled somewhere behind the house, in
the direction of the slave cabins, and the hound, Chalmette, answered with a gruff bark from the front
portico. Reine strained for other sounds, but none
impinged on the stillness.

*Ladylike desire…*

Had her response really seemed that way to the man
she was to marry? She hardly dared believe it. She had
felt the complete wanton, so lost in pleasurable sensation that she had come close to abandonment. If he had
decided to take her there on the card table with her
skirts rucked up around her waist, would she have
stopped him? She could not think, in all truth, that
she'd have had the willpower. What was ladylike about
that?

He didn't seem repulsed. Perhaps his experience
was with women of less-than-sterling virtue, the kind
who battened on the desires of men. Such females
must be more overt in expressing their ardor so as to
inflame their partners into paying for their company.
Yet if Christien considered her in the same light, what
did that make her?

He would show her the difference between con-
trolled and uncontrolled passion, or so he said. The
very idea sent anticipation surging along her veins. It
also terrified her. She was not herself around him. She
felt too much, hovered too close to some dangerous

sensual surrender that might destroy everything. She didn't trust him, but still less did she trust herself in his presence.

Squeezing her eyes shut, she gave a small shake of her head. She would not think of Christien anymore, would not wonder at what he might teach her. That way lay fevered madness she could not afford. It would be best to consider all that must be done for the wedding or, better yet, make her mind a blank. Some small degree of calm must be gained, one way or another.

Her bedchamber door creaked open. The abrupt jangle of her nerves and the odd, stiff position of her neck let her know she had fallen into a doze. The night had advanced, and heat lightning glimmered through the slats of her French door shutters.

*"Maman?"* Marguerite's eyes were wide in her small, pale face as she peeked around the hall door.

"Yes, *ma petite?*"

Her daughter eased into the room, then flew to catch Reine around the waist. She pressed her face against her, her breathing labored as she clung. "He's gone, *Maman,* he's gone."

"Who, sweetness? The *loup-garou?*"

"No, no. He is always there. It's Monsieur Christien. I had a bad dream. I went to his bedchamber. I knocked, but he didn't answer. I went in anyway, and he wasn't there. Oh, *Maman,* he wasn't there!"

The last was a cry of despair. Reine drew Marguerite with her to the settee, pulling her down beside her as she dropped back onto the cushioned seat. "Are you sure, *petite?*" she asked, rocking her back and forth, wiping tears from the small face with her fingers. "The bed is high, and perhaps you just couldn't—"

"I climbed up the steps. He wasn't in the bed. He's gone, gone away and left us."

"Oh, but surely not forever."

"I want him back, my Monsieur Christien! I want him back!"

"Not so loud, sweetness, or you'll wake everyone in the house. It could be that he hasn't gone far. Perhaps I could look for him. If I call Babette to stay with you, will you let me do that? Will you?"

Her daughter's arms tightened around her. She shook her head in refusal. As Reine spoke in a litany of soothing phrases interspersed with promises, however, her grip eased. Finally, she let Reine go.

Reine picked up Marguerite and took her back to her bed, tucking her in and lighting a lamp to leave burning on a side table. She summoned the nursemaid and left her rocking in a chair placed where Marguerite could see her. With another hug and quiet good-night, she left her.

Back out in the hall, she moved to the door of the room allotted to Christien. She hesitated, listening. Hearing nothing, she pushed her way inside.

Everything was neat, orderly, with no sign of disturbance. The frock coat he had worn when she saw him in the smoking room now hung in the armoire. He had changed his evening shoes for his boots and his dust coat was missing. It seemed clear that he had dressed for riding and left the house.

He had left the rest of his belongings behind. She

rested her forehead on the armoire's wooden door and allowed herself a sigh of relief. It had seemed possible he might have decamped, bag and baggage, out of sheer disgust for her behavior. At least she was spared that humiliation.

She had not heard him go, which suggested a stealthy departure. It was only an hour, possibly less, since she had heard him come upstairs. How far could he have ridden in so short a time?

Swinging with abrupt decision, she strode to her room. Without calling for her maid, she worked her way out of her evening gown by withdrawing her arms from the cap sleeves and twisting the bodice to the front in order to strip its tiny buttons from their loops. Skimming out of her petticoats, wishing she was not so tightly laced into her corset that she could not remove it as well, she took her riding habit of marine-blue poplin from its armoire hook. It was designed to be donned without aid for the sake of early-morning rides, a good thing at the moment. Settling it around her and doing up its hooks with fumbling haste, she stamped into her boots, flung the trailing skirt of the habit over her arm and hurried from the house. A short time later, she was cantering along the river road on her mare.

New Orleans was her destination, as it made no sense that Christien would go elsewhere. She kept a wary eye out for his dust trail ahead of her. Regardless of what she had told Marguerite, she had no intention of stopping him. She burned to know where he was going and what he meant to do there. The only way to discover these things was to follow him, once she had him in sight. With care and luck, she could manage to do that while hanging back on his trail.

The night air was oppressive, almost too thick to breathe. Gnats buzzed around her face, trying to sip the moisture from the corners of her lips and eyes. Mosquitoes rose in clouds from the occasional water-filled ditch, whining about her mount. Creatures scuttled across the pale track of the roadway of crushed oyster shells, rustling away into the underbrush. An owl called in the distance. On the far horizon, somewhere beyond the winding river levee, heat lightning glowed in erratic flashes.

She was less than a quarter of a mile out of town when she finally sighted Christien. He was a dark, broad-shouldered figure on horseback illuminated briefly as he passed a shanty tavern with a lantern hanging above the door. Reine drew her mare to a walk, guiding her into tree shadows until the space between them lengthened again. When she felt he was unlikely to recognize her even if he looked back, she picked up speed to keep him just in view.

He didn't make for his old haunt, the salons of the sword masters on the Passage de la Bourse. Nor did he turn toward the more sordid streets where he might have expected to meet with loose women. Instead, he left the levee street at rue St. Philippe and continued along its length for some few blocks. From there, he made another turn, crossed an intersection and came upon the side-street entrance of a house that fronted on rue Royale. He dismounted and hitched the black stallion's reins to a ring set into the wall of the house opposite. Removing his dust coat, he tossed it over the saddle and walked across to speak to the majordomo who guarded the door.

Reine, remaining well back in the side street, dismounted and secured her mare to a balcony post. On foot, she edged a little closer. A soiree was in progress at the rue Royale address, she thought, for light spilled from the French doors standing open onto the second-floor balcony. The strains of a waltz drifted down to the street, and the spinning shadows of dancers made a dizzying kaleidoscope in shades of gray upon what could be seen of the ceiling.

The event taking place would be a family party, Reine surmised, perhaps a birthday or anniversary celebration. The thought was dictated by the time of year; no hostess wasted funds or effort on an entertainment of any real magnitude during the summer. For one thing, it was far too hot to crowd into a single room for any length of time, almost too hot for the exertion of dancing. Mainly, however, the company in town was too thin. People of reasonable wealth and intelligence left New Orleans for their country places, for France or the watering places of Europe and the northeast during yellow fever and cholera season.

From a vantage point inside the recessed doorway of the corner patisserie, she saw the majordomo bow in token of agreement to Christien's request and in appreciation for the coin he passed him. As he disappeared inside, Christien moved back across the street, stepping under the arcade that protected the banquette.

In the shadow cast by the building, he propped one shoulder against the wall as if setting himself to wait.

What was he doing? Was his inamorata a lady attending the party, one he expected to slip down and join him? Was he in search of one of his swordsmen friends? If it was neither of these things, Reine could not imagine his purpose.

The minutes slipped past. A few more guests arrived for the soiree, and one or two departed. That was all.

Glancing around her, Reine pulled the veil attached to her riding hat about her face. A woman on the street alone was always a source of speculation, but doubly so at night. Tongues would clack if she were identified. That she had been besmirched by scandalized whispers already meant she could afford less than most in the way of speculation about her business.

By degrees, she became aware of how tired she was, also how on edge. The distant thunder and occasional flicker of lightning rasped her nerves. Her eyes burned as she watched the dim space where Christien stood. She tried not to fidget too much, for though she thought him unaware of her presence, she didn't trust him to remain so.

Activity at the doorway he watched slowed to nothing. Traffic in the street almost ceased, as well. Nothing seemed to be happening; Christien was doing nothing worthy of notice. He seemed, in fact, to have no purpose beyond idling away the time in contemplation of the house opposite him. Restless impatience grew inside Reine until she was on the verge of stalking from her hideaway and returning home.

The thought was banished as the downstairs entrance sprang open, throwing a rectangle of light into the street. A gentleman strode out, slamming the door behind him with a bang that echoed over the tile rooftops. Without pausing, he stalked across to where Christien waited under the arcade.

The swordsman straightened. He spread his feet a little, squaring his shoulders as he watched the gentleman's approach.

Reine came to frowning attention, as well, as the newcomer arrived within speaking distance. What was said as the two men met, she could not tell. Their voices were no more than a low rumble, and the back of the one who accosted Christien blocked her view. A sharp sound rang out, cracking like an openhanded slap. It was followed by more heated words. Abruptly, the unknown gentleman turned and walked off in the direction of the river. Christien collected his mount, then followed after him.

Tingling alarm slid down Reine's spine. She slipped from her concealment and moved quickly to the corner, then trailed the pair at a more sedate pace.

They strode with grim purpose until they reached the tree-shaded enclosure of St. Anthony's Garden, which lay behind the cathedral. In a pantomime of extreme courtesy, they each indicated that the other should go first through the gateway. Christien won the exchange, entering behind the other gentleman, carrying a long case that he had taken from behind his saddle. They walked to the center, where two intersecting paths divided the space into shrubbery-filled quarters. There they came to a halt.

Reine left rue Royale, slipping down the alleyway between the high walls of the cathedral and those of the government house next to it. In that darker conceal-ment, she paused behind a wax myrtle shrub that filled the garden's corner. Its sprawling growth provided a screen without obscuring her view of the deep-shadowed square of open area on its other side.

The two men conferred, then began to remove their hats and frock coats. They loosened their cravats and cast them aside. A grim word or two more passed between them, but Reine's heart was thudding so hard in her ears that she could not hear. Christien knelt beside the box he had placed on the ground, opening the lid. When he rose again, he held a long, glittering sword in either hand.

Reine drew a sharp breath as comprehension struck her. A duel, it was to be a duel. Yet this was no civil-ized meeting with carefully worded challenge and answer, appointed seconds and a doctor or two in attendance in case of injury. It was, must be, one of the infamous judgments-by-the-sword that were the specialty of the Brotherhood of *maîtres d'armes.*

Theodore had railed against such clandestine meet-ings in furious indignation. They were most unjust, he said, in that the superior skill and power was almost always on the side of the sword master. They were also beneath the notice of a gentleman, as the masters showed no regard whatever for the form and ritual that should govern such meetings. They were not duels at all in the strict sense, but degrading punishments meted out at the discretion of the men who deemed them necessary. She had often thought, while listening to his denunciations, that fear lay behind them. And what other than suspicion that he might be targeted for such a challenge could occasion such terror?

Christien gave his opponent first choice of the pair of swords. His opponent inspected one's length while holding it to the muted glow of the streetlamp on the far corner. Pronouncing it satisfactory, he moved to face Christien. They exchanged a slicing salute, then crossed blades with a bell-like clang. The command to begin rang out.

They were cautious in their forays at first, or so it appeared, each man testing the skill of the other as they shuffled from deep shadow to lighter darkness and back again. By degrees, the speed of their movements increased until they were striving in deadly earnest. Distant light slid along the edges of the swords, winking with starlike gleams. They attacked, grunting, recovered with swift aplomb from rigorous defense, rested a bare instant, then engaged again. They skipped forward, carrying a dazzling whirl of blades before them, and retreated while parrying with almost negligent flicks of the wrist and deep breaths from the challenged gentleman, which took on a harsh sound in the night.

Christien was magnificent. His lunges were clean and fast, his recoveries incredibly swift. His concentration was on the tip of his opponent's sword; it seemed he had none for anything else, certainly none for Reine's presence. Perspiration turned his shirt dark across the shoulders and down his back, and made his pantaloons cling to the well-developed muscles of his thighs. The look on his features, seen in glimmers of lamplight and lightning, was one of intent and driven intelligence. There was no anger or even dislike in it, but equally there was no relenting.

The impression sent horror and excitement down her back. Her pulse throbbed in her throat, and it was so difficult to breathe that she felt close to suffocation. Her eyes burned yet she could not look away.

What had the man who faced Christien done? How had he brought this retribution down upon himself? Would the sword master be so grim and without remorse toward all who required chastisement?

These questions had barely surfaced in her head when Christien drove forward in a lightning attack and the sudden shriek of steel on steel. His opponent gave a harsh gasp and staggered back. For an instant he hung with a sword tip, wetly gleaming, protruding from his shoulder. He dropped his weapon, brought up his left hand toward the dark gash that appeared on his shirtfront.

The *maître d'armes* stepped back with a hard pull, retrieving his blade. His opponent sagged at the knees.

Reine did not see him fall. With her eyes squeezed shut and hands clamped to her mouth to stifle her cry, she spun away from the dark garden. Sickness rose inside her, and she leaned her back against the rough stone of the cathedral wall, breathing in deep, silent gasps.

Even so, the outcome of this affair loomed large in her mind. What would be done for the wounded man now that he was down? What if he was so badly injured that he died? Yes, and what if the watch appeared to arrest Christien?

It could happen, as duels of any sort were forbidden by law. They were winked at, yes, but only if the men involved had social standing and were known to the judge. Public outcry had been strong of late concerning these summary punishments meted out by faceless sword masters.

At least one of them was faceless no more. She had seen Christien thrust a sword through warm flesh as if it was of no more concern than swatting a mosquito. She had seen and would never forget it.

It would be as well if no one knew she had been a witness. She was reluctant to have Christien learn of it, but had no wish whatever to be questioned by the authorities. There was nothing she could do by remaining that could not be taken care of with greater skill by a doctor. One would arrive soon, for she heard Christien tell the fallen man so. As she chanced a last quick glance, she saw Christien kneeling above him, using what appeared to be their discarded cravats to stanch the flow of blood.

Moving with the greatest of care, she eased backward a step, another, a half dozen. Turning then, she sped down the alley away from the rue Royale and St. Anthony's Garden. Scant seconds later, she emerged in the Place d'Armes. It lay empty and quiet, as did the streets around it. She looped her habit skirt higher over her arm and set off at a fast pace for the street where her mount was hitched.

Never had the road from town to River's Edge seemed so long or so dark and deserted. Reine rode what seemed like hours. She started at shadows, twisted in the saddle to identify strange sounds, flinched at the rumble of thunder overhead. The houses she passed slumbered with the closed eyes of barred shutters. Sounds were muffled, deadened by hot, too-still air. The thudding of her mare's hooves kept pace with her hammering pulse and racing thoughts.

She wished most fervently that she had never followed Christien, never seen the grim retribution he had meted out. He had been so implacable, so without pity. The man he had faced might deserve none, yet she was profoundly disturbed by that hardness.

She was also exalted by it. What manner of woman was she that his merciless prowess sent a secret thrill through her? If she had been a primitive creature living in the wilds, it might have made some small sense, but what use did a lady in civilized surroundings have for such attributes in a man? It must be a flaw in her nature, one part and parcel of her excess desires. At least she was now on her guard so could find a way to control it.

From behind her came hoofbeats at a fast gallop. She did not care to be overtaken on the road, for safety's sake if nothing else. Turning her mare's head, she left the shell-covered track, easing behind a growth of scrub oak and palmetto.

The riders came even with her place of concealment

and passed quickly down the river road. They were two in number. One sat his mount like a horseman, but the other was unused to the saddle if the wagging of his elbows and flopping of his feet in the stirrups was any indication. They spoke not a word, but appeared intent on reaching their destination with all possible speed. She could tell little more than that in the darkness, but was just as glad to avoid closer inspection.

Fearful the pair might notice her behind them if she took to the road again too soon, she waited until their hoofbeats had faded into the night and all was still once more, then waited some minutes more. Finally, she gathered her reins.

Before she could leave her concealment, the sound of hooves came once more. Her mare threw up her head as if to whinny.

Reine flung herself forward, covering the flaring nostrils with her gloved fingers. Lying along the horse's neck with its mane in her face, she could not tell what manner of traveler moved past this time. It seemed likely it was Christien, however, as the mare had attempted to signal a stable mate. She hoped so. It would be as well if he had not lingered at the scene of the duel. To aid the man he'd injured was a fine gesture, but not if he courted arrest.

A few more seconds of strain, then she was able to release her hold and sit up. Christien—it was him— had passed on out of sight. She gave a sigh of relief and urged the mare back onto the road.

The thunder that had threatened all evening seemed more ominous, the flickering lightning brighter. Mosquitoes seemed determined to eat her alive. Tension tied her shoulder muscles in knots, and she developed a cramp in the leg that gripped her sidesaddle's pommel.

Beyond her physical discomfort was the goad of her thoughts, which turned in endless, stinging circles. Was she doing the right thing with her alliance to the *maître d'armes?* If he meted out punishment so casually to a man for impersonal offenses, what might he not do to a woman who crossed him? Could she make it inside the main house without him discovering that she had followed him tonight? What could she possibly say if she were caught?

She could not wait to reach River's Edge and the safety of her bed.

At last she began to see the landmarks that told her the plantation was near: a dead tree where buzzards liked to roost, the ghostly shape of Bonne Espèrance, Theodore's family home, at the end of its overgrown drive. Relaxing a little, she began to think longingly of a restorative sherry and a bath for coolness and to rid herself of the smell of horse.

The muffled crack of a pistol shot shattered the night air. Reine's mount sidled and reared so she was nearly unseated. Holding the mare in, keeping her place with difficulty, she calmed the horse and brought her to a stand. Head up, then, she listened.

A dog barked somewhere in the distance. That was all.

The road curved ahead of her as it followed the river's winding embankment. Just beyond that bend was River's Edge. Reine rode forward with caution.

The dark form of a man lay across the road. His horse stood over him, tethered by reins that were still clutched in the rider's hand. She recognized the black stallion before she did its master.

Urging the mare to one side, she unhooked her knee from the pommel and half slid, half leaped to the ground. She ran forward, her long skirt almost tripping her so she stumbled to her knees beside the man stretched out on the crushed-shell roadway. He lay facedown. She reached to slip both hands beneath his chest and one shoulder, lifting with all her strength, then rolling him to his back.

His head lolled on the stem of his neck, turning toward her. His eyes were closed, his face unnaturally pale and marked by bloody cuts where he had struck the sharp oyster shells. His dust coat was torn along one side and marked by a dark stain. As she looked down at her gloved hands, the fingertips shone with something wet and blackish-red in the uncertain glimmer of lightning.

"Christien," she whispered in dismay. "Oh, Christien."

# 14

Christien woke with a jerk and the thudding boom of a gunshot in his ears. He lay still, staring into lamp-lit dimness while his mind grappled with where he was compared to where he should be, what he saw compared to what he remembered.

Thunder rumbled again, merging with the steady drumming of rain on the roof. Only thunder, not a gunshot at all.

He breathed deliberately, a slow rise and fall of his chest, and forced his taut muscles to relax. With care, he turned his head on his pillow, taking stock while squinting against the pain of the headache that stabbed behind his eyes.

He was in his rooms at River's Edge. Someone had undressed him and put him to bed. The bed curtains were looped back out of the way on either side, along with the mosquito *baire*. He was wearing a nightshirt, an item not usually a part of his wardrobe. His lower chest was tightly bound, with so much bandaging on the left side that his arm was held away from his body.

It hurt like hell there just below his rib cage. The

injury seemed strange because he could not recall being touched in that area or any other during the meeting in St. Anthony's Garden.

But no, he had been ambushed on the road back. He'd seen the flash of a pistol, heard its roar. He recalled now the wrenching blow as the ball tumbled him out of the saddle. He must have struck his head as he fell.

Frowning at the pleated yellow muslin of the tester above him, he considered who might want him dead. Friends of Barichere, the man he'd wounded during their meeting? They could have received word of the duel and decided to avenge the punishment. Lacking the nerve to make a challenge in due form, they might have taken their reprisal under cover of darkness.

To accept that explanation meant taking it for granted that someone close to Barichere knew where he was staying. It also assumed that Barichere, a man with a nasty temper and habit of beating his pregnant wife, the habit for which the Brotherhood had decreed his punishment, was capable of inspiring such loyalty. Neither seemed likely.

Two other possibilities remained. The first of them made Christien's head throb with a fiercer beat. Surely Cassard and his fascinating daughter were not so anxious to avoid the wedding and regain their property as to attempt permanent removal of the groom? As for the second…

The creaking of the hinge on his bedchamber door ended his ruminations. The crack between the panel and its frame eased open by minute degrees. He watched it with every muscle tensed for action, though he was by no means sure he could move. He felt as weak as a newborn pup, and had no weapon other than his fists. His sword case was not on the table beside the bed where he'd left it, nor could he spot it anywhere in the room.

The door swung wider. A small face appeared around its edge, one with bright blue eyes and a framing of fine hair that sprang in tendrils from the braid that confined it for sleep.

"*Monsieur,* you are awake!" A grin tilted Marguerite's small mouth as she saw him watching her.

"As you see." His voice had an unaccountable husky note. It must be from disuse, for what other reason could there be?

"*Maman* said I was not to wake you because you are sick. Did I wake you?"

"By no means." He lifted his right hand to beckon. "Come in, if you like."

"I do like," she said, skipping forward in a long nightgown of wrinkled cotton. She did not stop at his bedside but clambered up the bed steps to perch beside him as if it was the most natural thing in the world. The jouncing of the mattress made his side throb and sent pain shafting through his head in a sickening wave, but he clamped his teeth together and endured it.

Taking the fullness of her nightgown at the edges, the child spread it as she might a skirt, then tucked the hem around her feet. The glance she turned on him narrowed. "I came to find you last night," she said in a severe tone. "I was scared. You were gone."

"I do apologize," he said gravely, lying as still as he might if trying not to startle a butterfly into flight. "A gentleman sometimes has conflicting duties, you see."

"That's what *Grand-père* said. And you were hurted, too. But it was all right. The dream went away."

"Was it very bad?"

Thunder rolled again outside. Marguerite looked down at the knobs of her knees where they poked against the fabric of her nightgown. "Not so bad."

"Tell me about it," Christien said, watching the play of remembered fear and doubt as they moved over her piquant features. She was very like her mother in that moment, so earnest and enwrapped in practical courage.

"The *loup-garou* came again. He looked at me while I was asleep. He was scary and had marks on his face that were all ugly in the dark. I wanted to run but nothing would move. I only—only opened my eyes a little bit."

"He didn't touch you, didn't hurt you?" Christien asked, his tone as neutral as he could manage.

Her rumpled braid swung over her shoulder as she shook her head.

"He didn't say anything?"

She gave a small, nervous giggle. "No, silly. *Loup-garous* can't talk. They only come to bite you."

"Oh, is that right? And who told you that?"

"Babette."

This was, as he recalled, the name of her nurse. "Did she, now?"

"Demeter said it, too. She's a witch and lives in the woods. *Grand-père* said I would not be a mouthful so the *loup-garou* wouldn't bother with me. But I don't think he cares how little I am."

Christien had heard Cassard say that himself, though neither of them had considered the construction Marguerite might put upon it. "Has Babette or Demeter or your *grand-père* seen the *loup-garou?*"

"He goes away before anyone can wake up. I don't think he wants to see *them.*"

"Why do you think you're the only one he visits?" Though he refused to give credence to legends of *loup-garous*, it might be useful to discover the nature of Marguerite's fears.

Her voice dropped to a whisper and her eyes grew wide again. "He is like the wolf that follows Little Red Riding Hood in the story. He knows I'm little and have no sword."

The dread that shadowed Marguerite's eyes ignited rage in Christien's chest like nothing he'd ever known. He wanted to kill whoever was playing games with her, and annihilate the idiots who had planted such superstition in her mind. He was consumed with regret that he had failed her the night before, also that he might fail her again.

Clearing his throat, he asked, "What would happen if he came to the wrong person, someone who was not little? What if they chased him away?"

"He won't do that. He only comes to me."

The fatalism of that was telling, Christien thought. The *loup-garou* was singling her out in Marguerite's view, so she was the only one in danger. How lonely she must feel, and how hopeless.

For all the attention given her fear of this bogey-man, no one took it seriously enough to provide protection for her, such as assigning someone to sleep in the same room, allowing her to occupy a trundle or taking her into their bed. No wonder she had such dark shadows under her eyes and was so difficult to convince that it was bedtime.

"You have marks on your face," she said in a small voice.

"Do I?"

She nodded. "They look bad, but not like the *loup-garou*'s. Do they hurt?"

"Not exactly." They were nothing compared to the pounding in his head, though he was aware of a bruised soreness across his cheekbone.

"I could put salve on them the way *Maman* does for me," she offered.

"You would do that?" It gave him an odd sensation in the region of his heart that she would touch his injuries when she was so obviously repelled by what seemed to be *loup-garou*'s facial disfigurement.

She gave a nod that set her braid to bouncing. "It's over there, on the table. It won't hurt."

"I'm sure it won't." He watched with a suspended feeling in his chest as she crawled over the bedcovers, straddling his ankles to reach the bedside table. He caught a fold of her nightgown in his fist to prevent any chance of falling while she leaned to grasp the small glass jar of salve, but released it at once as she scooted closer to him.

Her touch was featherlight, like a spider crawling

over his face. It tickled and itched so mercilessly that he had to steel himself against pulling away, concentrating instead on the rain that poured down beyond the shuttered window. Yet he was entranced by the concentration in her small face, the way she held her bottom lip between her teeth as she worked, the thoroughness with which she searched out every small injury and the care she took not to hurt him.

Reine had bitten her lip in just that way as she measured him for his bridal shirt, he thought in distraction. Such mistreatment for so sweet and tender a surface; to see it had given him a hollow, hungry feeling in the pit of his stomach. He had been driven to kiss her or die from the need. Yes, and there in the smoking room while he played cards with her father, he'd watched her through the open sitting room door. She'd bit her lip as she sewed each careful stitch then. To soothe it later had been not just a yearning but a necessity.

"Where is your *maman* this morning?" he asked abruptly.

"It's not morning," Marguerite corrected him, still intent on her ticklish work. "That was a long time ago. Now it's night. *Maman* is getting ready for bed."

He had lost a day, Christien realized. The lamp burning on the bedside table was not left from the night's vigil, but had been brought to light the rainy evening as it closed in on them. The nightgown Marguerite wore indicated that she was on her way to bed, not that she had just come from there. Even now, Reine could be half-naked with her hair tumbling down her back in her bedchamber not far from where he lay.

He closed his eyes, the better to savor the image. Yes, and to prevent any hint of his inevitable reaction to it from reaching his small nurse.

In the quiet that fell, Christien became aware of voices calling back and forth elsewhere in the house. He could pick out an occasional word. Guessing the import of them presented no great difficulty.

They were coming closer. One in particular rang out clearer than the rest. Marguerite glanced over her shoulder, listening.

"Yes, *ma petite*," he said with wry humor in his voice. "Your *maman* is looking for you. You had best answer, for I expect she will check in here soon."

The result of that sally was not what he expected. Marguerite launched herself across the bed to return the jar of salve to the bedside table. Scrambling back again, she caught the sheet that covered him, lifted it and dove underneath.

Christien stifled a groan as the mattress bounced on its supporting ropes once more, but grinned at the same time. Reaching with one hand, he twitched the sheet over a small exposed foot, then lay back on his pillow. He let his eyelids drift almost shut, watching the door through the barest of slits between his lashes.

Rapid footsteps sounded in the hall outside. They paused. The knob turned in a slow revolution and the door panel swung open. Reine put her head inside in a move so like her daughter's that Christien's lips twitched.

She was coming in. He let his eyes close completely and lay unmoving, controlling his breathing to a steady cadence. Beside him, Marguerite breathed with quick and shallow movements, jerking a little as she stifled a giggle brought on by nervous excitement.

Skirts rustled softly as Reine came deeper into the room and stopped beside the bed. For long seconds, there was no movement, nothing, as if she was studying him. Then Christien felt the cool touch of her palm against his forehead. It was a delicious balm, but lingered only a second before she sighed and turned away.

She was leaving. That was not what he wanted.

Dredging up an artful sigh, he opened his eyes. "Reine? Don't go," he said in husky appeal. "Could I… Might I have a sip of water?"

Marguerite erupted from under the sheet, struggling up on her knees beside him. "I'll get it! Let me get it!"

Her foot tangled in the bedcovers as she reached toward the bedside table. She fell across his chest. He drew a hissing breath between set teeth as pain struck into his side like a burning lance.

Reine whirled with a wordless exclamation, sending the white batiste of her night robe and matching nightgown billowing around her along with the thick curtain of her unbound hair. She reached to pluck her daughter from the mattress, swinging her free in the same fluid movement.

Marguerite screamed and began to kick and flail in a frenzy. Reine, grim of face, took a firmer grip and turned toward the door.

"Don't take her away," Christien said through set teeth.

"What?" She swung back to face him.

Keeping his gaze rigorously above Reine's neck, away from the soft globes of her breasts outlined under her nightclothes where Marguerite was pressed against her, he tried again. "She didn't mean—didn't know…"

"She should not be here," Reine said. "I've been looking everywhere for her, we all have. I can't believe she was hiding from me. Yes, or that you were aiding her in it."

Christien could barely hear her above the child's heart-rending cries. His side ached, his head was pounding and he was laid up in bed when he should be at his strongest. It was suddenly too much. Unclenching his jaws, he spoke in firm reproof.

"Marguerite, enough!"

The girl fell instantly silent. She ceased struggling. Hanging in her mother's arms, she gave him a look of wide-eyed shock that turned slowly to misery. Above her head, Reine's face was set, her gaze watchful and without warmth.

Despite the strained atmosphere between them, it was a curiously intimate tableau there in the lamp-lit room with the rain falling beyond the windows. They might have been a family already, man, woman and child, all ready for a night of sleep in one another's arms. The rightness of it was like a blow to the chest for Christien, one far more agonizing than any mere gunshot wound. He wanted it, needed it to be real. What it took to make it so he would do, he swore in silent resolve, whether it meant courting Reine's father, mother, brother, daughter or, especially, the lady herself. He had lost his family once. This one, he would keep.

It was an instant before he could speak, and then he held his voice even only by the most stringent effort. "I didn't know anyone was searching for her until just a second ago. As for her hiding, it was meant to be a surprise."

Reine set her daughter on her feet, though the grim expression did not leave her features. If she believed a word of what he said, there was no sign of it. "I told her plainly not to bother you."

He divided a wan smile between the two of them. "She is no bother. At least, as long as she doesn't jump around."

"You have fever, you know," Reine informed him with something close to accusation.

"It's the rule with these things." He paused, more aware than he wanted to be of the throbbing that continued in his wound. Shifting a little in an attempt to ease it, he asked, "How bad is it?"

"You'll recover, barring blood poisoning. That is the considered opinion of Dr. Laborde. I sent Paul for him, and it was he who removed the ball from your side. He seemed competent."

"I'm familiar with his work," Christien said dryly. "He's thorough, though lacking in tenderness."

"It's as well that you weren't conscious while he was attending you."

"Just so." Laborde was the physician called out most often by the sword masters as he had an excellent reputation for healing wounds. Had the good doctor mentioned that he had seen him earlier, when called to Barichere? Surely not, or Reine would have mentioned it. Another reason for Laborde's popularity was his discretion. No doubt it was a coincidence that he had been chosen, or else Paul knew of his connection to those in the Passage de la Bourse.

"Did you see…that is, do you know who did this to you?" Reine spoke with distracted curiosity, her gaze on Marguerite. While they spoke, the child had wriggled from her grasp. She was climbing the bed steps once more, though she chose to sit near Christien's feet this time.

He gave a small shake of his head. "I saw nothing except the flash of the powder before the shot struck. Being so near River's Edge, I suppose my guard was down."

"You have no idea who might want to harm you."

"Not at the moment," he continued at once, before she could question the evasion. "To whom do I owe my gratitude for being brought to the house?"

"I found you, if that's what you mean. I heard the shot. By the time I reached you, the assailants were gone."

"Without finishing me off."

"I suppose they thought—thought there was no need."

She didn't look at him as she spoke but settled her gaze on the crystal water carafe on the bedside table, which had a matching glass turned over it as a cover. Recalled to his earlier request, perhaps, she moved around the bed, lifted the glass and filled it with water.

"Assailants, you said. You think there was more than one?" He watched her movements, noting without comment her reluctance to speak of his supposed death.

"It seems unlikely one man would venture to attack someone of your renown," she said with a small shrug.

"With a sword, you mean. A pistol evens the odds amazingly." He was not certain whether her implied compliment came from the truth, flattery or sly jib, but was gratified all the same. "I take it no one else saw the attack?"

"Not that I am aware." She set down the pitcher, then leaned over the bed and slid her hand beneath his pillow to lift his head. As he parted his lips, she held the glass to them.

He drank, but came close to strangling. Her scent of roses, violets and her own sweetness invaded his senses with stunning force. Feverish and supine on linen sheets he might be, but he was still aware of burgeoning heat and fullness in his groin. Her nearness set his brain rambling down paths far better left unexplored. It was just as well they had a small duenna sitting on guard, watching with bright, inquisitive eyes.

He signaled that he'd had enough water. As she straightened and replaced the glass on the bedside table, he spoke again. "I really am grateful for your timely appearance, you know, and for your care."

"You mustn't give me all the credit. It was Alonzo who directed the hands to bring you to the house on a shutter. He also undressed you and put you to bed."

"I did wonder," he said in a dry tone.

Her color increased in a fashion that made him wonder if Alonzo might not have had an assistant in removing his clothing. The idea was definitely stimulating. Before he could ask, however, she went on again.

"He will naturally be nearby while you are abed. You have only to ring for him."

"That's good to know."

Her lashes flickered, but she still didn't raise her eyes to meet his. "Dr. Laborde will be looking in on you to check your progress and change your dressing. He desired me to tell you that you should move as little as possible while you heal. You must not think of leaving your bed for at least three days, possibly more."

About that, Christien had reservations. It was his experience that wounds were less sore and mended faster if he moved around. But other matters were more important at the moment.

"As for your head, you have a mild concussion. He left a tincture of laudanum for headache as well as for the pain in your side. I will bring—"

"Thank you, no."

That got her attention, at least to the point of frowning at him.

"Truly, it will be—"

"No."

Her lips firmed and she looked away again. "As you please."

He eyed her with suspicion. He had not expected so easy a victory. It would not surprise him if she waited a short time and renewed the attack. A diversion might be useful.

"What about the wedding?"

"It's as well that plans for it have not been set."

"We will not put if off too long, I hope."

She sent him another flashing glance. "No."

He studied the wild rose color that stained the fine-grained skin over her cheekbones. It was a virulent reminder of the night in the smoking room and the stunned, deep rose-red that suffused her face after he had given her such unexpected pleasure. For an instant, the gripping ache in his groin was more distracting than the other aches he held at bay. It spurred his thoughts, giving him the glimmer of an idea.

"I've no patience with lying abed in the meantime. However…"

"Yes?"

"Enduring it would be easier if there was someone to read me the news sheets or even a novel or two. I mean, given that my head pounds like Thor's own hammer every time I move and my eyes feel as if they're crossing? A hand or two of cards might while away an hour or two, as well."

"Cards," she repeated, her voice flat.

It was a mistake to mention the last. He waited to be told it was impossible, or that he must apply to her father as the card player.

"I can play with you," Marguerite said with hope in her small face.

An ironic smile curved one corner of Reine's luscious mouth. "So she may, since she's no bother to you. My father has taught her all the more innocuous card games."

It wasn't precisely what Christien had in mind. Yet to disappoint the little one at the foot of his bed was impossible. "Thank you, Mademoiselle Marguerite. I will look forward to your fair company."

The child dimpled at him, a coquette in the making. Reine's face softened as she watched them, though it lasted only an instant. Stepping around to touch her daughter's shoulder, she said, "That must wait until morning. It's time you were in bed."

"But, *Maman!*"

"Monsieur Christien is tired now and should rest. Run along, *chère.*"

A petulant scowl pushed out the child's lower lip. "You must come, too."

"In a moment."

"Now," she insisted.

"Marguerite," Christien said, his gaze direct.

He thought for a moment that the girl would ignore him. She stared at him with mutiny in her small face, but finally heaved a dramatic sigh and climbed down from the bed. Her footsteps dragged as she left the room. The door closed behind her with a definite slam.

In the quiet that followed her departure, the rain thrumming on the roof and splashing from the eaves seemed louder, more insistent. Distant thunder made a dull counterpoint. The murmuring sound seemed to close them in together, in that house where everyone else had retired for the night.

A draft, left perhaps from the closing door, stirred

the folds of Reine's nightclothes. Christien looked away, being more aware than was comfortable of her shadowed curves within the layers of fine lawn. It would not do to be caught ogling his future bride, however much he might be tempted.

"I must ask you not to do that," Reine said abruptly.

"Pardon me?"

"Impose your authority in that way. You are not Marguerite's father."

"Not yet," he corrected.

"She is my child. Even when—after—we marry, I would prefer that you leave her care and discipline to me."

Anger stirred in his chest. It was not because she refused to allow him the right to command Marguerite, but because her stricture placed him firmly outside her tight-knit family circle. "She will become my responsibility as surely as if she were of my blood. If I must accept that, then I should have some say in her upbringing. No, wait," he said as Reine opened her mouth to refute the claim. "My purpose just now was not to override your authority. It was, rather, to reinforce it. To stand behind you will always be my object."

The anger drained slowly from her features. In its absence she looked suddenly weary. The pale and tender line of her throat moved as she swallowed. "I have managed these five years without your support."

"So you have, but why should you continue when I will be at hand?" He hesitated, then went on since he had no idea when an opportunity might come again.

"On this subject, will you consider allowing the big bloodhound to be in the nursery with Marguerite?"

Confusion rose in her eyes. "Chalmette? But why?"

"It seems he may be some protection for her."

"Protection."

Ignoring the flatness of Reine's voice, he said, "She thinks this apparition she calls the *loup-garou* haunts only her. If she can be persuaded the dog will alert the house to his presence or even keep him at bay, her mind may be easier." He waited for her answer, though half-afraid she would reject the suggestion merely because it came from him.

Reine stared at him for long seconds. Her lips firmed then, and she gave a brief nod. "It's little enough for the chance of a decent night's sleep, for all of us as well as for her. I will see to it."

"Excellent." He didn't smile, but he feared the sound of it was in his voice.

She turned toward the door as if she meant to call Chalmette inside at once. Pausing, she swung half around again, studying him from the corners of her eyes. "I really must ask again if you have any thoughts on who might want you out of the way. Yes, and would go to such ends to achieve it."

"Thoughts, possibly," he allowed, "but no conclusions."

"You are quite certain it doesn't come from some—some incident in your past? You are sure an enemy hasn't found you, some gentleman you may have bested in a duel or given other cause to wish you ill?"

He watched her while doubt rose inside him. It

almost sounded as if she knew more about him than she should. "None that I am aware of."

"I don't ask out of mere curiosity, you understand. My concern is for Marguerite and the rest of my family. If you are pursued by enemies, if you bring that danger to River's Edge, then the agreement between us must be ended."

His damnable reputation, that was the source of her doubts. To be required to defend his integrity went against the grain, but it appeared he must make the effort. "I have no string of deaths behind me that may require retaliation, despite what you might think," he said evenly. "If by chance there are those who feel obliged to take me to task for past deeds, then I believe I am capable of defending not only myself but your family, which will naturally become my own."

"I hope you're right."

"You may rely upon it," he said, his voice dropping to a deep and grating register. "No one touches those who belong to me. No one."

# 15

After days of steady stitching, Reine was almost finished with Christien's shirt. She plied her needle along the remaining few inches of the hem while holding it to the last rays of sunset through the French doors. Now and then she glanced up, stretching the kink between her shoulder blades caused by bending over her work, also resting her eyes by allowing them to linger on her patient. He was asleep with his arms relaxed at his sides and his head turned toward her on the pillow.

The sun's golden glow slanted across his features, giving them a bronze sheen like the mask of some ancient god. The coloration was fascinating, as was the thick fringe of his lashes, the strong line of his nose and pronounced cheekbone ridges of his Indian heritage.

The contrast between his skin and hers had been particularly marked that evening in the smoking room. Three days ago—almost four it must be now—how strange to realize when it was so fresh in her mind. Strange also to consider the two of them might never have met if he had not set out to win River's Edge. Propriety would have required that she ignore him even if their paths had crossed. Since circumstances had conspired to throw them together, she was free to see his attraction. Oh, yes, and feel it inside her.

Wanton, she had been so wanton during those moments of closeness between them. He had done his best to persuade her otherwise, but she knew better. For proof, she had only to consider how very affecting it was to trace the firm contours of his lips with her eyes now. Her body below the waist flooded with warm arousal at the mere thought of his mouth on hers once more. That she could feel such a thing in spite of his injuries and her misgivings concerning him was beyond disturbing.

He had proved a stoic patient, something she had seldom met with before. Her father lost his good nature when ill, damning all doctors as quacks. Her mother was inclined to moaning in self-pity while certain she required more treatment than she received. Marguerite was fractious to a point, but became limp and unresponsive in the grip of a fever. As for Theodore, he had been irritable and demanding, able to think of far more aids to his comfort than any one person could supply. He also had no tolerance whatever for pain.

No two men could be less alike.

Christien was immovable in his decisions; that much she had discovered on the first day. Unlike her father, he did not rant or bluster. Nor did he make extravagant threats as Theodore had once done. He simply said what he would do and then did it.

It was disconcerting. It was also infuriating when she wished him to do otherwise, as with the laudanum. Yet it could not be said that she didn't know where he stood.

At first, she thought he might be correct in saying he didn't need the tincture, was better off without it dulling his senses. He seemed to heal with amazing swiftness, going from supine weakness to sitting in a chair on the first day. By the next, he was walking around the bed, and she suspected him of walking longer and farther when she was not about. The cuts on his face had begun to heal almost at once. The bruising had faded away and the scabs became less every day.

His headache had not improved, however. Dr. Laborde insisted the laudanum would help. She had offered every treat she could think of in exchange for his compliance, but to no avail.

That had been her mistake; she should never have introduced the notion of rewarding him. He had taken up the suggestion so quickly she'd had no time to marshal a defense. She shook her head as the memory bloomed in her mind.

"I have no sweet tooth, at least not for pie and cake," he had said in tones of grave consideration as he lay against his piled pillows. "In fact, there's only one thing I can contemplate as a worthwhile exchange for swallowing your noxious draft."

She eyed him with lively suspicion. "And that would be?"

"A taste of something sweeter than cake to chase

away the bitter taste of it. Something close to the mead of the gods."

His gaze had been on her lips; she would have to be stupid not to guess his intent.

"Oh, no," she said, backing way from the bed.

"I think so, yes," he answered, laughter in his voice as he caught a fold of her apron, holding fast.

"Release me." She could have snatched free; she was almost certain of it. She might have caused him pain, however, and that was unacceptable. The devilish look in the velvet darkness of his eyes had nothing to do with her remaining near, nothing at all.

"I don't believe I can. Laudanum is a strong elixir, but not half so powerful as your kiss."

"Don't be ridiculous." She allowed herself to be drawn closer to the bed as he twisted her apron fabric around his fist.

"No, I swear it. You could make your fortune visiting the hospitals, though I don't know what you would do with the besotted fools who must surely follow you home."

"Nonsense."

"Not at all. I am a good example, being the most besotted fool of all."

For that outrageous claim she was allowed no answer. He drew her down until their mouths met. Wooing her with warm sweeps of his tongue, he set her on fire. As her lips opened, he took possession, engaging her tongue in a sinuous dance, drawing it into his mouth, allowing her to sample his in any way she chose.

She had been intoxicated by his humor and daring

as well as his fervor. Somehow, in the rapture of the moment, he eased her hips onto the mattress and drew her carefully into his arms. Thrusting one hand under the soft knot at the nape of her neck, he smoothed over her waist and down her thigh with the other. At her knee, he gathered her skirts in his long fingers, seeking beneath them until she lay in immodest acquiescence, drowning in hot splendor. She wanted his hand between her thighs, inside the slitlike opening of her pantaloons.

Shock at the fervor of that desire brought her upright again. It was she who pushed away at last, she who gathered her wits, poured the dose of laudanum in water and held the glass out to him.

She had not been so lost to all sense that she forgot her purpose. It was some consolation.

No matter the means, she had prevailed. He had taken the laudanum. Now his breathing was deep and even, and all trace of pain had smoothed from his features. It seemed his headache had finally been routed.

She was doubtful he could be kept abed more than another day. Only some purpose of his own had held him there so long, she felt sure. She caught him watching her now and then with what seemed to be a question in his eyes. She might have explored it, but feared she had no answer.

They had spoken only briefly of the night he was shot. He'd given not the slightest hint his mission that evening had any bearing on what happened to him. It could be from loyalty to his fellow sword masters, those others who made up the ranks of the Brotherhood. It could also be self-protection, because he didn't want anyone to know he had brought the threat of violence to the very gates of River's Edge.

As he was so reticent on the subject, Reine had neglected to mention that she had followed him, had come close to seeing him shot, possibly frightened his attackers away before they could finish their job. Or she claimed that as an excuse. It was better than being exposed as the sort of jealous, meddling female who would trail after a man and spy on him in that fashion.

Hot shame moved over her in a wave from just thinking of it. To actually confess it would be unendurable. Nevertheless, she was easier in her mind knowing his purpose in New Orleans had been the business of the Brotherhood. It meant he was not visiting another woman.

She should have guessed he would not be that kind of man. Nothing in his manner or his history suggested it; it was only her past experience that caused her to suspect him.

A quiet knock sounded on the hall door. She looked up in relief at the distraction. It would be Alonzo, for no one else had his quiet touch with such courtesies.

"A caller for Monsieur Christien, *madame*," the butler announced with his face set in lines of disapproval as he stepped into the bedchamber. "Shall I show the man up?"

The man, he had said, rather than the gentleman. It was a telling distinction. Reine glanced at Christien, sleeping so peacefully. She opened her mouth to declare him not well enough for visitors. Before she could speak, the new arrival stepped through the doorway behind Alonzo.

"Lucien Vinot, at your service," he said in quiet introduction as he moved deeper into the room. "And you will be Madame Pingre, I expect. I've heard much about you."

He was thin and tall, but ramrod straight with it, this Monsieur Vinot. His hair was steel-gray, a perfect match for his hooded eyes, and his clothing was an ensemble in stark black and white. Lines made deep grooves about his mouth so it appeared any attempt at a smile must break through untold layers of sorrow. He was pasty white, with a gray tinge to his skin not even the lingering light of sunset could relieve. It also picked out the faint quiver of his lips.

He did not look like a man Reine should know, yet it was necessary to put aside her sewing and deal with him. "Good evening, Monsieur Vinot," she said, moving forward to give her hand to the guest, keeping her voice low so as not to disturb Christien. "I am desolated to disappoint you, but my fiancé is sleeping, as you can see."

"I will not stay, but would only look on him a moment, if I may, just to assure myself that all is well with him."

The diffident words underscored the palsied tremor Reine felt in the man's hand. Her lack of welcome seemed suddenly petty and mean-spirited. "If I might offer you refreshment, perhaps you will be content to wait with me on the gallery until he wakes."

Vinot opened his mouth but was prevented from answering as Christien spoke from behind Reine.

"I'm awake now, *chère*."

She turned in surprise, in part for the term of affection but also because he had roused so easily from what she had thought to be drugged slumber. His eyes were clear and calm as they met hers, but carried a gleam in their depths that made her realize she had claimed him as her future husband.

Embarrassment assailed her. It was one thing to bow to the inevitable, but quite another to cooperate in it. She must take care or she would turn into one of those simpering, compliant females who doted on her bridegroom and invited all to congratulate her on attaching him.

That fear was wiped from her mind by another thought altogether. Suppose Christien had never been asleep? Was it possible? Could he have overcome the effects of the laudanum? She didn't care at all for the thought that he might have been observing her even as she was watching him. He saw too much as it was, this half-breed sword master.

"How providential," she said in polite response before turning back to their guest. "Well, then. Come, Monsieur Vinot, and take my chair. I will leave the two of you to talk while I see about wine and cakes."

It was an excuse. She could have directed Alonzo to bring what was required. Her purpose was to allow Christien and his friend a modicum of privacy. She had no intention of interfering with his friendships, and thought it as well that he should realize it.

She had reached the bottom of the stairs, was rounding the newel post on her way out to the kitchen, when Paul burst through the front door. He halted as he saw her, his face so pale his freckles stood out as tan blotches against the skin.

"Have you seen Papa?" he demanded.

"Not since midday dinner," she answered, as alarm brushed her. "What is it? What do you want with him?"

"Did you see that man, the one who just rode up?"

"I left him with Christien. What of it?"

"It's Vinot! I couldn't believe it, would not if I hadn't seen it with my own eyes. That he would dare come here is beyond anything."

"What are you talking about?" Reine searched her brother's face while wondering a little wildly if she should have left Christien alone with the man. Though recovering nicely, he was not at his full strength by any means. He had lost quantities of blood, so might be overpowered if this Vinot should have some connection to those who had shot him.

Paul pushed a hand through his hair, shoving the long strands away from his face. "You don't know? I thought you must by now."

"Tell me at once what you are mumbling about or I shall go into strong hysterics," she said with precision.

"Maybe I shouldn't."

The look her younger brother gave her was so like that of a gentleman bent on protecting fair womanhood from unpleasantness that it made her blood boil. "Now, Paul!"

"Oh, very well," he exclaimed, throwing up his hands. "Vinot is the father of the girl who was Theodore's little light of love. You understand what I'm saying?"

She had known there was someone though never the name. She gave a brief nod.

"He got her in the family way, then abandoned her, claimed she led him on. The thing is, she wasn't some loose Gallatin Street chit. She was an innocent, barely fifteen."

How very like Theodore, Reine thought in weary acceptance, to choose someone who knew less than he did of such liaisons. Meeting Paul's worried gaze, she asked, "Who told you?"

"Papa, for one, though it's common knowledge along the Passage de la Bourse. Vinot, you realize, is one of the oldest and most respected swordsmen to keep a salon on the street of fencing masters. He's a legend—or was until he closed his atelier two years ago. No one could touch him on the piste. He instructed every swordsman in the Vieux Carré who is worthy of the name. The number of duels he fought is beyond counting. He's truly formidable under the oaks. And this Vinot swore he would kill Theodore for what he did to his daughter."

Comprehension came in an instant. "That's what Theodore was running from when he fled town the night he was killed."

"Exactly. He was scared spitless of the old man, especially after the girl died in childbirth. He was so terrified out of his wits that he thought to hide out here. It didn't work."

Reine had assumed some difficulty had driven Theodore from New Orleans to Bonne Espèrance that fatal night, and from there to River's Edge. Gambling debts and duns from shopkeepers had been in her mind, however, no doubt because of her father's habits. Never had she considered anything so dire as this.

"You think Monsieur Vinot may have killed Theodore?"

"It makes sense, doesn't it? His wife died years ago and the daughter was his only child. She kept house for him in the apartment above his atelier. They say he was half-crazed by her death."

"But to be avenged in such a way." She winced from the thought of it.

"I agree it makes no sense. It should have been a clean, quick blooding from a sword instead of a cowardly attack. Yet Theodore refused to allow Vinot satisfaction on the dueling field."

He would, Reine thought. Admitting his faults and facing the consequences had never been Theodore's way. That he would desert a young girl in her need, refusing to acknowledge that he was the father of her child, seemed all too likely, as well.

How she wished she had known the facts two years ago. She might have grieved less for the life she had lost, that of a respected young matron of good family and impeccable repute, safe in her natural role of wife and mother.

"Vinot doesn't appear so fearsome," she said, continuing Paul's thought.

"Neither does Christien, but I would not depend on it."

"No," she said, the memory of swift-moving shadows and the vicious clash of blades in St. Anthony's Garden rising in her mind. She took a deep breath and released it again in an attempt at calm. "But if Vinot did away with Theodore, what of the attack on Christien? I had begun to think one might have led to the other."

Paul scowled at her. "In what way?"

"I'm not sure, but doesn't it seem something beyond mere happenstance must be at work?"

"Particularly as Vinot is here now, I do see what you mean. What reason did he give?"

"Only that he is a friend of Christien's. As I was leaving the room, he mentioned something about hearing he had been hurt."

"Friend." Her brother's voice was shaded with doubt.

"They are both sword masters," she said in an instinctive search for reason in an unreasonable situation.

"Something to remember." He looked away from her. "Could be I should look in on them."

"You were on your way to find Papa, were you not? I'll go back up."

"But what if—"

"Surely Monsieur Vinot doesn't intend violence against me. I've done nothing to him, after all."

The grim look did not leave Paul's face, though he turned away from her toward the front door. Over his shoulder, he said, "I'll be there as soon as I can, with or without Papa."

Yes, but what would he say when he got there?

Reine asked herself. What would he do? For that, there was no answer.

At the door of Christien's bedchamber again a short time later, she didn't bother to knock but swept inside. Behind her came Alonzo bearing a laden tray. She heard Christien's voice raised in what sounded like anger.

"I am in no danger of forgetting that she is the key—"

He broke off the instant the door opened, but the echoes lingered. Reine pretended oblivion to everything except her duty as a hostess as she directed Alonzo in placing his tray, dispensing cakes and wine and making everyone comfortable. When all was settled, she embarked on the kind of meaningless chatter that filled the quiet without straining civility.

Yet all the while, the phrase she had overheard rang in her ears with the dissonance of a cracked bell. It was all she could do to speak pleasant nothings while her thoughts clashed in her head.

What did it mean, what could it mean, that the man she was to marry was a friend to the father of the girl her dead husband had wronged? As with the attacks upon Christien and Theodore, there had to be a connection. That she was concerned seemed clear, for who else could Christien have been speaking of if not her?

Yet what an elaborate scheme it would have to be to encompass so much, from the disappearance of Theodore's body from the house to Christien's presence outside the Théâtre d'Orléans on that fateful night. From her father's gambling losses and the proposal that she marry the new owner of River's Edge to a duel in a dark garden. Revenge, though a powerful aim, hardly seemed sufficient for such a charade.

Yes, and what did it mean for her? Was the marriage proposed between her and Christien a farce? Would it be retracted at the last minute, or carried to its ultimate end as some particularly intimate form of reprisal?

She could feel the strain in her smile. It went with the weight in her chest, the leaden ache in her heart. How blighting it was to realize just how much she had begun to look forward to being married to Christien. That was at an end now, for how could she be happy with a man who might well see their alliance as an act of vengeance?

Her father arrived, panting from haste and with a pillow wrinkle in his face, as if he had been snatched away from a nap in some corner. Paul was close behind him, looking flustered yet older than his years. More stilted conversation ensued while wine and cakes were consumed.

After a time, Reine turned to Vinot. "Are you summering in the neighborhood by chance, *monsieur?*" she asked rather desperately.

"No, no," he replied with a small smile for the suggestion. "Though well aware that these open-crop lands are known to be less given to fever, I prefer it in town. If you are thinking of the ride along the river road, it's not so far for the sake of a friend."

"You must come to the wedding, then." She turned to Christien. "You did invite him?"

"It was in my mind to do so."

The glance he gave her was quizzical. She looked away, unable to bear the intimacy and remembrance in it. "That's settled, then. It will be pleasant for Christien to have someone present who is so well known to him."

"Surely the others will be coming," Vinot commented with a lifted brow. "The Conde de Lérida and his lovely condessa, O'Neill, Pasquale, Blackford, Wallace and their wives?"

"Wallace is in Kentucky just now," Christien answered. "He and Madame Sonia may or may not return to New Orleans come winter. The others are scattered here and there, but I have hopes they will be present, along with their baggage train of children and servants." He turned to Reine. "Marguerite should be entertained by the company. Speaking of which, where is she? It seems unlike her to miss the party here."

It hurt that he should think with such naturalness of her daughter's pleasure, Reine discovered. Also that he had considered those he would wish to be on hand for the wedding. He spoke so easily, it seemed impossible there should be anything sinister to the occasion.

Swallowing on an obstruction in her throat, she said, "Marguerite was in the kitchen just now, seeding raisins to be used as the eyes and coat buttons for the gingerbread men Cook is baking. Everyone will be expected to sample them in good time."

"Not I, if you will forgive me," Vinot said, getting stiffly to his feet. "It's time I said my adieus. With such cowardly attacks in the vicinity as Christien has suffered, I would not be on the road after dark."

The comment effectively ended the gathering. Though Reine's father tried as a matter of courtesy to persuade Vinot to stay to supper, the effort was half-hearted. Bowing with great cordiality, that saturnine gentleman took his leave.

Her father followed after the guest to show him out and wave him down the road. Paul made some excuse and departed in their wake. Reine was left alone with Christien.

She rose to her feet while marshaling a glib excuse having to do with preventing Marguerite from sampling too many gingerbread men. As she moved to set her glass with its dregs of *eau sucre* on the silver tray placed on the bedside table, Christien reached out and caught her wrist.

"Don't go just yet," he said, his gaze steady on her face. "Not until you tell me what is wrong."

"Nothing. Why should it be?" Her smile felt stiff, and a shiver moved over her skin, spreading from his warm clasp to every inch of her body.

"I don't know. That's why I'm asking."

She could tell him, could demand answers in anger and suspicion, but what would be the point? If he was involved in some nefarious scheme, he would only lie. If he was not, she would have revealed herself as an untrusting harridan. It was better to be certain of her ground before she said things that could not be taken back. "I'm tired, I suppose," she said in prevarication. "It's been a trying few days."

"You're sure you aren't angry over Vinot calling here?"

She met his gaze for an instant. "Should I be?"

"By no means. He has few friends, poor soul, and wants only to hold on to those that are left. But he is hardly your kind. Could be you were uncomfortable in his company."

"If I gave that impression, I'm sorry. You must have whoever you please to visit. This is your home, after all."

"Throwing my words back in my face, are you?"

Her lips tilted in the briefest of acknowledgments. "They seemed apt."

He watched her for a moment, his eyes searching while his thumb brushed back and forth over the pulse in her wrist in an absent caress. "We've become formal again of a sudden. Is it because you see in Vinot what I will one day become, a sword master who can no longer take to the piste?"

The slow caress of his thumb was driving her mad. She could far too easily imagine it elsewhere, skimming over the tips of her breasts, over her abdomen and lower, much lower. Her gaze rested on his mouth that looked parched from the fever that had only left him the day before, and her thoughts scattered in such disarray that it was an enormous effort to gather them up again.

"Why should it matter if you are unable to fence?" she asked, her voice husky in her throat. "You swore to lay down your sword when we are married."

"I did, didn't I? Is my pledge, by chance, the reason you've taken the pair of them away?"

She glanced around the room in puzzlement. "I don't know what you mean. I've done nothing with them. When did you last see them?"

His attention remained on her face for a considering instant before he lowered his lashes. "Never mind. Perhaps Paul has them. But if you're tired, why not join me here." He patted the mattress beside him. "There's plenty of room."

In her newly alerted suspicion, she questioned if his invitation might be a ruse to distract her from the subject of his swords. The pair of them in their flat box had been tied to the back of his saddle as he rode to New Orleans. They had been used in the impromptu duel there, but what had become of them afterward? Their box had not been with him when she found him.

"That's hardly a proper suggestion," she answered almost at random.

"I thought we were past that."

The low timbre of his voice awakened memories of a gaming table and her precarious perch upon it. It seemed possible he was right. More than that, the urge to simply abandon reserve and give in to his appeal was staggering. She would not have thought it possible a mere week ago. Now she longed for the illusion of safety she had found in his arms, for the comfort of lying down beside him and letting everything, all her duties, concerns, doubts and fears, drift away.

"What can be the harm," he asked in soft reason. "We will be man and wife in a few days, so free to take all our evening rests together. Besides, what is the difference between sitting here with me behind closed doors for hours on end and lying next to me for a few minutes? Everyone knows by now that I've been injured. Vinot even heard of it in New Orleans."

It was true enough. He must be seen as incapable of the physical exertion required for truly scandalous conduct. Added to that, she had no idea how long she might be at River's Edge once he healed. Anything could happen if Paul was right. One day soon Christien could simply tell her he had changed his mind and she and her family must leave his property. He could declare everything a mistake and ride back to New Orleans. A few days, maybe less, and she might never see him again.

He met her eyes once more in searching intensity. What he saw there she could not imagine, but he exerted a slow, even pressure on her wrist. She gave in to it, allowing him to draw her down beside him.

*Weak-minded fool.*

She castigated herself with that label in despairing silence as she kicked off her slippers and lifted her feet to the mattress, easing along his long length with care so as not to jar his wound.

*Depraved female.*

That description floated through her mind as she lay back, accepting half his pillow as he shifted over to offer it, then turned to rest in the curve of his arm that closed around her.

*Stupid, unprincipled wanton.*

She railed at her weakness as she rested against

him, but it was halfhearted at best. She really was tired, more so than she realized. The longer she lay at his side, the weaker she felt, the more depraved and less principled.

"Reine," he whispered, his warm breath stirring the tendrils of hair at her temple.

She drew back to look into his face, meeting the rich sable-black of his eyes, becoming lost in glimmering passion that lay there like a gold coin at the bottom of a wishing well.

"Stay with me," he said.

She heard but could find no answer. The choice wasn't hers to make while he held both her and River's Edge in his thrall like some ancient robber king. What did it matter, anyway, when this moment might be all she would ever have? To die a widow, unloved and unloving, as she had once planned, was not so great a thing, after all.

# 16

"Are you comfortable?" he asked, his voice like a caress.

She managed a nod. "I'm not hurting you?"

"Not my side, if that's what you're asking."

"You…you mean to say you're in pain elsewhere?"

"Reine, Reine," he said with laughter threading his voice. "What did I tell you about the danger of saying such things?" Taking her hand, which lay on her waist, he uncurled her fingers and spread them over the firmness at the juncture of his thighs.

Her eyes widened as she felt the heat and steel-like hardness of him. Inhaling sharply, she snatched her hand away.

He made no move to stop her, but lifted a brow as he smiled into her eyes. And abruptly she was light-headed with the onrush of purest, unbridled desire. Under its assault, she could not move. Warmth suffused her and she could feel a pulse begin to flutter in her bottom lip. Through her mind drifted his promise to show her just how Theodore had been a fool when it came to making love.

"Don't look like that," he whispered, his eyes growing darker as their centers expanded.

She could not answer. Her hand came to rest on his chest of its own accord. Beneath her fingers now she could feel the thick edge of his bandaging and, above it, the throb of his heart. Slowly, she spread her fingers, flattening her palm against that strong and steady beat.

"I did warn you," he said, the words almost inaudible before he reached to close his free arm around her, drawing her against him from breasts to ankles. His long, hard swordsman's fingers splayed across her back, a hold from which it might be impossible to break free.

She didn't want to be free, had no will to move away from the entrancing strength and firmness of him, the incredible rightness of being there with him at that moment. She reveled in the rich sensation flooding through her, tingling from every point where they touched, gathering in vibrant, near-painful pressure at the center of her being.

His lips were warm against her temple, her forehead, her eyelids. Perfect, perfect, the sense of being cherished that it brought, in spite of everything. Amazing, the heat of it that melted her very bones. It seemed she had been moving toward this place, this time, since the night they met, waiting for this moment. The glory of its arrival and his acceptance of it brought an ache to her throat and pressure behind her eyelids with the sting of salt tears. Mutely, she lifted her mouth, and sighed with a small moan as he took what she offered.

He tasted her, absorbed her, the touch of his lips a little dry from fever yet infinitely tender. He smoothed the surface of her mouth with his, collected the sweetness at the corners of her lips with the warm edge of his tongue, traced the line of their joining. She didn't mean to part her lips so soon, so eagerly; didn't know she had until it was done.

His hold tightened and a tremor ran along his arm. He rolled above her while deliciously invading her mouth. He swirled his tongue around hers, seeking her flavor, inviting imitation, inciting honeyed joy.

It rose inside Reine so fiercely that she strained against him, sliding her hand over the ridged muscles of his shoulders, curling her fingers around the taut column of his neck and pushing them into the crisp waves of his hair. She could feel the tight buds of her nipples pressing against the hard wall of his chest, her breasts molding to its muscle-sheathed planes. Rapture danced along her nerves to leave her pulsating in its wake, so exquisitely sensitive that she could identify the linen weave of the nightshirt he wore, sense the breath he held trapped in his lungs, recognize without effort the rigorous restraint he exerted over his needs, his impulses.

His taste, a mixture of wine and his own sweetness, intoxicated her. She twined her tongue with his, softly abrading it, following his withdrawal to skim the silken inner surface of his mouth. Drowning in languor and repletion, she let go of time and place. There was only wonder and the man who cradled her in magic and his sure strength.

He glided his hand from her back to the slender turn of her waist and over her hip. For an instant, he spread his hand there, drawing her tighter against him. Before she could absorb more than an instant of his heated hardness against her, he skimmed lower, gathering the fullness of her skirt in his fingers, sliding underneath to caress the bend of her knee. Even through the batiste of her pantaloons, she could feel the callused hardness and the heat of his palm as he brushed upward to her thigh.

He slackened his grasp, released her and eased away a short distance. Distress touched her. Then she saw that he was tugging at his nightshirt, gathering its fullness with one hand, trying to drag it off over his head. She aided him, freeing the yards of cloth, whipping the shirt away and letting it fall over the side of the bed.

Even as she stretched out her arm for that move, his hand was at her bodice, tugging the blouson summer shirtwaist she wore from her skirt and pushing it upward. Her arm became entangled. While she attempted to free it, he bent his head and nuzzled the soft valley between her breasts that he had exposed. A shiver moved over her skin, though whether from trepidation or anticipation she could not tell. In its wake, she was consumed by the need to strip away the layers of fabric that encased her, and with them to be rid of conventions and prohibitions, doubts and fears.

She pushed away a little and sat up to throw off the shirtwaist, unfasten the side hooks of the wide black band that held her skirt and the tapes of her petticoats.

With his eyes hooded, Christien tugged at the bow that tied her corset laces and loosened its tight pinch with a few quick jerks. He sent it flying then, along with its cover. While she kicked free of her skirts, he soothed the small red channels pressed into her skin by her whalebone corset stays, making gentle circles with his fingertips, following them with his lips.

She was enraptured by the concentration in his face as he performed that service, and by the concern. Yet all thought fled as he shifted his ministrations to the gentle mounds of her breasts, circling one peak until, in a sudden assault on the summit, he took the nipple into the heat of his mouth. It grew tighter, aching as he laved it, drew carefully upon it.

Heated pleasure surged through her. She arched her back, allowing greater access, offering unimpeded permission. Her pulse made feathery thunder in her ears. Heaviness gathered below her waist, throbbing between her thighs.

Even as he continued the delicate ravishment, he flattened his palm over her abdomen, smoothing in circles as if enthralled by the soft yet resilient surface. He eased lower in slow increments and questing intent.

He was no bungler, all inept arrogance and certainty that her pleasure was the same as his own. He knew the sites that stoked bliss, spreading it in engorging waves. Careful, unhurried yet certain, he closed his hand upon her, capturing her soft, moist folds, gently holding, pressing with the heel of his hand, separating with his long fingers.

Reine caught her breath, her stomach muscles shuddering in spasms at his slow incursion. Internal muscles fluttered, holding, opening again in invitation. She sighed as he pressed deep, stroking with such sureness that she was consumed by the most fervid of needs, the wildest of impulses.

She clasped his arm in her extremity, feeling the supple glide of the ropelike muscles as he moved. She needed, yearned for something more, something deeper. Her lips felt swollen, her brain on fire. She wanted him, wanted all of him, had to know what it was to make love to this man, to feel his strength against her, around her, within her.

He was so very strong, a latent force in the iron musculature of his body held subject by his iron will. His aura of power, in abeyance these few days spent in invalid's guise, surrounded them both, an effortless emanation that refused to regard his injury. It drew her strength from her, leaving her defenseless against him, also against her own urge toward surrender.

She didn't care. It might never come again, this perilous blending of bodies and intentions. Whatever happened, she would have this to remember. Whispering his name, she gave herself to the moment and to him, a gift he might not keep, might not value, but was his all the same.

He took instant advantage, exploring firm curves and soft hollows with a touch so thorough it could never be erased. Where his hands went, his mouth traced, as well, and the insistent lap of his tongue. Slow, painstaking, with no constraint upon will or imagination, he loved her while her breath sobbed in her throat and she writhed in his arms. And in her throes, she followed his example as best she might, learning his taste and texture while avoiding the bandage that wrapped his rib cage, listening for the catch in his breathing that marked his pleasure.

No access was denied her, no impediment given. She was free to take him as he would. And so she did until flesh and mind could stand no more. Lying beneath his perspiration-slick body, she captured his hard, silken length between her thighs, holding it poised against her softness while her very soul pulsated with rhythmic contractions and hot longing.

"Now?" he asked, the single word husky and not quite even.

"If you will, if you can. I do so need—" Her voice caught as he nudged against her and heat inundated her in rolling waves.

"No more than I. As for my will, it's as yours. For my ability, shall we see?"

She should not have doubted. Hard on his words, he gave a slow twist of his hips that opened moist, hot flesh, allowed him to surge inside in a single, swift plunge.

She caught her breath, holding it while the inner core of her expanded, throbbing in fierce welcome. Brushing lightly over his injury, clasping his hips, she pulled him deeper, wanting to be filled, needing all of him, aching to have him touch the wellspring of her existence before the meshing was too soon over.

Christien whispered wordless praise and promises against her hair, then raised himself above her. She almost cried out in protest at that small withdrawal, might have except for his steel-like slide against her inner walls. The muscles of his thighs bunched and gathered before he came down upon her again, plunging to greater depths.

It was an endless tumult then, rising and falling, blending without surcease or pause. He rocked her, gathered her, carried her with him into a physical realm where she had never before ventured, never dreamed existed. The gratification was beyond expectation or belief, an incredible upheaval of mind, body and senses. She reveled in it, met his fast and rhythmic pace, yes, and matched it while her chest heaved with gasping breaths and silent sobs.

With her eyes tightly closed, she exulted in the shuddering impact of his warm flesh upon hers that was warmer still, shivered with the inexorable mounting of sensual joy. No fastness inside her was left untouched or unclaimed. Thorough, tireless, as absorbed as a miner in avid search of gold, he moved with her, against her, letting her feel his strength, absorb his power, until she felt as if her utmost self was dissolving, molding to fit his.

Lost in infinite sensation, the spiraling apex of fulfillment caught her unawares. She cried out, tensing in every muscle while its spreading grandeur took her. He grasped her close, filling her so she pulsed against his hard heat, prolonging the pleasure to near insanity.

He began again then.

Gasping, swallowing tears, Reine soared with him, locked to him hot skin to hot skin, heart to heart. She opened her eyes and stared into his face, though it blurred above her. His gaze burned black and hot, almost primitive in its possessiveness. His teeth were clamped together so the muscles stood out in his jaws; his hair was damp with perspiration. And yet his restraint would not, did not, give way.

Exaltation sang in Reine's blood. She felt elemental, splendidly naked and glorified with it. They were, could well be, the only man and woman in the entire world to find this ultimate beatitude.

The sweet splendor took her again. The tears came, tracking into her hair, a salute to beauty and grandeur and the purpose of life, a backward look toward what had been glaringly absent in her marriage, an ecstasy beyond mortal dreams.

He plunged into her with a quick twist of his hips, and yet again with a harsh whisper of repletion. For long moments he hovered unmoving, a statue in bronze. Then he sighed and gathered her to him, sinking down beside her, burying his face in her hair. He held her while his chest heaved and their breathing, harsh and near-winded, slowed and grew even in the echoing stillness.

"Are you all right?" he asked, his mouth against the wet track where her tears had dampened her hair.

"Perfectly." The word seemed inadequate.

He shifted a little, rising up on one elbow as if to see her face. "You're certain I didn't hurt you?"

"I'm certain." She kept her eyes closed, in part to hold on to the feelings that were seeping away from her, but also for self-protection. She didn't want to see what he thought of her. "And you? Are you well?"

"Exceedingly," he answered with the ghost of a laugh in his voice.

"I only meant— I was speaking of your wound."

"It's well enough. Movement may have made it less sore—or could be I'm too sated to care. But we were speaking of you. If I was too rough—"

"No. Not at all."

"Why these, then?" He touched a thumb to her temple, collecting a tear on its hard edge.

"It's—nothing to do with you," she said over the knot in her throat. "Just all the things I never knew, might never have felt if…if you had not come to River's Edge. Yes, and how close I came to never knowing."

He was quiet for a long moment. When he spoke, his voice had a contemplative note in it. "The matter of Theodore's complaints, yes? You do see that men often blame bedchamber difficulties on their partners to cover their own lack."

"Why can't they simply learn what to do?"

"That would require admitting the fault, no easy thing for those whose pride is tender and easily damaged."

"They also have to care."

"That above all," he answered, his voice vibrating deep in his chest.

"But to go on for years…"

"It's far easier to assume the feelings of a woman matter not a whit. Or when their failure cannot be ignored, to mend their *amour-propre* at someone else's expense."

She had the feeling he was not speaking of her

alone. There was no time to question it, however. Running footsteps could be heard outside in the hall. Abruptly, the door sprang open.

Christien was already moving with swift purpose, whipping the top sheet from under them and wafting it over their nakedness. It settled in a drifting cloud of linen that half covered Reine's head. She had only the briefest glimpse of her daughter running into the room with a gingerbread man held in either hand and Chalmette gamboling behind her, tongue lolling and a grin on his furry face.

*"Maman!"*

Marguerite's cry was one of surprise as she came to a halt. She went on at once, her voice high-pitched with curiosity, loud enough to be heard all the way to the outskirts of New Orleans itself.

"What are you playing with Monsieur Christien? Why are you hiding in his bed?"

# 17

Reine's brother was at the table as Christien walked into the dining room. It was the first time he'd seen Paul since Reine had been discovered in his bed three days ago. The boy looked up and his expression turned surly. Dark color surged into his face. He rose from his chair.

"Don't leave on my account," Christien said in an even tone. "I'll go elsewhere. That's after an apology in any form you like for compromising your sister."

"I should call you out." Paul leaned his fists on the tabletop as he faced him across it.

"I beg you won't. It's enough to have everyone in the house disgusted with me without adding Reine to the list. She might well call off the wedding if I nicked her favorite brother."

"Could turn out you'd be the one nicked."

"So it might," he agreed. "Then you could explain to Reine."

The pugnacious look on the boy's face faded a degree. "You'd best not have any idea of skipping out on the wedding."

"The last thing on my mind, I assure you." God knew that was the truth, Christien thought. He would be a fool to abandon Reine, so exquisitely responsive to his least touch, so matched to his body in size, shape and impulses that he ached from just thinking of it. The trouble was, the choice could easily be taken out of his hands.

Paul looked away. After a moment, he resumed his seat. "I expected better of you," he said, the words a low mutter. "You were supposed to protect her."

It was a cut below the chest padding. Christien drew a quick breath against the sting, even as he studied the boy's tight features. He had disappointed Paul. It had been inevitable from the start; still he regretted it.

More than that, the charge leveled against him was just. He had failed Reine. His thought had been to see how far she would go in the game they played, if game it was indeed. He had failed to consider his own parched need of her. As a result, he had taken advantage of her with guile, deceit and such incredible joy that it made him weak-kneed to contemplate it. His punishment, as it seemed now, was the terror that she might discover just what he had done and all his reasons that had so little to do with simple pleasure.

He had almost confessed, there in those perfect moments before Marguerite arrived. He wished now that he had taken the chance. It would have been better than this fear that she would hear it from someone else.

Yet the worst of it was that he would take her again in an instant if given half a chance. There had been none since that evening; Marguerite's discovery of them, more or less in flagrante delicto, ended all chance of it. Reine had retreated, avoiding his bed-chamber as she might Bluebeard's chamber. Left with only the services of Alonzo, he had endured for a time. This morning, however, he had abandoned the hope she might return, and his invalid's pose with it.

"These things happen," he said finally, the words sober as he moved to the sideboard where dishes under silver covers awaited his choice. "It isn't as if your sister is some green girl seduced by visions of romance."

Paul shifted in his chair. "You're saying she co-operated."

"Nothing of the kind," Christien replied over his shoulder as he shuddered away from the smells of ham and bacon, opting only for a cup of black coffee. "In fact, I'm saying no more than absolutely necessary about what is a private matter," he continued in hard precision as he turned toward the table, cup in hand. "Any explanation to you or Reine's father will be to prevent the kind of stiff-rump posturing that may convince everyone within a hundred miles that the incident was worse than the whispers about it. In a few days we'll be man and wife, our vows blessed by the priest, the church and all who hear them. Let it be enough."

Paul looked away. His lips firmed for an instant before he spoke in gruff capitulation. "I suppose I must if Reine is satisfied."

Christien did not answer as his mind suddenly veered to hot, bright images of Reine's face at the moment of her fulfillment. A trickle of perspiration ran down the back of his neck that had nothing to do with the morning heat. It seemed a good idea to redirect the conversation before he embarrassed himself.

Reaching for the sugar bowl, adding a large lump to his cup, he spoke with a show of random interest. "About Reine's first husband. I believe someone said you identified the body."

"So I did." The boy frowned as he toyed with a piece of roll.

"Why was that? I mean to say, you were young for the responsibility at…what? Fifteen? Reine could not be expected to perform so unpleasant a task, of course, but what of Pingre's close male relatives? Surely there was someone more suitable?"

"I was there, was the main thing," Paul said without lifting his gaze from the roll he was crumbling. "Besides that, his old man was dead and he had no brothers. Madame Pingre, his mother, was prostrate over his disappearance. There might have been a cousin or two, but the body was in no shape to wait for them to arrive. I'd been fishing and sort of on the lookout for a floater, if you know what I mean."

"You found him, then?" The question was sharper than Christien intended, but he let it stand.

Paul gave a quick shake of his head. "A couple of fishermen in a pirogue did that. They brought him to the landing where I was wetting a line. King saw what was going on and came down pretty quick. He was the first to say it was Theodore."

"The overseer? Hardly the same as a blood relative."

"You'd be wrong there. Some say he was old Monsieur Pingre's, Theodore's grandfather's, by-blow, so an uncle to Theodore. The old man was something of a satyr right up to the day he died. King's papa was overseer here back when the place belonged to *Maman*'s father, you know, and not long married. His wife was pretty and a bit flighty in a backwoods style, or so they say. It's not that far from one place to another if you ride through the woods."

"So that's why he was so sure he could do as he pleased without being dismissed." Revealing the past scandal of his parentage might be the threat Kingsley had intended to use as leverage. The weakness of it, on top of the threat of Christien's reprisal, was likely why they'd heard nothing more from him. Well, that and the shooting. The overseer was Christien's best candidate for the ambuscade.

"King grew up next door to Theodore and so did I," Paul said with a twitch of one shoulder. "Didn't seem necessary anybody else should have to see…what was left of him. Anyway, the sooner he was put in the ground, the better."

"You were positive it was your brother-in-law, then?"

"I swore to it, didn't I?"

Christien had asked the question because something in the boy's manner rang an alarm bell in his mind. It clanged even louder now, particularly given the greenish pallor of his face. Picking up his coffee, he took a sip before he spoke again. "Must have been a horrible sight. Not many can stomach that kind of thing."

Paul waved a piece of roll at him. "Could we talk about something else? I'm trying to eat."

"Sorry. I suspect I'd have had trouble taking more than a quick glance."

"All right, I didn't look too close," the boy exclaimed, tossing the roll back on his plate with such force it tumbled out onto the tablecloth. "Does that make you happy? It was a man's body and it was found in an eddy just down the river. King said it was Theodore, too. That was good enough."

"It sounds to me," Christien said in a deliberately mild tone, "that you aren't so sure, after all."

"Don't be daft." Paul flung back in his chair with a scowl on his face. "Theodore was the only man missing around here and he hasn't shown up since. If it wasn't him, who else could it be?"

"You would know that better than I."

"Nobody, that's who. More than that, I don't like what you're getting at."

"And that would be?"

Paul faced him, his eyes blazing in his face, which had gone pale. "That somebody else was killed and shoved in the river to be found, that Theodore might still be alive. He's dead and gone, I'm telling you, has been dead and gone these two years and more. It was best for Reine to know it, to be sure so she could put on her widow's weeds and get done with all the folderol of mourning him. It was best that she stay here at River's Edge where she belonged and forget the idiot she married. So I said what I did, and I'm not sorry. I'll never be sorry."

Christien had his answer, for what good it did him. A humorless smile came and went across his face as he considered the cost of it. Looking up to meet his future brother-in-law's hot gaze then, he spoke with utter simplicity. "Nor will I," he said. "Nor will I."

Paul stared at him a long moment, then pushed to his feet. Dropping his napkin on the table, he stalked from the dining room.

Christien toyed with his coffee cup in brooding silence. He drank the lukewarm brew, then pushed the cup and saucer away from him. After a moment, he sighed, rose to his feet and went in search of Reine.

She was not to be found in the house. Her bed-chamber was empty, the door standing open while a pair of upstairs maids straightened the bed. The nursery was likewise empty. Madame Cassard, break-fasting in bed on café au lait and warm rolls, allowed her maid to inform him through a crack in the door that she had not seen her daughter that morning.

Monsieur Cassard, located on the lower gallery, had a neighbor with him whom he introduced as Monsieur Lavalier. His attitude was cordial in defer-ence to his guest, but his gaze was less than approv-ing. He seemed reluctant to be of assistance in locating Reine, but finally allowed that she had been seen heading in the direction of the stables.

Christien, taking his leave as soon as possible, turned his footsteps toward the plantation outbuild-ings. He was not happy with the thought of Reine anywhere near the stables. At least she was unlikely to be alone. Privacy was a rare commodity at River's

Edge, as he had discovered to his sorrow. Beyond that, the overseer was no longer around, nor was there reason to believe he might behave with anything less than respect if his path crossed Reine's. Christien couldn't be easy, nonetheless, and wouldn't be until he saw her.

She wasn't in the stable. The boy who was mucking out the stalls said he had saddled her mare a short time before, and also a pony for the small *mam'zelle*. The two of them had ridden off in the direction of the old Pingre place.

Christien, probing the bandaging at his waist with careful fingers, ordered his black stallion saddled. Mounting required clenched teeth and a leg up from the stable boy, but he made it. Gathering the reins, he sat for a moment, staring down at the young man who had stepped back out of the way.

"What is your name?" he asked, his gaze considering.

"Morris, *m'sieur*," the boy answered. "Though I'm called Mo."

"Was it you, by chance, who brought the stallion back to the stable on the night I was shot?"

He ducked his head in assent. "*Madame,* she came riding in like hell's hounds was after her. She says Alonzo and three more should come with her to carry you to the house, and I must take your horse."

"Riding?" Christien asked in puzzlement.

"*Mais oui.* A formidable rider, is our young *madame*. She fears nothing."

"No." Christien did not doubt it, yet she had not

mentioned riding out on the night he was shot. It was a detail that required attention. "I'm grateful for your care," he said, fishing a coin from his waistcoat pocket and passing it down to the boy. "Did you, perhaps, find a sword case behind the saddle?"

"Sword case? No, *m'sieur.* Nothing like that. It is lost?"

"Misplaced," he said easily. "No one has come across such a case along the river road?"

"I don't know. You want I should look?"

It was not likely a sword case lying in the ditch would go unnoticed. On the other hand, whoever found it could have it hidden away in hope of turning a coin on it. "I am fond of that set of rapiers. I might see my way to offering a reward if they should turn up."

"*C'est vrai?* I will look well, very well."

It was the best he could hope for, Christien thought. Giving the boy a salute, he rode from the dim stable into the hot morning sunlight.

The track he had been directed to follow led past the outbuildings and line of cabins that housed the hands, between the chapel and the overseer's cottage and on toward the sugar mill. From there it meandered through a grove of pecan trees, then alongside a drainage ditch that separated fields of corn and cow peas, coming out finally at a vast ocean of waving cane. Passing through the head-high stalks, it emerged in a field where cows grazed along with several head of mules and oxen and a few goats. More cane lay on either side, long walls of green. Straight ahead, however, the track became a woodland path running under great trees hung with vines and briars and with fern and spiked fans of palmetto at their feet.

There was no sign of Reine and Marguerite.

Christien was beginning to think he had come on a fool's errand when he heard a shrill cry and the deep bark of a dog. The hair rose on the back of his neck as he recognized both.

He kicked the black into a run, jumping him over a fallen log, ducking under a low limb and a dangling mass of wild grape vines. Through the trees ahead he glimpsed a clearing beneath the shade of a huge, old oak, saw the shapes of a horse and pony, caught a flash of color, heard Chalmette's deep woofs blending with Marguerite's cries. He slowed, pulled up the black.

It was the scene of an al fresco meal that lay before him, with a quilt in rainbow colors spread on the ground and a basket sitting on one corner. Reine was there in the middle of a patch of trodden grass. She had a blindfold over her eyes and her arms outstretched, turning this way and that while Marguerite danced around her, shouting and laughing, and Chalmette leaped about to join the fun. Now and then she made a swooping grab for her tormentors so the skirt of her riding habit of sturdy, rich blue cloth swirled around her, flapping down from where it was thrown over her arm. Chalmette barked and ran. Marguerite squealed and twisted her small body away, avoiding capture by a hairsbreadth.

The woods rang with such noise they had not noticed his approach. Christien slid from the saddle and tethered his mount to a low-hanging limb. Then he started toward them.

Chalmette saw him first. The big hound paused in his play and gave a low woof, wagging his tail in slow sweeps. Marguerite looked around, opened her mouth to call out to him. Quickly, Christien put a finger to his lips. The girl laughed, bright eyes dancing as she looked from him to her mother and back again.

He skirted a small briar thicket and moved into the clearing. A few long strides carried him within two feet of Reine as she bent a little at the waist, spinning back and forth with her head cocked to listen. Deliberately, he stepped into her path.

Her hands touched him, skimmed over the flat plane of his abdomen and grasped his waist. A rash of goose bumps ran across his shoulders and up the back of his neck, and he was suddenly awash in hot, urgent need. He stood perfectly still, breathing with strained control while her fingertips came to rest on the bandaging that still wrapped his waist.

Her lips moved, forming his name, forming a slow, strained smile.

Suddenly the clearing was brighter, wider, more verdantly green, a veritable paradise. And Christien wanted nothing more than to take this woman down to the quilt spread so conveniently nearby and make love to her in the small and perfect Eden as if they were the only two people in all the world.

"*Maman*, you caught Monsieur Christien!" Marguerite sang, gurgling with laughter, skipping, hopping, spinning around them like a small dervish. "Now it's his turn to be blind."

Oh, but he was blind already, or had been, Christien thought while watching with minute attention as Reine released him and reached up to remove the blindfold from her eyes. He loved this woman to desperation, had loved her from the moment he first saw her.

Oh, he had wanted her before, had schemed to have her, meant to have her regardless, but this was different. It was different and he had ruined it. She would never forgive him, might never again look at him as she did now, with clear, unguarded intimacy and somber remembrance. Yes, and a promise he did not deserve and never would.

"I didn't mean to intrude," he said in a low tone that had the sound of supplication to his ears. "I just couldn't resist."

"It's no intrusion. I brought Marguerite here, where we could be alone, to talk to her. She understands now, I think, that ladies and gentlemen share a bed when they are married."

"*Does* she?" he asked with a lifted brow.

Reine met his eyes, her own filled with rueful light. "To a point. She is happy, I believe, that you are to be her new papa."

*"Papa. Oh, Papa..."*

He drew a quick breath, shook off the flicker of memory. Taking Reine's hand, he lifted it to his lips. "So am I happy. And delighted indeed that you are to be my wife."

It was as simple and truthful a message as he could manage while Marguerite stood listening. Reine understood, he thought, for the blue of her eyes deepened, her lips parted and her grasp on his hand tightened a fraction.

It was more than he could bear.

He kissed her, a hungry meeting of mouths that tasted of remorse and desperation. Her lips were so soft and warm, like flower petals opening under his, flavored with nectar and sweet yielding. Need slashed into him. He might have taken her there, braced against the trunk of the great oak, if not for their small and far-too-attentive audience.

He drew back, his every muscle creaking with reluctance. Reine's lips were rosy, a little swollen, and she licked them with a small movement of her tongue as if to take in the taste of him. Her lashes veiled her eyes as she inhaled fast and deep, stepping away from him even as he reached for her again.

"Have you eaten?" she asked with a catch in her voice. "We were about to have our breakfast."

"Fried pies!" Marguerite cried, running back from where she had wandered away a short distance. "We have lots. And lemonade, too. Do you like fried pies and lemonade?"

"My favorites," Christien said, and turned to follow Reine the few steps it took to reach the quilt that was to be their table.

Marguerite skipped toward him and slipped her hand into his larger one, grinning up at him. Smiling down at her, feeling the clasp of her small fingers, so trusting, so accepting, Christien breathed deep against the spreading ache inside him, and cursed himself for a cretin.

The pies were made with dried apples folded into flaky pastry, an offering for the gods. The lemonade was tart, sweet and cool, the perfect antidote against the growing heat of the day. They tasted like ashes and acid in Christien's mouth, though he pretended to appetite and enjoyment. He ate only a few bites, giving half his share to Marguerite, who was still hungry when hers was gone, and feeding most of his crust to Chalmette.

Reine, watching him slip a piece to the dog that sat, slavering, at his right knee, spoke abruptly. "Should you be out of bed? I mean, Dr. Laborde did say—"

"I know." He gave her a wry smile. "But there are things it's better to meet while standing on your feet."

Color flooded her face. "If you mean my father and brother after the other night, I'm sorry. I should have been there to face them with you."

"It would have made no difference. Whatever was said, I deserved."

"Was it so very bad?"

He picked up a twig that had fallen onto the quilt where they sat, breaking it into small pieces. "Your father and mother aren't talking to me. Paul, unfortunately, is, or was. But I have no meeting under the oaks arranged for in the morning."

"I expect I should thank you for that," she said, her gaze clouded as she watched him.

"Not at all. Your brother seems to prefer a live husband for you to a dead seducer." He pitched the twig pieces into the grass beyond the quilt's edge.

"He said that?" she asked, her voice sharp.

"He was upset, and who could blame him? I should never—"

"Don't. Don't say that."

He met the rich blue of her eyes, and it was all he could do to hold that frank gaze. Guilt, hot and blighting, sat on his shoulders. He should have confessed what he was about days ago, when it might have mattered less. The longer he concealed it now, the worse it would be when she finally learned the truth. He had thought his purpose so important that it could be excused, had blithely assured himself her feelings would not matter, that he would take her any way he could get her. He had been wrong.

"No, I can't say it." His agreement was soft, certain. "But I can wish that you had not been exposed to more gossip, more…"

He trailed off, unable to complete the lie. Their exposure, if it could be called that, had been a fortuitous accident, one that could well accelerate events. He should be pleased, wanted to be pleased, because the sooner it was done, the better it would be for all of them. Instead, he felt a leaden weight of dread.

"It doesn't matter," Reine said, her gaze on her daughter, who had wiped her hands on the pinafore apron she wore and jumped up to play chase with Chalmette. "With everything that's been said, what is one small thing more? At least Marguerite is better."

She did seem to be, with a lighter look about her eyes and more healthy color in her face. "She sleeps well now after she is put to bed?"

"She does, excellently well," she answered. "Having Chalmette on the rug beside her made all the difference."

"She believes he will frighten away the *loup-garou,* then."

"She believes," Reine said with a slow shake of her head, "that he will growl loudly enough to bring you to her before anything can happen."

Christien pressed his lips together while a virulent curse feathered through his mind. He had failed Marguerite once by not being there. What if he failed her again?

"I hope she's right."

"Yes," Reine replied, her tone pensive.

Was it doubt he heard in her voice? If so, he had no right to complain, certainly no right to feel affronted. As he glanced away, his gaze slid over Reine's mare, which cropped grass near the clearing's edge with the pony grazing beside it. Into his mind seeped the comment made by the stable boy so short a time ago, that Reine had been out riding on the night he was shot.

"I didn't realize you were such a horsewoman," he said. "We must ride out together now and then."

"That would be lovely, particularly in the cool of the morning."

"Or late afternoon. We might even enjoy an outing by moonlight." He watched her face as he spoke, felt his heart trip and stagger as she swung toward him with a wide gaze that turned secretive the instant she met his eyes.

"That might be dangerous until we know who shot you," she said after a moment.

Had her alarm been only from concern? As much as he'd like to think so, he could not depend on it. Nor could he be certain she had no part in the attempt on his life. What better way to be rid of an unwanted groom? "There is that," he allowed. "Certainly, it would not be safe for a lady to ride out alone."

Her gaze moved past him, to the tree line beyond the clearing. "Yes, that would be unwise."

"I can't imagine a purpose strong enough to entice most females out after dark, anyway," he went on with grim determination. "It would have to be something of vital importance."

Her lips parted as if she meant to answer. The words went unspoken, however, as her attention fixed on the wooded growth at the edge of the clearing. Putting out a hand, she clutched his arm in a tight grip.

For a single instant, he was certain it was a ruse. Then he saw the color had receded from her face, leaving her lips blue-tinted at the edges. "What is it?" he demanded in soft concern, closing his hand upon her grasping fingers at the same time.

"There," she said, her voice hardly more than a whisper. "Someone in the trees."

He turned his head, locating Marguerite no great distance away, where she squatted in a flare of skirts to peer at something she had found on the ground. Chalmette, beside her, was watching the figure in the trees with his ruff raised and a sawing rumble deep in his throat. Christien followed the dog's fixed stare with a move as idle and without care as he could make it.

All he could discern was a dark form, hardly more than a shadow blending with the trees. It was already disappearing, melting into the thick growth of vines, briars and shrubbery.

"Demeter," Reine said on a sigh as she released him. "It must have been. She's forever slipping around, showing up when least expected." She gave him a brief look. "You may know she was Theodore's nurse-maid, also Marguerite's for a time. Her cabin is not so far from here, no more than a few hundred feet on the other side of the property line. Though River's Edge covers several hundred acres, it's pie-shaped like all the holdings along the river, narrow at the water's edge and spreading wider as it goes away from it."

"So your father told me," he said in some distraction. "Apparently your late husband's old nurse is no more anxious for my company this morning than anyone else."

"She doesn't know you."

"A situation unlikely to be remedied, it seems."

"Are you angry?" she asked, turning to search his face, alerted, perhaps, by some undertone in his voice.

"Now how could I be that?"

Demeter, if it was her, had paused to watch again from a more-distant vantage point, he thought. His trained woodsman's ears could no longer catch the stealthy sounds of retreat. What the old woman expected to see, he could not tell. Still, it seemed, in his present mood, that she should not be entirely disappointed.

"I don't know…" Reine began in doubtful tones.

He didn't allow her to finish. Reaching for her, he

swept her against him and lowered her to the quilt in a single swift move. He took her mouth in hard possession, allowing the spy to see while shielding her from Marguerite's view with his shoulders. He smoothed his hand from Reine's slender waist to her hips and pulled her tight against him. His fingers sank into folds of poplin over her hips, found firm, resilient flesh, molding it to his hand. She gasped, pressed the gentle mounds of her breasts against him, parted her lips.

He was almost lost in that instant. His lips softened, the pressure between them eased, and all he wanted was the same tender ravishment that he had found before, the same sweet surcease.

Not here. Not now.

To release her was like cutting off a limb. He did it, regardless, with a final salute on her wide brow and a wrenching movement that made him stifle a groan and hold his side. And he watched as she sat up and straightened her clothing, watched while breathing silent curses and equally silent apologies.

There was nothing to be done after that except push to his feet, help gather the remains of the outing and turn homeward. He gritted his teeth and gave Reine a leg up into her saddle. He put Marguerite onto her pony, then played at rear guard while mother and daughter walked their mounts back out to the track. When he was sure they could not witness the damage to his damnable male pride caused by his struggles, he dragged himself atop the black stallion. Catching up with Reine and Marguerite then, he rode with them back toward River's Edge.

Christien didn't look back, though not from lack of concern for what lay behind them. It was because he could not bear to be reminded of what might lie ahead.

# 18

$W_{hy}$?

Why, Reine wondered for the hundredth time, had Christien tumbled her to the quilt there with Marguerite so close by and where whoever watched could easily have glanced back to see? Why, when they had been embarrassed so recently by a similar straying from convention?

It wasn't as if desire had overcome him, she was almost sure. Something calculating and almost angry had been in his kiss, at least in the beginning.

She had returned it with fervor. Unbelievably, she had responded to him with everything in her. It wasn't that she had no control; she was quite able to deny herself most things, to avoid an entire spectrum of ordinary temptations. The problem was that being in Christien's arms was not ordinary in any sense of the word.

She had relearned a valuable lesson there in the woods. During these days of preparation before the wedding, she must not be alone with him, not ever. Even if she had not determined that for herself, it seemed her family meant to see to it. She could not move without finding her father or her mother at her elbow or Paul just behind her. If she and Christien were in the same room for more than two minutes, they were joined by Alonzo sent to bring wine or *eau de sucre,* by her mother with needlework in hand, Marguerite sent with a book to be read, Paul with some burning question about the finer points of fencing or her father with a yen to play cards. It would have been amusing if it weren't so inconvenient.

She could discover no opportunity to speak to her betrothed alone. It was frustrating when suspicion and unanswered questions clamored in her head.

He knew she had ridden out at night, she was sure of it. What else could be the point of his warning against it? If he suspected where she had been, however, surely he would have warned against venturing to New Orleans, as well. Failing that word of caution, she had to assume the worst of her secret was still safe.

It didn't follow, of course. Christien was not a man to put all his cards on the table.

It might have been better if she had made a clean breast of it. What might he be thinking otherwise? She would like to believe he suspected her of riding out to meet another man. Jealousy made a fine excuse for his reaction, after all.

Common sense prevented any such thing. Nothing that had passed between them thus far gave her reason to think he valued her beyond her usefulness as a bed mate and future mistress of his home.

He did desire her. That much was plain, though her rational French outlook prevented her from making much of it. Men were indiscriminate in their needs. She was at hand, would soon be legally available and was all too willing. Yes, she had to admit that even if the expectation that his injury prevented him from making love had lured her into a false sense of security. Small wonder that he had not waited until after the marriage.

What kind of union could come from such a beginning? What chance did it have with only passion and obligation to hold it together? Gallantry and good manners were no substitute for love and respect.

That prospect was bad enough, but what if the whole thing was about vengeance? Christien was a member of the Brotherhood, which righted old wrongs. If her future husband was prepared to risk death to accomplish that for a stranger, what would he not do for the sake of someone like Vinot, who had his gratitude and admiration?

With Christien back on his feet, a final wedding date was selected. Preparations began in earnest. It was not to be a grand affair, yet some attempt had to be made. Neighbors must be convinced that everything was as it should be, for one thing, but the people of River's Edge would be sorely disappointed if there was no celebration.

Accordingly, orders were written out and sent to various shops and warehouses in New Orleans. Steamboats began pulling into the landing before the house every day to off-load merchandise. There were kegs of spirits and wine, barrels of flour, molasses, pickles and sardines in oil; also boxes of raisins, nuts and candied fruits, and a nice selection of marzipan flowers to decorate the wedding cake. Blocks of ice buried in sawdust were shuttled to the barn and covered with canvas, then mounded over with layer upon layer of sawdust and hay.

The remainder of the wedding feast would be supplied from the plantation's bounty. As a start, two fine hogs had been selected for pit-roasting, chickens and ducks were being fattened, melons were cooling under beds and vegetables had been earmarked to be brought in from the fields.

Reine chose her gown. Made from cool, pale blue cotton voile, it featured deep flounces edged in pink ribbon. With it, she would wear a veil of finest *dentelle Valenciennes,* an heirloom that had covered the hair of her French grandmother on her wedding day, and carry a ribbon-tied nosegay of pink rosebuds from the China rose that still bloomed on the north side of the house.

England's young Queen Victoria had worn virginal white for her wedding a few years before, a style that found favor with the *Américains* above Canal Street. Reine had scant interest in the mode. She was hardly a virgin, for one thing. Added to that, ladies of the Vieux Carré seldom took notice of fashion originating anywhere other than Paris.

Marguerite, much to her satisfaction, was to be dressed very like her mother, except the flounces of her confection would be edged with narrow white lace. A seamstress had arrived from New Orleans with two assistants to cut, fit and sew both gowns, as well as one in indigo-blue muslin printed with palm leaves for the mother of the bride.

The majority of the arrangements fell to Reine. Her mother was too dithery to undertake the many decisions necessary, and her father considered he had done his part by choosing the wine for the wedding supper. Paul virtually disappeared, spending most of his daylight hours on the river. Christien seemed content to rely on her judgment, answering any question she put to him by saying she must have it exactly as she wished.

Her bridegroom's days were dedicated to plantation matters. No new overseer had been hired since Kingsley's departure, and he seemed content to act in that position with the aid of Samson, the work boss, as tall as a barn door and almost as wide, with feet the size of horse troughs and a grin like the sun rising. The two got along well from all appearances, and were often seen riding over the property together.

Christien did take Marguerite up in front of him on his black stallion from time to time, a gesture that thrilled her and benefited her mother. And he continued to play cards with her father, removing the worry that he might return to the gaming dens to escape a household upset by the wedding preparations. He also wrote out the notes inviting his friends to the ceremony and gave careful instructions to the stable hand entrusted with delivering them over the far countryside. Other than that, he listened carefully while she told him that he was to escort her mother into the chapel, as was the custom, and then follow Father Damien's lead for the remainder of the ceremony. He dutifully accompanied her on a visit to the priest, which included a homily on the responsibilities of married life. Yet there was one important detail on which he remained elusive.

In late afternoon just three days before the wedding, she sought him out where he sat on the upper gallery. "About the gentleman who will act as your best man," she said as she walked toward him. "You did write to ask someone?"

"I did."

He sat up with the contraction of lean muscles as he spoke, making as if to rise. She forestalled him with a brief gesture. "But you haven't heard from him. He hasn't told you whether he is willing."

"He is apparently undecided."

"But you must have someone," she said in vexation.

Leaning back again, he rested his head on the rolled back of his wicker chair, clasped his hands over his waistcoat buttons and propped his booted feet on the railing. "Don't fret, *chérie,*" he said with a smile. "If he can't be here, another of my friends will take his place."

Another of the sword masters, he meant. "Your attendant must walk with Marguerite as we all enter the chapel, you know."

"I'll see to it he is someone who will look after her."

That he understood her concern so easily gave her a tight feeling in her chest. A part of it was gratitude, but not all by any means.

He was so very handsome as he sat there smiling up at her, yet it would be a mistake to think him indolent or off guard. His recent activity seemed to have accelerated his convalescence. Latent power lay coiled beneath the starched linen and beige cotton suiting he wore, and the mind that directed it was never quite at rest, had not been, she was almost sure, since he arrived at River's Edge. Even now, a shading of wariness lingered in the blackness of his eyes, so she felt suddenly that he was not quite so relaxed as he appeared.

"I suppose that will have to do," she answered, and turned to go.

He reached to catch her hand in a light clasp. She stood quite still, willing her heart to continue its natural rhythm, knowing it was impossible.

"It will be all right, *chère*," he said, his voice deeper than before.

She met his gaze, tried a smile, though it was not quite steady at the edges. "Are you quite sure?"

His eyes grew darker and his smile faded to nothing while he searched her face. After a moment, he lifted her hand to his mouth, brushed her knuckles with his warm lips and let her go.

If he had meant to reassure her, the effort was a failure. The disquiet that lived inside her these days seemed to expand, filling her universe.

Back inside the central hall, she went at once to her bedchamber, stepped inside and closed the door. She leaned against it with her eyes tightly shut. Her hand still tingled from the touch of Christian's lips and she cradled it against her chest. Her knees felt weak, and it was all she could do not to slide down to the floor.

In her mind bloomed the sequence of events that had taken place in his bedchamber, his bed, his arms. Dear heaven, how they haunted her. She had relived them so many times that the least little thing could send her spiraling into the sensations he had roused in her, the exquisite feelings he had drawn from her very being. She had not known she could feel such rampant desire or such need to be close to a man. Nothing in her first marriage had prepared her for it.

These past several nights, she had lain in an agony of need for his touch, his taste. The urge to go to him had grown so strong that she shook with it. Twice, she had risen from her bed and got as far as the door, only to draw back again. She would not appear the love-starved widow, unable to conceal her cravings, nor would she court the mortification of being found out again. Most of all, she could not bear having the glorious magic that had flowed between her and Christien besmirched by exposure to censure and disdain.

The wedding day would arrive soon enough. Afterward would come the wedding night and the three days of seclusion with her new husband. Time enough, then, for passion and naked splendor without hindrance. How strange that she would yearn so for that time when she was marrying a stranger who might have a different goal altogether. She would never have believed it, never. Somehow, she would, must, wait until then.

* * *

It was the night of the fifth day after Christien rose from his sick bed that Marguerite's tormenting specter returned. Reine was not asleep. Sheer exhaustion ensured an hour or two of rest immediately after she crawled between the sheets, but then she woke to stare wide-eyed into the darkness while her thoughts moved in endless circles. Or else she was bathed in perspiration and barely able to breathe because of dreams that fled so quickly she could recall nothing of them except that they were terrifying.

She sat up this night as she heard Chalmette growl. The noise was low in his throat and constant, like a bull saw cutting through a cypress log.

Alarm jangled along her nerves. She flung back the sheet that covered her knees and slid from the bed. Swiftly yet as silently as possible, she moved to the door that connected to the nursery.

Inside, she paused, wishing she had stopped to light a candle. The room was dim because of its tightly closed shutters, the only illumination coming from the faint moon glow through their slats. Though it was designated as a nursery and had the usual rocking chair, doll bed and toys set here and there, it was merely another bedchamber with a large half-tester bed that made a darker shadow against one wall.

Chalmette ceased growling and padded toward her from somewhere near the bed's foot. He nudged her thigh with his big head. She reached down to trail her fingertips over his lifted ruff as she held her breath, listening.

Nothing.

"Marguerite, *chère?*" she called out in a strained tone.

Bedcovers rustled. A sleepy voice came out of the darkness. *"Maman?"*

Relief swept through her. She released the breath she didn't know she was holding, sought for a normal tone. "Did I wake you? I'm sorry. I thought I heard Chalmette."

"Yes, but it's all right. It was the *loup-garou.* Chalmette scared him away."

The words, spoken so easily, sent a chill down Reine's back. "Did he, *chère?* One moment, then. I…I'll be back."

A few strides took her to the hall door. It stood open a few inches, she saw with grim disturbance. Snatching it wide, she sailed through, then paused to stare up and down the dark space.

Nothing moved that she could see. The French doors that opened onto the back gallery were closed, their stacked panes showing as rectangles with feeble moonlight behind them. With quick steps, she moved toward them. The steel rod that barred them hung from its wall hook unsecured. She compressed her lips as she stepped out onto the gallery.

All she could see at first were the gently shifting shadows under the great live oaks as moonlight struck through leaves moved by night wind. She waited, trying for patience as she pressed against the wall behind her.

There. A shape, gray and ghostlike, slowly disconnected from a tree trunk. It eased away in the direction of the barn, sure-footed and familiar with the way. After a moment, it disappeared into the darkness.

Marguerite's *loup-garou*. It was not a werewolf or spirit of any kind, definitely not a figment of childish imagination.

It was a man.

The urge to shout, scream, to raise the alarm, was a sharp ache in her throat. She couldn't make a sound. Her tongue felt glued to the roof of her mouth, her heart thundered in her chest.

She was too terrified of just who the *loup-garou* might turn out to be.

Reine returned to Marguerite and sat with her until she slept again. Leaving the door open between the nursery and her bedchamber, she returned to her bed, but not to sleep. Over and over in her mind, she saw the figure of the man as he faded away from the house. She asked herself time and again what kind of fiend would visit a child's nursery in the night, careless of the terror he caused. She sought for reasons, and could find only one. She asked herself what she was going to do about it, but could not settle on an answer.

Morning came, and she was still undecided. As the sun rose, however, the problem was wiped from her mind.

The steamboat *J. T. Danson,* bound for Natchez, pulled into the landing to deliver three hogsheads of rum. It also dropped off a body that its deckhands had pulled from the river a mile or two downstream.

It was Kingsley. The overseer had a slit in his chest, one that exited his back in the manner of a wound caused by a sword thrust. Caught in the same eddy that had rendered up Theodore's body instead of carrying it downstream, he had been in the water for some time, perhaps even several days.

Reine, watching in sick dismay from the upper gallery as the body was loaded in a wagon and driven toward the cool shelter of the barn, knew one of her unsettling questions from the night before had been answered. The overseer was most definitely not Marguerite's *loup-garou.*

The sheriff arrived before noon. Reine's father received him on the lower gallery with coffee, wine and cakes. All cordiality, he did not wait for the lawman to question him, but explained with regret that Monsieur Kingsley had been released from his position at the plantation some two week before, perhaps a little more. Man to man, and with some reluctance, the reason for his discharge was given. Perhaps he had been despondent over the loss of his position, yes? Or, given the overseer's temper, he had annoyed the wrong person?

But of course, the sheriff must make the investigation. He should feel quite free to question whomever he liked. Yes, naturally his daughter's prospective groom, Monsieur Lenoir, would make himself available. The famous sword master and new owner of River's Edge had sent the man packing, true. One could see, most easily, how Kingsley might have a grudge against Lenoir for it, but what earthly reason could Lenoir have for injuring the dead man?

Ah, so he had died of a sword wound, but what of that? Half the men in the parish owned such weapons. More, the Kaintucks who plied their keelboats up and down the river favored knives easily long enough to make such a wound. It was ridiculous on the face of it, this suspicion. Monsieur Christien Lenoir's word that he had no involvement must be accepted with the same courtesy as his own. Yes, or that of his son, Paul, for that matter. As for the unfortunate man's corpse being found close by, well, River's Edge had been his home. The late Monsieur Kingsley could be put off the place, but no one had the power to remove him from the neighborhood.

There was more in that vein, but it all came to the same thing in the end. The sheriff questioned Christien and Paul, spoke to Alonzo and the other house servants and nosed around the cabins behind the big house. He did not, quite naturally, trouble the ladies of the house as they could have nothing to add to the mystery. After a fruitless few hours, he prepared to depart, though he did not appear completely satisfied with his investigation.

Reine, in her guise as hostess, moved down the steps to the garden gate to bid him farewell. Smiling with every show of ease, she invited the official and his wife to the wedding. He appeared gratified by the offer of hospitality, though uncertain his missus would feel up to the frolic. He would leave Kingsley's body with them to be buried at their discretion, he said as he stepped into his gig, being that the man belonged on the place, as you might say. Finally, he wheeled away down the drive in a cloud of dust.

Watching him go, Reine feel a shiver run down her spine. Who had killed Kingsley? Her father's suggestions were plausible. She would like to believe he was right, and the overseer had met his end at knifepoint after the quarrel. That was better than wondering if Christien had resumed his midnight rides as the Nighthawk.

Regardless of how he had died, they would bury Kingsley in the family graveyard with his mother and father. Any man's death deserved that much respect.

A burial so soon before the wedding. It was not a good omen for marital bliss.

# 19

The great day arrived in a blaze of summer sunlight. By midmorning, it was stiflingly hot. No sign of a breeze stirred the air. The leaves drooped on the trees. Cicadas sang from their hiding places in the topmost branches, but few birds called. The smells of wood smoke and cooking pork from the fire pits behind the outdoor kitchen hung heavy in the still air, mingling with the scents of baking cakes, caramelizing sugar, chicken and onions frying and coffee roasting. Subdued voices could be heard from the cabins as the field hands had been given a holiday. A sulfurous, waiting quiet enveloped the place, one that made it seem too much trouble to move, almost too much effort to breathe.

Christien's guests began arriving before midday. None had been in New Orleans, it seemed, but had been sojourning at various plantation houses here and there or along the more salubrious coastal areas. Being early on the scene would allow them time to rest from their travels, then bathe and change their clothing before the wedding. It also gave them an opportunity to visit with the groom and one another.

Reine was on hand to greet these swordsmen and their wives. What a lot of them there were; she was amazed, having gained the impression that Christien had only a handful of acquaintances. Glancing at him as he stood beside her on the steps, introducing his friends as they alighted from their various equipages, she wondered what other surprises he might have in store for her.

The first to arrive was Gavin Blackford, an Englishman judging from his accent. He was blond, quick-spoken and devilish in his humor. He was married to a most soignée lady with the unusual name of Ariadne. Their offspring toddled ahead of them up the front steps, a pair of blond imps, Arthur and David, one boy barely a year old, so still in skirts though definitely male, and another perhaps a year older. Both had the unselfconscious beauty and bounding energy of golden-fleeced lambs.

Hardly had they disappeared upstairs than a cavalcade of three carriages and a wagon appeared. In the first vehicle were Monsieur and Madame Pasquale, carrying small twin girls who were like mirror images of each other, and preceded by a boy with the features of an angel by Michelangelo who appeared near Marguerite's age. The second carriage held a half dozen boys in their early teens, no two of whom seemed to share looks, parentage or nationality, and had a young gentleman of serious mien cantering alongside as an outrider. A ladies' maid, nursemaid and tutor occupied the third equipage, while baggage for the large family filled the rear wagon. Monsieur Pasquale, or Nicholas,

was as handsome as his son in an Italianate style, and
Madame Pasquale, calm and nunlike in a soft gray
ensemble, was introduced as Juliette. Their eldest son
on horseback, or rather foster son, was Nathaniel, if
Reine had it correctly, though his foster siblings all
called him Squirrel. The twin babes were Claire and
Chloe; the younger boy was Edouard; the tutor,
Gaston; the maid, Marie-Therese; and the nursemaid
was called ZaZa.

Reine's head was spinning with names by this time,
yet there were still more to come. Monsieur Caid
O'Neill appeared in short order, a stalwart, brown-
haired gentleman who had emigrated from Eire, so it
seemed, though his vivacious wife Lisette was French
Creole to her fingertips. Their older children, a boy and
a girl, were Sean and Celeste Amalie, and the babe
Lisette cradled in her arms was Marie Rose.

The first arrivals trooped back down the stairs to
greet the rest as if it had been years since they had last
met instead of the few weeks since the end of the
season. They jostled one another on the portico,
embracing, talking, laughing and exchanging stories
as if they meant never to disperse. They were still
there when a pair of glorious carriages were sighted,
both lacquered in burgundy and black, with a liveried
coachman on the seat and a coat of arms on the door.
From these alighted the Conde and Condessa de
Lérida, Rio and Lina, a pair dazzling in their warm-
hearted sophistication. Behind them came their five
children in stair-step ages from about eight to a babe
in arms, each with an attendant.

Marguerite, who had joined Reine and Christien on the steps to welcome their guests, was beside herself with excitement over having so many playmates. Long before the advent of the conde and condessa, she was involved in a wild game of chase that seemed to have no beginning, no end and no rules, but involved at least a hundred players, possibly more. The de Lérida children, piling out of the carriages, ran screaming to join the mob while their parents looked on with what seemed relief and resignation. The conde, gathering tutors and nursemaids with no more than a glance from dark, commanding eyes, directed them here and there to keep watch.

"I fear my daughter is the cause of the melee," Reine said. "Being an only child, she isn't used to so much excitement."

"It will do them no harm, I'm sure," the condessa said with a smile.

"Especially after being cooped up in the carriage for so many miles," the conde added as if finishing his wife's thoughts were the most natural thing in the world. "And the respite may do their parents a world of good. We love them devotedly, you understand, but…"

"Yes, *but*," Reine agreed with the kind of rueful laugh only another parent could share. She had thought perhaps these illustrious guests might be too high in the instep for River's Edge. Instead, they seemed perfectly at home there.

In fact, the sword masters with their wives and children had every aspect of a large family, each of them intimately familiar with the other and concerned with their problems and joys of the moment. She had seen real families that were less comfortable together. And every one of them greeted Christien like a brother or dear uncle, kissing him on both cheeks in friendly salute or slapping him on the back, hugging his knees or clamoring to be picked up, asking after his injury and listening to his response as if they truly cared whether he lived or died.

He was a part of that great, warm circle. Reine, on the other hand, was outside it.

It didn't matter, of course; she could not expect to be accepted as one of them on so short an acquaintance. Why she should wish to be was hard to tell. She had her own family, after all.

Regardless, there was something about that close group, some shared experience or circumstance, that turned them into a powerful, almost invulnerable force. They existed beyond the ordinary rank of New Orleans society, were somehow above it.

Reine's father, on hand to welcome all to River's Edge as nominal host, was able to make himself heard above the noise after a time. With superb aplomb and Christien's gracious permission, he drew the gentlemen to a shaded gallery where they would partake of planter's punch liberally spiked with rum and cooled by some of the precious wedding ice. Reine was able to ascend the stairs with the ladies to make certain they were comfortable in their bedchambers.

River's Edge boasted six such accommodations, five

of which were already in use. For the advent of these guests, then, some rearrangements had been made. Reine had vacated her room, for she would dress for her wedding in her mother's bedchamber as was the tradition. Later, she would share Christien's bedchamber, of course, a prospect which made her tremble inside every time she thought of it. Paul had been ousted from his bed, as well, and would sleep on the back gallery for the duration. Marguerite had been moved to a trundle in her grandparents' bedchamber, though Reine was by no means certain she would remain there. The arriving couples would each have a bedchamber for their use, then, while the great upstairs hallway would become a dormitory lined with cots and pallets to accommodate the various offspring who would not be sleeping in a trundle or cot in their parents' bedchamber. Those boys who wished it could join Paul on cots under mosquito *baires* on the back gallery. Reine suspected that Nathaniel, being no great number of years older than Paul, might avail himself of the opportunity, and perhaps one or two of the others, as well. Dressing rooms and the servant quarters in the attic would naturally expand to hold the extra attendants.

Poor Chalmette would be relegated to the front portico once more. That was, if he didn't sneak back in as some child went in or out.

In truth, where people or animals would sleep was not a matter of great moment, Reine thought. The festivities would last far into the night, possibly even until dawn. People could, and no doubt would, snatch a few winks wherever exhaustion overcame them and a quiet corner could be found.

The wives of the sword masters talked and laughed among themselves with the greatest of ease. They teased one another, questioned without restraint, spoke of problems with husbands and children with unusual freedom and little self-consciousness. They were interested in everything, particularly how Reine and Christien had met and how he had proposed, how the two of them would go on after the wedding and what she meant to wear for the ceremony. Somehow, without Reine quite knowing how it happened, they all crowded into the bedchamber where she would dress to have a look at her wedding gown.

The ensemble was pronounced lovely, just the thing, particularly the heirloom lace veil. Much was made of Christien as a bridegroom, with great attention to his physical attributes and smiles over his manners and birthright as a descendent of the Great Sun; he could not have been more honored for that connection if his heritage had stemmed from some glittering title of the ancien régime. There were a number of roguish and sidelong glances as they spoke of his great height and impressive physique. Reine was forced to smile and laugh but could not be quite as easy with such frankness.

"You must insist that he give up the Brotherhood," Caid O'Neill's Lisette said. "He will cling to it as an oath of honor, but you will have no peace otherwise. To watch and worry while he goes out at night to fight duels in the dark—no, no, it's not to be borne."

"Have I the right to ask that of him?" Reine inquired with a small frown between her brows. "It's his life, after all."

"But not his alone any longer. The life the two of you will make together is more important. A husband's allegiance must change when he takes a wife. His responsibility to her and to their children should take precedence over the Brotherhood and its purposes. Christien would be the first to agree that nothing matters quite so much."

Would he indeed? Reine was not so sure. "Is it usual for these sword masters to give up the Brotherhood when they marry?"

"But of course. Others will carry it forward, you may be sure, those who have no families or responsibilities. They must become the vanguard."

"I wish I knew exactly where Christien goes and what he does," she said, almost to herself.

"We have all felt that urge, I think," Lisette said.

"Indeed," soft-spoken Juliette agreed. "And I expect he will tell you in time if you truly care, truly want to know."

"You seem so sure, while I'm not sure at all."

"Oh, *chère*. When Nicholas and I first met and agreed to marry, we were strangers as surely as you and Christien," Juliette said with a smile. "I thought the Holy Mother had sent him in answer to my prayer to save my family, and who is to say she did not? But there were secrets between us. He thought me the most innocent of novices since I had been promised to the church. I was certain he was Casanova personified for that was his reputation. Once, at Tivoli Garden, I almost gave myself to him while in disguise, thinking he did not know who I was. But he knew all along, as he confessed afterward, a misunderstanding that gave me many unhappy hours. I thought he was attracted to some loose woman, you see, when he was never in doubt about who he held in his arms. The point I would make is that you must trust each other and speak what is in your heart. Don't let secrets come between you."

It seemed good advice. The trouble was finding the courage to implement it.

Yes, and the time, as well.

The day that had seemed so long suddenly picked up speed, rushing toward evening. Before Reine knew it, her mother appeared at her side, saying it was time for her to bathe and dress.

The wedding was finally at hand.

# 20

A zinc tub shaped like a lidless coffin, one brought by steamboat downriver from Pennsylvania, was a prized possession of Reine's mother. It had already been filled with tepid water when Reine entered the bedchamber used by her parents. That coolness was an excellent thing in the furnace heat of the waning afternoon. The bedchamber was stuffy and over warm, though not so hot as the rooms on the opposite side of the central hall, including that used by Christien, which lay on the southwest corner of the house.

That room would become their bridal chamber, where the two of them would spend the next three days in seclusion. It would surely be too hot for night-clothes. Well, or for much in the way of clothing during the day. A few more hours, and she and Christien would be expected to go inside and shut the door, closing out everyone and everything. They would lie together in the wide bed and what happened behind the filmy gauze of the mosquito *baire* would be no one's business except their own.

A flush suffused her, one that had nothing to do with

the heat of the afternoon, nor of undressing before her mother and her maid and stepping into the cooling water in the tub. At least she was left alone while she bathed.

She had washed her hair in soft rainwater the day before and brushed it dry while sitting on the gallery in the morning sun. Now she soaped herself with fine-milled soap scented with lavender and roses, squeezing water over her arms and shoulders and down her back as she rinsed it away. Lying back in the tub, enjoying the coolness, she closed her eyes. It was the most peaceful moment she had known in days, possibly since that first morning when she saw Christien riding toward the house.

By degrees, she grew aware of the rumble of male voices. Christien and his friends must have gathered on the side gallery just outside the bedchamber, she realized. It wasn't too surprising since that portion of the upper gallery was shaded. She was happy that he had such company, for the past few days had not been easy for him. Her mother had steadfastly refused to remain in the same room with him, her father had been less than his cordial self, and Paul had gone so far as to avoid his company. Her bridegroom appeared to disregard these slights, but she was sure he felt them. It was good that he could relax with those who accepted him without reserve.

Idly squeezing water over her drawn-up knee, she wondered if the gentlemen, particularly Christien, had any idea that she was just on the other side of the French doors, also what she was doing, what she was wearing. Or rather, not wearing.

Their voices turned serious after a few minutes. She caught a few words here and there that made her think they were discussing the war in Mexico. She hardly listened, being unable to grasp why it was necessary to invade that country. Her only concern was that the fighting might continue until Paul was old enough to go. Already, a number of his friends had slipped away to sign up at the big rallies in New Orleans. Some few had come back from the Rio Grande campaign bearing their war wounds like badges of manhood. Some would never return.

A lull came in the rumble of conversation. Into it, then, the Irish gentleman, Caid O'Neill, spoke in lazy, almost random comment. "I thought Vinot would be here. He is still to stand with you as best man?"

"I expect him at any time," Christien answered without elaboration.

"I look forward to seeing him. It's been quite a while since I've had the pleasure as he gets out so seldom."

"This is a special occasion."

Vinot was to be best man? A rash of goose bumps ran down Reine's arms as she absorbed the news, heard the portent in Christien's voice. She had nothing against the older sword master, but she could not be easy in her mind. Why him, when there were others who would excite far less speculation?

It was the custom for the bride's nearest female relative to have the best man's escort. Usually that was a sister or cousin, but Reine had promised that place to Marguerite. If Vinot was to act as Christien's attendant, then he would walk into the chapel with her daughter. What a mismatch it would be.

Slow anger gathered inside Reine as she considered further implications. Christien had deliberately kept this from her. He had known she would not care for his choice of best man, must have guessed her parents would object to having as a member of the wedding party the father of the young woman Theodore had wronged. It was like a slap in the face, an additional mark against any chance for happiness together.

Her thoughts scattered as she realized the men were speaking again.

"If he doesn't appear, you know you may count on any one of us," the conde said in his intriguing Spanish accent.

"For which you have my gratitude, though I don't doubt he will be here." Christien's voice turned grim. "Too much has gone into arranging this experiment and it means too much for him to fail."

Experiment? What experiment was this? Could Christien be speaking of their wedding? The very idea chilled Reine to the bone in spite of the evening heat.

"You're sure you want to go through with it?"

That was Nicholas Pasquale speaking, she thought; she caught the hint of Italian in his voice. It appeared the other sword masters knew exactly what Christien intended. Was that proof his presence at River's Edge was an affair of the Brotherhood as she had once imagined? Was she truly about to be married in an act of vengeance?

"I've never wanted anything more," Christien said, his voice flat.

Reine surged to her feet in a sluicing cascade of water. Reaching for the towel laid ready, she whipped it around her. As the lap of water subsided in the tub, she realized the voices on the gallery had stopped abruptly. Absolute quiet reigned now from that quarter.

They knew someone had heard, or at least suspected it. What they could not know was who was in the bedchamber, who had been in the tub. She stood unmoving, waiting to see what they would do.

"Reine, *ma chère,*" her mother called out as she swept into the bedchamber without bothering to knock, "have you fallen asleep in the bath? I thought you would ring ages ago. If you are not to go naked to your groom, we must get you dressed at once."

Outside on the gallery, there came a scraping of chairs. Booted footsteps retreated with varying degrees of haste. "Christien, Christien," Gavin Blackford said, his voice lilting with risible humor as it faded toward the back of the house, "where is old Diogenes with his lamp when it's required? Sacrifice is one thing, but no man claiming such a notion should be enthralled to the point of anguish by a bridal bath. What, oh, what, have you neglected to tell to us?"

What indeed, Reine thought with her lips set in a tight line. What indeed?

An hour later, Reine stood in front of the cheval mirror in her mother and father's bedchamber. The skirt of her gown, with its graduated flounces, had been lifted and arranged around her until it stood out like a soft blue-and-pink cloud. Her veil of fine Valenciennes draped her shoulders in perfect folds while framing her face with its dainty scallops. Her bouquet of small pink rosebuds tucked into a silver holder and backed with a fine lace handkerchief, both items presented by her groom in his *corbeille de noce* along with the gold hairpins in her hair and the lovely cameo necklace she wore, had been placed in her hands. She was ready, or as ready as she was likely to be this evening.

"You are so pale, *chère,*" her mother said in a fretful tone.

"All brides are pale," dark-haired Ariadne Blackford, pale of complexion herself, said bracingly. "It's the anticipation—though we will not say of what!"

"There, that has brought the roses," Juliette Pasquale declared warmly as she peered over Reine's shoulder. "Lina, have you any Spanish papers? She could use a little more color in her lips."

"Are you suggesting I use such aids to nature?" Lina, the Condessa de Lérida, inquired with a sparkling look.

"I know you do," Lisette O'Neill chimed in with great frankness. "We all do, *naturellement.* I believe I have a packet in my bag." Tugging at the strings that held the top of the reticule on her arm, she drew out a small red sheet and presented it with a flourish.

Reine murmured her thanks and took the paper, moistening her lips before putting it between them. The results were an improvement, she thought, but then anything would have been. Her lips had been so bloodless they were almost blue. It was not the wedding night that concerned her, however. It was the reasons behind this empty excuse for a marriage.

She should call a halt here and now. No reason existed for her to go through with it. She need only speak the words and keep on saying them until everyone heeded her. She should shut herself up in her room until all the guests and relatives went away and left her alone. If Christien tried to persuade her, she need only refuse to speak to him. If he put them all out into the road, so what? It had happened to others before them. They would survive.

Oh, but could her mother survive the clattering tongues and pitying glances? Could she ever respect a daughter so lost to propriety that she fell into bed with a stranger before the wedding, and then refused to speak her marriage vows afterward?

What of the public pillory of whispers and sneers, the avid relishing of yet another scandal? Reine might have faced it for herself, but how could she inflict it on her parents or Marguerite?

Her father was past starting over, she knew, no matter how valiantly he might face the change. As for her mother, Reine could not support seeing her decline into greater frailty, was unable to bear it on her conscience. She must marry Christien.

With that final decision made, Reine lifted her chin, summoned a smile and pronounced herself ready. Moving from the bedchamber with her mother, Marguerite and the escort of swordsmen's wives who had crowded around for the finishing touches of her toilette, she walked to the head of the stairs.

The others left her there while they trooped down to form the obligatory procession to the chapel. The last to go was Marguerite, who caught her hand and pulled her down a little to whisper in her ear.

"You look beautiful, *Maman*," she said. "Monsieur Christien will think so, too."

"Thank you, *ma petite*." Reine spoke against the lump in her throat as she hugged her daughter. Then she watched her go carefully down the stairs in her ankle-length gown and long, bright hair, watched until Marguerite blurred into what appeared to be the form of a small angel.

It was her turn to descend. She lifted her bouquet to her face, breathing the scent of roses, praying silently for composure, for courage, for faith. Holding them at her waist then, she squared her shoulders. She put out her right foot and began the long descent.

Christien moved from the salon, coming to a halt at the bottom of the stairs. Dressed in a gray frock coat of impeccable cut, worn with a black waistcoat embroidered in silver, darker gray trousers and black boots with a glassy polish, he took her breath away. His linen shirt, fresh from her needle, was snowy white and fit to perfection, and his cravat was of white silk shot with silver thread.

He had promised not to embarrass her with his choice of wedding raiment. He had kept that pledge.

One or more of his trips into New Orleans in these past days must have been for fittings with his tailor as well as to choose his *corbeille de noce* gifts for her. If she had not known he had other motives, other loyalties than to her, she would have been touched by the effort. She did know, so refused to be impressed by his sartorial perfection or be made stupidly maudlin, refused to acknowledge the sting of tears behind her eyes.

Yet she could not but notice the exotic and sensual attraction he acquired from the contrast between the darkness of his skin and the pristine paleness of his linen. It made him look so foreign it was impossible to believe she had lain in his arms, had taken him inside her, had shuddered to the purest pleasure of his touch. Yes, and surely would again. Soon, so soon.

He held out his hand as she reached him. She put her fingers in his. For a single instant, she met his dark and somber eyes with their half-hidden glimmers of gold. She was transfixed, unable to look away, to move, to think what they must do next. His gaze searched hers, looking for…what? Some sign of whether she realized his perfidy and meant to renege? Let him wonder. It was little enough by way of retaliation.

He smiled and kissed her fingers, all loving urbanity, before placing them on his arm. Turning, he moved with her out the front door and down the steps. There he ceremoniously passed her hand to her father.

All occurred exactly as if should, yet it seemed a foretaste of his desertion.

The way to the chapel was lit by lanterns hanging from the great limbs of the live oaks, by pine-pitch torches that flared with orange-and-blue light, and by distant flashes of heat lightning. Reine and her father led the way, the hem of her skirt and petticoats whispering over the dusty grass. Following them was Chris-

tien with her mother on his arm, and behind them
came the tall, thin figure of Vinot, arrived at last, who
smiled down at Marguerite as if charmed beyond
measure. A handful of cousins followed—those who
lived nearby and could not be slighted. After them
walked the whole panoply of sword masters and their
wives and children, and also the nursemaids and tutors
assigned to watch over them. Bringing up the rear was
Alonzo and those house servants who could be spared
from last-minute preparation for the wedding supper.
So trooping through the late-evening shadows they
went, under the murmuring oaks, through pools of
lantern light illuminating the pathway, past the torches
whose acrid black smoke hung on the still evening air.

"You are all right, *ma chère?*" her father asked as
the white walls of the plantation chapel came into
view.

"Perfectly, Papa," she answered, keeping her voice
as even as possible. If she said no, said she didn't want
this marriage, she was sure he would support her. She
could not force him to make that choice.

"I wish you every happiness, you know. Though I
expect it will come easily if you will only put your
trust in Christien."

Trust. How peculiar that he should mention it.
"Have you reason to think that might be difficult?"

"No, no. I am quite confident in my mind about this
business after these days of getting to know him. I
believe he has your best interests at heart."

"I'm sure he does." She smiled automatically at the
dark brown faces of the field hands gathered outside

the chapel to see the wedding procession, lifting a hand in recognition of their murmured good wishes.

*"Chère…"* Her father tipped his head as if trying to look around her veil into her face, perhaps disturbed by the odd note in her voice.

"Yes, Papa?" She turned a clear gaze upon him.

"Nothing." Glancing away, he heaved a sigh. "Nothing at all."

The massed bouquets of fern and China roses that decorated the chapel were already drooping in the heat. The candles in the floor candelabra set here and there oozed wax, adding to the suffocating airlessness without doing a great deal to brighten the surrounding gloom. Their fitful light gleamed here and there on the painted faces of saints in their niches, the gold-leafed crown of the Holy Mother, the peaceful agony of Christ on his crucifix. It picked out the shimmering vestments of Father Damien where he awaited them behind the low railing that enclosed the altar.

Reine gave her bouquet to Marguerite to hold. Her father kissed her cheek and gave her gloved hand into Christien's keeping once more. Her fingers shook a little as her groom's closed firmly around them. The two of them performed a small genuflection, then he opened the small gate in the railing. They passed through to approach the altar, leaving the others behind as they must leave them behind when they were married.

Rustling, whispering, the gathered guests found seats, including the hands from the quarter who filed in to take the rear benches. The priest gestured, and more rustling ensued as all knelt. The benediction for the bride and groom began.

Though Reine closed her eyes, she was excruciatingly aware of the man so close beside her—his height, his strength, the brush of his sleeve against her bare forearm below her veil. The blood throbbed in her veins, rushing so strongly that she felt a little lightheaded. It was difficult to breathe against the press of her corsets. She could feel perspiration gathering at the nape of her neck, creeping slowly from her hairline under the covering of Valenciennes.

Thunder rumbled, so low and far away it was a mere jarring of the thick air. Reine's grasp tightened involuntarily upon Christien's. He turned his head to glance at her, for she heard the quiet shift of his clothing. Greatly daring, she opened her eyes and looked up at him.

His eyes held concern and the faint gold reflections of candle flames. As he searched her face, his firmly molded lips curved in a smile of such warm beguilement that she felt her heart alter its beat. Her own lips answered it without her volition. The moment stretched while the fluttery panic inside her slowly faded away.

The die was cast; there could be no turning back now. Whatever happened in the hours, days and years ahead, she would have this brief moment of perfect rapport to remember.

A gust of wind swept through the chapel, a draft that entered through the double doors standing open to the sultry night. It brushed over the gathering and out through the doors inset on either side behind the altar. Thunder rumbled again. Father Damien ended his blessing. He looked up with a signal for those congregated to regain their seats. Obediently, they followed his lead.

The priest stood as if turned to stone. His wide gaze was fixed on the wide, dark rectangle of the open entrance doors. His lips moved in what appeared to be a silent and near blasphemous exclamation.

Reine turned her head to follow his line of sight. At her side, Christien did the same. A quiet whispering filled the chapel as the congregation swung around in their seats to see what held their attention.

A man was poised there with his feet set wide and his hat in his hands. He shifted, took a step, then another, pacing forward with deliberation. His sardonic gaze moved over the priest, the altar, the candles and flowers, the gathered friends and family. Then he met Reine's eyes and his full lips moved in a grim smile that twisted the scarred ruin of his face into a sneer.

"Stop the wedding," Theodore called out in angry demand. "The bride requires no husband. She has one already."

# 21

*Theodore Pingre. At last.*

Cries and exclamation rang through the chapel. Madame Cassard screamed and sagged into her husband's arms. Paul whispered an oath, his eyes wide with shock as he clutched the back of the seat in front of him. Reine stood in stunned immobility, as deathly pale as a statue in chalk-white Parian marble.

Christien had scant attention for the chaos. Every particle of his being was centered on the threat posed by Pingre.

He would have known him anywhere, he thought, in spite of the sunken scars that separated his face into mere lumps of flesh half curtained by a straggling growth of beard. The shape of his head, the way his hair grew, the set of his shoulders were features carefully memorized from his portrait. Then there was his supreme arrogance, as if no single person in the chapel had value except as they might serve him.

Vinot had been so certain that Pingre was alive. Christien had been less convinced in the beginning. Lately, however, he had grown as positive as his old mentor. It had been only a matter of smoking him out of his hiding place. He wasn't proud of the method used, but the results could not be faulted.

Beside him, Reine inhaled with a harsh gasp, as if her breath had been trapped in her chest until that moment. Her gaze was not on Pingre, however, but on Vinot and her small daughter, who stood next to him. Dread and despair limned her face, darkening the blue of her eyes.

Marguerite stood between the old sword master and the man Vinot hated with a passion so virulent he was almost unhinged by it. The child stared at her father, her eyes wide and her small face a perfect match for the white lace that edged her dress ruffles. Her small, pale lips opened but no sound came from them, not even a cry.

*Papa. Oh papa...*

A single thought seized Christien's mind, and with it came the blackest of revulsion. Reine knew what he and Vinot had done. She might not guess the whole underhanded scheme, but she understood why he had arrived at River's Edge, why he had proposed marriage, why he had almost made love to her in a wooded clearing. She understood and was sickened by it, not for herself alone but because he had involved Marguerite.

He had used a child to further the cause of revenge. What kind of monster had he become that he inflicted pain on others in order to remove that of a friend? He prattled of honor, but where was it in this?

Reine turned her head, lifting her eyes to his face with such desolation pooled in their depths that he felt it as a blow to the heart. He whispered her name, taking a step toward her. And was cut to the quick when she backed away.

There was no time to explain even if he could find the words. Vinot was easing Marguerite behind him as he stepped out into the aisle. Head high, shoulders back and an expression of terrible retribution on his thin face, he squared off in front of Pingre.

"So you are alive, after all," he said, his voice like a lash.

Pingre halted as if he'd hit a stone wall. His face turned a sickly yellow hue in which the scars stood out like purple ribbons. "You!"

"You thought never to see me again? But of course, you expected to hide like a coward from a father's wrath. You are a miserable excuse for a man, Pingre, taking your pleasure with a young girl too innocent to know your kind, leaving her to bear your bastard alone, yes, and die for it. You will pay for what you did, one painful sword slash at a time. Name your seconds!"

"You malign me, old man. Your daughter was free enough with her favors, as pretty a young wh—"

"Stop there! Shut your filthy mouth or I'll kill you where you stand."

"Gentlemen!" the priest cried out in protest. "This is a house of God."

Christien, moving with precision, left the altar and passed from the enclosure to stand beside Vinot. He expected Reine to remain behind, but heard the soft whisper of her skirts as she followed him up the narrow aisle.

Pingre snapped his teeth together on the words he'd

been about to say. His eyes glittered and his lips protruded as he stared around him. His gaze passed beyond Christien and Reine, tracking over those assembled as if searching for a friendly face.

There was none.

"I see how it is," he said, throwing back his head. "This was a trap from start to finish. Clever, Vinot, using a younger sword master as decoy, one who could worm his way into River's Edge and set my wife up as bait. Did you agree to it, *madame?* Is it your pleasure to see me die so you may be a widow in truth?"

"I was told you were dead," she said, the words falling from her lips in a leaden whisper. "I wore mourning for the full two years, and you let me do it."

"What of it?"

"Your body...Paul saw it."

"It was my old uncle who died, rather. He had passed on a few days before so served well as my corpse after a week in the water and with my alliance ring on his finger. My mother's suggestion, that, before she shook the dust of Bonne Espèrance from her skirts."

A murmur ran over the wedding guests. More than one lady pressed a gloved hand or handkerchief to her lips in token of sick revulsion.

Bitterness corroded Pingre's tone as he stared around him. "I was to join her in Paris. But that was before she heard how hideous I had become. She rescinded her invitation, would not send the fare. I was to remain here with nothing—no money, no amusement—in a hovel with a nursemaid too withered to tend anyone. I could rot for all she cared. But I mean to have money, yes, and to rejoin my dear mother."

He had been in hiding from what he had become as well as from Vinot, Christien thought, hiding with nowhere to go. He could pity the poor devil if not for the knowledge that his soul had grown as twisted as his face.

"Enough," Vinot said with a slicing gesture of one hand. "Do you accept my challenge?"

"Willingly," came the answer. "If I can't best an old man like you then I deserve what comes to me."

"But you will not be meeting me," Vinot said with austere satisfaction in his voice. "As you pointed out, my day as a swordsman is done. I hereby claim the right to appoint a champion. For the post, I choose the best pupil ever to grace my salon, my Sophie's old playmate, Christien Lenoir."

Christien expected it, of course, had known it would come from the moment Pingre walked through the chapel doors. Not so, the rest of the guests. A babble of voices erupted again, questioning, explaining the dueling code that allowed the substitution.

Beside him, Christien felt the movement when Reine turned toward him. He glanced at her, caught the stark question in her eyes. He saw, and realized suddenly that he held the power to free her from Pingre, to rearrange their lives to suit himself. All he had to do was forget the meticulous punishment Vinot had decreed for his daughter's seducer and simply kill the man.

Pingre gave a snort that might have been meant for

a laugh. "Why not?" he inquired in tones of scorn. "An old man or a cripple, it's all the same to me. Besides, I owe Lenoir something for daring to touch my wife."

Christien gave Pingre his attention once more. "And how do you know I'm a cripple?"

Pingre laughed, a crude sound. "I know more than you imagine. I hope you enjoyed my wife's devoted nursing, for it will be the last you'll have of it."

"You plan on resuming your place at her side."

"With you out of the way and Vinot turned feeble, there's no reason why I shouldn't." Pingre turned his misshapen grimace on Reine. "Unless you can think of one, my dear wife?"

Christien longed to hear Reine denounce her husband, to swear she would never return to his home and his bed. She did neither. Turning from them both, she crossed to where Marguerite stood half hiding behind the skirt of Vinot's frock coat. She took her daughter's hand, drawing her to her side. Looking neither right nor left, she turned her back and walked from the church into the thunder-edged night.

Christien watched her go and waited to see if she would give some small sign, some fleeting glance or change of expression that might indicate whether his life or death meant anything to her. There was nothing. Though Marguerite craned her neck to look back over her shoulder with her small face a mask of fear and woe, her mother stared straight ahead. And why not, when he had done nothing since the day he arrived at River's Edge except make use of her, one way or another?

The pair moved beyond the light until only the pale

shapes of their light-colored clothing could be seen in the darkness. Christien watched until the last pale shimmer was gone.

Savage in his disappointment then, he turned his concentration to the duel that was to come and the man who would be Reine's husband again once it was over. That was, of course, if he did not kill him first.

Pingre had moved, taking a step as if to follow after his wife and daughter. The look in his eyes was grim, his jaw set.

"I wouldn't," Christien said in soft warning. "You aren't wanted, for one thing. Then, we have unfinished business here."

The look Pingre turned on him was so bleak he felt an errant flicker of sympathy. It went out immediately as he spoke.

"They would not have walked away from me before you came."

"You should have staged a resurrection sooner. Why didn't you?"

"I'm here now," Pingre said by way of an answer. He looked Christien up and down, allowed his gaze to rest on his side where the pistol ball had been removed. "My seconds will call on yours."

"As you prefer." Christien lowered his voice. "Your friend Kingsley won't be among them, however. What a pity."

"He's no great loss, being less than a gentleman."

Few would be a loss to Theodore Pingre, Christien thought. "You used that excuse for refusing to meet Vinot two years ago, as I recall," he said. "I'm no more of a gentleman by your lights, but you've agreed to meet me."

Pingre's lips lifted in his one-sided smile. "Even a gentleman must stoop now and then to kill a snake."

Christien might have resented the insult more if he had not felt it held some truth. The salient point in it was that Pingre intended a fight to the death rather than a mere bloodletting. Inclining his head, Christien said, "He can try."

Hatred flared in the other man's eyes, along with an edge of cunning. "Till the meeting, then," he said, and turned away, moving from the chapel into the rain that had begun to fall, swaggering into the gray evening as if everything he'd planned had been accomplished.

Perhaps it had, Christien was forced to admit. Pingre had certainly halted the wedding. He had also ended any pretension Christien might have had toward taking his place. Neither was unexpected; still, virulent anger for it burned in his mind.

Pingre's seconds would arrive at River's Edge in the morning, most likely. The time and place for the meeting would be hammered out between them and his own men. Doctors would be agreed upon and messages sent to request their presence. Time must be allowed for both participants to settle their affairs and make their wills. Make it two days, then, before he would face Pingre.

An awkward silence had settled over the chapel. People looked at one another, at a loss as to how to proceed in these unusual circumstances. As it length-

ened, Monsieur Cassard eased his comatose wife into
Paul's arms, where the boy stood beside them. With
slow steps, he gained the chapel aisle and faced the
wedding guests. He opened his arms as if to embrace
them all.

"My friends and family," he said in a tone of solemn
reason, "this affair has not ended as expected. It is a
great disturbance to us all. Nevertheless, you were
promised a feast and I would not have you disappointed. Let us put aside these troubles and return to
the house. One must eat, yes? One must drink and
dance to good music, no matter what has happened or
how heavy the heart. If we can't rejoice in a wedding,
we can at least celebrate being together."

It was that simple. The guests dashed back to the
house through the pouring rain. A modicum of nor-
mality was restored by everyone's need to dry off and
rearrange their toilettes. Good food and drink did the
rest. The party was soon under way.

Christien and the other sword masters retreated to
the quiet of the upper gallery. There outside his bedchamber, with the rain falling in steady streams from
the roof behind them and the noise covering their
voices, they put their heads together.

Caid and Gavin drew the long straws for the right
to act as his seconds. A message was sent to Dr.
Laborde requesting his presence at River's Edge once
more. Meeting places were discussed, keeping in mind
the need to avoid disturbing the ladies or attracting
official attention. The wooded clearing at the edge of
the property was chosen, the one where Christien and

Reine had caught sight of what must have been Pingre skulking in the shrubbery.

When there was no more to be decided, the others dispersed to reassure their wives about the coming event and find something to eat. Christien remained where he was, having missed being a husband by a hairsbreadth and hunger being the least of his needs. Moving to the gallery railing, he leaned one shoulder against a post and stood staring out at the rainy night.

Frustration and anger were live coals inside him. The need to find Reine and make her listen while he explained, to make her see the need for what he and Vinot had planned, warred with his loyalty to his mentor and to the Brotherhood.

If only the wedding procession had moved faster, if the priest had spoken more quickly, things might have been different. He would have stood some small chance of being declared Reine's legal husband. A man who played at being dead while allowing all the legalities attached to that condition to be invoked could not expect to come back to life at will. Yet here Pingre was, claiming his wife and daughter as if he had never given them up.

Such a dramatic public reappearance had not been anticipated. A private confrontation had seemed more likely, even one at swordpoint or the wrong end of a pistol. Of course, that had been tried and Christien had the half-healed gouge in his side to prove it. The spectacle tonight was likely the answer to that failure.

What would happen now? Did Pingre anticipate returning to his old life? Would he dare face public scrutiny and attempt setting up residence at Bonne Esèrance again, demanding his rights as a husband and father?

It all depended on the outcome of the duel. What that might be none could say, least of all Christien.

A prickling moved across the back of his neck. The air seemed to shift to a more silken warmth. Reine. So attuned was Christien to her presence that he turned before she fully materialized out of that dimly lit hallway behind him.

She appeared as pale as the gown she still wore, her wedding gown of light blue with its pink ribbon edging. She had removed the lace veil, revealing her hair piled into a crown of ringlets from which a single, shining curl had escaped to lie alongside her neck.

"Madame Pingre," he said, his voice abrupt.

She paused a bare instant before she came on again. *"Monsieur."*

He had meant to keep some kind of distance between them. It was impossible. Never in this life would he forget how she had looked as she descended the stairs toward him earlier. No bride had ever been more beautiful; nothing had ever so touched his soul as the acceptance in her face as she put her hand in his. Now he stood and watched her come toward him as if gliding on the hems of her skirts, and could hardly bear the thought that this time, this hour, was supposed to have been so different.

They would have stayed at the family gathering long enough to accept due congratulations and reply to the toasts. After an hour or so, Madame Cassard would have come for Reine and taken her upstairs, helped her undress and put her to bed. When all was ready, he would have been summoned. Entering the bedchamber that was theirs to share, he would have closed the door and locked out everyone and everything except the two of them.

How perfect it would have been to hold her close while they made love to the rhythm of the rain, then fell asleep listening to it pound on the roof. He had almost had that, almost, even if he did not deserve it.

"Have you eaten?" she asked as she drew near.

He shook his head. "Later, perhaps."

"Alonzo has put back a plate for you. It's on a warming rack before your bedchamber fireplace, waiting on your convenience."

"I must remember to thank him." Christien did not make the mistake of thinking Alonzo had arranged the food on his own. He knew to whom he owed the undeserved consideration. "You managed to eat something?"

"I wasn't hungry. As you say, possibly later."

If the wedding had taken place, they might have shared a private supper of champagne, small delicacies and each other. Casting around his mind for something to counteract the effect of that thought on his unruly body, he thought of Madame Cassard. She had been half carried from the chapel to the house, reviving only in the coolness of the rain.

"How fares your mother?"

"I've just come from her. She's resting with a cloth dampened with lavender water on her forehead and her tisane nearby. I expect she will be all right in the morning."

"I'm glad to hear it. She seemed overcome by Pingre's appearance."

"Yes, it was a shock," Reine said shortly. Her gaze touched his face and moved away again before she went on. "But not to you, I think."

"Not entirely."

"Nor was I surprised."

His gaze sharpened on her averted face. "What are you saying?"

"I should have told you earlier," she said with a small shake of her head. "I'd like to remedy that, now that matters have turned out so differently."

He wasn't sure, quite suddenly, that he wanted to hear. There were too many secrets at River's Edge, few of them completely harmless. He turned toward her, putting his back to the post behind him and crossing his arms over his chest.

She stepped to the railing next to him, putting one hand upon it and placing the other on top as she stared out at the falling rain.

Her nearness did strange things to his equilibrium, he realized with a silent groan. He could catch the tantalizing fragrance of roses, lavender and warm female. It was with extreme effort that he gathered his thoughts again, found sufficient words to convey some kind of meaning.

"What would this thing be that you wanted to tell me? Perhaps how you knew your husband was alive?"

"To say I actually knew would be a bit strong," she

said as a frown crossed her features. "I began to suspect two days ago."

"How was that?"

She told him, relating how she had heard Chalmette in the night, had gone to Marguerite's room, then looked out to see an oddly familiar form in the darkness outside the house. She ended with her daughter's claim that the *loup-garou* had come to her room but Chalmette had scared him away.

"You think Pingre has been the *loup-garou* that's haunted her." He felt his heart ease into a calmer beat as he spoke. Reine's knowledge of Pingre's masquerade as a dead man did not, apparently, extend back to the beginning.

Her eyes caught the lamplight from the hall in a blue flash as she flung him a quick glance. "I've tried to make excuses, to allow him some feeling as a father. He may have wanted to see her, so satisfied the need by slipping into her room to watch her sleep." She clenched her hands into fists and slammed them on the railing. "Yet how could he bear hearing her cry out as if in nightmare at the merest glimpse of him? How could he not understand he was frightening her to the point of illness? What kind of monster believes his fatherly impulses are more important than the welfare of his daughter?"

The questions were unanswerable. Christien let them go. "Chalmette scared him off that time."

She gave an unhappy nod. "He knows Theodore, of course, but there is little love lost between them. Theodore used to kick him out of his way when we visited here. Chalmette even bit him once, when he and Paul came to blows after Theodore's teasing got out of hand."

"Dogs have an instinct about people," Christien allowed, "particularly when it comes to protecting those they love. But why didn't you call out to me when you caught sight of Theodore? Or tell me later, if it comes to that?"

"It seemed doubtful you would believe the *loup-garou* was real. More than that, I had no idea what you might do."

"Do?" he asked while holding his anger under stringent control. "What would I do except chase down this specter and show him to Marguerite for what he was?"

"It would not have been a particularly salutary lesson for her if what he turned out to be was dead!"

"I wouldn't do such a thing."

"Perhaps not, but I could hardly depend on it. You were—you are—a virtual stranger. You are also the Nighthawk, chief among the Brotherhood of swordsmen, a man who takes to task those who prey on women and children and makes them pay in blood for their sins."

A stranger, she called him. A stranger, though she had lain beside him in his bed, and more, much more. He turned to grip the railing as she was doing, his hold so fierce he could not feel the ends of his fingers. "How do you know that?"

"About your nighttime activity? I followed you. What of it?"

"You did what?" He was stunned, not least because

he could not believe he had failed to notice her behind him. Where had his mind been? As if he couldn't guess.

"I watched you leave in the midnight hour of your first evening here. It became necessary to know if you were going to another woman."

"To Vinot, I only went to see Vinot."

"But I wasn't to know that. I'd had one husband who felt climbing into the beds of other women was his birthright. I had no use for another."

"You trailed after me on the night I was shot, to make certain I would honor our vows." The pattern was clear now. She had been out riding, all right, just as Mo, the stable boy, had told him.

"I suppose."

"Yet you were prepared to speak your vows while fearful you had a living husband lurking about the place."

She gave him an unhappy look. "To call off the wedding on the evidence of a shadow glimpsed for one moment seemed foolish. Besides, I hoped I was wrong."

"You hoped…" he began.

She went on as if he had not spoken. "Don't tell me you hadn't some idea that Theodore was alive. You proposed our marriage in order to force him into the open, but would have gone through with it without turning a hair if it hadn't worked."

"Oh, yes," he said, his voice hard and his gaze raking her face, which had taken on the high color of anger, "I'd have done that."

"To see if I would refuse at the end, no doubt,

proving that I knew I was not a widow. I'm sorry you were cheated out of that final act. The truth is, no one at River's Edge guessed Theodore might be alive until it was nearly too late."

"Forgive me, but that seems hard to credit when Marguerite was terrified of him."

"Don't be ridiculous. To her, he was just a phantom, a monster from some ancient superstition."

"She caught a glimpse of him that night in front of Davis's theater, I would swear to it. It frightened her, so she ran into the street and almost died. He appeared a monster to her, yes, because of his scars, yet must have looked enough like his portrait to trigger some form of recognition. When I held her as we lay in the street, she said… I thought she was calling me her papa, but she must have been trying to say he had been there."

Reine pressed her lips together, turning from him. "She did ask about him after that, but I'd told her many times that her papa was in heaven."

"So she turned him into a *loup-garou* to explain why he was still here."

A tear gathered at Reine's lash line and overflowed, making a wet track down her face. "I failed her. I'm her mother, and I didn't believe her so did nothing. I should have talked to her more about her nightmares and allowed her to tell me her fears. I should have known what was happening."

"The blame is not yours," he said in grim certainty.

He leaned on the railing, staring into the wet night through the streams of silver rain that cascaded from the roof. He had to hold on to something to prevent himself from reaching out to take Reine into his arms to comfort her, to sweep her into the open door of his bedchamber, which was not so far away.

It was impossible. She was a married woman; to touch her would be to commit adultery. In something over twenty-four hours, he would meet her husband with sword in hand. He could be forced to kill him, longed to kill him for reasons that clamored in his head with the force of a hurricane. He wanted to dispatch Theodore Pingre for Sophie, for Marguerite, and most of all for Reine, so she would be free of him.

To kill Theodore could be judged as murder given his skill. It would also be a tactical error. That Pingre had returned from the dead would be a seven-day wonder—add the coming duel and tongues would wag for years. If Reine should marry the man who sent her husband back to his grave, she would be suspected of collusion in the crime and branded as unfit for decent society.

He couldn't do that to her. Pingre's resurrection proved conclusively that she was no murderess. She was effectively freed of her status as a social outcast. To return her to it by dispatching her husband, then demanding she marry him as planned, would be self-serving beyond words.

Yet how could he permit Theodore Pingre to claim her?

# 22

Christien had been different tonight.

It was not to be wondered at given what had occurred, still it troubled Reine. He had behaved with such formality, as if already putting distance between them in preparation for the parting that must surely come. He had called her Madame Pingre in that odious fashion that made it clear he considered her a married lady, therefore open to censure for what had taken place between them in his bedchamber. He had listened to what she had to say, then bowed and left her alone with her doubts and fears and endlessly turning thoughts.

How strange to think of Theodore as being alive. In these past two years, she had grown quite used to the idea that he was gone. Never had she prayed to be a widow, but the role had suited her.

Not that she was so hardened as to wish for his death now, much less suggest to Christien that he arrange it. She would not be human, however, if she didn't reckon the chances.

No, she didn't want Theodore to die. She only

wanted the situation to be as it had before he returned. That was clearly impossible. No matter what happened, nothing would ever be the same.

She returned to the evening party, if it could be called such a thing; Theodore's appearance had cast such a pall it seemed more a wake than anything else. Voices were hushed and conversation lagged. That was except for the whispers in corners. The music played by a trio of musicians on violin, French horn and pianoforte had a lugubrious sound and few were inclined to dance. Appetites were meager, though inroads were made on the chilled wine and spirits served over ice. The children, a part of the gathering by country French tradition, were made fractious and noisy by confinement and the strain that hung in the air, causing parental tempers to fray.

At last, the rain slackened and soon ceased altogether. Guests not staying in the house began to depart. The musicians packed up and climbed into their carriage to return to the city. By midnight the swordsmen and their wives and children were all that remained.

With no incentive to extend the evening, everyone dispersed. The younger children were put to bed in the hall and older boys relegated to the back gallery. One by one, the bedchamber doors closed on their occupying couples and the gleam of lamplight from under the doors vanished. Reine checked on Marguerite, pulling the mosquito *baire* a little closer around the head of her trundle. Then she turned to look at her mother in the tester bed before searching out a quilt in order to make herself a pallet somewhere.

The bedchamber was quiet, lit only by a candle under a hurricane globe. Her mother was sound asleep behind her mosquito netting, with her braided hair trailing over one shoulder and her hands folded on her chest. All strain was gone from her features, wiped away by sleep and the laudanum with which Reine had laced her tisane. She snored gently.

The door opened behind Reine. Her father paused on the threshold, then came forward. "She looks peaceful, does she not? More so than in some time."

Reine met his gaze. A moment of communication passed between them before she said, "I was thinking the same thing just now."

"You will stay with her, perhaps, in case she wakes and needs another of her tisanes? You know just how to make them to please her."

"You mean sleep here?" She indicated the place next to her mother.

"Yes, yes, certainly, as the bridal chamber is denied you. You must not seek a chair or curl up in a corner somewhere after this disaster of an evening. I confess to being exhausted, and you must be a hundred times more so."

Now that he had mentioned it, she was weary beyond all bearing, almost to the point of being unable to think. She gave a small nod. "Where will you sleep?"

"I will be quite comfortable on the gallery with Paul and Nathaniel. Vinot is there also, you know, as he must stay for this business of a dawn meeting."

"Are you sure?" she asked doubtfully.

"Most certainly. Though night air is said to be poisonous, I can't think it true. We always slept outside in hot weather when I was a boy. I'll quite enjoy the change."

She went to him and gave him a hug, pressing a kiss to his cheek. "You're an old humbug, and I won't take your bed, but I am grateful for the offer all the same."

"Please, *chère*. I would be much easier in my mind with you there beside your mother."

It required further protests and more assurances, but exhaustion won in the end. Her father changed in the dressing room, covering his nightshirt with a foulard dressing gown. Taking an extra pillow and giving her a cheery good-night, he let himself out into the hall. Reine undressed, slipped one of her mother's nightgowns over her head, blew out the lamp and crawled under the *baire*.

Sleep that had threatened to drop her in her tracks only a few moments before deserted her now. She was insufferably hot. Her borrowed nightgown was too tight in the neck, so it strangled her every time she turned over. She seethed with unsettled longing, was haunted by images of what should have been taking place in these midnight hours. She pictured Christien alone in his bedchamber. To ease from her bed and go to his would mean running the gauntlet of children's cots and pallets that lined the hallway, but might be managed. He would not turn her away; she was almost sure of it.

It was pride more than the consciousness of sinful intentions that kept her in place. He had thought her capable of living a lie, of concealing the truth about Theodore's disappearance. He had never expected to marry her, but meant only to lure her husband from his hiding place with the fiction. He had foisted himself upon her, upon them all, without regard for how any of them might be hurt by it. He had desired her, made love to her, taught her to anticipate married bliss, but had no permanent place for her in his affections or his life. If she went to his bed now, it must be as a supplicant, a female so lost to her own worth, so at the mercy of her desires, that nothing else mattered.

She couldn't do it, though her heart stung with the salt of her unshed tears.

No, she couldn't.

Could she?

She stared into the darkness while her mind turned in endless circles to reach, finally, the inescapable negative answer. And when she had accepted it, taken it deep inside her, sleep came down like a hammer blow.

Bright sunlight poured in gold streams around the shutter edges when she woke. Its heat was already stifling, made harder to bear by the steamlike rise of moisture left from the rain. Reine's mother was awake and surprised to find Reine beside her, though she apparently approved the arrangement.

As she complained of thirst, Reine slid from the bed and poured water for her from the bedside carafe. She thought of getting dressed, but all she had to wear was her wedding gown. She borrowed a dressing gown from her mother to use until she was certain Christien was awake and Alonzo could remove her clothing from where it had been transferred to the armoire in his room. Until then, she was trapped here. Her father would have to act as host to their guests until she could join him.

So much that must be put back the way it was before. Everything. Almost everything.

"Ring for café au lait, will you, *chère?*" her mother asked. "I believe I could relish a roll, as well. I do hope one or two are left from last night."

"I'm sure they are," Reine said, summoning a smile as she moved to do as she was bid, turning the bell crank set into the fireplace mantel. "It's good you're feeling better."

"I do seem to be," her mother answered. Then her lips flattened. "Theodore did come back, yes? Or did I dream it?"

Reine turned sober, as well. "He was there, at the chapel."

"But changed, so changed. Oh, Reine…"

"Don't think about it."

"The wedding didn't take place, did it? I mean…"

"I know what you mean. No, it didn't."

"All praise to *le bon Dieu* that you were spared that much. Oh, but the talk! How people will smack their lips over such a rich morsel. It's not to be borne!"

"If not this, then it would be something else," she replied in clipped tones. "They must always have something to enliven their dull lives."

"But all of us are touched by it, as I'm sure you must agree. The question is what will happen next."

"After the duel, you mean?"

"Duel? What duel is this?"

The words were edged with alarm. It was clear her mother remembered next to nothing of the events at the chapel. Choosing her words with care, Reine told her what had transpired.

"*Alors,*" her mother said in fading tones. "Do you think… Is there a chance Theodore may not survive?"

Reine could not tell whether dread or anticipation was uppermost in her mother's voice. "One always exists in these things."

"I was only thinking of you, you know. Well, and of how awkward it would be to have him here again, to sit at the table with him, know he is sleeping just down the hall and…and all the rest. He is quite…quite hideous, *chère.*"

*All the rest.*

That phrase covered so much, including Theodore coming to her bed with his rage and bitterness, his maimed face and his body made corpulent by inactivity and indulgence.

"As you say," Reine answered in spite of the sick feeling in the pit of her stomach. "He may have other plans. It has been his choice to stay away all this time."

"But why? I don't understand."

"Morbid fear of Monsieur Vinot, it appears. Now that he has seen him and discovered how frail he has become, he is less impressed by his past reputation. But of course, it's Christien who will meet Theodore."

"How can he? He is not fully recovered from his

injury," her mother said in querulous tones. She paused. "Perhaps they will kill each other."

*"Maman!"*

"Dreadful for me to say, yes, but it would make everything much more comfortable."

She didn't mean it, Reine thought. Surely she did not. "By no means," she said at her most prosaic as she opened the door to Alonzo, who had arrived with their morning coffee on a breakfast tray. "We should all of us miss Christien, *ma chère maman*—Paul, Marguerite, Papa and, yes, even you." Taking the tray, she gave instructions concerning her wardrobe, then turned back into the room. "Now," she said with a smile for her mother, "would you care for butter on your breakfast roll?"

It was past midmorning when Reine finally left her parents' bedchamber. The cots and pallets in the upper hallway were empty, of course; she had heard the children playing for two hours and more, seen them running here and there from the bedchamber window that she had thrown open to the brief morning coolness. Blindman's bluff and hide-and-seek seemed to be their principal choices for entertainment, though she had also seen them partaking of a breakfast of melon slices.

Marguerite had apparently dressed herself, or perhaps Lisette O'Neill or Juliette Pasquale had seen to it. Thinking it might be best if she had a look at the results, just in case, Reine moved out onto the upper gallery. From that vantage point, she framed her mouth with her hands for carrying quality as she leaned over the railing and called her daughter.

Marguerite did not appear.

Reine was not altogether surprised, given her high excitement over having playmates. She called her name again, letting the last note keen through the great oaks and out across the nearer cane fields.

Still no Marguerite.

Young Sean O'Neill came running from the rear of the house. *"Mon cher,"* she called down to him when he was close enough to hear, "have you seen Marguerite?"

"No, *madame!*" He turned his earnest, choir boy's face up to her. "Not in a long time."

He was gone again the moment the words left his mouth. From where he had disappeared behind the house came high-pitched children's laughter. Listening closely, Reine could make out the voices of several of the children. Her daughter's voice was not one of them.

Concern touched her, but she dismissed it. Sean was playing with the other boys, most likely, while Marguerite would be somewhere with the girls. Or she might have visited one of the swordsmen's wives who had a baby, hanging over the cradle watching the little one nap, or else in a dressing room where it was being bathed. She could be in the kitchen, with her grandfather, or even with Christien. There was no need to panic.

Turning swiftly, Reine moved back into the house and through its width to the rear gallery. From that vantage point, she could see an expanse of yard where most of the other children played, as well as the track that led to the barns and other outbuildings. She counted the various offspring of their guests, but could not locate Marguerite's bright head.

Down the stairs she went in a billow of skirts, almost running as she moved out the front door and around to the side gallery. Her father and a half-dozen other men lounged there. They must have received the seconds sent by Theodore already, for they seemed to be discussing the terms of the duel. She had no time for that now, no attention for anyone except Christien.

"Marguerite," she said with a catch in her voice as she met his dark eyes. "Do you know where she is?"

He came to his feet in a single smooth movement, a frown of concern descending over his features. "I thought she must be with you."

"No, and I don't see her with the others." She glanced past him to her father and the other swordsmen, who had risen to their feet. "Has anyone seen her this morning?"

"Don't upset yourself," her father said, moving to put a hand on her arm. "She has to be here someplace."

That soothing platitude grated on her nerves. She wondered in a flash of insight if her mother ever felt this way when he spoke so to her. "Help me look, then," she said in a resolute tone. "If you'll make sure she isn't hiding out for the sake of some game, I'll check the kitchen."

Christien said not a word. He merely looked at the other swordsmen with a lifted brow. That brief gesture sent them fanning out under the trees in every direction. Stepping from the gallery, then, he jogged off in the direction of the stables.

He meant to see if. Marguerite was showing her new friends her pony or perhaps the kittens recently brought from hiding by the barn cat. She should have thought of it, Reine told herself, might have if not for the disquiet that gripped her. That Christien had that presence of mind made her throat tighten until she could not speak. Placing her hand on her father's where he comforted her, she squeezed it, then swung from him in the direction of the kitchen.

Cook had not seen Marguerite since she gave her *pain perdu,* day-old bread dipped in egg batter, fried and sprinkled with sugar, to go with her breakfast melon.

Lisette O'Neill said she had hung over her shoulder while she was nursing her baby, but went away saying something about the kittens in the barn who suckled just the same.

One of the upstairs maids had retied the sash on her apron when it came loose.

Alonzo had seen her carrying a kitten, trying to make Chalmette let the little thing ride on his back.

No one had seen her for at least an hour, however, possibly two. A thorough canvassing of the shadows under the oaks turned up no sign of her, nor did it help anything to call the other children in and line them up in a row to be questioned.

Reine turned from all those sober young faces. She turned from the concern of their parents, who hovered behind them, also from all the people from River's

Edge who had been called out by the alarm bell. She turned from Paul's pinched and concerned features, from her parents' pale devastation, from the grim set of Christien's mouth.

She turned and faced the river. It was all that was left.

She didn't want to think of it. The very idea brought such harrowing images, the body identified as Theodore two years ago, a child lost from a steamboat just downriver in the spring and Kingsley's body only days ago. Still, the possibility must be explored.

"No," Christien said, stepping swiftly to her side. "She isn't there." He hesitated. "At least, there's no sign of her along the bank in either direction."

He had accepted the possibility and seen to it. Whether it was from experience, scrupulous effort or to save her from the harrowing necessity made no difference. It was done, and done well.

Reine closed her eyes, feeling the hard pounding of her heart and the tearing pain inside that presaged heartbreak. She felt it and she knew that she loved this man, would always love him. And it was not for the way he looked, his strength or prowess with a sword. It was not for how he touched her or the way he could draw forth her most fervent responses.

No, she loved him because he understood how she felt with sure instinct, her terrors as well as her joys. It was because he bent his strength and his will to sustain hers without expectation of return. It was because he saw her for what she was and did not turn away, but accepted everything about her. Yes, even the fact that she belonged to another man.

It was then that Chalmette appeared, trotting from the direction of the barn. Around his neck was a crude kerchief of osnaburg. Attached to the fabric was a sheet of foolscap.

Paul whistled and the big bloodhound veered in his direction. He looked tired and footsore, and had a line of dried blood along one side that might have been made by a briar but could have come from a knife. He crouched at Paul's feet, whining a little as he looked up into his face.

Paul loosened the knot that held the foolscap. With only the barest glance at it, he handed it to Reine.

Her hands shook as she took it, so it was an instant before she could make out the words. The handwriting was familiar, though it had been more than two years since she had last seen it.

*My dear wife,* it ran, *I have our daughter.*

"It's from Theodore," she whispered, looking up, her vision obscured by tears. "He has taken Marguerite."

"Where?" her father demanded. "How did he get to her?"

Reine didn't answer. She was reading again, though a tear splashed onto the paper, blurring the words. She dashed it away in sudden dread that she might obliterate something important.

*I have taken her as surety for the affair of honor that will take place in the morning. If you care to see her again, you will make certain I survive it unharmed. This you will arrange with Lenoir. I leave the method of persuasion in your hands.*

"Reine?" Christien asked, his voice urgent as he watched her face.

She handed him the note without a word. Then she watched in her turn as his skin turned gray beneath its coating of copper-bronze. And when he cursed in softly vicious phrases, she echoed them in her mind.

Theodore had Marguerite. If Christien harmed him in the duel, then he would make certain she never saw her daughter again. He would not kill her, surely he would not, but he might take her far away if only to punish Reine.

"Vinot must withdraw the challenge," Christien said abruptly. "I'll send my seconds to arrange it with Pingre's friends."

Hope leaped inside Reine's chest only to fade away again. "You can't do that. He will take the utmost pleasure in claiming you were too cowardly to face him."

"It doesn't matter."

"But it does. I can't imagine he will let it go without a public confrontation. Besides…"

"What?" Christien looked from her to her father, then past him to the other sword masters.

"He only asks that he be allowed to survive," she said in deliberate clarification. "He doesn't demand to be victorious."

"He will expect it," Christien said, the words as certain as they were hard.

"Then he should have said so."

He shook his head. "It's Marguerite's safety at stake here."

"He's her father. Surely he won't harm her. But if

he thought you'd believe he would…" She stopped, biting the inside of her lip until she tasted blood.

Christien met her eyes, his own dark with rigorous consideration. He gave a slow nod. "You're right. He would prefer a meeting where my hands are tied."

"Yes, but I can't ask…"

Hot color rose into her face as she remembered the words of the note. Theodore misjudged her if he thought she would stoop to using her body to persuade Christien to let him live. He misjudged Christien, as well, if he considered it might be necessary.

"And need not," he said, answering her thought before glancing again at his friends. "He can't have taken Marguerite far, not if he expects to be at the dueling ground in the morning. We—my friends and I—can search him out, descend in force and bring her back."

"No!" The answer was instinctive, though the temptation to leave it to his strength and ingenuity, and that of his formidable friends, was almost more than she could bear. What was it he had said once? Ah, yes. *No one touches those who belong to me.* If she allowed it, he would certainly hold true to that vow.

He would, yes, but at what cost?

"No," she said again with a small shudder. "If Theodore saw or heard you coming, he might be maddened enough to do something he would not otherwise. I fear he isn't entirely…responsible." What she truly feared was the he was insane, and had been since the night he was attacked at River's Edge.

"We would take every care to make certain that doesn't happen."

She met the fierce darkness of Christien's eyes, her own drowning in liquid terror and sorrow. "I know, and I would trust to your word if anything less were at stake. But I can't in this, not when it's Marguerite's life."

He returned her regard for interminable seconds while his hands knotted at his sides. Then he inclined his head. "She is your daughter, therefore it will be as you prefer. Let Pingre have his way. With luck, it will make no difference."

Christien would have to face Theodore with this threat hanging over him. He dare not use his full skill for fear of reprisal against Marguerite. With the lingering effects of his injury, he would be at a double disadvantage.

Could he surmount the difficulty so as to snatch some form of triumph from the meeting? Or must he accept the denial of justice for Vinot's daughter and, yes, the danger of dying on Theodore's sword?

Between the safety of lover or child, there could be only one choice for Reine. She would allow Christien to stay his hand, would accept that sacrifice from him if she must.

The question was whether she could live with the consequences.

# 23

"He has your rapiers."

It was Gavin Blackford who made that observation as they stood in the wooded clearing with the great oak tree, waiting for Pingre and his seconds to get ready. The English swordsman should recognize them, Christien knew. The beautifully wrought dueling swords had once belonged to Ariadne, Gavin's wife, before she sold them to Christien, and had been purchased by her in Paris and brought to New Orleans. It was unlikely there was another pair like them in Louisiana.

"I can't say I'm surprised," he answered.

"Like the frog with the fly stuck to its nose, it does rather leap to the eye. They were lost on the night you were shot from the ambuscade, therefore…"

"Therefore, I am to be killed with my own weapon as I refused to oblige Pingre by dying from that injury."

"Only if you accept what he offers. Others are available."

That was certainly true. Every former *maître d'armes* present had his sword at hand this morning, from habit if not necessity. Gavin and Caid had brought theirs as a matter of course since it was always possible that some mischance or display of temper during a duel would require their forceful intervention. "I see no reason to object. They would have been my choice if still in my possession. Could be poetic justice will be served."

"His thought, as well, or so I would imagine."

"Then we are equal."

"Unless he has altered the blades in some manner."

Christien lifted a brow as he met his friend's bright blue eyes. "Your province, I think, to see that no such mischief occurs."

"Oh, yes, and I will govern it as I can, but he's a wily beast and bent on execution."

"He's welcome to try."

"Oh, all my piastres would be on you, except for the minor handicaps of a great bloody rent in your side and a child's life hanging in the balance. Tell me, should I chance it?"

Despite the brutal obscurity of their phrasing, Gavin's words usually had a point to them. Christien had learned to take note. "If you're asking whether I'm fit, the answer is yes, within reason. If you want to know whether I can ignore the welfare of Madame Pingre's daughter in any degree, you should know better."

"No, no, you mistake me," the English sword master said with the ghost of a smile. "I inquire only for how you will neutralize the danger to the innocent while still, and inevitably, belaboring the guilty."

"I haven't decided," Christien said with a frown. "When I do, I'll let you know."

"Excellent," Blackford answered with fine cheer, "as long as you have it in mind."

Christien had thought of little else from the moment he read the note from Marguerite's father. The problem had been clearing the rage from his mental processes.

That Pingre would use his daughter as a shield was beneath contempt. It was also of a piece with his night attack on the man who dared propose a second marriage to his wife. He had been content to remain safely dead while she was the grieving widow in retreat from clacking tongues. He might care little for her as a woman, but she represented his name, his heritage, his value as a human being while she still mourned him. The prospect of a new life for her he viewed as a betrayal, one as cutting to his pride as deliberate adultery. He could not allow it.

The reaction was not unexpected. What they had not counted on, he and Vinot, was the lengths Pingre would go to in order to remove his rival. They had looked for him to surface in order to reclaim his rights as a husband, even at the risk of a meeting over his past deeds. They had planned no defense against attempted murder, had not imagined he would hold his own daughter hostage to protect his miserable hide.

It was a costly mistake for which Christien took full responsibility. His task now was to make sure the price wasn't more than Reine could pay.

Gavin and Caid laid out the piste, removing any broken branches, twigs, briars and vines that might trip the unwary and marking the boundary lines with powdered lime dribbled from the bunghole of a wooden keg. By rights, the task should have been overseen jointly with Pingre's seconds, but they had declined the office. They were sure the former sword masters had a better grasp of the requirement than they did. More than that, they were unlikely to dispute with such dangerous gentlemen if it was not to their liking. They were quite free to do as they pleased.

All was done, rather, with the greatest of fairness, the lines being drawn so neither man would have the rising sun in their eyes. Pingre was allowed to call the toss of the coin for position. To Christien went first selection of the two weapons presented. They took their places as the sun came up, striking through the trees, sending their long shadows slipping ahead of them over the grass.

A warm breeze stirred the leaves overhead to a soft murmur, like an audience waiting for the play to begin. Birds whistled in the distance. A grasshopper left the area with a clicking sound, as if its knees were popping. Somewhere a dog barked and cattle lowed, waiting to be milked. The sky overhead was rinsed to palest blue by heat and sunlight.

Pingre was sweating, Christien noted. For all his base preparations, he was still nervous of the outcome. As well he should be.

The man's gaze moved over the gathering, from the few distant neighbors to the swordsmen and on to Paul, who stood to one side. Chalmette drooped next to him, his long face hangdog and lost without little

Marguerite. The man's eyes settled on Vinot, a thin, dark form in the forefront of the gathered spectators. It seemed Pingre felt the need to keep an eye on the father of the young woman he had wronged. That was also wise of him. Not that Vinot would interfere at this point; he was far too experienced in these affairs for that kind of error. Yet neither would he permit the slightest deviation from the rules of conduct.

In the pitiless light of day, it was easy to see one reason Pingre had elected to remain hidden from society. To a man of overweening pride, vain of his appearance and his attractiveness to women, the destruction of his face must have come as a blow. Healing would have taken months; the scars would never go away. Pingre's beard concealed some part of the damage, but its unkempt state added to the feral, not quite human, look of him. It was no wonder Marguerite had seized on the name she had given him.

"Salute," Gavin called.

Christien swept up his blade in crisp respect for an enemy in this ritual form of combat. Pingre's movement was sloppy, with a derisive edge that plainly showed respect for nothing and no one, least of all himself.

*"En garde!"*

Their blade tips came together with hard purpose. They watched each other above them, gauging will, strength and purpose.

"Begin!"

Christien allowed Pingre the first attack, deflecting it with a parry in quarte and a riposte that taught a quick lesson in caution. He would not attempt a lightning coup, would not essay a crippling blow, but neither would he be easily touched. They settled then to a series of small passages to see precisely what each was made of.

Pingre was a competent swordsman. At a guess, he had spent much of his time practicing over the past two years. How had that been accomplished if he seldom ventured into town?

"You are to be congratulated on your skill," Christien said conversationally. "Who has been your *maître d'armes?*"

"No one you would know."

"Try me. You might be surprised."

"A gentleman sent from Paris by my mother, Monsieur Thibaut. He was with me for a year."

"Long enough to instruct you in the finer points, yes, and perhaps instruct a sparring partner."

"As you say."

The answer was short, though not merely because Pingre was reluctant to admit he was right, Christien saw in the middle of an adroit parry. He was also growing winded. He might have practiced, but it was without the dedication that builds endurance.

It also came to him in a flash of memory who Pingre's partner must have been, the only man it could have been.

"To kill your sparring partner was somewhat rash. What did Kingsley do to deserve it, I wonder? Oh, but permit me to guess. He failed to kill me but demanded to be paid regardless."

"Greedy bastard deserved to die. He tried to blackmail me. Me! We fought. He went into the river."

"An accident, was it? I had thought it a duel."

Pingre made a sound that might have been a grunt or a laugh while parrying in his turn. "Oh, yes. Naturally."

"Though like Vinot and myself, you did not consider Kingsley a gentleman, I believe. Your standards seemed to have undergone considerable revision." His opponent obviously felt he could get away with his ridiculous claim. What then did he intend to say was behind Christien's own death? The right of the cuckold husband to defend his honor? It would not be the first time such a defense was used.

"A man doesn't choose his enemies." Pingre hurtled into another attack, this one with more brawn than finesse, as if made bold by his own rhetoric.

Christien, defending, was aware of the growing strain in his side. He thought the scab covering it had broken for he could feel a warm trickle inching into the waistband of his trousers. "And there is no enemy like family, is there? I say that because I heard a rumor Kingsley was your uncle."

"That lout was no kin of mine."

"No? Your honored grandfather may have thought differently. But say he wasn't, one need not feel bound to uphold all the honorable conventions with such opponents, yes? What ruse did you use to defeat him?"

Contempt twisted the man's misshapen mouth. "He was a cowhanded farmer pretending to be a swordsman. I needed no ruse."

"I am a different proposition, apparently."

"So you are."

"Yet to drag a child into the business is a drop down the scale, even for you."

"When you are a *maître d'armes?* Not knowing your level of expertise, I arranged extra protection. I think now I could have taken you without my little safeguard."

It was exactly what Christien wanted Pingre to think. Toward that end, he had done little more than skirmish while keeping his more expert stratagems in reserve. "Do you indeed?" he inquired, all affability. "Or do you only contemplate some underhanded trick like a shot in the dark or a slash in the back? I should warn you the Brotherhood is more than a name or a handful of men fighting in the dark against those who choose to become bestial. It's a circle of friends dedicated to hardihood, prowess and honor, each one of whom stands ready to resent injury to the others to the last red drop of his blood." He smiled in deadly earnest. "We do choose our enemies, you see."

To one side, where stood Dr. Laborde, come from town that morning, his seconds, Gavin and Caid, looked at each other. Behind them, where Pasquale and the Conde de Lérida stood, there was a similar shift. Though Christien had scant attention to give them while parrying rapidly in tierce, he had the impression that they came to attention like soldiers awaiting battle, a lethal phalanx of friends. And he heard the quiet hiss of blades being drawn.

"Fine lot of good that will do you when you're dead," Pingre, unheeding, answered with a sneer.

"Oh, but I didn't tell you all of it," Christien answered without raising his voice. "They each adore their wives and children and cannot suffer them to feel fear or pain. This tenderness is extended to every child anywhere who cries in the dark. Learning of an injury to the one, they draw their swords against the man who caused the hurt. And they will not rest until every single tear that falls from the sweetling's eye has been avenged."

Counter threat to threat against Marguerite; it was the best Christien could do. Hard on the words, he sprang forward into an attack with his most polished ruse behind it and every ounce of his will. His blade clashed with Pingre's, slid edge to edge in a shower of sparks, slithered past guard and handle and reached warm, yielding flesh.

Pingre screamed in shock and rage as he fell back with his free hand clamped to his neck. Christien dragged his rapier free with a wrenching pull, stepped back out of guard position.

Gavin moved forward with sword in hand, a bulwark between Christien and his opponent. Turning toward him, he asked, "Are you satisfied, Monsieur Pingre?"

Murder shone from the eyes of Reine's husband, even as blood appeared on the collar of his shirt, soaking it, running down the sleeve to drip onto the sword still in his hand. He wanted to answer in the negative; that much was clear. It was also plain to be seen that he lacked the expertise to gain the victory he craved or the nerve to go on without it.

"I'm satisfied," he said in guttural defeat.

Christien waited for relief to take the tension from his muscles. It didn't come. His bow was stiff, his movements almost jerky as he turned away.

Pingre growled low in his throat, the sound erupting into a roar as he sprang forward. Whipping around, Christien saw the bared teeth, the twisted lips, blood-streaked sleeve and raised blade. Taken unawares by trust in unwritten rules, he flung up his sword even knowing it could not meet Pingre's blade in time.

There was no need.

The attack was stopped by a mighty, ringing clang with myriad echoes as four men leaped forward, Caid, Gavin, Nicholas and Rio, swords upraised in their hands. The movement set them between Christien and his enemy, a ring of steel between him and death. So they stood, holding Pingre's blade aloft, their cold, implacable faces turned against him. Then as one, they heaved him backward.

Gavin snatched the man's rapier as he stumbled, falling to the ground. As Pingre scooted away on his haunches, putting distance between him and his judges, the Englishman flipped the retrieved sword back toward Christien. It landed upright in the grassy earth, waving slowly back and forth, shining and bright in the morning sun.

Christien watched it an instant, then looked up, looked toward where Reine's husband had lain sprawled, cursing with liquid rage in his eyes.

He was up and running.

Pingre was sprinting through the woods toward the

old playhouse where his ancient nursemaid, Demeter, lived, running toward his family land, his old family home. He was running toward the one place where he might keep a small child locked away from sight.

He was running toward Marguerite.

# 24

River's Edge was deathly quiet. The men had left before dawn, departing without breakfast, with no fanfare or word of farewell. A duel was not usually an affair to the death, and to treat it so was like asking for ill fortune; still, that careless sangfroid seemed to fly in the face of reason. Or perhaps, Reine thought, she was simply pained that Christien had not kissed her goodbye.

She could not bear to think of where he was going or why, much less of what might happen. Dread consumed her. She was torn between visions of Marguerite confined somewhere, crying in terror or pain, and Theodore hacking at Christien while knowing he could do little more than defend himself.

Oh, but was that true? Christien had never agreed to stay his hand completely. He had exercised great patience in his quest for vengeance. Might he not feel it took precedence? What if he decided a fatal, or near fatal, injury for Theodore was more likely to remove the danger to Marguerite than letting him return to wherever she was being held?

Where was Marguerite while this duel was taking place? Who was holding her? Who did Theodore expect to injure her, possibly even kill her, if he was defeated? The questions revolved endlessly in Reine's mind, had since the moment Theodore's note was put into her hand.

There was only one answer that she could see. It had to be in the same place, with the same person who must have hidden him away so long. And who should that person be, the only human being who loved him, had always cared for him as if he was her own?

Who else except Demeter?

He could not think his old nurse would harm Marguerite. No, not even at his direct order. If Marguerite was to pay for any harm inflicted upon him by Christien, then he must exact the price himself.

Surely he would not hurt his own daughter? She was so tender and innocent, so trusting. And yet she had called him a *loup-garou,* a monster of the night.

Reine flung out of bed with her mouth set in a straight line. She dressed with haste, pulling on her riding habit. She could not depend on the outcome of this dawn meeting, refused to sit with her hands folded while others decided the fate of her child. There should be time while the duel was in progress to get to Demeter's cottage and back again. She could not take the back way, for that led past the site of the duel, but there was another, longer route. If she could not snatch Marguerite away from such a feeble jailer, then she had no right to call herself a mother.

Scant minutes later, she was leaning over the neck

of her mare, racing down the drive. At its end, she turned onto the river road that ran past the Pingre plantation on its way to New Orleans.

Bonne Espèrance was shuttered, the covered door openings like empty eyes as it sat at the end of its overgrown drive. The whitewash on its walls had turned gray with mold and mildew, the canvas on the gallery floors had begun to rot and dead leaves lay in drifts on the steps and before the front door. Reine trotted past, ducking under a tree limb broken off in the recent rainstorm but still hanging from one of its shading oaks. Beyond the house was order of a sort, as the land was still being worked, but drainage ditches were clogged with weeds, barn and stable doors sagged and a miasma of stagnant water and outdoor privies hung in the hot morning air.

At the back of the big house was a garden that had become a jungle of overgrown shrubs, wild roses and briars hidden in knee-high grass. Leading from it was a trail that meandered away into the forested no man's land between Bonne Espèrance and River's Edge. Dismounting, looping the mare's rein around the arm of a lichen-covered statue at the garden's corner, Reine set off down the trail at a run.

The playhouse was half-buried in honeysuckle and wisteria vines. Its windows on either side of the center door gave back only reflections of the surrounding woods. The door stood open and an orange tabby sat on the sill with its paws tucked under its chest. As Reine stepped inside and glanced around, the cat rose with dignity and stalked off toward the big house.

Nothing moved inside the small cottage. Its single room smelled of wood smoke, fried food and unwashed bedding. An iron pot sat over dead coals in the single fireplace. Against one wall, a cot of canvas over a wood frame served as both bed and settee. Through the open back door could be seen a small porch where sat a bench holding a wash basin. Next to it was the first steps of an outside staircase that led to a minuscule sleeping loft. Over its post was draped a man's coat with a pair of boots beneath it.

The silence was deep, broken only by the buzzing of a fly against a windowpane.

No one was there. No one had been there for hours, perhaps not since the day before.

Whirling in a flare of skirts, Reine ran back toward the big house. This time, she approached from the rear. Mounting the steps with caution, she crossed the lower gallery to reach its center set of French doors. They were not barred. The handle turned under her hand. She caught her breath, hardly daring to think what that meant, as she eased inside.

Bonne Espèrance had been constructed in the French fashion so all rooms opened into one another. The only way to get from one end of the house to the other without passing through multiple salons and bedchambers was to use the galleries. The central doors where Reine entered opened into the summer dining room, which, in common with most of the major rooms, had double doors on either side for airflow during the summer heat.

More silence greeted her there, along with festoons of spiderwebs and dustcover-wrapped tables, chairs, sideboards and even chandeliers. A deserted feeling hung in the long room, which made Reine believe Theodore's mother was unlikely ever to return from her sojourn in France.

She had left her injured son behind, left him in the care of only an old nursemaid. Had she really expected Theodore to join her in due time as he said, or only thought to outdistance the scandal and him with it? Reine didn't know. She should have known as his wife, she thought. That not knowing seemed as much a tragedy as the rest of it.

Shaking off the unwanted introspection, she skirted the dining table under its dustcover of old linen sheets, stepped over the long tubular shape of the room's carpet, which had been rolled up and pushed to one side. Tobacco leaves had been sprinkled inside for protection from insects, for the dusty-sweet smell rose from the roll as her skirts brushed against it. Smothering a sneeze, she made for the enclosed staircase that rose between the dining room and the butler's pantry on the north end of the house. She eased up the treads as quickly as she dared.

The stairs decanted into a salon wrapped in more dustcovers. In that main room, which, like the dining room below, had access to both front and back galleries through French doors, she hesitated. Four bedchambers opened from it. On the north front corner was the bedchamber she had once shared with Theodore. Marguerite's old crib was in one corner of it, and her old toys, just as they had been left two years before. It was both habit and instinct that urged her toward it.

*"Madame,* why you here?"

She stopped abruptly as Demeter emerged from the gloom, standing in the open door of that room. "You know why," she answered after a moment.

"M'sieur Theodore, he'll not like it."

Reine gave her a hard stare as she lifted her chin. "I don't care what he likes. I've come for my daughter. You can hand her over to me or I will take her."

"She be the child of M'sieur Theodore."

"And he's been such a devoted father to her these past two years, hasn't he? You know he cares nothing for her. Did he tell you to kill her if he doesn't come back from the dueling ground."

"Never would he do this thing!"

"I can show you the letter threatening it. Step aside, Demeter. Marguerite is going home with me."

Inside the room, there came the creak of a wooden bedstead, the rattle of slats. Marguerite called out in high-pitched distress. *"Maman!"*

Reine expected her to come running. Seconds ticked past and she didn't appear. By degrees, the explanation for it came to Reine. She could not come. She was being restrained, perhaps tied up in some manner. Rage unlike any she had ever known washed through her.

She stepped toward Demeter and kept moving. She was going to her daughter if she had to walk over the old nursemaid.

At the last moment, Demeter shifted to one side. Reine ran the last steps that took her into the bedchamber.

It was in chaos, as if someone had raged around it,

inflicting as much damage as possible. The doors of
the armoire hung askew. The clothing she had left
behind, evening gowns and capes, day gowns unneeded
while she was in mourning, had been dragged from it
and cut into ribbons. The toilette articles on her dressing
table were smashed, with powder and perfume spilled
into the wreckage. The bed had been torn apart, the
mosquito *baire* ripped from its metal rings, pillows dis-
emboweled of their feathers and cotton pulled by
handfuls from great cuts in the mattress. Lying on its foot
was the sword used to inflict all the damage, a cavalry
saber that had once hung over the fireplace mantel,
beneath a portrait of Theodore's great-grandfather as he
had appeared when he wore it as a musketeer of the
ancien regime.

Reine noticed the destruction with only the outer
fringe of her attention. Her gaze went at once to the
crib that stood in the corner. She plunged toward it.

*"Maman,"* Marguerite cried with tears filling her
eyes and her arms thrust through the crib's slats in supplication. The small bed was too short for her, so she
lay at a cramped angle across it.

Reine cursed softly, repeating words she had heard
Christien whisper as she saw the strips of torn sheeting
that encircled her daughter's small waist and ankles
and that bound her to the slats. With hands like claws,
she dragged at them, desperate to free her. They were
knotted several times and of linen too stout to give to
anything except a sharp blade of some variety.

"Get me a pair of scissors, a knife, anything," she
said over her shoulder. All the time she spoke, she

was pulling at the bindings around Marguerite's waist, trying to push them down over her small hips.

"M'sieur Theodore won't like this at all," Demeter said in querulous repetition. "Wait for him, *madame*. Soon, soon, he comes. Ask him. He will give her to you if you ask."

She was to beg, as if Theodore had the right to keep her child from her. Perhaps he did in a legal sense; she didn't know. But no right existed that allowed him to take her and tie her up like an animal. Reine half turned toward the nursemaid, stabbed a finger toward the saber. "There, hand that to me at once."

"Think, *madame*," Demeter said, even as she bent to take up the weapon and pass it to Reine. "You will only anger him."

"He doesn't know what anger is," she snapped. Leaning over the crib, she lifted a strip of the binding, passed the blade under it and slashed upward. With vicious strength then, she cut the other strips that held Marguerite, feeling as if she could tear the crib itself apart with her bare hands.

The final strip of linen came unwrapped. Leaning the heavy sword against the crib, Reine snatched away the pieces and flung them from her. Reaching with both arms then, she picked up Marguerite and caught her in a close hug, rocking her back and forth. And she couldn't tell whether that movement was to calm her daughter or soothe her own shuddering rage.

"Oh, *madame*," Demeter said in a tone like two sheets of foolscap rubbing together, "you don't know what you've done."

Reine didn't answer. With Marguerite's arms still around her neck and her small legs clamped about her waist, she strode across to the door once more. She passed into the large salon, ghostly under its dust cloths and dimness caused by closed shutters, then turned toward the dark entrance to the stairwell. Shifting Marguerite so she sat on her hip, Reine turned in that direction.

Theodore appeared ahead of her, rising from the lower floor like a demon from hell. A grim smile tugged the good side of his mouth upward. "Going somewhere, *chère?*"

She halted where she stood. He didn't pause but stepped into the salon and bore down upon her. Reine glanced around a little wildly. Another staircase led down from the front gallery beyond the salon's French doors. But those doors were locked inside their barred shutters. She could never get through them before he was upon her.

"I told you he would not like it," Demeter muttered, backing away from them both, sidling along the wall until she reached a protective corner.

Reine barely heard her as she turned back toward Theodore. "Step aside, if you please," she said with resolution. "I'm taking Marguerite home."

He laughed. "Now, why would you do that when you are both where you belong?"

His hair hung in sweaty strings, she saw, his shirt limp and damp with perspiration, and dirt smudged his pantaloons. A long streak of red ran down his sleeve, spreading from a cut in the fleshy part of his neck, just above the collar of his shirt. She moistened her dry lips, holding her daughter closer as Marguerite began to make small whimpering noises. "It seems you survived the duel. Christien, Monsieur Lenoir, must have honored his intention to let you live. It's over. You can let us go now."

"What of this?" He hunched his shoulder toward the neck wound. "I said nothing about being bloodied. I don't call this honoring anything."

"Did you think he would allow you to slice him to pieces at will? You could not be so foolish."

"Are you quite sure he didn't?" He gave a snorting laugh, jerking his chin toward his injury again. "With the exception of this pitiful attempt at defense, of course."

Horror congealed her blood, turned her heart as cold as ice. Was it possible Christien had failed to protect himself? Where was he now? Where were the others, the seconds and the doctor who should have seen to Theodore's wound? Had they gathered around Christien as he fell, leaving Theodore to fend for himself?

"He…he wouldn't do that," she whispered. "Marguerite isn't even his child."

"No, she's mine." His gaze turned reflective. "Or so we must suppose. You, *ma chère,* were so avid in your passions it's difficult to be sure they never overcame you with another man. Perhaps she belonged to King, *hein?* He confessed, while drinking to our success at shooting Lenoir from the saddle, that he'd always had a yen to get under your skirts. Not that it was any surprise, I'd seen him watching you. Maybe he did more than think about it."

"That's a vile thing to say." Odd, but she could see a resemblance between the two men now where she never had before, something in the eyes and red wetness of their mouths.

The discovery was made with only surface attention while she shuddered inside with cold dismay, crying in the depths of her soul for Christien.

"Vile to be forced to think about, but there you are. A man gets these fancies while laid up with a broken head and only a piece of battered meat for a face."

"Don't!" she whispered, wishing she could shield Marguerite's ears. The urge to run beat up inside her once more. She might have chanced it, might even have tried fighting past him if she had been alone. But she had little hope of succeeding while Marguerite clung to her, hiding her face in her neck, growing heavier with each passing second.

"As you will," he said in a travesty of consideration.

"You killed Kingsley. Is that why, because he was unwise enough to…to…"

"To admit he lusted after you? Oh, no, it was for something far more important, a matter of money."

If that was supposed to put her in her place, it failed. Revulsion wiped away self-consciousness. "I'm relieved. I would hate to be the cause of a man's death."

"Of course, there's always Lenoir. We don't have to guess about him now, do we? Everybody knows exactly what the two of you have been up to."

The last words were savage, but she barely flinched

at them. "What do you care?" she demanded as rage returned, pushing aside her fear. "It didn't matter what was happening with me or Marguerite until another man came into it."

"Would you have wanted me to care? Would you have tended my wounds and nursed me with such dedication as you gave Lenoir?"

"You—you were my husband. It would have been my duty to nurse you."

"I am still your husband," he said with snide satisfaction. "And I have been reminded there is a world beyond this tomb of a house. I mean to step into it, now that Vinot is too feeble to prevent it. I knew I had only to wait, that it was a mere matter of time."

"Do you really believe he will stop now? He's waited as well, waited all this time for revenge."

"Could be he won't live that long."

"That's your answer to everything, is it, to kill those who stand in your way?"

He lifted a hand in negligent dismissal. "It has the advantage of being permanent."

"You're a monster! You care about nothing and no one except yourself. You terrified your daughter to no purpose all these weeks, you shot Christien from the dark like a coward, you killed Kingsley. And now—"

"Now I have you where I want you, and here you will stay."

"You expect me to live here with you? Never, it's impossible."

"Maybe you prefer the sword master? Too bad. He'll never have you."

"You mean…"

"I'll kill you before I let another man have what's mine."

He seemed to be saying Christien might be alive to possess her. Sudden hope leaped inside her. It gave her courage in spite of Theodore's threat, the swollen veins in his forehead, the flat, hard look in his eyes.

It was then that a shout sounded outside the shuttered French doors at the front of the salon. They rattled in their frames as a fist beat on them. "Reine! Open the door! Reine!"

Paul.

He could not get in. The shutters were made to withstand hurricane winds. The rusty iron bar that closed them held firm.

No matter. Her brother's arrival was the distraction Reine needed. As Theodore swung toward the pounding, she shoved past him, speeding headlong for the stairs.

She was met by a swarm of men coming up, a cadre with grim faces and flashing steel in their hands. Mercurial and golden Gavin Blackford was there, with Nicholas Pasquale at his shoulder. Vinot followed. On his heels was Caid O'Neill with the courteously lethal Rio, Conde de Lérida, pushing them from behind. And at their head, like a dark angel of inhuman grace and strength, was Christien. Or perhaps it was his ghost, for his eyes were empty of everything except the promise of death.

She halted, teetering on one foot while fierce, breathless joy jolted through her. She could not speak, could make not a sound. It was Marguerite who cried out in welcome, reaching toward him.

This was no time for a reunion. They were blocking the way.

In stumbling haste, Reine retreated into the salon again. The swordsmen streamed around her, past her, carrying her with them as they filled the room to its echoing, plaster-friezed ceiling, making the cloth-swathed chandelier swing in a gentle arc to the shuddering thunder of their arrival. And beneath it all could be heard Paul crashing into the shutters again and again.

Theodore was no longer there. Pale and cursing, he flung away the instant they came in sight, disappearing into the front bedchamber. His running treads made a hollow, thumping sound on the bare floorboards.

Christien lunged after him. Reine, in a flash of memory, saw the destruction inside and what had caused it.

"The saber," she cried out. "He's after the saber!"

Whining death sang beneath her warning. Swinging the heavy battle sword with both hands, Theodore sprang from the bedchamber in fury. He advanced, slashing right and left, his teeth bared as he cleaved the air in his search for flesh and bone.

Christen leaped back from the first great, slashing strikes. Then he stepped into them, catching a wild blow on his rapier. Metal bit and shrieked. The blue fire of sparks dripped around their feet. But the heavy saber, wielded with manic strength, could not be held.

Gavin lunged to take the next clanging charge. He absorbed it, throwing Theodore back. But Reine's husband, wild in his rage, whirled away, slicing at Blackford again as he turned, a swipe the Englishman parried with a twist of his wrist.

*"Mon ami,"* Vinot began, exchanging a swift look with Christien.

"Watch him," Caid O'Neill warned.

*"Le diable,"* the conde exclaimed in virulent dread.

Too late. Theodore's murderous, whirling, slicing path, like a dance to the rhythmic crash of Paul's shouts and repeated blows on the shuttered doors, took him to where Reine stood. He reached out, hooked an arm around her neck and dragged her against him. The saber flashed, and she felt the sharp sting as its edge pressed against her throat.

"No, no, no," Marguerite moaned, clutching at the blade that threatened her mother. Keening, crying, she pushed at it in hysteria, her small hands slicing along the edge, beginning to bleed. Reine, boiling with a mother's fury, shot up her hand to catch the saber's hilt, thrusting it from her and her child, fighting Theodore's strong arm that threatened to slice down with it again.

Shutters banged open at the French doors. Daylight sprang into the room from the front gallery. Glass shattered and Paul catapulted into the salon with the great hound Chalmette, teeth bared, at his side.

All heads turned in that direction. Chalmette crouched while his rumbling growl rolled over those assembled in the violent tableau, and his red-tinged gaze fastened on Marguerite in her distress. Christien, his eyes black and utterly without remorse, looked from Chalmette to Theodore.

And then he stepped aside.

Chalmette, eyes feral, gathered powerful muscles, began his leap from halfway across the room. His great body soared, suddenly silent, forefeet tucked, teeth bared. Theodore tried to slash out, but Reine tightened her one-handed clutch on the saber's hilt, swinging her weight from it. Theodore began a guttural scream.

The hound slammed him backward as he took his throat. Reine was dragged down with the pair. She heard the saber hit the floor and clatter away, heard distinctly the sound of crunching bone.

Marguerite landed on top of her, still screaming, strangling her with her small arms. Reine rolled with her in swift escape from the melee. Then she covered her daughter's face, breathed curses and prayers into her bright, sweet-smelling hair.

Theodore's screams ceased. Chalmette growled once more and was quiet.

"Papa," Marguerite whispered. "Oh, Papa."

# 25

"Alonzo said you're going."

It was Paul who spoke, standing in the bedchamber door with his hand on the knob as if ready to bolt if need be. Christien did not look up from the careful folding of his hand-stitched white linen shirt. Smoothing the collar, placing the cuffs just so, he settled it into the top of his portmanteau with the care he might use with a newborn babe.

"It's time," he answered.

"Why? Everything is back the way it was. I mean, Theodore is gone, Reine is a widow, and you still own River's Edge."

"I signed the deed back over to your father."

Paul bent an outraged stare upon him. "Why would you go and do a thing like that?"

"I had my reasons." Christien gave him a wry glance as he buckled the bag's leather straps. "But if it's your lack of a sparring partner that worries you, you will always be welcome in any salon on the Passage. I'll pass the word to make it so."

"That's not it at all," the boy said. "You're needed here."

"What's required is my absence. The sooner I'm gone, the sooner the gossips will find new meat." He didn't meet Paul's eyes as he spoke. Mature beyond his years, that young man had too much of his sister's skill at discerning hidden motives to take the chance.

"You think that, then you're a fool. They'll just want to know what you found out that made you take off."

Christien's smile turned ironic around the edges. "An excellent shot by way of argument. It might even have found its mark if I didn't understand too well the local outrage over what Pingre pulled on her."

"So you'll cut and run, leave Reine to pick up the pieces on her own."

"She has you."

"It's not the same."

Nothing Paul said was new to Christien. He'd turned it over in his mind like a chicken scratching in a dung heap during the long hours since they all returned to River's Edge. What he had discovered was about as savory. The truth was, he didn't deserve to stay, could find no earthly excuse that wasn't ignoble and preeminently self-serving. That being so, he'd spoken to Vinot, also the other sword masters, before they gathered up their families and departed, had listened to their advice and made his plans. Now all he had to do was dredge up the guts to act on them.

"Look," he said, trying for patience. "I came here under false pretences. I had a purpose and followed it like a berserker with a bloodied knife, cutting down whoever got in the way. I could use all my good intentions as a shield, but what good is that? There are still two graves to be accounted for. I'd rather not add to the total."

"You saved the ones who matter."

Christien's smile was tight as he lifted his portmanteau from the bed. "I'll take that as my epitaph. Do you know where I might find your sister?"

"Outside, walking under the oaks. She said not to let you go without saying goodbye."

It was confirmation, if any was needed, that what he was doing was just as she expected. He made no reply beyond a grim nod of understanding, not the least reason being because his throat was too tight. With portmanteau in hand, he left the bedchamber, went past Paul down the hall and quitted the big house.

His black stallion was waiting at the mounting block. He tied his portmanteau behind the saddle, atop the box that held his swords. Giving his mount a shriveled apple from his pocket to pacify him, he went in search of Reine.

She had her back to him as he came upon her under the oaks, a solitary figure in a black gown with gray trimming that blended with the evening shadows. The mourning was for Pingre, of course; who else? And the sight of it sent a ripple of fury along his veins. He paused a moment to allow all vestiges of it to fade, also to gather his defenses, before he moved forward again.

She swung to face him, the hem of her skirts stirring a small drift of dust from the grass. Her eyes were dark blue and liquid yet calm, her hands lightly clasped at her waist. She tilted up her chin a fraction as she searched his face.

"So you're really going," she said, the words like ice tinkling against a crystal julep glass.

He inclined his head. "It seems best. The furor over this business will die down faster if I'm no longer around."

"It's for my sake, then."

"And mine." He indicated her black dress. "I don't think I can stomach two years of watching from afar while you mourn Pingre twice over. Besides, I have no right to be here."

"Because Theodore died? It wasn't your fault."

He allowed himself a wry smile. "Wasn't it? I tried to usurp his place. I deliberately enticed him out of hiding in the name of justice. Though I may not have struck the death blow, I was the instrument of it all the same."

"Or you could say he caused his own death. If he had been different, had acted otherwise…"

"That isn't the worst of it."

She met his eyes, her own shadowed with equal parts of dread and fortitude. "What…what do you mean?"

He looked away, unable to watch her while he said it. "I have no right to River's Edge. I cheated your father out of it. He was playing deep the night I won it, but would not have staked so much if I hadn't goaded him into it. And when everything he owned was on the table, I palmed an ace and it was mine."

"But…why?"

"An extreme action of the Brotherhood, if you will. Vinot was certain Pingre was alive. He'd heard whispers, thought he saw him once in a Gallatin Street dive despite his being almost unrecognizable. He asked my help in forcing him out of hiding."

"And you obliged."

Something in her voice disturbed him. He turned back to search her face, but saw only pale composure and pride. "I owed him so much," he said after a moment. "He took me in, taught me everything I knew. Sophie, his daughter, was like a sister. How could I refuse?"

"Yes, certainly."

"If you think…" he began, a frown growing between his eyes.

"Apparently, I've done little enough of that," she said in brittle self-condemnation. "It never occurred to me a man would go so far to settle an old debt."

She thought he had taken her into his bed as part of his ploy to bring Pingre out into the open. Anger that she understood him so little robbed him of words for an instant. When he could speak, his voice was harsh. "No. That had nothing to do with it. The cheating, the proposal and all the rest, but not that."

"You never intended to marry me."

"It was doubtful from the first that the wedding would take place. Pingre was almost certain to show up beforehand." That did not answer what he would have done if her husband had not appeared. Not at all.

"You had a lucky escape, then."

"I don't know about that…." he began.

"Never mind. We are better for your coming here, when all is said and done." She went on quickly before he could inquire deeper into that assertion. "You saved Marguerite from the *loup-garou*, and we must be thankful for that much."

"I would have said you saved her. If not for you—"

"Don't!" She turned swiftly away. "I can't bear to think of it. If I had not held on to the saber…"

"If you had not held on, he might have cut your throat when Chalmette took him down, or Marguerite's. But don't think about it. Push it to the back of your mind until the pain of it is gone."

"Is that what you do?" She gave him a quick glance over her shoulder.

Was it? He hardly knew. Christien only shook his head. "How is Marguerite? Her poor little hands—will they be all right?" He'd wanted to slaughter Pingre for the sweetling's frantic terror and bloodshed, had been preparing for it when he saw Chalmette ready to make his leap. Stepping aside to allow it had seemed right. Yet somewhere inside him was lingering regret that he had not struck the final blow. He did not care to be remembered by Marguerite only as the man who killed her father, but he could have counted the deception he'd undertaken as worth something if he had ended his persecution.

"Children are very good at pushing horror into the back of their minds and closing the door on it," Reine said softly, "though I don't say she won't need more attention for a time or have nightmares. At least their monsters will no longer visit her in the flesh. Anyway, she's in the kitchen at the moment, displaying her bandages to everyone who will look and being hand-fed cookies and milk. Well, and sharing them with Chalmette, who is even more her trusted companion than he was before."

"The cuts weren't serious, then?"

"One or two went fairly deep, but she has use of all her fingers."

"And your mother?"

Reine's lips moved in a grave smile. "She's still asleep, the first untroubled rest she's had since…well, since that night two years ago. She is literally spent with blessed relief, I think. She thought she'd killed Theodore that terrible night. It was she who damaged his face so badly, you know."

All this time, Madame Cassard had been hiding what she thought was her guilt as a murderess. It explained a great deal, Christien thought. The pity of it was that all her fear and repentance had been for nothing. Another black mark against Pingre that he'd allowed it, hidden behind it.

"What actually *did* happen that night?" he asked. "Your father told me a little when I first came, and you added to it, but I've never quite gotten the straight of it."

"There's little enough to tell. Less than we once thought, anyway." A tendril at her temple waved as she shook her head. "You know Marguerite had been ill. Theodore was driven mad by her crying, so went into town. Everyone at Bonne Espèrance was upset because of his uncle, who hovered near death from a wasting sickness. Demeter was tending him, making batch after batch of one of her concoctions for pain, so had little time for a mere childhood complaint. The stomach upset was passed to the dying man, so they claimed, and he passed away. Everything was so strained that I brought Marguerite home to River's Edge."

It seemed noteworthy that Reine had thought of River's Edge as home in spite of having been married for several years, Christien noted, but he only nodded his understanding of the situation she had laid out.

"Her fever was extremely high, but finally broke in the middle of the second night here. She fell into a natural sleep and the crisis seemed over. I left her in my bed in the bedchamber where I'd slept before I married. It had been hours since I had sat down, days since I'd snatched more than a quick nap, and suddenly I was exhausted but starving. I meant only to find a little something to eat and drink in the kitchen, then go back upstairs. But I woke up with my head on the kitchen table and screams ringing in my ears."

"Marguerite's?" His voice was sharp.

"My mother's," she corrected. "Later we told everyone it was because she'd found Marguerite lying in a pool of blood on the bed. Actually, she had heard Marguerite crying and got up to see to her. She found Theodore with her. He'd returned from New Orleans, discovered Marguerite and I were gone and everything in an uproar because of his uncle. He came on to River's Edge and made his way to my bedchamber. He was a little drunk, I think, and stumbled around, waking Marguerite, so she started crying. When my mother came into the bedchamber, he had picked her up from the bed and was cursing as he shook her violently, trying to make her be quiet. *Maman* was… She never…"

She paused, searching for words. Christien provided them for her. "She had a difficult childhood, I believe."

"Her father, my American grandfather, was a strict Calvinist who did not believe in sparing the rod for man, woman, child or beast. I suppose she saw Theodore as cut from the same cloth. She picked up a silver poker and hit him in the head, then kept on hitting him until…"

There seemed no point in lingering on that scene. "I see. And then?"

"I'm not quite sure. Theodore apparently got away from her somehow and staggered out of the house. By the time I arrived, he was gone, though there was a trail of blood spots down the stairs and out the front door. I assume he went to Kingsley's cabin and then was taken to old Demeter's place back in the woods."

"And she took him in."

"He was her baby," Reine said simply.

Christien nodded. Never would he forget the terrible grief of the old nursemaid as she fell to her knees beside her charge with silent, endless tears running in rivulets down the tobacco-colored wrinkles of her face. Afterward, she had disappeared into the woods. It had seemed a kindness to let her go, though he wondered how long she could live with such pain and sorrow at her great age. A basket of the sweets she loved had been taken to her little house, he knew, having been told earlier that Alonzo was away on that errand. The work boss, Samson, would take men out to look for her if she didn't appear soon. It was all they could do.

"Within a day or two, Theodore must have heard that he was feared dead, also heard the speculation that a prowler or thief had set upon him, as we, my parents and I, suggested," Reine went on in a somber tone. "No doubt it seemed a good thing to let everyone think for a while that he was dead, though we were ignorant of his reasons. Later, I suspect he preferred that no one see his face."

"Or he knew Vinot had not given up looking for him, would never give up."

"Possibly."

"Therefore, the subterfuge of digging up his dead uncle and putting him in the river, knowing he would almost certainly be unrecognizable by the time he was discovered."

"Which he was, except for the ring that had been placed on his finger, Theodore's alliance ring that was a match for mine." Her voice turned bitter. "A nice touch, that."

"The corpse was Kingsley's part in the business, I imagine," Christien said thoughtfully.

"For which he was well paid, you may be sure, then and afterward. He assured me over and over that the search for Theodore had turned up nothing, right up until the moment his body, or what we assumed was his body, was pulled from the river. It seems now that Kingsley may have thought I knew the truth but was keeping quiet for reasons of my own. Please believe me when I say I had no idea Theodore had been living less then three miles from River's Edge all this time."

"A scarred husband would have been better than a murdered one, given the gossip," he said in understanding. "But your husband saved his hide at your expense. He allowed you to be whispered about as a murderess, to become a social outcast, and did nothing to stop it."

"I'm sure he thought I deserved it, that what happened was my fault for leaving his bed and his home in the first place—it's how he would have placed the blame. If he had to live in isolation, he probably felt it only fair that I do the same."

"Until I came along."

"Yes, until then." She paused. "Where will you go now? What will you do?"

It was a good question. He felt completely unsettled, unable to go forward, unwilling to go back to the Passage de la Bourse and endless days of teaching young fools the art of sword play. "I may sign on for Mexico. A good, straightforward fight doesn't sound too bad for a change."

She met his eyes, and he thought her fingers turned white at the ends where she gripped her hands together. "You'll be going to war," she said in flat acceptance.

"Fighting is what I do best, after all."

She opened her lips as if to protest, to give him an alternative, to ask him not to go. Or maybe that was wishful thinking on his part. Watching her, he was swamped by memories of the taste of those lips, of the feel of her skin against his, the glory of her tight, moist heat surrounding him, taking him deep inside her. And he wanted her, wanted her daughter and the rest of her family, wanted River's Edge and all that had almost been his with a fierce ache that made his head pound and his heart feel boiled in acid. He wanted, passionately, all the things he could not have.

So he took the little he might be allowed, sweeping her against him and setting his mouth to hers, a taste for eternity. Then he put her from him and walked away.

It was a damn good thing the black whinnied when he saw him coming, or he might have walked all the way to New Orleans.

# 26

*Gone.*

Christien was gone, riding away down the drive. He had left her life as abruptly as he had entered it. She should be glad, should be overjoyed that she need not be married against her will, Reine told herself. She should feel nothing except relief that River's Edge was returned to her father and everything was as it had been before. Yes, literally everything since she was once more a widow—this time, a true widow.

Christien had used her. He had made his outrageous proposal for one purpose only, to draw Theodore from hiding and make him proclaim himself still her husband. What she felt, her fears and feeling of being trapped in unwanted obligation, had meant nothing and less than nothing. All that mattered was that Theodore should pay for his crime against Vinot's young daughter.

The ruse had worked. Justice had been served up on a silver platter, and now it was done.

Christien was going to war. In that strictly male milieu he would be in his element, at risk of having to kill or be killed. Either way, he was unlikely to return.

Why could she not be glad? Why should she feel this painful emptiness, as if he had taken a part of her with him?

Christien was gone.

She had been suspicious in the beginning about how he had gained ownership of River's Edge. In time she had been lulled into false security caused by the idea there was something personal in it. She had thought, more fool her, that he might have become enamored after their few moments of close contact outside the theater that night. She had imagined that something about her and Marguerite had appealed to him on some deep level of which he was hardly aware, so he had been compelled to claim them as his ready-made family. Apparently, she had been wrong.

And yet he had made love to her. He had taken that advantage. Well, or she had given it to him. The caresses, the feelings, the whispers of fervent appreciation had meant nothing. What lived in her memory as an unforgettable experience had been no more than a brief pleasure to him. How strange that it should be so, that he could banish all emotion from the act of love, turning it into a physical coupling no more meaningful than taking a drink when thirsty.

It was quite otherwise for her.

She had grown used to having him in the house, to the security of thinking him somewhere about the place during the day or just down the hall at night. She had become accustomed to thinking of him as her future husband, had begun to anticipate with secret joy the long days of making love without let or hindrance.

She had thought more often than was comfortable of exploring all the myriad ways to stoke desire, tending it until it became a consuming flame.

It wasn't going to happen. Christien was gone.

She was a widow this time in truth, with the most graphic proof of the death of her husband. The funeral mass had been held followed by a quiet burial. The funeral meats had been eaten, such as they were being the remains of the abortive wedding feast, and everyone, everyone except her close family, was gone. She was finally alone.

She would be a solitary widow for all the days and weeks of her life, the years she had no idea how to fill.

She would survive, of course. Women had done it before her and would do it when she was gone. It was what they did.

Christien had cheated in order to acquire her home. She had half suspected it in the beginning, thought it an indication of how important being at River's Edge had been to him, how determined he had been to make a place for himself. She had been right in the main, though wrong in the details. Yet he had fit so well into all their lives, Marguerite's and Paul's, her father's and even her mother's. Yes, and hers. Dear heaven, but how he had fit into her life, her future, her bed and her body.

*Gone, gone, gone…*

At a small noise from the direction of the house, she turned to see her mother emerging onto the gallery with her father carefully supporting her. He seated her in one of the wicker chairs and she smiled up at him as he moved to take the one next to her. She glanced around then with a look of childlike wonder on her face.

It was the first time her mother had been out of the house that Reine could remember since before she had attacked Theodore. That was other than to travel to New Orleans or to make the short trek to the chapel as she had for the wedding. Reine had taken it as a sign of illness that she lacked the strength or energy. It had never occurred to her that her mother might have been afraid. Now that Theodore was dead, however, here she was.

"Well," she called out as she made her way toward where her parents sat, "this is an occasion!"

Her mother lifted a shoulder in a most Gallic gesture, considering that was not her heritage, giving her a tremulous smile. "I was suddenly weary of being shut away."

"Oh, *Maman,* did you really think Theodore was outside here somewhere?"

"I couldn't be satisfied in my mind that he was dead. He reeled like a drunkard when he left the bed-chamber but was able to walk and scream curses at me. I couldn't imagine what happened to him."

"You were right to wonder," Reine answered, leaning to kiss her mother's soft cheek. "He would have sent word or at least come back as soon as his cuts were well if not for fear of Vinot."

"He was truly terrified of him, I do believe that," her father said in corroboration. "Even before that poor girl died in childbirth, he was fascinated by the exploits of the Brotherhood, was always collecting stories about the nighttime deeds of the sword masters, particularly the Nighthawk."

"But where is Monsieur Lenoir?" her mother said, gazing around with her brows drawn together in puzzlement. "I thought I saw him with you a moment ago."

"He was saying his farewells. It seems he has to leave us."

"Not permanently, I hope."

Reine exchanged a quick look with her father, who wore a frown on his cherubic face. "I fear so," she answered. "It seems he gained title to River's Edge by dishonorable means so felt compelled to rectify the error."

"Nonsense," her father said with a snort. "I had every intention that he should have the place, did my all to make it so."

"Papa!" she exclaimed. "You mean he didn't cheat you at the card table?"

"But yes, though he was a veritable amateur at it, *ma chère*. I could have stopped him at any time, and without the least scandal. All it would have taken was a small sleight of hand of my own."

"But to give away everything, Maurice," his wife said in protest.

"No such thing. I saw how he looked at Reine that night in front of the opera house. You were not there, my love, and I was too far away to be of use, but never have I seen such stunned and hopeless yearning on a man's face. He was needed at River's Edge, for I'd grown weary of Kingsley's tricks but had no aptitude for growing sugar and no love of it, either. To lead Lenoir toward the proper result required a certain cunning, I will allow, but I did not do too badly, *hein?*"

"It really was your suggestion that he propose marriage," Reine said in dazed acceptance.

"No, no, I only allowed him to see the benefits so he conceived the idea himself. It was child's play when permitting him his heart's desire."

"I believe you were mistaken, Papa. Christien— Monsieur Lenoir—merely required a means of enticing Theodore out into the open."

"I don't say that wasn't part of it, but he could have accomplished the same thing by merely courting you. Oh, no, *chère.* He meant to have you."

This was no time to mince words. Besides, she hadn't the patience for it. "What stopped him?"

Her father glanced at her mother with a roguish look in his eyes. Matching amusement rose in her mother's face. Reine, hearing the echo of her own words, thought of Christien's methods of ensuring that she guard her tongue and felt a hot flush burn its way to her hairline. Still, she refused to back down.

"I think, perhaps," her mother answered in her light voice, "that it was a species of gallantry. He feared that to marry you out of hand so soon after the fiasco of the wedding and Theodore's death would make you notorious indeed. And naturally he could not remain here indefinitely without it."

"But you and Papa would have been here for respectability. He would have been no different from any other houseguest."

"Except that everyone knows already that he won the place at cards, had made his proposal and was accepted. Only consider what the gossips might have made of it if he had simply stayed on afterward. They would have been certain the two of you were living in sin, and…well."

They probably would have been, so her mother thought. It was likely she was correct.

"You don't think he was simply glad to quit River's Edge after everything that happened?" Reine had to ask it. Too much depended on the answer to allow uncertainty.

"It troubled him, I believe. He's not an unfeeling devil, after all, unlike some we could name. But neither is he the kind of man who runs away from a sticky situation. At least, not without the best of reasons."

"Yes. Yes, I expect you're quite right," she said in distraction. Gallant, indeed, and to the last, she thought. She might have known.

She had no use for gallantry, as she had told him more than once. She did not have to accept it, nor would she.

"*Maman,* as you are so recovered, do you feel you could be happy having Christien in the house on a permanent basis?"

"Why should I not, *ma chère?*"

"You called him an angel of death and seemed to fear him so."

"Ah, yes, sometimes things are not clear to me. If Monsieur Lenoir was an angel of death, it was not I he was after, but Theodore. You will forgive me, I know, if I say that was quite acceptable. And now, now it is over."

"Darling *Maman*," Reine said, swooping down to give her another swift kiss where she sat, "you are a wise woman."

"As are you, my daughter, as are you."

Reine didn't hear. She was already whirling away toward the house, calling to a stable boy to saddle her mare as she went.

She rode like a storm wind, with the veil on her hat streaming out behind her and her long habit skirt rippling back along the mare's flank. Her heartbeat kept pace, pounding with the same hard rhythm as the hoofbeats. She tried to think what she would do and where she would go to find Christien if he reached town ahead of her, but came to no conclusion. She would have to decide that when she got there. In the meantime, she set her face forward and refused to think that her *maman* and papa might be wrong and she on a fool's errand.

Less than a mile out of New Orleans, she caught sight of a tall, familiar horseman riding toward her. Gladness sang in her heart even before she was certain of his identity. Drawing her mare to a walk, she eased along as she waited for Christien to come up to her. They met finally under the cool dusk of a huge live oak that sheltered the crushed-oyster-shell road.

"What is it?" he asked in gruff concern, pulling up as he drew abreast of her. "Has something happened at River's Edge?"

"Something more, you mean?" Her smile had a

wry edge. "Not this time. I meant to overtake you before you reached town, but here you are coming back. Did you leave something behind?"

His features relaxed though his dark eyes remained keen as he searched her face. "You might say so. Or I could admit I turned around because I have no place to go. The war in Mexico is over."

"You mean it's ended?" she asked, trying to assimilate the abrupt announcement. "Just like that, after all these years?"

"So I was told by a man I met on the road. Mexico City has fallen to General Scott and his army. The government has conceded defeat. It's only a matter of time before a peace treaty is signed."

"There's no need for your sword, then."

He shook his head. "I'm not quite ready to beat it into a plowshare, but I thought…" He stopped, looked away.

"What?"

He made a quick gesture of defeat. "I thought Paul might have use of a fencing partner."

"No doubt," she said. "He aspires to be your equal one day."

"I promised Marguerite I would keep her safe from the *loup-garou,* and though one has gone forever, who can say? There may be others about someplace."

"Indeed," Reine said with difficulty caused by the knot of tearful joy in her throat.

He met her gaze an instant, his own shadowed with the faintest stirring of something that might have been hope. "Your mother called me a dark angel. It seemed necessary to make certain she knows I mean her no harm."

"By odd chance, she came to that conclusion on her own just this evening." He could be so formidable with a sword in his hand and the prospect of death in front of him. It was touching beyond measure that her family's approval meant so much to him.

"It occurred to me your father might fall back into his old habits if I'm not there." He paused, took a deep breath. "And it would not suit me at all if he should lose River's Edge to another man who might be delighted to take you with it."

"Now, there you need have no qualms," she said with deliberation. "I would never agree to such a thing again."

He gave a brief nod, gathered his reins as he looked away. "I suspected it, but had to be sure."

"So you might. I object to having such base advantage taken of me or being married only out of guilt and convenience. Oh, yes, and as a goad to bring a dead man back to life."

"Don't," he said with the same grating sound in his voice as the shells that crunched under their horses' restive hooves. "It wasn't like that. I wanted you as I've never wanted anything in my life. I held you in my arms that night in New Orleans and felt I had found all I had lost—home and family and a love so strong nothing could change it, nothing stop it. I vowed to do whatever I must to protect you and Marguerite from Vinot's plans, but also swore to do whatever it took to have and keep you, if I had to sell my soul to the devil for the chance. And I nearly did. I cheated, lied, used the tenets of the Brotherhood for my own ends, played on an old man's grief and became a hunter of men in that goal. I lost my one chance because I couldn't see that I had become all the things you most despised."

"Not entirely," she said softly. "You could have killed Theodore to remove him from your path, but you didn't."

His laugh was sardonic as he looked away down the road behind her. "I wanted to, God knows. And I wished to high heaven I had when he ran away, back to where he had left Marguerite. I knew it would destroy you if he harmed her in any way, and I had misjudged him, had let him live to do it."

"Because you are a master at arms, and gallant with it."

"For what good it did me. Or you."

"Oh, but I have a tendre for men who use swords but know their limits," she said, her voice lilting with the joy rising inside her. "In fact, I could never marry just any man for the sake of River's Edge. Being something of a half-breed myself, mixed French Creole and *Américain,* I must have such a one as my husband, a *maître d'armes* of mixed blood who is also the last Great Sun of the Natchez. He is the only one who could ever please me."

His head snapped back toward her. "Reine…"

"Is that not clear enough for you?" she inquired, her gaze steady for all its hot brightness. "I can be more precise. Only one man could ever persuade me to give up my widow's weeds this time, just one. He is the man who made certain, finally, that I would wear them. You may not have taken Theodore's life to save Marguerite, but you were there to see that Chalmette had time for the deed."

He swung down from the black stallion in a lithe and powerful movement, stepped to her mare and pulled her down into his arms. She was ready, had already unhooked her knee from the pommel and leaned toward him. He held her close, allowing her to slide down his body while an expression of granted happiness so intense it was close to agony lay over his features.

"Reine," he said again in a husky whisper, and kissed her while standing there in the middle of the road. He caressed her back with his strong hands, captured the thick coil of hair at the nape of her neck in the cage of his fingers while he took possession of her mouth, her life.

"Not here," she gasped when she felt his warm hand close over her breast, when she could struggle free enough to breathe, to form coherent words. Taking his hand, she drew him off the road, behind the bulwark of the great oak's wide trunk.

He came willingly enough, only pausing to gather the reins of their horses and draw them with him. He ground-tethered them with a quick gesture before taking her into his arms once more.

"Madame Pingre," he said in low threat, "do you recall a lesson on watching what you say?"

What had she said? She could not recall with any accuracy, not while his hands molded her curves to his touch and the dusk drew in around them, hiding them in its gray folds. Her voice no more than a whisper, she asked, "What of it?"

"I am the only man who can please you, so you said. It was, just possibly, true at the time. Shall we see if it can be true again?"

She really must watch what she said. She must watch carefully for the right thing, the proper and most innocently salacious comment she could discover that would bring him to her, devilishly smiling like this, into her arms, into her heart.

"Why not?" she said on a swift intake of breath as he moved closer, fitting his hips into the cradle of her thighs.

"Oh, why not?"

\* \* \* \* \*

# AUTHOR'S NOTE

Historical detail fascinates me, particularly as found in the news sheets of old New Orleans. With their notices of arrivals and departures of ships and steamboats, seasonal merchandise, operatic performances, subscription balls, dancing, drawing and fencing lessons and a thousand other things, they are like moments in time captured on microfilm. Using these sources to make life in the Vieux Carré as depicted in the Masters at Arms series as true as possible was a labor of love.

Several of the *maîtres d'armes* mentioned in passing, including Gilbert "Titi" Rosière, Bastile Croquere, Jean "Pepe" Lulla and Marcel Dauphin— were living masters. They, with their companions, played their parts with style and grace until the beginning of the Civil War. By the war's end, the way of life that made their profession necessary and profitable had vanished and so they faded from view. It has been my pleasure to allow them to live again.

My love affair with men who wield swords is not over, however. I'm currently researching the waning days of knights in shining armor, circa 1485–1495, when medieval austerity began to give way to the glories of the Renaissance. My next three books will be set at the court of the reigning king of England, the first of the Tudors, Henry VII. Into that turbulent and colorful lifestyle, rife with scandal and danger, I've placed the accursed Three Graces of Graydon, sisters who bring disaster to any man who attempts to possess them without love. As I write now, my mind swirls with velvet and pearls, mottos and pennons, the rights of kings, pele towers, battlements and medieval manners. I am excited about bringing this era to life, and hope you enjoy its vivid grandeur, as well.

*Jennifer Blake*

Caney Lake
April 19, 2009

# ACKNOWLEDGMENTS

"Louisiana, a state of mind," the ad copy reads, and so it is. The sweep of the state's past extends from the seventeenth century under the Sun King Louis XIV through the panoply of colorful and outrageous characters to the events in today's newspaper. Many authors have sought to capture the scope and spirit of this long stretch of history, extolling a piece here, a piece there, and I am indebted to every one of them. I am particularly grateful for Herbert Asbury's *The French Quarter*, where I first saw mentioned the famous *maîtres d'armes* and their curious place in New Orleans society; for *Gumbo Ya-Ya: A collection of Louisiana Folk Tales* by Lyle Saxon, Robert Tallant and Edward Dreyer, with its excellent description of the life and customs of the aristocratic French Creoles of the Vieux Carré, as well as the flavor of their speech and their manifold superstitions; for *Gentlemen, Swords and Pistols,* Harnett T. Kane's treatise on dueling in the antebellum south; and *Louisiana: A Narrative History* by Edwin Adams Davis, filled with succinct descriptions of events in various time periods. Eliza Ripley's *Social Life in Old New Orleans*; Grace King's *New Orleans: the Place and the People*; Stanley Arthur's *Old New Orleans,* Albert E. Fossier's *New Orleans: the Glamour Period, 1800–1840,* and particularly Benjamin Moore Norman's famous guidebook written in 1845, *Norman's New Orleans and Environs,* were all invaluable.

A number of great volumes on fencing remained close at hand during the writing of the Masters at Arms series. These include *The Duel* by Francois Billacois, *Harnessing Anger,* by Peter Westbrook, *The Art and Science of Fencing* by Nick Evangelista and, most useful of all because of its teaching techniques, *On Fencing* by Aldo Nadi. I am also most appreciative of the online sites about fencing and historic swords, not to mention the kindness of their owners and visitors in sharing their expertise on a subject I knew little about when I began writing about swordsmen six years ago. Nor can I neglect this opportunity to thank, once more, the staff of the Historic New Orleans Collection and Williams Research center, Chartres Street, New Orleans, for their patience in searching out books, papers and endless rolls of microfilm to feed my craving for historic detail. Librarian Robin Toms and her staff at the Jackson Parish Library, Jonesboro, Louisiana, deserve all praise, too, for keeping me supplied with reading material even in the face of my spotty record for returning it.

Finally, huge thanks are due to the most gentlemanly agent in the book business, Richard Curtis, for his sublime faith in this project; to my lovely editor, Susan Swinwood, for her unfailing support and sensitive editing; and to the art director and production crew at MIRA Books for turning what was only a vision in my mind into a grand reality. They are all the best.

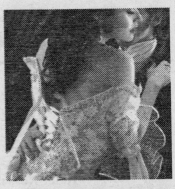

# DEANNA RAYBOURN

> "Let the wicked
> be ashamed,
> and let them be
> silent in the grave."

These ominous words are the last threat that the darling of London society, Sir Edward Grey, receives from his killer. Before he can show them to Nicholas Brisbane, the private inquiry agent he has retained for his protection, Sir Edward is murdered in his home.

Determined to bring her husband's killer to justice, Julia Grey engages Brisbane to help her investigate Edward's demise. Together, they press forward, coming ever closer to a killer who waits expectantly for Julia's arrival.

*Silent in the Grave*

"[A] perfectly executed debut."
—*Publishers Weekly* (starred review)

*Available wherever books are sold.*

**MIRA®**

**www.MIRABooks.com**

MDR2817

# REQUEST YOUR FREE BOOKS!

## 2 FREE NOVELS
## FROM THE ROMANCE COLLECTION
## PLUS 2 FREE GIFTS!

**YES!** Please send me 2 FREE novels from the Romance Collection and my 2 FREE gifts (gifts are worth about $10). After receiving them, if I don't wish to receive any more books, I can return the shipping statement marked "cancel." If I don't cancel, I will receive 4 brand-new novels every month and be billed just $5.74 per book in the U.S. or $6.24 per book in Canada. That's a saving of at least 28% off the cover price. It's quite a bargain! Shipping and handling is just 50¢ per book in the U.S. and 75¢ per book in Canada.* I understand that accepting the 2 free books and gifts places me under no obligation to buy anything. I can always return a shipment and cancel at any time. Even if I never buy another book, the two free books and gifts are mine to keep forever.

194 MDN E4LY  394 MDN E4MC

Name _____ (PLEASE PRINT) _____

Address _____ Apt. # _____

City _____ State/Prov. _____ Zip/Postal Code _____

Signature (if under 18, a parent or guardian must sign)

### Mail to **The Reader Service:**
**IN U.S.A.:** P.O. Box 1867, Buffalo, NY 14240-1867
**IN CANADA:** P.O. Box 609, Fort Erie, Ontario L2A 5X3

Not valid for current subscribers to the Romance Collection
or the Romance/Suspense Collection.

**Want to try two free books from another line?**
**Call 1-800-873-8635 or visit www.morefreebooks.com.**

* Terms and prices subject to change without notice. Prices do not include applicable taxes. N.Y. residents add applicable sales tax. Canadian residents will be charged applicable provincial taxes and GST. Offer not valid in Quebec. This offer is limited to one order per household. All orders subject to approval. Credit or debit balances in a customer's account(s) may be offset by any other outstanding balance owed by or to the customer. Please allow 4 to 6 weeks for delivery. Offer available while quantities last.

**Your Privacy:** Harlequin Books is committed to protecting your privacy. Our Privacy Policy is available online at www.eHarlequin.com or upon request from the Reader Service. From time to time we make our lists of customers available to reputable third parties who may have a product or service of interest to you. If you would prefer we not share your name and address, please check here. ☐

**Help us get it right**—We strive for accurate, respectful and relevant communications. To clarify or modify your communication preferences, visit us at www.ReaderService.com/consumerschoice.

# JENNIFER BLAKE

| | | | |
|---|---|---|---|
| 32619 | GALLANT MATCH | ___ $6.99 U.S. | ___ $6.99 CAN. |
| 32454 | GUARDED HEART | ___ $6.99 U.S. | ___ $8.50 CAN. |
| 32405 | ROGUE'S SALUTE | ___ $6.99 U.S. | ___ $8.50 CAN. |
| 32213 | DAWN ENCOUNTER | ___ $5.99 U.S. | ___ $6.99 CAN. |

*(limited quantities available)*

| | |
|---|---|
| TOTAL AMOUNT | $ _____ |
| POSTAGE & HANDLING | $ _____ |
| ($1.00 for 1 book, 50¢ for each additional) | |
| APPLICABLE TAXES* | $ _____ |
| TOTAL PAYABLE | $ _____ |

*(check or money order—please do not send cash)*

To order, complete this form and send it, along with a check or money order for the total above, payable to MIRA Books, to: **In the U.S.:** 3010 Walden Avenue, P.O. Box 9077, Buffalo, NY 14269-9077; **In Canada:** P.O. Box 636, Fort Erie, Ontario, L2A 5X3.

Name: _____
Address: _____ City: _____
State/Prov.: _____ Zip/Postal Code: _____
Account Number (if applicable): _____

075 CSAS

*New York residents remit applicable sales taxes.
*Canadian residents remit applicable GST and provincial taxes.

**MIRA®**

**www.MIRABooks.com**

MJB0210BL